THE DANGEROUS GAME

MARI JUNGSTEDT

Translated from the Swedish by Tiina Nunnally

CORGI BOOKS

TRANSWORLD PUBLISHERS
61–63 Uxbridge Road, London W5 5SA
www.transworldbooks.co.uk

Transworld is part of the Penguin Random House group of companies
whose addresses can be found at global.penguinrandomhouse.com

First published in Great Britain in 2015 by Doubleday
an imprint of Transworld Publishers
Corgi edition published 2015

A CIP catalogue record for this book
is available from the British Library.

ISBN
9780552168762

Typeset in 11/13½pt Giovanni Book by Kestrel Data, Exeter, Devon.
Printed and bound in Great Britain by Clays Ltd, St Ives plc

Penguin Random House is committed to a sustainable future
for our business, our readers and our planet. This book is
made from Forest Stewardship Council® certified paper.

1 3 5 7 9 10 8 6 4 2

For my beloved daughter, Bella

It was a warm day in May, and she was strolling alone through the streets of Milan. After a while she came to a large, paved piazza in front of a church. The square was filled with pigeons. White, grey, and some that were almost a shimmering blue. The birds fluttered around each other in a sort of lustful mating dance. Some strutted about contentedly on the sun-warmed paving stones, here and there casually pecking at a few crumbs. Lining the big open square were park benches bolted to the ground. A mother with a baby in a pram was trying to read the newspaper while her two little girls raced about. They were playing with multicoloured rubber balls, bouncing them on the pavement as they laughed merrily. A young man with rolled-up shirtsleeves stood at the sole vendor's stand, selling burnt almonds in little paper bags. He was sweating in the heat, and his curly hair stuck to his forehead. He kept mopping his face with a handkerchief. The sweet scent of the almonds wafted towards her, prickling her nostrils. She was hungry and had plans to meet someone for lunch in the old part of town. That was where she was now headed, yet she took time to pause and enjoy the scene. A group of schoolgirls wearing green-checked uniforms had sat down on blankets placed in a circle to listen to their teacher, who, with sweeping gestures, seemed to be recounting the history of the church. A couple obviously in love sat on one of the benches, kissing. Seated on another were three elderly black-clad women, chatting in the shadow of the cypress trees. Surrounding the entire piazza were well-maintained blocks of flats with brightly painted window frames. She smiled to herself as she crossed the square and continued along the winding lanes in La Brera, the oldest neighbourhood in Milan.

Several hours later she was back at the same piazza, on her way to meet with her agent. She was in a hurry. The lunch with her new male acquaintance had been unexpectedly pleasant and lasted longer than anticipated. She was almost feeling a bit infatuated. She looked forward to the time soon to come when she would be working in this Mecca of the fashion world. Her head was brimming with thoughts about the man she'd just met.

When she reached the square, which had previously been so lively, she stopped short and looked around in bewilderment. The scene had dramatically changed. On the ground lay several dozen pigeons, lifeless and bloody. It was alarmingly quiet. The elderly women, the playing children and the amorous couple were gone.

She took in a deep breath. It looked like a war zone, just minutes after a massacre. With one blow the harmony had been replaced by devastation and death. The beautiful pigeons lay scattered about, their plumage stained with blood. Their eyes were closed, their throats limp, their beaks resting on the ground. Under one bench she saw a ball that had been left behind. She raised her eyes and discovered that the pigeons who had survived were huddled close together, perching on the window ledges of the surrounding buildings. The birds were utterly silent. Not a sound could be heard. She looked down, and noticed a red spot on one of her shoes. She stared at it with revulsion. Was that pigeon blood? Her cheeks flushed with an inexplicable feeling of shame.

In distress, she grabbed the coat sleeve of a man who happened to walk past, asking him what had happened here. He shrugged. Didn't he understand what she'd said?

Before she rushed off to go to her meeting, she cast one last look at the dead pigeons. Her mouth was dry, and her head was throbbing. She couldn't comprehend how all that effervescent life on the square could have been so cruelly replaced by such bleak destruction.

The taxi pulled up in front of the Grand Hotel and smoothly came to a halt. The hotel was located in the heart of Stockholm, with a view of Gamla Stan, the old part of the city, and the palace, across the water. The magnificent baroque castle was one of the largest in Europe, but right now half of it was hidden by the November haze. And dusk had begun to settle in. The dark, cold water of Strömmen was teeming with ducks, swans and seagulls hoping for breadcrumbs from the passers-by. Lined up along the quay were the white boats with names like *Norrskar*, *Solöga* and *Vaxholm* – a bittersweet reminder of the now-distant summer when these boats took passengers out to the archipelago.

The man in the back seat paid the cab driver in cash without saying a word. Under the black overcoat he wore a leaden-grey Armani suit, a silk tie in the same hue and a white shirt with a starched collar. He had on sunglasses even though the weary, late-afternoon light barely penetrated the clouds. Maybe he's on drugs, thought the doorman who hurried to receive the guest. Or it could be that he simply didn't want to be recognized. Maybe he was just another of the countless publicity-shy celebrities who had come and gone during the almost 150-year history of the hotel.

The doorman, impeccably outfitted in his black

frock coat and top hat, opened the back door of the cab.

'Good afternoon, Sir. Welcome to the Grand Hotel.'

He bowed and took a step back.

The passenger fumbled with the change he'd received from the cab driver and grabbed his briefcase before getting out.

A second later he dropped his wallet, but he was so quick to pick it up that the doorman had no chance to assist him. When the man bent down, his flawlessly pressed trousers hitched up to reveal that he was wearing tube socks with his custom-tailored suit. White tube socks. The doorman frowned. A clear breach of style. Not a VIP, after all, more likely some yokel trying to blend in, though without being entirely successful. The lack of baggage probably meant that the man was on his way to the bar, or that he was meeting someone for an early dinner. He watched with interest as the man disappeared through the glass doors of the hotel.

The doorman liked to amuse himself by making up stories about the guests. They came from every corner of the earth. Arabian princes, American pop stars, Greek ship-owners, government ministers and heads of state, kings and queens. Celebrities as varied as Albert Einstein, Martin Luther King, Grace Kelly, Charlie Chaplin, Nelson Mandela, and Madonna had stayed at the hotel. For thirty years the doorman had stood sentry at the entrance to the city's most famous hotel, and by now he was used to almost anything. Yet he never tired of thinking about the guests – their lives and cultures, and where they'd come from.

He went back to his post behind the stand just inside the entrance.

Through the big glass windows he had a clear view of any approaching guests. He kept an attentive eye on all the passers-by on the street, looking for anyone who might be heading for the hotel.

It wasn't long before the man with the sunglasses returned from the lobby. He seemed to be in a hurry and came striding towards the exit with his gaze fixed straight ahead. There was clearly something odd about him, something that didn't seem right. It was the way he was moving. His gait was tightly controlled, almost stiff, giving the impression that he was unusually reserved or suffered from aching joints. Or, for some other reason, he was either unable to move naturally or chose not to do so. He seemed nervous, but harmless enough. A poor guy who had ended up in a setting where he felt extremely uncomfortable. No cause for concern.

The doorman smiled as he thought about the tube socks and reached for one of the evening newspapers that had been placed in the side compartment of his stand. Absent-mindedly, he began leafing through the paper.

The next minute he had completely forgotten about the man in the taxi.

Only a few hours before the launch of Stockholm Fashion Week, things were fairly chaotic in the improvised dressing room behind the stage in the winter garden of the Grand Hotel. A dozen long-legged models were crowded together with hairdressers, make-up artists, stylists and assistants helping the models into their clothes. Everyone was busy pinning up hair, curling lashes, fastening belts, tying laces and adjusting the drape of the garments.

Jenny Levin was perched on a bar stool, having her face powdered as she observed the confusion. She enjoyed the seething activity and nervous frenzy before a show, the hectic atmosphere in which everyone involved focused a hundred per cent of their attention on specific tasks. She was a newcomer, having worked as a model for less than a year, but she already felt right at home. As if I was born to do this, she thought, casting a satisfied look at herself in the mirror. Her coppery red hair had been drawn up into a big loose knot on top of her head, with a few tendrils hanging down here and there. It looked as if the strands had come loose by accident but, like everything else, that was merely an illusion. Every little detail had been carefully designed and styled.

Jenny knew that her face was considered beautiful.

She had high cheekbones, almond-shaped green eyes and a fair, unblemished complexion with a light sprinkling of freckles.

She opened her mouth slightly as the make-up artist applied red gloss to her lips. Jenny stood five foot eleven in her stocking feet. Her childlike face gave her the look of a fifteen-year-old, even though she was already nineteen. Her innocent, fresh beauty, combined with an indefinably mysterious look in her eye, prompted people to think of a wood nymph, which was perfect for the current trend. Ideally, a model was expected to look like some sort of creature that had sprung straight out of nature.

Growing up in farming country on the Swedish island of Gotland, Jenny had suffered from a complex about her height and her skinny figure. But now she'd developed a whole new view of her appearance. Attributes which in her former life had been considered anything but attractive were suddenly being hailed as lovely.

After her lipstick was done, she suppressed a yawn and stretched out her long, slender legs. She hadn't had much sleep last night. Thinking about the reason for this, she felt a spark of heat in her nether zone.

In the middle of the room the hair stylists were all working hard on their assigned models, supervised by their boss, André, who was casting a critical eye over their work. It was his job to make sure that each hairdo was exactly as the designer and stylist had intended. He was a short Frenchman, dressed in baggy jeans, a black T-shirt and suede sandals. With hairbrushes stuck in his back pockets, spray bottles gripped between his knees, and hairpins poking out from the corner of his mouth, he confidently and professionally added last-minute touches to make each hairstyle perfect. All the models had long, thick hair that required several steps to bring it under control. First, their hair had to be carefully brushed out, blow-dried, and subjected to a flat-iron, then sprayed and combed back with impressive vigour. The young women patiently sat in their chairs, their faces impassive. Occasionally, one of them would be asked to stand up while André applied the hairspray. That caused him a certain amount of difficulty, since he barely reached even to their shoulders.

As a final touch, each model was given the most amazing shiny hair extensions, which were either skilfully fastened to the hair piled high on their head or allowed to flow freely past their thin shoulders.

Along one wall of the room, every single bar stool was occupied in front of the team of make-up artists who were busily applying mascara and blusher and lipstick. They had been directed to keep the make-up toned down and discreet in order to create a more natural look. The focus was supposed to be on the lips, which were being painted a strong red under layer after layer of gloss to give them as moist and drenched an appearance as possible. 'Think fish,' the stylist had said when she issued her instructions. A great deal of time was also devoted to applying the base foundation, since the models had to have a smooth and even complexion. Any blemishes were concealed, eyebrows plucked, a bruise on a thigh was covered with make-up, a spot carefully hidden with the most expensive cream available. And a lustrous lotion was rubbed on the legs of all the models to give them an attractive gleam on stage.

Along the other walls stood dozens of clothes rails mounted on wheels, each one labelled with a model's name and photograph. This was where their outfits for the evening had been hung, in the order in which they would be worn. Jackets, dresses, trousers, scarves, belts, hats and caps, as well as jewellery stowed in plastic bags. Lined up in neat rows on the floor underneath were shoes and boots – different ones for each creation. A stunning mix of bright-blue suede sandals with stiletto heels, coral-coloured platform shoes, grey thigh-high boots, and screaming-pink plastic shoes with blocky heels. The shoes were adorned with rivets, buckles and glittery gemstones. All the heels were at least four inches high, which meant that most of the girls stood close to six foot three when they were dressed and ready to go.

The models moved with accustomed ease from make-up to hairstyling to wardrobe. From time to time, they were forced to take brief breaks while waiting for assistance. During that time one model might pick at a salad, while another talked on her mobile phone, and someone else simply sat idly, looking bored. Others would get deeply immersed in a conversation, as if they were sitting in a café, and totally ignore the commotion going on around them. One dark-eyed beauty was merrily cavorting in front of a mirror, wearing shorts so skimpy that her legs seemed to go on for ever; another, who was critically examining her fringed, pink suede dress, wore neon-coloured nail polish that shone against her dark skin.

Garments and accessories were put on at the last minute. Nobody paid any attention to the fact that so many bodies were constantly being clothed and unclothed. Bare breasts and thongs were revealed without the slightest embarrassment. All the models had boyish figures with straight shoulders, flat stomachs, tiny breasts, and narrow hips. Long arms, long legs, big feet. Hollowed cheeks, protruding collarbones, muscular backs.

Having finished with make-up, Jenny Levin was squatting down in the middle of the room, wearing only a thong as she buckled her elegant snakeskin shoes with the sky-high heels. She stood up and looked around for the woman who was supposed to help her put on the stunning and glittery bandage dress that was to open the show. No bra. The designer wanted the contours of her breasts to be visible under the tight-fitting garment. At that moment, the woman showed up, and together they managed to get Jenny into the glossy sheath without disturbing her hairdo.

Sometimes, Jenny was seized with a feeling of unreality in the midst of everything. She found it hard to comprehend how her life could have changed so completely and so quickly. Only a year ago she had been just an ordinary schoolgirl. Each day was like all the others. She took the school bus to the secondary school in Visby, went to classes, and stopped for coffee with a few of her classmates in the city before heading back home. At the weekend she went riding, and in the evening she went out with friends. Often a bunch of them would hang out together and watch videos. Or if someone's parents were away, they'd have a party at their house, drinking strong beer and home-distilled alcohol.

With one blow her whole life had changed. Suddenly, she'd become used to the most expensive champagne in the hottest nightclubs – places that she'd previously read about only in magazines. Now, she was frequently seen in photographs mingling with celebrities. She wore the most beautiful clothes and was greeted with admiration wherever she went. It was incomprehensible.

When only ten minutes remained before the start of the show, the tempo behind the scenes escalated. Even in the dressing room everyone was aware that the audience members were beginning to take their seats on the other side of the curtains. Suggestive techno music was pulsing from the loudspeakers, adding to the air of anticipation.

Jenny went over to the wall one last time to check the list showing the order in which the models were to appear. She was first, and of course she knew why. There was no doubt that she was the star of the group. And this was particularly exciting because, tonight, he would be sitting out there. She had decided to pretend not to notice him, as if he had no effect on her.

In her mind she went through the eight different garments she would wear during the course of the show. She cast a quick glance at the rack of outfits assigned to her; everything seemed to be in order.

The stylist gathered all the models, by now giggling and giddy, for one last run-through. Lined up behind the curtains, they looked like women depicted by the nineteenth-century French artist Toulouse-Lautrec. With their elaborate hairdos, extravagant dresses and bright-red lips, they could easily have stepped out of a painting of the red-light district in Paris more than a century earlier.

The stylist sternly admonished the glittering beauties to stop whispering and urged them to focus on the task at hand. It was almost time. She put on a headset so she could stay in contact with the technicians. A minute to go. On the other side of the curtains they could hear an expectant hum of voices from the six hundred invited guests.

The make-up artists quickly moved among the models, doing some last-minute touch-ups, as the hair stylists sprayed and poked at their hairdos.

Jenny was caught up in the mood; she loved this moment. Seconds before the show started, her mind cleared of all thoughts. She stared attentively at the stylist, waiting for her cue. Then the curtains parted and she stepped out on to the catwalk. A gasp passed through the audience when they caught sight of her. She paused for a moment and couldn't help smiling. She looked for his face and found it at once.

Then she moved forward.

A pale November light strained to make its way through a few gaps in the heavy cloud cover. All the stones worn smooth by the water lay untouched on the shore. No one had walked along that stretch of beach in a long time. The sea was grey, with hardly a ripple. Far off in the distance, leaden waves lapped steadily at the scattered boulders that seemed to have been randomly tossed into the water.

Anders Knutas, who had just stepped out on to the front porch of the summer cottage, shivered and pulled up the collar of his jacket. The air was fresh but raw, and the damp cold seeped through his clothes. There was almost no wind. The bare branches of the birch tree down by the gate didn't move. They were covered with drops of water that sparkled in the morning light. The ground was spongy with tiny yellow leaves that had fallen when the autumn chill crept in. But a few roses were still blooming in the garden, glinting like red and pink will-o'-the-wisps against all the grey; they were reminders of another season.

He headed out along the muddy gravel track that wound its way parallel to the sea. Their cottage was a couple of kilometres beyond Lickershamn, an old fishing village on Gotland's north-west coast, also called the Stone Coast. Nowadays, it was a summer paradise with only a few permanent residents. At this time of year it was peaceful, and he enjoyed the quiet.

Knutas, who was a morning person, had slipped out without waking Lina. She was sleeping soundly, as usual. It was no more than eight o'clock on this Saturday morning, and he had the road all to himself. It was uneven and muddy, with countless potholes that had filled with water after a night of rain. Lying upside down on the grass-covered strip of land next to the sea were several flat-bottomed rowboats, one of which belonged to Knutas. He loved to go out fishing, and he was a long-standing member of the Lickershamn fishing association. Brown trout, salmon, flounder, cod and turbot were plentiful in these waters. He usually went out with his neighbour Arne, who was a fisherman and one of the few people who lived here year round.

Along the road grew reeds that had now yellowed and withered, a few bushes with beautiful, gleaming red rose-hips, and a gnarled apple tree with a dozen or so yellow apples still clinging to its branches.

Further away, steep chalk cliffs rose dramatically out of the sea. The big *rauk* called Jungfrun, the Maiden, was sharply outlined against the sky, keeping watch over the small harbour, where only a couple of fishing boats and a few rowboats were now moored. There wasn't a soul in sight.

On Friday afternoon, Knutas had left police headquarters early and picked up Lina after her shift on the maternity ward of Visby Hospital. Then they had driven out to the cottage. Arne had phoned to tell them that a tree on their property had fallen in the latest autumn storm, which had swept over the island with such violent force a few days earlier. So they had decided to spend the weekend cleaning up. Their marriage had been going through a lengthy rough patch, and they were both making a real effort to find their way back to each other. And, lately, things seemed to be going well.

During the past year, he'd sometimes thought that divorce was inevitable. Lina had become withdrawn and didn't seem to need him in the same way as she had in the past. She did more things alone, took weekend trips to Stockholm, and spent time with her female friends. She and Maria, who was a photographer, had spent all of October on the West African islands of Cape Verde, documenting the high rate of mothers who died in childbirth. Maria wrote the report and took the photographs, while Lina contributed in her capacity as a midwife and researcher. When Knutas offered some mild objections to Lina taking the trip, she had angrily declared that in the developing countries the death rate among women giving birth was an enormous problem that deserved attention. He shouldn't even try to stop her going.

Knutas had never imagined how lonely it would be without Lina. Their twins, Petra and Nils, were seventeen and seldom at home. Petra had always been sports-minded and loved outdoors activities. She'd been playing floorball for years, but her biggest passion was orienteering, to which she devoted almost all her free time. Several evenings a week she went to track practice, and when she had no floorball matches at the weekend, she went with her friends to Svaidestugan, outside Visby. That was where the local orienteering community had a clubhouse, and there were also a number of different types of training trails. Healthy hobbies, of course, but recently Knutas had hardly seen her at all.

Nils was the exact opposite of his sister. He was totally uninterested in anything having to do with sports or exercise. He belonged to a theatre group and played drums in a band that practised every evening. Knutas was glad that his children had so many interests. And both of them did well in school, so there was no real reason to complain. They were in the process of separating from him and Lina, which also meant that they, in their role as parents, had to do the same. Lina didn't seem to think this was a problem. She had adapted to the situation and at the same time had found new activities to keep herself busy.

Like that trip to Cape Verde, which, for Knutas, had been sheer torture. On that first evening when he came home from work, he'd felt as if the walls were echoing with emptiness all around him. Outside the windows the autumn darkness had settled in even though it was only four thirty. He'd switched on all the lights in the house and turned on the TV, but he'd been unable to fend off the feeling of being abandoned. And it got worse each day. If the children were spending the night somewhere else or didn't come home for dinner, he lost any desire to cook or even make a cup of coffee for himself.

He had suffered through the silence of that month, without fully working out whether the empty feeling was because he was missing Lina in particular, or because he missed having someone else's company in general.

The day before she was due back home he was suddenly seized with a great surge of energy. He cleaned the whole house, filled the refrigerator and pantry with food, and bought fresh flowers, which he put in a vase on the kitchen table. He was determined to do his utmost to be loving and considerate.

And it had worked. They'd started talking more to each other. Their relationship seemed deeper, more intense, and they'd drawn closer.

On Friday afternoon they had cleared the toppled tree from their property, then raked up leaves and burnt them on a bonfire. They ended the day by cooking a good meal together, and then sat in front of the fireplace, drinking wine and talking. Before going to sleep, they had made love. It almost felt like old times.

Knutas drew the fresh sea air deep into his lungs and continued walking. He passed the home of one of the permanent residents and saw smoke coming from the chimney. Off in the distance, he noticed light in a window. A flock of black jackdaws was perched in the treetops. With a loud shriek they all took off at once when he approached. The sea birds, clustered on rocks out in the water, reacted the same way. As they rose up into the sky, he realized how many there were.

The fishermen's huts that were lined up down by the harbour were all empty. Some of the larger ones had been turned into summer homes with kitchenettes and bunk beds.

Knutas sat down on a bench and gazed out at the sea. One evening in September, they'd gone swimming here on their last visit to the cottage. He thought about Lina's voluptuous body and soft white skin. Her long, curly red hair, her smile and warm eyes. He was still very much in love with her.

When he got back, he saw her sitting on the porch wearing a long grey cardigan and thick socks, with her pale, freckled hands wrapped around a coffee mug. She waved and smiled at him as he came walking along the road. He waved back.

When they reached the road that connected the peninsula of Furillen to Gotland's north-east coast, Jenny rolled the car window down halfway and breathed in the sea air. She hadn't been here in a long time, and she'd forgotten how beautiful it was. Solitary, barren, and nothing but sea, sea, and more sea. In the distance she saw several wind turbines reaching towards the sky, their blades turning slowly in the light breeze. The beach was deserted, the road bumpy and dusty, the landscape bare and rocky; the higher up they drove, the more stripped everything looked. Like a moonscape, devoid of all traces of civilization.

The photographer Markus Sandberg was driving; she sat next to him in the passenger seat. There were two other people in the rental car: Maria, the make-up artist, and Hugo, the stylist, who were both going to work on the photo shoot, which was expected to last three days. They were quietly talking in the back seat and seemed to be completely absorbed in their conversation.

So much the better. That meant Jenny could enjoy the company of her companion in the front seat. As often as she dared, she let her eyes rest on Markus. She couldn't believe how attractive he was, so mature, so worldly. He was one of the fashion industry's most sought-after photographers and a favourite of the agencies. He'd travelled the globe with all the most famous models and stylists, working for the best magazines. He was nicely suntanned, with several small tattoos on his muscular arms and a silver bracelet on one lean wrist. He had a dark stubble on his cheeks, full lips, and intense, deep-blue eyes. His hair was thick and almost black, with no hint of thinning, even though he was close to forty. But that was hard to believe. Jenny thought he looked much younger. Maybe thirty at most. Markus was careful about maintaining his appearance. He worked out at the gym, shaved only enough to be fashionable, and spent a lot of time in front of the mirror styling his hair. 'I've devoted my whole life to appearances,' he'd cynically explained when she teased him about being so vain. 'Both professionally and in my personal life. If I don't take care of how I look, what would I take care of? It's the only thing I know how to do – making myself and other people look our best. Beauty is my great passion in life.'

At first glance, the clothes he wore seemed casual and thrown together, as if everything he'd put on just happened to look right. A scarf wrapped around his neck, a pair of jeans faded in the proper places, a seemingly simple print shirt. But, on closer inspection, his clothing turned out to be from one of the foremost designer labels. He looked fabulous even with no clothes at all, she thought, longing for night-time, when they would share a bed. Markus had insisted on staying in one of the separate cabins that belonged to the hotel and were intended for guests who wanted to be left in peace. Personally, she wasn't exactly thrilled about the arrangement. It didn't sound especially appealing. Markus had told her that the cabins had been built at some distance from each other and about a kilometre from the hotel itself. They were barely visible because of the surrounding shrubbery and trees. They had no electricity or running water, with only paraffin lamps for light and wood stoves for heat. She had promised to sleep there with Markus. The one positive thing was that it would be easy for her to slip out, spend the night in the cabin, and then return to her room in the hotel early in the morning without being seen.

So far, their relationship was a secret. She wondered how long it would be before they could show their love openly. Markus was a bachelor, and he had no children. When the other models talked about him, they always claimed that he'd stay single for ever. They also pathetically agreed that he was completely unreliable. In the past, he'd photographed girls for various men's magazines, and he'd developed a reputation for constantly changing girlfriends. At first, Jenny had been bothered by the fact that he'd taken nude photographs, but now she no longer cared. Everybody had to start somewhere, after all. Although she did try to avoid looking at his old photos of those girls with the big boobs. The models looked like they were eager to have sex with the photographer at any moment. She'd also felt a bit shy in the beginning, since he was so used to seeing such shapely women naked. She was embarrassed, and that made it hard for her to relax when she was with him. But he'd managed to convince her that none of that mattered; it belonged to his past, and he wasn't proud of that work. Plus, she was more beautiful than any other woman. So she had decided to ignore all the spiteful gossip about Markus. Including the fact that he had never had a serious relationship with any woman.

She studied his handsome profile. Maybe it was simply because he'd never met the right person. In her mind, Jenny pictured the two of them sitting together on the veranda of a huge luxury hotel near the sea with several little children playing around them. What if she was the one to finally snare him? She laughed at the thought.

'What's so funny?'

Markus's eyes were smiling behind his sunglasses. A dimple appeared in his unshaven cheek.

'Nothing,' she said. 'Nothing at all.'

She turned to look out of the window again. It was wonderful to come out here after the hectic fashion week in Stockholm. What a contrast to the noise of the big city. Right now, they were passing the abandoned limestone quarry where water had formed lakes in the huge pits. Far below, she could see the hotel, which looked so small and insignificant from this distance. The Hotel Fabriken had been built on the grounds of a former limestone factory. It stood in the middle of an expansive gravel-covered lot, surrounded by pyramid-like heaps of crushed limestone. A few factory buildings remained, reminding visitors of the industrial operations that had once been carried out on the property. Still present were an old stone crusher, a warehouse and the solidly constructed wharf that stretched out into the water, from which ships loaded with limestone had headed out to sea in the old days. In the middle of everything stood a caravan shaped like an egg, with shiny aluminium panelling. It looked out of place, like some sort of vessel that had just landed from outer space. She wondered if it was available for hotel guests.

An efficiently run business had operated on this site into the early seventies. After that, the military had largely taken over the land, and for the next twenty years or so Furillen had been a restricted area of Gotland, and foreigners were not permitted access. By now, most of the barbed wire had been removed, and the old radar stations remained as memorials to a bygone era.

When she was a child, Jenny had sometimes come out to the peninsula with her parents. They would take hikes in the barren landscape, walk along the deserted shoreline, or pick strawberries in the woods. Her mother knew a secret place where they could always find plenty of berries.

Now Jenny had returned for a completely different purpose. Who would have believed that the next time she set foot on the peninsula it would be as a celebrated fashion model?

A year ago, she'd been discovered by a scout from one of the biggest modelling agencies in Stockholm. She'd gone to the city with her family, and the scout had stopped her on the street to ask if she'd be willing to pose for some fashion photos. Feeling both surprised and flattered, she'd gone with him to the agency office and had auditioned during a photo shoot that very afternoon. The next day, the scout had phoned to invite

Jenny back to the agency along with her parents, since at the time she was under eighteen. Her mother and father were impressed by the agency and its intentions, so they gave their permission, and with that the matter was settled.

Jenny quickly became popular, and it wasn't long before her diary was fully booked. Since the modelling was going so well, she quit school after Christmas and started working full time. She travelled to Milan, Paris and New York, each photo session more successful than the last. Everyone seemed to appreciate her unique look. She was soon a well-known Swedish name within the international fashion world. And after being photographed for the cover of the Italian edition of *Vogue*, which was the most prestigious magazine of all, she became one of Europe's top models. The money poured in, and the amounts were greater than she could have ever imagined.

Now she was sitting here in this car, on her way to an exclusive photo shoot with one of Sweden's foremost photographers. Not to mention that she was in a romantic relationship with him. Markus had stressed that they needed to be cautious at first. It was a sensitive matter, since he'd recently broken up with a model from the same agency, and she seemed to be having a hard time accepting the fact that she needed to let him go. Diana would sometimes phone in the middle of the night, and he would have long-drawn-out conversations with her. So things weren't exactly without complications at the moment. Markus thought that if they made their romance public, Diana, who was very temperamental, might hit the roof. It was better to wait.

*

Now the road was heading down a steep slope. Again
Jenny turned to look at Markus. Of course she could be
patient.

'I can't believe it's that late!'

Karin Jacobsson threw off the blanket and climbed out of the big double bed. She was naked, and her short dark hair stuck out in all directions.

'What?'

Her companion sat up, looking startled. He squinted at the glare when she turned on the ceiling light.

'I can't understand how I could have overslept. That never happens!'

Karin kept on grumbling as she dashed for the bathroom. He couldn't help casting an admiring glance at her lean, supple body before the door closed behind her.

'Could you make some coffee?' she called. 'I've got to have a cup or I'll die.'

The next second he heard the shower go on. How could anybody move so fast? She was like a little ferret, he thought as he plodded off to the kitchen. An extremely sexy ferret.

Five minutes later they were sitting across from each other in Janne Widén's big, bright kitchen in Terra Nova, a residential neighbourhood outside Visby. It was on this very street that they'd first met, six months earlier.

Karin tapped in Knutas's number on her mobile. As usual, he answered at once.

'Listen, I've overslept,' she said. 'Yes, really. No, but it's true. Once in a while even I have to . . . Okay, okay, never mind. I'll be there as soon as I can. Oh, is that right? So there's no hurry? Not really, but . . . So I can take my time? That's great. See you later, then. Okay? I'll get there when I get there. What? No, nothing special . . . Just a little tired. Mmm. No, it's no problem.'

She ended the conversation and looked at her new lover who was sitting across the table. She smiled, showing the gap between her two front teeth. When she spoke the tone of her voice had completely changed.

'So. The meeting with the county police commissioner was cancelled. I've got nothing on my schedule until lunchtime.'

'What luck! And all I have to do is stay here and pack.'

'What time does your plane leave?'

'Six o'clock. Then I change planes in Stockholm. And that plane leaves at eight thirty tonight.'

'I can drive you to the airport.'

Janne was going to Spain for a week with one of Sweden's most famous pop singers to take some PR photos. He poured more coffee into Karin's cup.

'He sure asks a lot of questions, by the way. Your boss, I mean.'

'Oh, he was just surprised. He and I always used to be the first ones to arrive at the station in the morning. I don't think I've ever overslept before. Not once in the fifteen years I've been on the force.'

'That's incredible! You're so bloody disciplined. I have to say that it's liberating to know that even you can muck things up once in a while, my little Miss Perfect.'

'Cut it out,' she said, smiling. 'Just because I like things to be neat and tidy. And, besides, I have to set a good example.'

Karin Jacobsson was the assistant superintendent of the criminal police in Visby and the closest colleague of Detective Superintendent Anders Knutas. They were good friends and had worked together for many years, but they almost never socialized outside working hours.

The autumn had been relatively calm, with no major incidents; everything seemed to be proceeding smoothly. To be honest, Karin had been doing her job more or less on autopilot. For the first time in ages she'd met a man with whom she felt comfortable, and now she'd even fallen in love with him. So she wanted to spend as much time with Janne as possible. As if that wasn't enough, she'd also taken steps to renew contact with her daughter, Hanna, whom she'd given up at birth for adoption. And their relationship had its complications.

When she'd eaten the last bite of toast, Janne stood up. With a mischievous glint in his eye, he picked her up and carried her back into the bedroom.

'What are you doing?' she asked, laughing.

'It's only nine o'clock. We need to make the most of the time before I leave. And you said you don't have anything until lunch, right?'

The interior of the hotel was designed in an austere, modernist style that presented a stunning contrast to the details remaining from its factory days. They entered a lobby with a gleaming stone floor and a ten-metre-high ceiling. A lovely blonde woman standing behind a small counter built into the wall welcomed them and handed out the room keys. Then they each went off in a different direction. Markus was going to scout photo locations with Sebastian, the art director. Jenny barely had time to drop her things in her room before she had to head to make-up. Every minute counted.

Two hours later, she was ready for the photo shoot, for which she would model ten different outfits. Markus was waiting for her in the main lounge, where he would take the first pictures. As luck would have it, at the moment there were no other guests staying at the hotel, so they could work in peace.

It was a large grey room that seemed to exude quiet harmony. The furniture consisted of severe-looking steel-framed armchairs upholstered in a leaden-grey woollen fabric, low concrete tables, stainless-steel lamps, and white leather sofas. Black curtains, white limestone walls. A beautiful shimmer of light flooded the room from one wall that was covered from floor to ceiling with little glass cubes. Outdoors, a few scraggly pine trees were visible on the rocky shore, and beyond was the sea – dark, foaming, and at the moment inhospitable. Along the walls of the room stood heavy log benches with sheepskins in various hues of grey. In one corner of the bright room a black bicycle had been parked; in another stood a big fan on wheels. A large TV was fastened to the wall. From the ceiling hung an overhead crane with long chains, recalling a time when the building had housed a factory.

Markus wanted to use only natural light. He needed daylight for these photos. Nothing else. The photos were for a fashion spread to be published in one of Sweden's biggest fashion magazines. Jenny was wearing a short checked skirt and a purple top with a wide belt around her waist. Grey tights and purple suede boots that reached to her thighs. She wore a light amount of eye make-up and clear lip gloss. Her hair had been curled to look natural and had then been classically styled.

Jenny was the only model, and everyone was giving her their full attention. Hugo, the stylist, checked every fold of her clothing. He wore a belt that held safety pins, tape and various clips. Maria, the make-up artist, had to stand on tiptoe in order to touch up Jenny's lip gloss and to dab a bit more powder on her face. Jenny was cheerful and relaxed, happy to let everyone do their jobs, whistling softly and chatting as she stole glances at Markus. He took a few test pictures of her in the room. The purple of her outfit stood out nicely against all the grey.

Then the photo shoot officially got started, and the

change in mood was instantly noticeable. There was a different vibe as everybody focused on what the model was doing. Jenny's eyes took on an intense look as she stared into the cold lens of the camera. She struck various poses and flirted with the camera, sometimes with a trace of a smile and a mocking expression. In between shots the make-up artist and stylist stepped in to powder her face, to push back a strand of hair that was out of place, or to straighten a fold of her skirt. Occasionally, Jenny would hum and dance, clowning around to keep up her energy. She didn't want to freeze up. Although there was no real risk of that happening with Markus as the photographer. He inspired her. They were a perfect team. With small, delicate movements, she altered her poses, moving her hand from her hip, raising one leg, changing the way she sat on the edge of the leather sofa. The grey, modern furniture, the industrial setting, the high ceiling, the polished floor, the sheepskins, the concrete – everything provided an effective contrast to her tasteful elegance. As soon as the camera began clicking, something changed in her. She lit up from inside, glittering so brightly that sparks practically flew all around her, and the charm she radiated had a strong effect on the rest of the team. Everyone became even more meticulous and finicky about the details, even more anxious for the photos to be as good as possible. The hours flew by. They moved to other rooms, then went out into the forecourt. An old Opel from the fifties was driven into place and Jenny lovingly leaned against it.

She willingly obeyed all the directions that Markus gave her.

The door opens and she hears the usual hearty voice say, 'Good morning. Seven o'clock. Time to get up.' Without looking at her, the nurse comes in, turns on the ceiling light, and opens the curtains. It's still dark outside, but light shines in from the other buildings, reminding her that she's in hospital, that she's not well, that she is not part of normal life in the world. The buildings loom like ominous grey monsters outside her window. The hospital is so big that it even has its own street name in the neighbourhood.

Agnes turns on to her other side. Away from the light, away from reality, evading all reminders that there's a world out there, a life that's continuing, a life that she could have been living, but it's about to run away from her. At least that's how it feels right now. Even though she's only sixteen.

This is the worst part of the day. Waking up. All she wants is to stay asleep and not have to wake up to yet another hell. The battle to eat as little as possible and to get rid of as much energy as she can, without the nurses noticing.

She doesn't know how long she'll be able to keep doing this.

Agnes wishes that she could stay in bed under the covers, yet she's painfully aware that she needs to hurry and get up in order to jump at least thirty times in the bathroom before breakfast. Otherwise, it will be unbearable to force down enough yoghurt and toast to satisfy the nurse.

For a moment she wrestles with the dilemma, and then, with a great effort, she sits up and gets out of bed. She sticks her feet in the fleece slippers and casts a glance at her room mate, Linda, who is lying in bed with her back turned. She never says much. Agnes goes out to the corridor and into the bathroom. So far, she's still one of the lucky few who are allowed to close and lock the door when using the toilet. For some inexplicable reason, they still trust her, even though they think it's taking a long time for her to gain any weight. They don't seem to have worked out what she's been doing.

The bathroom is cramped, with only enough space for a toilet in front of a small sink. There is no window or mirror. After she finishes peeing and washing her hands, she gets started. It's not easy with so little space. She can't do her arm exercises in here; that has to wait until the afternoon in the warm room. Here she can only bounce up and down. She pushes off with both feet, jumping straight up, as high as she can manage. After only a few jumps she's out of breath. Her heart is hammering in her chest as if protesting such rough treatment. Her legs ache; they're fragile after such a long period of malnutrition. Agnes grits her teeth and keeps counting, whispering the numbers to herself: 'Ten, eleven, twelve.' The whole time she's scared that a nurse might knock on the door. If she's forced to interrupt her exercise, it won't have the same effect, even if she continues later on. She needs to jump at least thirty times in a row, otherwise she'll be lost.

Soon, she's sweating profusely and breathing even harder. She perseveres, fighting so much to keep going that she tastes blood in her mouth. They say that she's emaciated, that she'll die if she doesn't put on weight. Right now, she has no idea how much she weighs, because that's not something they ever discuss in here. The patients are weighed once a week but aren't told the results. The last time she checked her weight back home in Visby, the scale showed ninety-five pounds. Since she is five foot nine, that meant her BMI was fourteen. She doesn't think that sounds dangerous. There are plenty of girls who are much thinner. 'Twenty-one, twenty-two, twenty-three.' No one has knocked on the door yet, but she knows there's a great risk that soon she'll be interrupted. She closes her eyes for a moment, as if that might make it harder for anyone to discover what she's doing. She makes a great effort to quiet her breathing so she won't be heard. She's starting to feel dizzy, and her heart is pounding in her fragile chest. 'Twenty-seven, twenty-eight, twenty-nine.' She has reached her goal of thirty, so she sinks on to the toilet. Leans back, shuts her eyes. Waits until her racing pulse calms down. When she has recovered sufficiently she gets up and splashes cold water on her face. She takes off her nightgown and rinses her armpits. She won't have time for a shower. She usually does take a shower in the evening before going to bed. That gives her the chance to do her last exercises for the day. When she finally opens the bathroom door, she breathes a sigh of relief. Now she'll be able to handle breakfast.

Dinner was served in the dining room, which had been furnished in a discriminating modern style that matched the rest of the hotel.

Filled with anticipation, they all took their places, hungry after the long day's work. Jenny looked at the others seated around the table. Hugo had turned out to be a steady rock. Always on hand to offer assistance, from safety pins to fabric glue to accessories that suddenly seemed essential because the light was coming in at an unexpected angle and required something other than what had been planned. He was the consummate professional and always understood precisely what Markus meant when he talked about the fold in a garment, a polo-neck, or the heel of a boot. At the same time, he had his own self-assured view of things. If, on occasion, he disagreed with Markus, Hugo would persist in arguing until he got his way.

He had straggly hair that stuck out all over, and he wore glasses with heavy black frames. He chose elegant clothes, displaying an infallible sense of style that was striking without being garish. And he was always so upbeat, which rubbed off on the others. He had told Jenny that he'd recently become engaged to his boyfriend, whom he'd known for only a few months. Maybe that was the reason for his good humour.

When everyone had a glass of wine, Hugo gave a toast to celebrate the excellent work they'd done that day. Sebastian Bigert, who was the art director, and Anna Neumann, the producer, raised their glasses and smiled. They seemed nice, although Jenny hadn't talked to them much. Kevin Sundström, the photographer's assistant, was a young guy on his first photo shoot outside the studio. For that reason he was a bit confused and over-eager, but a real charmer who looked after her needs. He was constantly running off to get Jenny coffee and water. He was always asking her if she wanted anything else, his eyes flirting with her from under the black fringe of his hair. Jenny had met Maria Åkerlund eight days ago during Stockholm Fashion Week, when Maria had done her make-up several times. She had a confident and steady air about her, even though she wasn't very old. Twenty-five at most, Jenny guessed.

Everyone was sitting at the dinner table, except Markus, but they weren't going to wait for him. He was usually late. The three-course meal consisted of new beets with a locally produced goat's cheese, grilled turbot with potato purée, and chocolate trifle for dessert.

Jenny ate everything with good appetite. Hugo raised his eyebrows when he saw her empty plate.

'That's the way she is,' Maria explained. 'She can eat almost anything, and she never gains even an ounce. No wonder she makes people mad.'

She gave Jenny a big smile and then raised her glass in a toast. The Amarone tasted fabulous, and they all drank several glasses of the red wine. Jenny started feeling the effects, which made her giggly and light-headed.

Several times during the meal she had discreetly checked her mobile. The others were sure that Markus would turn up at any moment, if for no other reason than he must be hungry. There was no food in the cabin where he was staying.

Jenny went outside to smoke a cigarette and give him a call, but she couldn't get through. When she asked the desk clerk about this, she was told that the mobile coverage at the cabins wasn't good. The guests could seldom be reached by phone, and that was the reason why most of them wanted to stay there. To get away from the outside world.

When it was close to eleven, the party broke up.

'He probably fell asleep,' said Hugo. 'See you tomorrow.'

Jenny's pulse quickened as she thought about Markus. It seemed so unlikely that he would simply have fallen asleep out there. He must be longing for her as much as she yearned for him. Earlier in the day he had whispered to her that he could hardly wait to be alone with her. What if he'd decided to skip dinner and had been waiting for her all this time? He'd told her that he had brought along a bottle of champagne, which he'd stowed in an insulated bag in the car. She felt weak-kneed at the thought of how considerate he was. He cared too much about her to have simply written her off this evening.

Jenny hurried to her room to touch up her lipstick and spray on more perfume. She slipped her toothbrush into her handbag and put on a warm jacket. It wasn't really cold – the temperature was several degrees above freezing – but she could hear the wind blowing outside the window.

When she stepped outside, she saw that it was pitch dark beyond the dimly lit forecourt. The old stone crusher up on the hill looked ghostly and frightening in the darkness. She couldn't make out much of the sea, catching only a glimpse of the black expanse as she listened to the roar of the waves. The remaining massive piles of crushed limestone loomed against the sky.

She found a women's bicycle among the row of ungainly military bikes lined up along the wall of the hotel. Several of them had toppled over in the wind.

The gravel appeared white in the dark; the feeble glow from the bicycle lamp wasn't much help in finding her way. Far off on the horizon she saw a few faint red dots of light.

She tried not to think too much about her surroundings, focusing instead on her riding. Markus had said that it wasn't far to the cabin.

She soon found herself approaching the wind turbine on the hill. Its powerful white tower disappeared into the dark sky. She could hear the huge blades spinning; the sound of their rotation penetrated through the rush of the wind and the roar from the sea down below. The closer she got, the louder the sound. She heard a steady swishing, a rhythmic whooshing. As she passed directly underneath, the three arms turned overhead like knife blades slicing through the night air. The base of the tower stood right next to the road, and she could have almost touched it if she'd reached out her hand.

It felt as if the wind turbine was a great roaring beast, very much alive. But she had to ride past; there was no way to avoid it.

She pedalled as hard as she could and felt a certain relief once the wind turbine was behind her. Now she entered the woods. The road levelled out, and the wind wasn't as strong among the trees. Tightly packed on both sides of the road were spruce trees, pines, shrubbery and dense thickets. She happened to cast a glance into the woods and noticed a menacing dark strip of sky with patches of grey. The faint moonlight that managed to filter through the trees created sinister shadows. 'Don't look,' she murmured to herself. 'Don't look to either side. Keep your eyes on the road. Don't look into the dark.'

The road out to the cabin was longer than she'd thought. By now she was regretting the whole venture. She had sobered up and wanted to turn around. She looked over her shoulder, but she could no longer see the hotel, which was somewhere far below her. It was almost midnight, and they all had to get up at six in the morning to work. What was she thinking? Finally, a blue shed appeared at the side of the road. Relief made her dizzy. She had to be close. And the cabin lights could supposedly be seen from outdoors. She tried to remember what Markus had said.

'Leave the bike at the shed. The path is too rough for a bike. Walk twenty metres to your right and down the slope towards the sea. Be careful. It's really steep. You'll see the light from the paraffin lamps and the fire burning in the fireplace through the window. The light will guide you.'

She jumped off the bike and leaned it against the shed. She couldn't hear the wind turbine any more. The sound was drowned out by the increasing roar of the sea. She walked down the slope and glimpsed a faint light a hundred metres away. That was lucky. Otherwise, she would never have dared go through what seemed like impenetrable thickets. She had a hard time making her way forward. Several times she stumbled over roots and loose stones. Branches slapped at her face, and she bumped into trees that she couldn't see in the dark.

Suddenly, without warning, the light went out in the cabin, and it was pitch black all around her.

Johan Berg jolted awake. He was lying in bed in Roma, feeling sweaty from the nightmare he'd been having. In his dream he'd started smoking again. How banal. Reluctantly, he climbed out of bed, careful not to wake Emma. The stone floor felt cold under his bare feet. He used the toilet and then went out to the kitchen. He poured himself a glass of water and looked at the digital clock on the cooker. It was a quarter past midnight. A sense of uneasiness still lingered from his dream, and he was too restless to go back to bed. He looked in on the kids. All four were staying with them this week. They were sound asleep. Eleven-year-old Sara and Filip, who was ten, were Emma's children from her previous marriage. They came to stay every other week. Johan and Emma also had two children together: Elin, who was three and a half, and Anton, who would soon have his first birthday.

Johan sat down on the sofa in the living room and looked out at the garden. It was partially lit by the white glow of the street lamps. The apple trees had lost almost all their leaves. He was not looking forward to winter. He listened to the wind blowing outside the window. That damned wind. He still wasn't used to the winters on Gotland. They seldom had what he considered a real winter. The paltry amount of snow usually lasted only a few days before melting and disappearing. Elin and Anton had really had only one chance to play in the snow, and that was when they'd gone to visit his mother in Rönninge, a suburb south of Stockholm where Johan had grown up. In a few years he was hoping that they'd be able to go to the mountains at least once a year. That was something he'd done before he met Emma. She, on the other hand, had never been skiing.

He yawned. He ought to go back to bed, because he had to go to work in the morning. Johan liked his job as a reporter in the local Visby office of the Regional News division. He was back at work now, after taking a six-month paternity leave, and he had to admit that he looked forward to every single workday. Of course, he had enjoyed being at home with Anton, and also with Elin on those days when she wasn't at the day nursery. But all the daily chores, the lack of stimulation and little contact with other adults had taken their toll on him. Much more than he'd ever imagined. Maybe it was different for men who took leave from work to stay at home with the children. Women were better at networking and making contacts. And many mothers had got to know each other at the prenatal clinics. But for men, it was easy to end up feeling isolated. He'd felt very lonely as he pushed the pram through Roma, going from the Konsum supermarket to the nursery, to the playground, and back home.

Yet, right now, very little was going on at the editorial office. There was hardly any news worth reporting. They found themselves in a strange in-between period, here in the middle of November. All Swedes should really go into hibernation, he thought. At least for a month. In December, they had the Christmas holidays to look forward to, at any rate. At the moment life was nothing but dreary darkness. Everybody looked pale and worn out, sniffling with colds and generally morose. He was at heart very fond of Pia Lilja, his camera woman, but this past week they had ended up quarrelling several times at work. They were the only staff members of the news division in Visby, and sometimes they acted like an old married couple, grumbling about nearly everything. Pia was also feeling frustrated, in terms of both her work and her personal life. Her affair with a shepherd from Hablingbo, which was the longest relationship she'd had so far, had recently ended. And a temporary job in Stockholm that she'd been hoping to get had gone to someone else.

Something needs to happen, thought Johan. It doesn't matter what it is, as long as we can have some story to work on. Otherwise, Pia was going to scratch out his eyes with her long, turquoise-coloured fingernails.

He sighed, then got up and went into the bedroom. Emma was wrapped up in all the covers. He lay down, put his arm around her and fell asleep.

She needed to stay calm. Not lose control. It was only darkness. Out here in the middle of nowhere, she was all alone. Just her and nature. Like back at home on the farm in Gammelgarn. Nothing dangerous about it. Jenny could feel that her cheek was bleeding. No doubt they would give her hell for getting all these scratches on her hands and face.

Then she worked out what must have happened. Markus had turned off the paraffin lamp because he'd given up hope that she might come out to the cabin. He probably hadn't been able to resist sitting down to go through the day's photographs, and then he'd forgotten all about the time until he realized that it was too late for dinner. And then the battery on his computer had run out, or he'd simply felt too tired to do any more work and decided to go to bed.

Her courage bolstered, she continued on.

Suddenly, she could make out the wall of a building a few metres away. The cabin stood in the midst of thick undergrowth and, nearby, a big rock jutted up from the hillside like a *rauk*. Now she remembered. Markus had laughed and pointed to the tag fastened to his key. His cabin was called 'The Rauk'. So she was in the right place. It was a cabin with unpainted wooden cladding and a slender chimney made of sheet metal.

There was only one window. She called Markus's name several times. No answer.

Jenny stepped on to the porch and found a padlock on the plain wooden door. She felt hope slipping away as she yanked on the door handle.

She was worn out and freezing, and now the bloody door was locked. A padlock on the outside. Wasn't Markus even here? At that moment she felt drops of rain on her face. She peered into the darkness but could barely see anything at all. Then she noticed another small hut a short distance away.

Hunching forward as the rain started coming down harder, she stumbled over roots and stones as she headed in that direction. She held out one hand and ran her fingers over the wall. A hasp. She opened the door, and a faint, unpleasant smell wafted towards her. It was the outdoor latrine. At least she could get out of the rain. She sat down on the closed lid. What the hell should she do now? Why had the light vanished if Markus wasn't even inside the cabin? Maybe the fire in the fireplace had died out, or the flame of a paraffin lamp had gone out on its own. But would he have left a light burning if he was going to leave the cabin? She didn't understand.

Raindrops were pelting the metal roof. Where was Markus? The most likely explanation was that he'd gone over to the hotel when he realized that she wasn't coming to see him. In that case, she was all alone out here in the wilderness.

That realization brought her to the verge of tears, but the next instant she got hold of herself. She was a big girl now; she could take care of herself. She considered her options. In reality, there were only two choices. She could cycle back to the hotel, take a hot shower, dry herself off and then crawl into bed. Then she would at least get a few hours' sleep. But she shuddered at the mere thought of stumbling over the rough terrain in the dark and the rain.

The alternative was to try to get inside the cabin. If Markus had gone over to the hotel, he would find her room empty and realize that she was here.

She would need some sort of tool to pick the lock. She searched her pockets and found a pack of cigarettes and her lighter. She'd forgotten all about them. She lit a cigarette and inhaled the smoke deep into her lungs. She looked up at the ceiling and listened. It wasn't raining nearly as hard. Thank God for that. She glanced at her watch. Ten minutes to one. This was insane. She had to be in make-up by six o'clock. She pushed that thought away; it was too stressful at the moment. She took another drag on her cigarette.

Jenny rummaged through her shoulder bag. In her make-up bag she found her toothbrush and birth-control pills, as well as a couple of hairpins. To her great relief there was also a pair of tweezers. Now she should have a good chance of picking the lock. It seemed like a small and simple padlock. She opened the door of the latrine and tossed out her cigarette butt. The cabin was only a few metres away. She was wet and cold. All she wanted was to get indoors.

She made her way back to the cabin and stuck a hairpin in the lock. She cursed as she twisted it in every direction, but the lock was stubborn and refused to budge. Then she tried the tweezers, wiggling them back and forth. Finally, with a little click, the lock opened.

He was lying just inside the door, on his stomach, face down on the floor. She stared at his body in horror. She recognized Markus instantly, even in the dim light. With a sob she reached for a shelf near the door and found a box of matches. She struck a match and lit the paraffin lamp hanging close by on the wall. The minute the light filled the room, she screamed. He had a deep wound in the back of his head, and blood had gushed out on to the floor. The small cabin was a chaotic mess with things tossed all about, a toppled chair and smashed cameras littering the floor. Markus had big gashes in his arms and hands. There was blood everywhere.

Panic-stricken and sobbing, she dug her mobile out of her bag. Her hands were shaking as she tapped in Maria's number, but the call didn't go through. Shit. That's what the desk clerk had said. There was no signal out at the cabin.

The call came into the police station at 1.17 a.m. A nearly incoherent woman spoke to the officer on duty. After it had been checked with the hotel owner out on Furillen, her confused report turned out to be true. The famous fashion photographer Markus Sandberg, who was working on a photo shoot there, had been found gravely injured in the cabin where he was staying. Sandberg had been assaulted with an unknown weapon, but he was still alive.

An hour later, Anders Knutas and Karin Jacobsson were in the first vehicle to arrive at Hotel Fabriken. From there they were to be escorted to the cabin where Markus Sandberg had been found.

As soon as they pulled into the gravel courtyard in front of the entrance, the owner came out to take them to the crime scene. He was a well-known figure on Gotland. He had once been a fashion photographer himself, but he'd left the profession to open the hotel in this isolated location. Knutas had met him several times before under various circumstances. Right now, he looked paler than usual.

'Hi.' He greeted them curtly. 'The ambulance just left with Sandberg and that model, Jenny Levin. Damn, this is so awful. Follow me in your car. I'll lead the way.'

Before they could say anything, he jumped into an SUV and started up the engine. Knutas and Jacobsson dashed back to their car as Knutas shouted instructions to their colleagues in the other vehicles.

'Sohlman, you come with us. And the dog unit, too. The rest of you stay here and take care of things in the hotel.'

Several minutes later they parked as close as they could to the cabin. There they found a path that only a few people knew about. The rain had stopped, but the ground was muddy. As cautiously as they could, they made their way through the undergrowth. Their torches provided only scant light. They soon reached the remote cabin.

Knutas peered inside the open door. The interior had been ransacked, and blood was spattered all over the floor and walls. Crime-scene technician Erik Sohlman came over to stand next to Knutas.

'Jesus, what a mess. It won't be light for hours. And it wouldn't make any sense for us to start our technical work until then. We don't want to risk disturbing any evidence.' He ran his hand through the red mane of his hair as he looked around. 'We should focus on catching the perpetrator. Whoever the madman is who did this.'

An impenetrable darkness had settled over the little community of Kyllaj, a lonely outpost with only six permanent residents located right on Gotland's east coast. In the old days it had been a fishing village, but over the years it had become transformed into a summer paradise for tourists. There was a short sandy beach, a row of boathouses and a marina for small boats. Now that it was November, the hustle and bustle of the summer seemed a distant memory. The place was deserted. No shops, kiosks, or any other form of commerce. Only houses that had been closed up for the winter, standing there like abandoned stage sets waiting for the springtime sun and their owners to return.

On the outskirts of the village was a larger house made of limestone that belonged to a local family. They had gone abroad, so the house had been rented out to an author who wanted to get away from civilization to write in peace and quiet. He couldn't have chosen a better place. Kyllaj's isolation suited him perfectly. He was thrilled when he discovered the advert in the newspaper: 'Limestone house on Gotland for lease for an indefinite length of time. Modern amenities, located in Kyllaj. Sea view and large garden. Free rent in exchange for gardening and general maintenance.' The timing couldn't have been better. He had just gone through a difficult separation, and at the same time had been awarded a grant that he was planning to use to write his next book. He needed to get away from the city, away from his daily routines. He needed a quiet place to write. And the house had turned out to be exactly what he was looking for.

The dog was his only companion. She never nagged him or interrupted, and she didn't care when he ate or slept. She simply adapted to whatever he did. When he sat down in front of the computer for yet another writing session, she would obediently curl up under the desk, heave a big sigh and fall asleep. She was a quiet and undemanding companion who gave him constant and unconditional love. Thanks to her, he went out every day for long walks that helped him to clear his head while also getting some fresh air and exercise without needing to sweat. At night she lay at his feet, which he found comforting on those occasions when he felt too alone in this isolated setting. The dog was definitely an author's best friend.

By now, Olof Hellström had been living in the house for six months. And his book was practically finished. At Christmastime, he would go back to Stockholm.

He was spending this particular night writing. That was often the case. There's no one else I need to consider, he thought, rather bitterly. He was sitting at the kitchen table, with only a candle for light as he worked on the last chapter. He was astonished that, once again, he'd actually managed to write a whole book. The months in this house had done him good. His publisher would be pleased and he was ready to face the big city again.

Every once in a while he would look out at the darkness. The house stood close to the sea, its black and endless expanse visible outside the window. Now and then, the moon would peek out from the clouds and cast a white glow over the lawn leading down to the water.

He heard a sound outside. A faint clattering, like the sound of a boat motor. He gave a start. Who the hell could that be? Hardly anybody came out here in the winter.

The dog growled from under the table. She sensed that something wasn't right. Olof hushed her, then decided to leave her in the house. On his way out, he put on his jacket and grabbed a pocket torch.

The night air was cold and fresh, with almost no wind. The boat motor was now clearly audible. He walked briskly across the grass, soft with night-time dew.

The clattering sound had slowed, sounding intermittent, as if the motor might be shut down at any second. That meant the boat was about to dock. And even if it was an ordinary fishing boat, that would be odd. Those boats always left from the small-boat marina, which was further away. Here the shore was rocky, and there was only a private dock that belonged to the house. Olof Hellström suddenly felt uneasy. He didn't want to get involved in anything.

A two-metre-high stone wall ran along the shore on this side, hiding him from view. He turned off his torch well before he came to the wall. The fact that a boat had arrived here in the middle of the night was so unexpected that he didn't want to make his presence known. When he reached the end of the wall, he cautiously peered around it.

Down by the water a beacon emitted a red light towards the sea to guide boats into the harbour. In the glow from the beacon he saw a man pull up next to the dock and climb out of a small fibreglass vessel that was hardly bigger than a rowboat. Surprised, Olof watched as the stranger shoved the boat back out to sea instead of tying it to a mooring post. The man wore dark clothing and seemed in a hurry. He dashed across the wooden planks and headed for the road. Olof Hellström was puzzled and didn't know what to do. Should he shout, or not? He decided not to. Then the man stopped and turned around.

Olof stood there as if paralysed, and waited. He now regretted not bringing the dog.

Dread wriggles its way like a poisonous snake through her stomach as time for the next meal approaches. A voice screams inside her that she won't. But no one hears. No one is listening. No one cares. What she feels or wants is no longer taken into consideration. She has become dehumanized, degraded into some sort of living doll that must get fatter at all costs. Just so that the staff on the ward can improve their statistics and boast of the results. As a human being, she is worth nothing.

She and her personal nurse, Per, trudge down the corridor towards the dining room. There they will pick up their lunch and carry it on trays to the food lab, which is a room that is used by those who can't handle eating with the rest of the patients in the dining room. Agnes has brought along a device that tells her how much she should put on her plate and how fast she should eat. It's like a little computer attached to a plate that functions as a scale. Everyone on the ward has their own device. Agnes calls hers the Widget. Each food portion weighs 250 grams and has to be eaten in twenty-five minutes, in accordance with the guidelines that have been individually designed for her. If she eats too slowly, the voice of the actor Mikael Nyqvist issues from the device, telling her that she has to speed up.

Usually, it takes her an hour to finish the food. Mikael Nyqvist gets to speak several times.

The patients had been allowed to vote on which voice would speak from the Widget. The choice was Rikard Wolff or Mikael Nyqvist. And Nyqvist won. She doesn't know why. Maybe he was asked first. At any rate, he agreed to be the human voice for seriously ill patients suffering from anorexia. Maybe it was his way of doing a good deed. Sometimes Agnes turns off the sound when she can't stand listening to his admonishments any more. But usually she appreciates his company. It's almost as if Nyqvist is right next to her in the room and she doesn't have to be alone with the nurse, who is always sitting across from her like some sort of prison guard.

The room is small, windowless and claustrophobic. A pine table and two chairs, one on each side, are the only furniture. A clock on the wall ticks relentlessly, demonstrating with the utmost clarity what a wretchedly long time it takes for her to eat the food. The colourful runner on the table jeers at her. The chairs scrape on the floor as they sit down. Per sits across from her. He's the nurse she likes best in the clinic. She guesses he must be about twenty-five, but she has never asked. Sometimes she can't bear his presence either. On certain days he seems preoccupied, like today. Then it's easier to fool him.

Agnes stares at her tray. A glass contains 8.25 millilitres of milk, and she has to drink every drop. Milk is difficult, as are all dairy products. It feels so fatty and thick. As if the milk settles in a layer inside her guts and stays there. Making her heavy.

The lunch is in an aluminium container. She lifts the lid and stares at the fish. It's in a creamy sauce. Dread seizes hold of her. How in the world is she going to eat that? She turns on the Widget, taps in her password, and instantly hears Nyqvist saying, 'Set the plate on the scale.' She does as he says. 'Serve the food.' She begins spooning out the contents of the aluminium box until the digits on the display reach one hundred and turn green – a hundred per cent. No more, no less. If she puts only ninety per cent on the scale, the Widget goes on strike and won't continue. There's no use trying to cheat.

As always, she's amazed at the huge amount of food in front of her. It rises up like an unconquerable mountain. A heap of mashed potatoes, a piece of cod with egg sauce, two wedges of tomato, several slices of cucumber and a couple of lettuce leaves. She also has to get down a glass of milk and a piece of white bread with Bregott cream cheese. All this food in twenty-five minutes.

Unconcerned, Per starts eating while, inside Agnes, a war commences in which obsessive thoughts wrestle with each other. The battle is right in front of her. What matters now is to eat as little as possible without drawing Per's attention.

Agnes has become an expert at finding topics to talk about. She is able to distract a nurse by starting up a conversation that becomes so lively that he or she forgets to stay on alert every second. She's very good at chatting when she's in the right mood.

And all she needs is a second to get rid of at least part of the serving of food. At first, when the nurse is paying closest attention, she proceeds cautiously. She starts by cutting up the fish into tiny pieces. She stirs the mashed potatoes with her fork, dabbing at them and moulding little bits into various shapes. If she divides up the food as much as possible, maybe it won't stay inside her body as long. Maybe it will burn off more quickly. Everything depends on getting the horrible stuff out of her body as fast as possible.

Carefully and discreetly, she moves the glass of milk, making drops spill down the outside. She clanks her fork and knife on the plate for extended intervals before putting a tiny little piece of food in her mouth. She chews for a long time, frequently pushing out a dab of mashed potato and sauce on to her lips. Quick as lightning, she wipes it off with her napkin. Agnes wipes her lips many times during the meal. Every bit she avoids eating is a victory. The spilled sauce is a triumph.

But Nyqvist protests when she eats too slowly. 'Eat a little faster.'

Agnes chats eagerly about all sorts of things in order to distract Per. Breadcrumbs land on the floor as she urgently makes a point about something. When Per looks down at his plate to take another bite of food, a piece of fish swiftly disappears into the pocket of Agnes's hoodie. She leans forward a bit as she talks, managing at the same time to poke her finger into the mashed potatoes, which she then wipes on the underside of the table. She pretends to scratch her head, but what Per doesn't notice is that at the same time she sticks the rest of the bread and cream cheese on to the back of her neck, underneath her hair. And she keeps on in that way. By the time they leave the room an hour later,

Agnes has managed to sneak away almost a third of the designated portion of food. It has gone better than expected. Per must be tired today, preoccupied with his own thoughts.

Her anxiety has diminished. At least for now.

The phone was ringing and it was only five thirty in the morning. Fear gripped Johan as he rushed to take the call. In a matter of seconds he managed to remind himself that all the children were staying with them so, no matter who was ringing, it couldn't be about his kids. He felt a flash of relief before he picked up. It was one of Emma's closest friends.

'Hi. It's Tina,' said an agitated voice. 'I'm sorry to wake you, but something terrible has happened.'

'What is it?'

A moment of hesitation before she said apologetically, 'I think I should talk to Emma first. It's about my daughter, Jenny.'

'Sure. Let me get her.'

Johan hurried to the bedroom to wake Emma. For once, she came wide awake immediately, as if she could hear in his voice that something serious had happened.

Johan went out to the kitchen to make coffee as he waited. When Emma had finished talking on the phone, she came into the room and sank down on a chair.

'Tina is at the hospital with Jenny. She was doing a photo shoot on Furillen, and very early this morning she found that the photographer, Markus Sandberg, was lying injured in his cabin. He'd been assaulted.'

'Good Lord. Was he badly hurt?'

'He's alive, but his injuries are life-threatening. They took him by helicopter to the hospital in Stockholm.'

'How's Jenny?'

'In a state of shock, of course. But she's not hurt. By the time she turned up, whoever attacked Sandberg had disappeared.'

'Did some sort of quarrel lead to the attack?'

'No, everything was normal at the photo session yesterday. But Markus didn't make it to dinner, so Jenny went looking for him and found him lying on the floor, beaten to a pulp. Nobody knows who did it.'

'Where did she find him?'

'In a cabin on Furillen. One of those little remote cabins that belong to the hotel. The police want to interview Jenny when she feels up to it. Apparently, the doctors have given her a sedative.'

The next second, Johan was on his way back to the bedroom to get dressed. The fact that Markus Sandberg was the one who'd been assaulted made the news a much hotter story than if the victim had been unknown to the general public. Sandberg had an odd career behind him. He was one of the few photographers in Sweden who was a household name, largely because of his reputation as a scandalous porn photographer, and because he'd been the host of a controversial TV programme on a commercial channel. The programme was accused of being sexist and demeaning to women, and it didn't last long. But enough episodes were broadcast that the name Markus Sandberg became etched into the public's consciousness. There was no mistaking his personal appeal: with his warmth, humour and charisma, he was a big hit among viewers. And even though the programme was cancelled, he continued to turn up on various game and quiz shows on TV. He always acquitted himself well, and gradually people forgot about his dubious past. He then shifted gear to become a full-time fashion photographer, and suddenly he was appearing in all sorts of contexts. He was a judge for various fashion and beauty contests, and he published a photography book that catalogued Swedish fashion through the ages. Markus Sandberg had certainly succeeded in building a new brand for himself, and that had been irrefutably confirmed in the summer when he became a regular interviewer on the radio station P1.

Johan eagerly tapped in Pia Lilja's phone number. Since she answered at once, he assumed that she'd already heard what had happened. He quickly told her what he knew.

'I was just about to ring you,' said Pia. 'Julia, a girl that I know, called to tell me about it. Her mother is a cleaner at the hotel. Are you going to contact the police?'

'Yup, although I thought we might as well head for Furillen first. We can always interview the police later, but we need to get pictures.'

'Definitely. I'll gather up my equipment and we can leave as soon as you get here.'

By 7 a.m., after Sandberg had been discovered out on Furillen, the investigative team was already gathered at police headquarters in Visby. Knutas noted that his colleagues looked tired and pale in the merciless white glare from the fluorescent ceiling light. November certainly was a gloomy month.

The most important team members were all present: Assistant Superintendent Karin Jacobsson; Detective Inspector Thomas Wittberg, who was a real charmer; and the somewhat reserved spokesperson, Lars Norrby. Technician Erik Sohlman would stay for part of the meeting, but then he had to return to the crime scene on Furillen. The forensic work would get started as soon as there was enough daylight. Chief Prosecutor Birger Smittenberg had also been called in. Knutas had great confidence in the prosecutor and liked to have him participate from the very outset.

'Well, friends,' Knutas began, 'you've all been awakened in the middle of the night, and we now have an unusual case in front of us. Early this morning the photographer Markus Sandberg was the victim of a murder attempt by an unknown assailant at the Hotel Fabriken on Furillen. Do all of you know who Sandberg is?'

Everyone sitting at the table nodded.

Knutas went on. 'The perpetrator attacked the victim, possibly using an axe, but that hasn't yet been verified. This information is based on a statement from the medics. I plan to talk to the doctor at the hospital as soon as we're done with this meeting. What we do know is that Markus Sandberg was seriously injured, and it's unclear whether he'll survive. He was taken by helicopter to the neurosurgery division of Karolinska University Hospital. He has been heavily sedated and will be undergoing surgery soon, if that hasn't already happened. All right, then. Sandberg was found by no less than Gotland's own Kate Moss – the Swedish celebrity and fashion model Jenny Levin, from Gammelgarn. Does everyone here know her?'

Again, they all nodded.

'He was found inside a small cabin that belongs to the hotel. It's about a kilometre from the main building, and he was supposed to spend the night there. When he didn't turn up for dinner, Jenny got worried, so later she cycled over there to check on him. And that's when she found him.'

'Check on him?' Wittberg queried, raising his eyebrows. 'I've seen those cabins. They're called "hermit retreats" and are deep inside the woods. What time did she get there?'

'A few minutes past one. The call came in at 1.17, but it took a while for her to find a place where she had mobile coverage.'

'Why would she go out in the dark so late at night to "check on him"? Was it purely out of concern for a colleague? I doubt it.' Wittberg shook his head with the golden curls.

'She was worried. I think the whole crew was probably a bit concerned. As I mentioned, Sandberg never turned up for dinner.'

'Right,' snorted Wittberg, looking at his fellow officers seated around the table. 'Those two are having an affair. She was going to spend the night with him. That's obvious. And Jenny Levin isn't just anybody, let me tell you. She's probably the hottest model in Sweden at the moment. She was discovered only a year ago, and her rise has been nothing short of meteoric. I was just reading about her in *Café*.'

'Of course you were,' said Jacobsson caustically.

'She's bloody gorgeous,' replied Wittberg, laying it on thick as he grinned at Jacobsson. He loved teasing his colleague.

'Maybe so, but that has nothing to do with the matter at hand,' said Knutas sharply.

It was well known that Wittberg was a real playboy. Almost every woman who worked at police headquarters had at one time or another been in love with the suntanned and buff ladies' man. Except for Karin Jacobsson. They often worked together, and she always kept Wittberg at a safe distance, although the two of them couldn't help bickering. Sometimes they behaved just like siblings.

Knutas continued, 'At the moment Jenny Levin is in hospital. We'll have to wait to interview her. So far, we have no specific leads regarding the perpetrator. None of the hotel staff noticed anything out of the ordinary. Nor did any of the crew doing the photo shoot, and they were the only guests at the hotel. But we'll see. After Sandberg was discovered, everybody out there was upset and confused, of course, and no one was thinking clearly. Right after this meeting, we'll start by conducting the necessary interviews. Hopefully, they've all had a chance to calm down. Four staff members sleep at the hotel: the hotel owner and his wife, the restaurant manager and a cleaner. They were all questioned at the scene, but they'll be coming here this morning, along with the other staff. We've cordoned off a large area around the cabin, and a dog unit is patrolling the site. We need to start knocking on doors as soon as possible.'

'Knocking on doors?' said Norrby. 'How many permanent residents live on Furillen?'

'None, as far as I know. But there are a few homes in the area around Lergrav. The question is: How should we handle the press? This is going to attract a lot of attention. Markus Sandberg is a very well-known photographer, and as soon as the reporters get wind of the fact that Jenny Levin was the one who found him, they'll be after us like sharks. What do you think, Lars?'

'I suggest that we hold a press conference as soon as we can,' said Norrby, giving Knutas a challenging look. 'That's essential, given the situation.'

There had been a certain tension between the two men since Norrby had been passed over for promotion a few years earlier. Knutas had chosen Jacobsson for the position instead.

'Okay. We might as well take on the whole bunch at once,' Knutas concluded, slapping the palm of his hand on the table as if to underscore his words.

'Who was on the crew at the photo shoot?' asked Wittberg.

Knutas put on his reading glasses and leafed through his notes.

'There were five people in addition to Jenny and Markus. A stylist by the name of Hugo Nelzén, an art director named Sebastian Bigert, a photographer's assistant named Kevin Sundström, a producer, Anna Neumann, and also Maria Åkerlund, who's a make-up artist. So seven people in all.'

'How well do they know each other?'

'I have no idea. That's something we'll find out today. Everyone is on their way over here to be interviewed.'

'Were there any other models?' asked Wittberg. 'If so, I'd be happy to interview them.'

'You're hopeless,' said Jacobsson, but she couldn't help smiling.

Knutas was starting to get a headache, and his stomach was growling. He rubbed his forehead and then glanced at his watch. Seven thirty. He'd been up since one thirty but hadn't yet had anything to eat.

Sohlman stood up. 'If there's nothing else, I need to go. I've got a lot of work to do out there.'

'Okay.' Knutas looked intently at everyone seated around the table. 'Our colleagues have been searching all night for the perpetrator, and they've set up roadblocks at several places in the area. More officers are also on their way out to Furillen right now. The dog unit will continue to search. Who knows? Maybe the assailant is still there, hiding out someplace. As I mentioned, we'll do a door-to-door in the vicinity this morning. It's important for us to talk to as many people out there as possible. Those of you staying here at headquarters will help to conduct the interviews. As far as the press conference is concerned, I suggest we hold off on that for a while.'

Norrby frowned and looked as if he wanted to protest, but he restrained himself. He settled for muttering his displeasure.

'For now, the media will have to make do with a press release,' Knutas went on. 'We need to find out more about what happened before we talk to any reporters. It remains to be seen what we'll learn today, and whether the victim even survives. I'll stay in contact with the hospital. The media interest is going to be huge, so we need to be prepared,' he said, turning to look at Lars Norrby, who didn't always find it easy to deal with journalists when the pressure was on.

Jacobsson stopped Knutas as he was heading for the door.

'How come you know who Kate Moss is?'

'Why shouldn't I know who she is?' he remarked, giving her an inscrutable look.

'I can't imagine that you'd be interested in fashion.'

'I don't know what you mean. I'm a virtual fashion maven,' said Knutas, plucking at the checked shirt that he'd bought at the Dressmann menswear shop five years ago.

Jacobsson couldn't help laughing.

'Shall we grab a bite to eat?' she asked.

'Sure. But I don't want to eat too much. I have to think of my figure. I've heard that, this winter, thin is in.'

It was still dark when Pia Lilja headed for Furillen in the TV van. Johan sat in the passenger seat, talking to the duty officer on the phone. No other police officer was available. When he finished the conversation, Johan turned to look at his colleague.

'He would only confirm that an incident of aggravated assault took place in a cabin that belongs to the hotel, and that the victim has been taken to hospital. Of course, he refused to identify the victim or give any details about the attack. At any rate, the police are on the scene, but they can't do much until daylight. So far, no one has been arrested.'

'Aggravated assault,' said Pia, snorting. 'I think it sounds more like attempted murder. Apparently, it was a real bloodbath, according to Julia's mother. And Markus Sandberg isn't just anybody. Right now, he's hovering between life and death. It might well turn out to be murder.'

'Nothing on the TT wire service yet. We're probably the only ones who know the identity of the victim. I'm going to ring the morning editor.'

Johan phoned the main editorial office of Swedish TV in Stockholm and explained the situation. The editor told him to report back as soon as he knew more. For the moment they would put out a simple statement on the news wire. They would wait until later to publish the victim's name.

When Pia and Johan pulled up outside the hotel, they could see at once that something major had happened. Lights were on throughout the building, and several police vehicles were parked nearby.

They went into the lobby and were met by a uniformed policeman, who stopped them from going any further.

'No journalists in here. The hotel is off limits.'

'Can you tell us what's going on?' asked Johan.

'No. I need to refer you to our spokesperson, Lars Norrby.'

'Is he here?'

The cop gave him a weary look.

'I don't believe so.'

'Is there anyone on site that I could interview?' Johan was trying to quell his irritation.

'No, not at the moment. Right now, the investigative team needs to do its work in peace and quiet. We're dealing with a serious crime here, and we need to catch the perpetrator.'

'So you haven't arrested anyone?'

The cop pressed his lips together. Then he said, 'I can't comment on the state of the investigation. I need to refer you to Lars Norrby, our spokesperson.'

Johan cast a glance around the hotel lobby, which was deserted. They went back outside.

'What a sodding sourpuss,' sniffed Pia. 'Julia's mother, Birgitta, has worked here as a cleaner and breakfast waitress for several years. She sleeps at the hotel at night. She said we should wait for her here.'

They sat down at a table that was made of concrete so as to withstand the elements year round. Johan looked about.

'Damn, what a creepy place.'

He surveyed the dimly lit gravel forecourt and the stone crusher on top of the hill. A feeling of doom hovered over the place.

Suddenly, they heard footsteps approaching across the gravel. A blonde woman in her fifties appeared.

Pia jumped up to give her a hug.

'Hi, Birgitta. How's it going?'

'Oi. What a horrid thing to happen. Especially out here, where it's so quiet. The most peaceful place you could imagine. We're all really upset.'

Birgitta shook hands with Johan.

'It's probably best if we get started right away,' said Pia. 'Could we go somewhere else to do the interview? Otherwise, there's a risk that Mr Police Officer in there will try to stop us.'

'Sure. Come with me.'

They walked around to the side of the building, and Birgitta opened a door to an empty room. There were no corridors inside the hotel; all the rooms were entered from the outside. It was a lovely room, sparsely furnished. A generous-sized bed with fluffy pillows dominated the space. The whitewashed walls were bare. Several sheepskin rugs were spread out on the stone floor.

'Okay. This is fine,' said Pia. 'Let's get going.'

The camera began to roll.

'What were your thoughts when you heard about what happened?' Johan began the interview.

'I was shocked. Couldn't believe it was true. I never would have imagined that something like that would happen here on little Furillen. It's terrifying.'

Brigitta looked around, as if afraid that the perpetrator might be hiding in the bushes in the dark outside the window.

'What's the mood like inside the hotel?'

'Everybody thinks what happened is really awful, of course. So it's not exactly cheerful here at the moment. Nobody can believe it. This is the calmest and most peaceful place you could imagine. At the same time, it's lucky that we don't have other guests at the hotel at the moment. But, as I said, the mere thought that an assailant has been sneaking around in the bushes . . . We're really shaken up. All of us.'

'What can you tell us about the victim?'

A slight blush appeared on the woman's cheeks, and she fidgeted a bit.

'I know Markus Sandberg because of . . . well, because of that TV programme he once had. I know it wasn't very good, but I still couldn't help watching it, because everyone was talking about the show. Plus, he's been out here several times for work.'

Johan let her talk, even though he wasn't sure that they would reveal the victim's identity when the report was broadcast. It might be too soon for that. On the other hand, they were dealing with a photographer who was well known to the public. But, naturally, his family needed to be informed first. The decision to make his name public or not would come later.

'What do you know personally about the attack?'

Birgitta grimaced and shook her head.

'From what I've heard, he was seriously injured. Covered with blood and badly beaten. I don't know whether the weapon was an axe, but it was something like that.'

'So the attack occurred inside the cabin?'

'Yes.'

'Who found him?'

'Jenny was the one who found him. She cycled out there.'

'Why would she do that?'

Birgitta shrugged and didn't comment.

'Then what happened?'

'She rang the police, and the officers and medics were here in no time.'

'Have you personally noticed anything strange or different out here lately?'

'There is one thing. About a week ago a man phoned. Sometimes I work on the reception desk. In a place like this, you have to be able to do a bit of everything, especially in off-season.'

'Oh, really?'

Johan automatically moved closer.

'Yes. The man asked some odd questions. He wanted to know how many guests were staying at the hotel right now and how many we expected in the coming week. And then he asked if there were any special events planned. So I told him about the fashion photo shoot and the fact that certain parts of the hotel would be off limits for a few days. Then he wanted to know more details, and he actually got a bit rude. Finally, I asked him who he was and whether he was a reporter. But he hung up without answering.'

Knutas went back to his office after having breakfast with Jacobsson. That had done the trick. His headache was gone, and he was feeling much better. He phoned Karolinska University Hospital and was put through to the doctor in charge, Vincent Palmstierna.

'Markus Sandberg has suffered very serious injuries,' Dr Palmstierna began. 'We're doing all we can but, unfortunately, I have to tell you that the prognosis is uncertain. There is every indication that he was attacked by someone wielding an axe, using both the blunt part and the blade.'

'What are his chances of survival?'

'It's hard to tell right now. He is heavily sedated, and we're keeping his body cool in order to regulate the cerebral metabolic rate and reduce the swelling. He has been given multiple blood transfusions, and he's probably going to need quite a lot of surgery.'

'How would you describe his injuries?'

'He suffered several cerebral haemorrhages where the axe struck the skull. Unfortunately, so-called subdural haemorrhage also occurred, meaning there was bleeding under the brain's dura mater. He has lost his right ear, and his jaw was shattered. He also has defensive wounds on his arms, where the assailant struck him with the blade of the axe. He has some nasty, deep gashes on his hands – at the base of the thumbs and on the tops of his fingers. Also on the outside of both his upper arms and his forearms.'

'Christ.'

Knutas grimaced. He pictured again the chaos they'd found inside the cabin and imagined the struggle that must have caused it. Then he went on, 'What happens now?'

'As I said, we're going to need to perform several operations, and we have to reduce the swelling in his brain. A number of surgical procedures will be carried out to deal with his crushed jaw, and also his ear. He'll be under heavy sedation for at least a week, maybe longer. Provided he manages to hold on, which isn't guaranteed.'

'But, if he does survive, will he remember anything about the attack?'

'We should probably hope that he doesn't recall much about the event itself. On the other hand, total memory loss is quite unusual. I mean, when it comes to his life as a whole. But it's reasonable to expect that he'll have partial amnesia.'

'Is it possible that he'll make a full recovery?'

'To be honest, it's much too early to speculate about that, especially since we don't yet know whether he'll pull through. But, in general terms, I can say that, given the nature of his injuries, it's highly unlikely. He will probably suffer some hearing loss and have difficulty articulating his thoughts. He may have long-term problems with headaches, difficulty concentrating, an inability to handle stress and, as I mentioned, partial amnesia. On top of everything else, he'll have permanent facial damage. There's no doubt about that.'

Knutas thanked the doctor and ended the call. With a heavy sigh, he leaned back in his chair. So there was little hope that Markus Sandberg would be able to identify his assailant. They would have to direct their efforts elsewhere. Even though Furillen was one of the most isolated places imaginable in winter, it still seemed reasonable that someone must have seen or heard something. A perpetrator always left behind evidence of some kind.

He had just taken out his pipe and was filling it with tobacco when the phone rang. It was the officer on duty. He sounded as if he had urgent news.

'I've got a man on the line who has something to tell you. Just to warn you: he's rather long-winded.'

'Okay, put him on.'

'Hi. My name is Olof Hellström, and I'm calling from Kyllaj. I'm renting a house out here. Well, I live in Stockholm, but the thing is, I'm a writer and I've been staying out here to work on my new novel. I've just reached the final stage and am doing some last-minute revising, and—'

'Okay, okay. Get to the point,' said Knutas brusquely. He might as well make the man realize from the start that this was no time for lengthy explanations.

The man on the phone sniffed to show he was offended but went on.

'I think I saw the guy who attacked that person out on Furillen last night.'

Knutas took a deep breath. Could it really be true?

'What makes you think that?' he asked tensely.

'I was sitting up late last night, writing. Then I heard

the sound of a motor out on the water below my house. I got curious, so I went down there to see what was going on. A small boat pulled up to the dock. A man jumped out, and I was very surprised to see that, instead of tying up the boat, he shoved it back out to sea. I had left my dog up at the house. I have a golden retriever, but I thought that—'

'Go on.'

'Well, anyway . . . The man ran off the dock and then disappeared. I didn't see which way he went.'

'And you didn't try to follow him?'

'No. And I didn't let him know I was there either. The whole scene made me nervous. I didn't know who he was, or what he was up to. And, at the time, I had no idea that anything had happened out on Furillen. But then I heard the news on the radio and thought there might be a connection.'

Knutas had got out a notepad and pen while Olof Hellström talked.

'What did the man look like?'

'Normal build, a little shorter than average, maybe five foot nine or ten. He was wearing dark clothing.'

By this point, Hellström seemed to have grasped that it was best to keep his answers brief.

'What kind of clothing?'

'I don't know. I only caught a glimpse of him.'

'Did you see his face at all?'

'No. I'm afraid not.'

'Do you have any idea how old this man was?'

'Hard to say. He seemed youngish. Not an old man, by any means. I'd guess in his thirties, or maybe even close to forty.'

'Did he see you?'

'No. At first I thought he did, because he stopped and turned around. But then he disappeared. I stayed where I was for several minutes, but he didn't come back. Then I went down to the dock and looked for the boat, but it had already drifted away.'

'Do you know what time it was when you saw this man?'

'Hard to say. I don't keep track of the time when I'm working. But it was night-time and, since I was still feeling wide awake, it couldn't have been very late. I'd guess one o'clock, maybe two.'

'Okay. As I'm sure you realize, this is very important information, and I need to ask you to come down to headquarters as soon as possible.'

'No problem. I can leave right now.'

Jenny Levin arrived at the police station after lunch on Tuesday. She had recovered from the shock and was ready to give her statement. Jacobsson and Knutas, who were going to handle the interview, went to meet her in the reception area.

In her high-heeled boots, Jenny was even taller than Knutas, and she was more than a head taller than Jacobsson. With her long red hair, freckles and pale skin, Jenny reminded Knutas of Lina as a young woman. Her eyes were bright green. Her hand felt cool and limp, her handshake fleeting. She sat down in the chair they offered her, crossing one long, jeans-clad leg over the other. Knutas noticed that her thighs weren't much wider than her calves.

There was something magnetic about the young woman sitting before him; she possessed a radiance that was irresistible. Her movements were lithe and graceful.

Jacobsson sat in a corner of the room. She was present as a witness to the interview and would refrain from speaking.

Jenny Levin seemed nervous. Her eyes flitted about, and her hands didn't stop moving. She kept clasping and unclasping her long fingers.

'How are you feeling?' Knutas asked kindly. He filled

a glass with water and slid it across the table towards her.

'Not so good,' she said, looking at him unhappily. 'I'm really worried about Markus.'

She took a few cautious sips of water.

'I understand.' Knutas gave her a sympathetic look. 'Can you tell me what happened yesterday evening, after all of you had finished working?'

'We worked pretty late. It was six o'clock by the time we stopped. Everybody was tired and wanted to rest before dinner, so we decided to meet again at eight. Markus didn't turn up, but we thought he'd arrive at any moment. He was staying a short distance from the hotel, in that cabin.'

'Why was he staying out there?'

'He'd been to the hotel before on a photo shoot, but he hadn't stayed in a cabin, and this time he wanted to try it.'

'So how long did the dinner last?'

'A long time. We had a proper three-course meal, which meant it went on for several hours. We also drank a lot of wine while we talked.'

'Didn't you think it was strange that Markus never appeared for dinner?'

'Yes, we did. And we tried to ring him, but there's no mobile signal out at the cabins. We thought he was probably working on the photos and forgot about the time, or maybe fell asleep.'

'Do you know what time it was when you finished dinner?'

'Not exactly. Eleven, or maybe twelve.'

'Then what did you do?'

'I tried to phone again, and I also sent a text, but he still didn't answer. The others went to bed, but I decided to cycle out to the cabin and check on him.'

'Why did you decide to do that?'

Patches of crimson appeared on Jenny's throat. She bit her lower lip.

'Because I . . . was worried about him. I was wondering what had happened to him.'

'So when you set off on the bicycle it was close to midnight. Is that right?'

'I think so.'

'What time did you have to start work in the morning?'

'The photo shoot was supposed to start at eight, but I had to be in make-up two hours before that.'

'So, six in the morning? And yet you went off in the middle of the night to see how Markus was doing?'

Jenny began to fidget again.

'I suppose that might sound odd, but I was worried and I didn't think it was very far away.'

'How did you know where to go?'

'Markus told me how to get there.'

'I see.'

Knutas frowned and jotted down a few words on his notepad.

'What happened after you set off for the cabin?'

'It was much further and more difficult to find than I'd thought. If I'd known how bad the road was, how dark it was going to be, and how hard the place was to find, I'd never have gone out there. But after a while I found the cabin. The door was locked from the outside, but I used a pair of tweezers to pick the padlock.

Markus was lying inside on the floor, and he was covered in blood. I turned on a paraffin lamp and saw what a mess the whole place was. It was horrible.'

She shuddered and folded her arms, hugging herself as if she were freezing.

'Take all the time you need,' said Knutas in a soothing voice. 'I know this is difficult. But it's very important that you try to recall everything you saw in the cabin, every single detail, no matter how irrelevant it may seem.'

Jenny sighed heavily before going on. Her voice was fainter as she spoke.

'Markus was lying on his stomach, so I couldn't see his face, but I knew it was him. The whole back of his head was bloody. And his arms and hands were covered with big gashes. It looked like somebody had been hacking at him with something . . . I didn't really take in that many details. A chair had been overturned, and I noticed broken glass on the floor. A lot of smashed camera equipment and a broken paraffin lamp. I ran outside and tried to find someplace where my mobile would work. Then it didn't take long before the hotel owner came out to the cabin, along with the producer for our crew. The three of us waited together for the ambulance to arrive. It took a long time. Maybe an hour. I'm not sure.'

'Forty-five minutes, according to the police report.'

'Oh. Then the medics took care of Markus, but he was in really bad shape. So it was a while before they could put him on the stretcher.'

'Okay,' said Knutas. 'Try to remember if there was anything else you happened to notice earlier in the day. Was there anyone you didn't know hanging about? Was someone acting strangely? Did you see a car or a motorcycle?'

'No, nothing. There was nothing unusual about the photo shoot, and nothing special happened.'

'Do you know if Markus has ever been threatened in any way?'

'No. Never.'

'How well do you know him?'

It was obvious that Jenny didn't want to answer that question. Now the red patches spread from her throat to her face.

'We haven't known each other very long,' she replied evasively. 'I'm new to the fashion business.'

'How long have you worked as a model?'

'About a year.'

'Do you work full time?'

'Yes, now I do. I quit school. Temporarily. I'll go back to it later.'

'How many times have you met Markus?'

Jenny licked her thin lips. She seemed to be considering the question. And was reluctant to answer.

'Hmm. I don't know. It's hard to say. The agency I work for often hires him.'

'And you've only met on the job?'

'What do you mean?'

Knutas stared intently at the young woman, who was obviously nervous.

'Isn't it true that you and Markus Sandberg have been having an affair?'

Jenny sighed, looking resigned. She seemed to have been expecting to hear him say those words.

'Yes, that's right,' she said quietly. 'We've been seeing each other. But we didn't want anyone to know. Not yet.'

'Why not?'

'It doesn't matter to me, but he wanted to wait.'

'And what's his reason for that?'

'He said it would interfere with our work, that the agency might not send us out on assignments together if they knew about it. Robert, who's the boss, has made it clear that he doesn't like people who work for him to have romantic relationships with each other. And Markus has a difficult ex-girlfriend who refuses to accept that it's over between them.'

Knutas's ears pricked up.

'A difficult ex? What's her name?'

'Diana Sierra. She's been a real pain. Won't let him go. She keeps ringing him all the time, and sending text messages.'

'Is she a model, too?'

'Uh-huh. Unfortunately. And for the same agency. Luckily, she does a lot of work abroad, so I haven't run into her yet, and I hope I never do.'

'I understand. That should be all for now. Thank you for coming in,' said Knutas. 'We'll let you know if we need to ask you any more questions.'

'Do you have any idea who did this?'

'Not yet. But we have plenty of leads to follow up. Don't worry. We'll solve this case.'

Knutas patted her on the arm.

He hoped that he was right.

The corridor extends through the entire ward. Agnes jogs mechanically from one end to the other. She has a hard time sitting still. She needs to work off as much energy as possible, even though the opportunities for doing so are very limited here. Much to the annoyance of the staff, she is always coming up with new excuses for getting up and moving about. For instance, she needs to fetch the newspaper she's left on her nightstand. When she comes back to the communal lounge she stands there reading an article for two minutes, then returns to her room to put the paper back. Then she continues on to the art room, stares at the felt-tip pens for a few minutes, and heads back to the lounge. There, she rummages about in the games cupboard but doesn't find anything of interest, then remembers that she has a pack of cards somewhere in her wardrobe and she could play patience. Back to her room again, where she looks through her belongings until she finds the cards, but by then she has lost any desire to play. Maybe she could knit something. So once again she returns to the art room and looks at all the different kinds of yarn, but she can't make up her mind which to choose. Now and then, one of the nurses says to her, 'Sit down.' Agnes complies, but the next second she jumps up again. She has thought of something else.

Finally, her list of excuses runs out, and she makes do with plodding back and forth along the corridor. When Per appears, she stops and pretends to be studying a picture on the wall.

'How's it going?' he asks.

'Okay. I'm just a little restless.'

'I can understand that. It's not so strange.' He glances at his watch. 'I've got meetings right now, for another hour or so. But how about a game of backgammon later on? And, this time, I plan to win.'

'Sure.'

Agnes gives him a wan smile. It's lucky he's here. Otherwise, she wouldn't be able to stand it. Per gives her a quick hug before he disappears into his office and closes the door. She sighs and continues her endless wandering.

They've made an attempt to spruce up the decor so the place won't seem so depressing. The walls are painted a warm yellow, the curtains have a pattern of different-sized red circles against a yellow background. The chairs are also covered in a colourful fabric. And the framed posters on the walls show scenes of rugged mountains, a deep-blue sea, a sunset, and a summertime meadow filled with fiery red poppies that remind her of Gotland.

She doesn't like the way they've tried to make the ward more cheerful. As if that would help anyone who's being held here. They're trapped in this hell. The patients move like automated zombies from the food lab to the communal lounge, from the art room to the warm room. Her life has come to a standstill; she is imprisoned in her obsession and sees no way out. Anxiety frequently threatens to suffocate her. Sometimes, she can't breathe and, occasionally, she is seriously convinced that her heart will stop beating. That she's going to die in this place. The warm, yellow interior feels like a slap in the face. It's like a children's hospital, she thinks, where kids with cancer or some other terminal illness lie in bed surrounded by stuffed animals and cheerful drawings. It's too bloody macabre.

She reaches the end of the corridor and turns around. Passes the art room for what must be the tenth time. She sees Linda and Sofia sitting there, making beaded trivets. Beaded trivets! That's what little kids make in childcare centres. The one thing they want to do here is diminish the patients, she thinks. Make us non-people. And she does feel like a non-person. She has lost all hold on real life, can hardly remember what it's like. Sometimes, she tries to recall what things were like before, to remind herself that she really did have a perfectly ordinary life, just like everybody else. She has nothing to do here, so the only sensible thing is to think about life outside. Transport herself there in her mind. Think about things that she used to do before she came here, about the friends she had, and about school.

Yet she avoids thinking about Mamma and Martin. As soon as they appear in her mind, she tries to escape and think about something else. It's too painful.

But now, as she walks along the corridor, the memories come back, whether she likes it or not.

The accident happened on a perfectly ordinary Tuesday in February when she was only thirteen. The weather had changed overnight; the temperature dropped and the roads were slippery. Mamma was going to pick up Martin in Stenkumla, where he'd been visiting a friend. Agnes remembers the conversation as if it were yesterday. She was the one who had picked up the phone when Mamma rang from the car. Her happy, eager voice saying, 'We'll be home soon, just need to swing by Atterdags and pick up some shopping. We'll eat at seven. Meatballs and potatoes with gravy and lingonberries.'

But that dinner never happened. One minute after they said goodbye to each other, a long-distance lorry coming from the opposite direction had skidded into a vehicle, veered into the other lane and then run head-on into her mother's car. The police said afterwards that she had had no chance of avoiding the collision. They died instantly. Both Mamma and Martin.

Agnes heard the news less than an hour after she'd talked to her mother on the phone. Someone rang the bell, and her father went to the door. Agnes was upstairs in her own room, so she didn't hear what was said. She remembers only seeing her bedroom door open a short time later, and Pappa's face. How he came in, as if entreating her, his hands held out, his lower lip quivering, terror in his eyes. Yes, that was what she saw. Pure terror. No grief, no despair. It was too soon; all of that would come later. She knew at once that something serious had happened. She stared at his mouth, his trembling lips. He tried to say something. He reached for her hand; his own was shaking. She remembers his voice. It sounded metallic, hollow. 'Something terrible has happened, Agnes. Come here and sit next to me.' He took her arm and walked her over to the bed, where he sat down. She sank on to the bed beside him. A sound had started up in her head, way in the back, but it was getting louder by the second. A wave of resistance surged inside her. No, she refused to hear what he was going to say. She didn't want to know. She wasn't ready. She couldn't do it, she wouldn't. She wanted to escape, run as far away as possible. She was looking at the bedspread through a blur. She was already crying, even though her father hadn't yet told her anything. She didn't want this to be happening. She was only thirteen years old, just a child. Wasn't prepared for something like this. She wanted to shut her eyes and cover her ears. Why weren't Mamma and Martin home? Why didn't she hear her mother's cheerful voice downstairs in the front hall, as usual? Why wasn't Martin pulling off his shoes and jacket and opening the fridge, like he always did the minute he stepped in the door?

'There's been an accident,' her father said. He squeezed her hand. Tears were now falling on to her fingers. 'Mamma and Martin were in a car accident.' She stared angrily at the bedspread. The pattern billowed before her tear-filled eyes, moving up and down, back and forth. The sound in the back of her head was getting louder. 'It was a lorry. It was a bad crash, Agnes. They didn't make it. They're dead. They're both dead.' His voice broke and she broke and the whole world broke. At that very instant. Right there and then. She hardly remembers what happened after that. Somebody came. They drove to the hospital. White coats, worried eyes, cautious gestures. Someone took them into the room where Mamma and Martin were lying. Two metal-framed beds, next to each other. Each of them lying under a blanket. Their bodies and faces covered. Her mother and brother. They no longer existed, and yet there they lay. She remembers noticing the clock on the wall. It was seven o'clock exactly. Right now, they should have been eating dinner, the four of them sitting at the kitchen table. Just like always.

Meatballs and potatoes with gravy and lingonberries.

The investigative team met for a second time late on Tuesday afternoon. They had a lot of material to share and go over. During the day, everyone had worked on the Hotel Fabriken interviews. Officers had been sent out to knock on doors, and Sohlman had returned from Furillen after spending the whole day supervising the technical examination of the crime scene.

Knutas started the meeting by giving his colleagues an update on Markus Sandberg's condition. He had undergone surgery and was heavily sedated. So far, he was alive, but his condition was still critical. Knutas then reported on the latest developments in the case, especially what he had learned from the writer Olof Hellström in Kyllaj. The witness thought that he had seen the perpetrator with his own eyes.

'How reliable is he?' asked Chief Prosecutor Birger Smittenberg.

'I see no reason to doubt what he told me,' said Knutas.

'But there's no real evidence supporting his story,' Jacobsson interjected. 'We've inspected the dock where the man supposedly came ashore. There are no traces of blood, no footprints or anything else that might confirm the author's claim.'

'Didn't he wait to ring the police until after he found

out about what happened on Furillen? He could just be a crank,' said Wittberg.

'What about the boat?' asked Norrby. 'If he's telling the truth, we should be able to find it.'

'It's still missing,' said Knutas with a sigh. 'Tomorrow we're sending out a helicopter to look for it. Right now, there's none available.'

'Any tyre tracks?' asked Sohlman, who hadn't had time to get involved in the search that had been done in Kyllaj.

'We found a lot of tracks, but it's hard to make any sense of them. It rained overnight, you know. And people sometimes drive down there to take a walk or let their dogs run about. Things like that. We'll have to see. So far there are no solid leads.'

'Are there any other witnesses of interest in Kyllaj or in the vicinity?' asked the prosecutor. 'Besides Olof Hellström, that is.'

'No, there are only a few permanent residents, and nobody who lives on the road saw anything unusual last night. As far as we know, at least. We haven't been able to get hold of everyone yet.'

'What about the axe?' the prosecutor went on. 'Has it been found?'

Sohlman shook his head.

'No, I'm afraid not.'

'He could have thrown it into the sea, of course,' said Jacobsson, sighing. 'I don't think we're going to find it any time soon.'

'I'm afraid you're probably right,' Knutas admitted. He turned to Sohlman. 'Okay, Erik, we'd like to hear more from you. What can you tell us?'

Sohlman got up and pulled down the screen at the front of the room as he began talking.

'First, I'd like everyone to see what it looked like inside the hermit's cabin. I think that's important so you'll understand what sort of person we're dealing with here. Or at least what his state of mind must have been when he launched the assault.'

He signalled for Jacobsson, who was sitting nearest the wall, to switch off the light. The first picture showed a modest cabin, not much bigger than an ordinary garden shed, with unpainted wooden cladding. There was one window and a door. A plain metal roof and a thin metal pipe for a chimney. In front stood a simple wooden bench. Underneath was a small, blue insulated bag.

'Do you see that bag there?' said Sohlman pointing. 'Inside is a bottle of Dom Pérignon and two champagne glasses. Apparently, he was expecting a visitor. And I assume it was Jenny Levin.'

The steps leading up to the door consisted simply of two logs that had been placed upside down in the gravel. Surrounding the cabin stood bare trees with white, ghostlike branches, a few withered juniper shrubs and some dwarf pines whose boughs had been twisted by the wind. Visible a short distance away was the latrine, along with a *rauk* jutting up from the undergrowth. The photograph revealed nothing of the drama that had been played out inside the cabin.

The next picture was also devoid of drama. It showed a forged-metal plate with six hooks fastened to the wall. From the hooks hung a wooden washing-up brush, a couple of clothes hangers, a dark-blue linen hand towel and a pair of old-fashioned scissors. But, in the next picture, which was a close-up, they could see that there was blood on the hand towel and also spattered on the wall. The next photo showed the entire interior of the cabin. It was a room with dark, greyish-brown wood panelling, an unmade bed in one corner, a small table next to the window and a beautifully designed chair, which had toppled over. There was also a wood stove made of black cast iron. On the light-coloured pine floorboards lay a sheepskin rug, and next to the stove stood two brown-paper sacks containing neatly stacked wood, with sections of newspaper stuck in between. On the floor lay a shattered paraffin lamp and other pieces of glass. Several smashed cameras were strewn about. There was blood everywhere – on the wood in the sacks, on the ceiling, on the window facing the sea. On the sheepskin rug and on the floor.

'It was a vicious assault, as you can see,' Sohlman went on. 'We've found strands of hair, crumpled balls of paper and cigarette butts that we've sent to the crime lab in Linköping. There are lots of fingerprints in the cabin, of course, but they could be from any number of individuals. There are footprints in the gravel out-side but, unfortunately, they're not very clear because Jenny Levin and our own officers have walked through the area. But there are a few clear prints from an old rubber boot, size seven and a half. Sandberg's camera equipment was smashed to pieces, but his computer survived. It was stowed away inside a cupboard. His wallet was on the windowsill, untouched, with cash and credit cards inside. His mobile phone is missing but, if it's turned on, we should be able to trace it. The weapon used by the perpetrator was most likely an axe. We haven't found it at the scene. This was clearly a crime committed by someone in a state of intense rage.'

'What about the door?' asked Prosecutor Smittenberg. 'Was there any sign of forced entry?'

'No. It could be that the victim and the perpetrator knew each other. I can't say. But why would Sandberg even bother to lock the door way out there in the woods? There doesn't seem to be any reason to do that. But the perpetrator fastened the padlock on the door when he left, so Jenny Levin had to pick the lock with a pair of tweezers. Here's something interesting that we found.'

The photo on the screen showed a close-up of a piece of jewellery. A shiny green stone shaped like a beetle, with tiny legs and antennae.

'This earring was found on the floor under the victim's body. Markus Sandberg does not have pierced ears. We need to find out whether it belongs to Jenny or any of the hotel staff. The cabin hasn't been used in months, but it was thoroughly cleaned after the summer season. Of course, it's possible that the earring was left there by a previous guest, but it could also belong to the perpetrator.'

He paused for dramatic effect.

'I've been saving the best for last,' he added, with some irony. He reached for his glass of water and peered solemnly over the rim at his colleagues seated around the table.

'Now that you've seen the cabin, I'm going to show you the victim. Be prepared for the worst. These pictures are not very pretty. We got them from the hospital. So here is Markus Sandberg as he looked when he arrived.'

Everyone was paying rapt attention. Jacobsson closed her eyes halfway. She still had a hard time looking at victims who were seriously injured or dead. After fifteen years on the police force, she realized that she probably would never get used to it.

Even though the officers in the room were all very experienced, they gasped when the pictures of Sandberg appeared on the screen. He was unrecognizable. His face was swollen and lacerated, his jaw crushed, leaving a gaping wound with teeth and bone fragments sticking out of the remaining pieces of flesh. One side of his skull was covered in blood, and his right ear was missing. He had deep, nasty gashes on his hands, upper arms and forearms.

No one said a word as the photos were shown. Afterwards, they all continued to sit in silence. Not even Sohlman said a word. What kind of person would do something like this? Who were they looking for?

Knutas woke at five in the morning and couldn't go back to sleep. Lina's side of the bed was empty. She was working the night shift at the hospital. Feeling restless, he got up and made some coffee. Gloomily, he stared at the total darkness outside the window. Winter lay ahead, a grey, cold haze that would last four months, with the days getting shorter and night falling sooner, only a few hours after lunch.

The cat purred and jumped up on to the kitchen table, wanting to be petted, then slipped outside when Knutas opened the front door to fetch the morning paper. The November chill made him wince. It had been a cold night. He steeled himself, then hurried down to the letterbox, still wearing his dressing gown. Back inside the warm house, he sat down at the kitchen table and poured himself a cup of coffee. The entire front page was devoted to the assault out on Furillen. Knutas was startled to read that the police suspected the weapon used was an axe. The article referred to last night's Regional News report, which had been broadcast on TV. Johan Berg again. That man had an infernal ability to dig up more details than the police wanted to reveal. Even though Knutas was annoyed, he couldn't help feeling a certain admiration for the reporter. And there was really no harm done. The information was bound to leak out sooner or later, and in the best-case scenario, it might bring in more tip-offs to the police.

He quickly scanned the rest of the article. Nothing noteworthy, nothing that the police hadn't made public. He managed to listen to the news on the local radio station before he had to leave for work. It was largely the same as he'd read in the paper.

He put on warm clothes and set off. It took him twenty minutes to walk to police headquarters on Norra Hansegatan. He enjoyed this part of the morning, before the city awoke. He was all alone on the quiet streets. Snowflakes were drifting down from the sky, melting the moment they touched the ground.

The only visible lights on in the police station were on the ground floor. As usual, Knutas greeted the officer on duty and exchanged a few pleasantries. Then he went up two flights of stairs to the criminal division. The light was on in Karin Jacobsson's office.

'Hi,' he said in surprise when he saw her sitting at her desk. 'You're already here?'

'I couldn't sleep.'

He paused in the doorway.

'Any special reason?'

'No. Just the usual ghosts.'

'Would you like some coffee?'

'Sure. That'd be great.'

Knutas came back with two cups, setting one down in front of her before taking a chair across the desk from her.

'Did you see the news on TV last night?' he asked.

'No, we were busy with other things.'

'Apparently, Regional News reported that we suspect an axe was used in the assault.'

'I saw that in the morning paper. Not totally unexpected. Berg must have gone out to Furillen and talked to someone. Everybody who works at the hotel knew about it.'

'I can't believe that people have such a hard time keeping their mouths shut.' Knutas shook his head. 'Anything new?'

'Not really. Except that the earring that Sohlman found in the cabin keeps getting more and more interesting. Nobody seems to want to claim it. Evidently, it doesn't belong to Jenny Levin or to any staff member or previous hotel guest. That particular hermit's cabin was recently built, so very few people stayed there before Sandberg. And the very cooperative and efficient receptionist has managed to contact almost all of them. At the moment, all indications are that the earring belongs to the perpetrator.'

'So we know one thing about him,' said Knutas dryly. 'He has at least one pierced ear.'

'As for Sandberg's computer, it's going to be examined today,' Jacobsson went on. 'Let's hope that it can tell us something useful. I've also started going through all the interviews and I've found at least one interesting thing. The cleaning woman who works at the hotel, and sometimes works on reception as well, reported that a man phoned the hotel about a week before the attack and asked some strange questions. When he heard a photo shoot was scheduled at the hotel, he asked detailed questions about the arrangements. The cleaning woman thought it was a bit odd, so she asked if he was a reporter. He hung up without answering.'

'Did he give his name?'

'No.'

'We need to trace that phone call. Does she remember what day he rang?'

'Actually, she does, because she was brought in when a staff member called in sick. Not last Saturday, but the previous Saturday. She's positive about that. She even remembers what time he phoned, because she was listening to *Melodikrysset* on the radio and was annoyed at being interrupted.'

'Bravo. Could you follow up on this today?'

'Of course. We also have the reports from our colleagues who knocked on doors in the surrounding areas on Furillen, but they don't tell us much. There are so few houses that are occupied this time of year, and the only people we were able to contact didn't see or hear anything. An old man who lives right near the road claims that he definitely would have woken up if a car or motorcycle went by during the night. He's a light sleeper. But all he heard was the ambulance. By the way, we still haven't found the boat, but the helicopter will go out there as soon as it's light. And no boat has been reported stolen. Today we'll continue to search around Lergrav, Valleviken and the other communities in the vicinity. We'll also try to talk to anyone who wasn't at home yesterday in the houses along the road to Kyllaj.'

Jacobsson clasped her hands behind her head and stared up at the ceiling. Knutas looked at her for a moment without speaking. She was thin and petite, with short dark hair and big brown eyes. He noticed that she looked unusually pale, with dark circles under her eyes. But she'd said she hadn't slept well. He liked her face. It was so sensitive. He'd been working with her for years, ever since she'd arrived as a trainee at police headquarters in Visby. He was almost fifteen years older than she was, but he never thought about the age difference. That's so typical for a man in late middle age, he thought, with a good dose of self-contempt. We never want to admit how old we are. We're constantly deceiving ourselves. But what did he know about Karin's perception of things?

'Do you often think about the age difference between us?' he said, surprising himself by asking such a question out of the blue. He hadn't intended to say anything. The words just slipped out.

Her cup banged as she set it down on the desk.

'What did you say?'

'Oh, er, I was just wondering if you think that . . . well, if you notice that there's almost fifteen years between us,' he said, embarrassed.

'What do you mean? Are you asking me whether I think you're old?' She broke into a smile, revealing the gap between her front teeth.

'Just forget it,' he said, getting up.

She grabbed his arm.

'Anders, seriously, what do you mean?'

'It just occurred to me that I never think about the age difference between us, but maybe you do.'

'It's not something that I do think much about, I have to admit. Not often, at any rate. And we're just co-workers, after all. If we were together, it would make a huge difference.'

She laughed annoyingly and gave him a poke in the side. Knutas felt like an idiot. There was something about Karin, something that he'd probably never fully understand.

The wind was gusting harder across Kyllaj on this cold November morning as Eduardo and Dolores Morales drove towards the sea in their rental car. They had come to Gotland a few days earlier from their home in Seville in southern Spain to take part in a conference dealing with the depletion of fish stocks in Europe's inland seas. Since they shared a keen interest in the history of fishing in various countries, Kyllaj was one of a string of fishing villages along the Gotland coast that the couple intended to visit. They wanted to take pictures that would become part of their ever-growing collection of photos from similar communities all over the world.

They got up early, enjoyed a hearty Scandinavian breakfast in the dining room of their hotel in Visby, and then set off to the north-east. Kyllaj was first on their list; then they would visit Lergrav, before continuing north to Bungeviken and Fårö.

They parked the car near the small-boat marina, which was deserted. All the boats had been taken in for the winter. Dolores Morales pulled up the zip on her heavy jacket before getting out of the car. The wind nipped at her cheeks, making her eyes water. The cold and the dark in these regions were indescribable. At this time of year, the sun set by four in the afternoon, and then it was pitch dark. She couldn't for the life of her understand how the Swedes could bear it. It was beyond comprehension that anyone had come up with the absurd idea of settling this far north. Right now it was 3 degrees Celsius, with a north wind. The receptionist at the hotel had said this was nothing. Winter hadn't even started yet. The truly bitter cold would arrive in January and February, when the seawater surrounding the island had cooled down completely. Then the temperature might drop to minus 10 degrees Celsius, or even minus 15, although that didn't happen often on Gotland. Dolores Morales and her husband were experienced travellers, so they'd had the good sense to bring along appropriate warm clothing.

The fishing village consisted of a row of sheds down by the water, a small harbour with room for a dozen boats, and several wharfs. A few racks for drying fishing nets stood side by side, and two posts held beacons that came on at night to guide boats into the harbour.

As a matter of course, they headed off in different directions and methodically began to document what they saw. There was a feeling of complete desolation about the place, as if they found themselves at the world's end, far from any real civilization. They peered in the windows of those sheds where the curtains were open and saw, as expected, mostly fishing gear, nets, and various tools.

Dolores was just about to suggest that they go back to the car and have a coffee break when she discovered that the padlock on one of the sheds was open. When she got closer, she could see that it had been cut. Someone had used pliers to cut off the lock. She looked around for Eduardo but didn't see him. She called his name but, apparently, he didn't hear her. Curiosity got the better of her, and with some excitement she opened the door to the shed.

It was dark inside, and the air was musty and damp. She looked about. Shelves loaded with tools and all sorts of fishing gear covered one entire wall. Hanging on another wall was a clumsily painted portrait of a smiling, bearded fisherman with a pipe in his mouth. She saw a rickety table with a paraffin lamp, a box of matches and a mug with dried coffee dregs in the bottom. On the floor stood a battered chest. She lifted the lid and found inside weekly tabloids and magazines that seemed to be forty or fifty years old. Many of them had cover photos of smiling women, some bare-breasted, some wearing bikinis. Somehow, they looked so innocent. She read the word *Se*, which was printed in white inside a red circle, and guessed that it must be the name of the publication. The date was 1964, which proved that she'd guessed right about the age of the magazines. She smiled at the sense of nostalgia that the covers conjured up in her. Those were the days.

She and Eduardo had met in the Basque country in the small town of San Sebastián. The fight for independence in that region of Spain had been heating up, and they were both only twenty years old. She had been so naive back then. Such an idealist. And what was she doing now? Documenting old fishing villages. Why, and for whom? she thought as she let go of the lid of the chest so that it closed with a dull thud. But the sound was loud enough to startle a mouse out of the shadows and send it racing across the floor. Dolores

Morales was certainly not the type of woman who would be upset by something like that; she couldn't care less about the mouse. But what did it have in its mouth? Something long and yellow. The light was dim inside the shed, and the mouse had quickly disappeared into a corner. But it had definitely been carrying something. She found a torch on a shelf, then glanced out of the window, but Eduardo was nowhere in sight. By now, he must be wondering what had happened to her. She switched on the torch and began searching for the mouse. She didn't see it, but she did hear tiny claws scratching at the wooden floor. She aimed the beam of the torch at the floor and then at the walls lined with shelves. Ashes in the wood stove, a rusty drill, a saw, a glass jar containing freeze-dried coffee, a tin that she was curious enough to open. She smelled something sweet, although the tin was empty except for a few crumbs in the bottom. She recognized the fragrance of cinnamon and ginger. Then she realized what it was. Those typical, crisp biscuits that the Swedes served at Christmastime. *Pepparkakor.* As she looked around the space a little more, she finally realized what the mouse had been carrying. Next to the biscuit tin was a fruit platter with several old banana skins. Looking more closely, she saw that they weren't that old – maybe from a few days ago, at most. Someone had been here recently.

She turned around and discovered an old America-trunk that was slightly open. The lid was crooked and hadn't been closed properly. Hesitantly, she went over to lift it. A suffocating smell rose up, forcing her to take a few steps back. Inside was a bundle of clothes,

Mari Jungstedt

and Dolores couldn't believe her eyes when she picked
up one garment after another: a pair of bloodstained
jeans, a blood-soaked T-shirt, a sweatshirt, a down
jacket, a pair of gloves and a knitted cap. The jacket,
T-shirt and pullover were not only covered with blood,
they also seemed to be soiled with what looked like
vomit. Her suspicions were confirmed when she lifted
the jacket closer to her nose. Her stomach turned over.

That was as far as she got when she heard a thud and
something scraping at the window. Dolores screamed
when she saw her husband's face pressed against the
pane, and then a man tackled him from behind.

The next second she was looking into the eyes of a
stranger.

114

The whole family was having breakfast when the phone rang. Johan took the call, since Emma was always so stressed in the morning. She had to be at work earlier than he did, so she was usually in a hurry. It was Tina. He asked her how Jenny was doing.

'Okay, considering the circumstances. Thanks for asking. She's home now, and she'll be staying here for a few days. She needs time to recuperate.'

'That's understandable,' said Johan. 'But there's something I'd like to ask you.' He cleared his throat and paused for a moment before telling her what he'd been thinking about, wondering how best to approach Tina. 'This may seem a bit intrusive right now but, since I'm a journalist, I have to ask whether you think Jenny might agree to be interviewed. She's an important person in this story, as I'm sure you realize. And I promise not to ask any questions that she doesn't want to answer. You can also look at the piece before we broadcast it. And you can be present during the interview, too, if you like. I actually think it might be good for her to talk to me. Then she can always refer to the interview if other reporters start pestering her. She can tell them she has already said as much as she's going to say. And it's better if I do the interview rather than someone else. Don't you agree?'

115

There was a brief silence before Tina replied.

'I don't know,' she said doubtfully. 'This whole thing just happened yesterday. I need to ask Jenny, and I want to hear what Fredrik thinks, too. Can I get back to you in a few minutes?'

'Of course.'

'I was actually calling to talk to Emma. But she'll be home for a while yet before she has to leave for work, right?'

'Sure. And I really appreciate it that you're willing to ask Jenny about this.'

Johan hung up the phone, saying a silent prayer that she'd come back with a positive answer. Just then, Emma came into the kitchen.

'Who was on the phone?'

'Tina. She wanted to talk to you, but she'll call you right back.'

'Oh?'

'Uh-huh. I asked her if I could interview Jenny, so she was going to talk to her and let me know in a few minutes.'

'You just couldn't resist, could you?'

He heard a hint of sarcasm in her voice. Emma had never had much patience for the way journalists were always on the hunt for the next big scoop. Or their irrepressible delight when they were the first to break a news story. She had personally been subjected to a media onslaught, and she wouldn't wish it on her worst enemy. Luckily, she had benefited from Johan's ability to handle such situations. Although, when it came right down to it, he was just as hungry for a good news story as his colleagues were. She could see the gleam of anticipation in his eyes as he thought about how close he was to snagging the one interview that every reporter in Sweden was hoping for at the moment. Like a bloodhound on the trail.

Ten minutes later Tina rang again. Jenny had agreed to do the interview.

The farm was in Gammelgarn in the eastern part of Gotland. Located as it was, high on a hill, the buildings were visible from the road. Johan and Pia turned off on to a straight gravel road with expansive fields, lying fallow now during the winter, spreading out on either side. The old farm was built in the typical Gotland style of greyish limestone, with a main house, a sheep barn and a big old barn used by the family as a shop selling sheepskins during the tourist season. Johan had been here many times before. Tina and Emma had been friends for ages, ever since teacher training college. Johan liked Tina and her husband, Fredrik, and enjoyed their company. The two couples got on well together, and regularly met for dinner.

As Pia parked the car in the yard at the front, Tina came out of the house and waited for them on the porch. Two lively Border collies raced about at top speed, wagging their tails in greeting.

Johan gave Tina a hug, thinking that she looked a bit worn out.

In the kitchen, they found Jenny sitting at the table holding a cat on her lap. She got up to hug Johan and shake hands with Pia.

Jenny looked more beautiful every time he saw her.

It had to be at least six months since they'd last met, because she'd been doing so much travelling recently. Her hair hung over her shoulders in a thick, shiny red curtain. Her almond-shaped, inscrutable green eyes had an intense look to them. Long, thin legs in jeans, and a simple V-necked red jumper. She wore no make-up, no watch or any jewellery.

They filmed the interview in the kitchen. Jenny sat there with the cat curled up on her lap, a lit candle on the table, a fire crackling in the wood stove. Outside the window sheep with heavy woollen coats could be seen scattered over the fields, grazing. The collies lay under the table and sighed.

With much emotion, Jenny told Johan about the terror and panic she'd felt as she wandered in the woods, trying to find the hermit's cabin in the night. Her shock when she discovered Markus and all the blood inside it. Her uncertainty about whether he was dead or alive. Her fear of the assailant, not knowing whether he might still be out there somewhere in the dark. And how she had sat in the latrine, feeling so alone and vulnerable.

And, in no time, they had the whole story, as told by the key person in the drama.

'What is your relationship to Markus Sandberg?' Johan asked at the end.

'I'm in love with him,' she said, quite candidly. 'We've been seeing each other for a while, but not for very long. Only a few months. We wanted to keep it private for a while.'

Johan gave a start. What the hell? He hadn't heard

anything about this before. He cleared his throat and tried to restrain his glee.

'Why is that?'

Jenny blushed. She was clearly reluctant to answer the question.

'It's not something I want to discuss on TV.'

'So why have you decided to say anything about the relationship now?'

'Because, er . . . because of what happened to Markus. I feel like I might as well tell everyone what the situation is. So that . . .'

'What do you mean?'

'Well . . . you never know . . .'

'What do you never know?'

'Whether the man who did this . . . I mean . . . whether it had something to do with our relationship.'

'Are you saying that jealousy might have been the motive?'

'I don't know, but . . .'

Jenny Levin fell silent and turned to look at her mother. It was obvious she wanted to end the interview.

Tina was sitting in the corner, listening. She stood up at once.

'I think that's enough now. Okay, Jenny?'

She nodded. Johan put down the microphone.

'Sure. Of course. You can stop the camera,' he said, turning to Pia.

'But I need a few still photos,' she told him.

'Okay, but let's wait a few minutes.'

She turned off the camera and set it on the tripod

before going outside to the front porch to have a smoke. Pia hated it when Johan told her what to do.

'Sorry,' Johan said to Jenny. 'Was I too tough on you?'

'Not really, except for the last part . . .'

'About your relationship with Markus?'

'No, about why I've decided to talk about it now. It's because I'm so scared. Scared that this has something to do with us.'

'You mean that Markus was attacked because he's with you?'

'Uh-huh. I think that might be one reason.'

'We're not filming this, right?' Tina interrupted them.

'Of course not,' said Johan. 'And, as I said, we won't use any material that you're not comfortable with. If you like, you can come over to the office and watch the report before we broadcast it.'

'No, that's okay,' said Tina, patting Johan on the shoulder. 'I trust you.'

Johan turned back to Jenny.

'Are you thinking of someone in particular who might react to the fact that you're together, you and Markus?'

'Not really,' she said hesitantly. 'Not really.'

'Do you have an ex-boyfriend who might be jealous?'

'No. At least, I don't think so. I've only had one long-term relationship, and it ended six months ago.'

'Did he break it off, or did you?'

'I did, actually. But he was fine with it. There wasn't any drama or anything.'

'How long were you together?'

'About a year.'

'What's his name?'

'David Gahnström. He's from here in Gammelgarn. We're neighbours. If you step outside you can see his parents' farm over there.' She looked out of the window and pointed. 'But he'd never do anything like this.'

'Are you still in touch with each other?'

'Uh-huh. I always see him when I come here. He's one of my best friends, and he still means a lot to me, but not in a romantic way. We grew up together, so we have a special relationship.'

'Okay. What about Markus?'

'I know that he's had a number of girlfriends, including one named Diana, and she's been really difficult. She keeps ringing him up. She works for the same modelling agency but, luckily, she does a lot of photo shoots in New York.'

'Does Markus still have much contact with her?'

'Er . . . I don't know. I don't think so. It's over between them. Or he broke it off, at least. But she seems to be having a hard time accepting the fact.'

Jenny turned to gaze out of the window.

'Are you worried about your own safety?'

She looked at Johan again.

'I don't really know. Maybe a little.' She shrugged her thin shoulders.

'Do the police know about all this? That you and Markus are together?'

'Yes. But you're the only reporter I've talked to.'

'Thank you, Jenny. I really appreciate the fact that you let me do this interview.'

Johan glanced at his watch. 'Okay, we hope that Markus gets well soon.' He gave Jenny a hug. 'Could we take a few photos?'

She nodded. Pia had finished her cigarette and come back into the kitchen. She gave Johan her sweetest smile and her voice dripped with sarcasm as she said, 'So why don't you go outside and say hello to the sheep in the meantime. You'll just be in the way here. And I'm sure you and the sheep will get on famously together.'

The man who had Eduardo Morales in a neck lock looked surprised when Dolores came storming out of the shed, but he didn't let go of the slender Spaniard.

Dolores spoke excellent English, since she'd been an environmental activist for Greenpeace. Now, she shouted angrily, 'What are you doing to my husband? Release him at once!'

She rushed over to the stout Swede and made a futile attempt to yank his arm off Eduardo. But the man didn't budge.

'Are you out of your mind? Let him go, or I'll call the police!'

At the word 'police', the man did loosen his hold slightly. He turned to look at Dolores.

'Who are you?' he asked, in faltering English. 'What are you doing here?'

'We're Spanish tourists, and we're studying various fishing villages on Gotland. My name is Dolores Morales, and this is my husband, Eduardo. We're from Seville.'

Now, the man finally released Eduardo and offered to shake hands with Dolores.

'Please excuse me. My name is Björn Johansson. I live over there, in Lergrav.' He pointed a rough finger towards a spot along the shore. 'There are good fishing houses there, too.'

A smile appeared on his wrinkled and weather-beaten face.

Dolores was still cross, and Eduardo was coughing as he held one hand to his throat, as if to emphasize that the attack hadn't gone unnoticed.

'Why did you attack my husband?' she demanded to know, glaring at Björn with her brown Spanish eyes. 'Are you in the habit of assaulting tourists?'

The man waved his hands in a dismissive gesture.

'No, no, not at all. Something terrible has happened. Over there on the peninsula. You can see it from here. Furillen.'

'Furillen?' Dolores said. It was one of the strangest names she'd ever heard. 'What happened over there?'

'Last night, a man was beaten almost to death. Someone hit him again and again with an axe, and the police think that the murderer got away in a boat and then came over here.'

Dolores opened her eyes wide in alarm. Her husband tapped her arm, and said something in Spanish.

'Excuse me,' she said. 'I need to translate what you said for my husband. He doesn't speak English.'

Dolores rattled off a long stream of Spanish, waving her arms about as she did so. That prompted an even longer and equally incomprehensible volley of words from Eduardo.

'I need to show you what I've found,' Dolores then said, tugging at Björn Johansson's jacket. 'Come inside.'

The burly man followed them into the shed.

Cautiously, Dolores opened the lid of the America-trunk to show him the contents.

The Swede didn't touch the clothes. One glance was enough for him to realize what he was looking at.

Without a word, he took out his mobile and dialled the number for the police.

The investigative team was having a meeting when the next important call came in from Kyllaj. The discovery of the bloodstained clothing was such a spectacular find that Knutas wanted to go out there in person. The Spanish couple and the neighbour who had made the call were asked not to leave until the police arrived. This discovery bolstered the theory that the writer who was staying in the fishing village really had seen the perpetrator.

'Now the question is: Where's the boat that he used?' said Knutas in the car.

Jacobsson was driving, as usual.

'No one has reported a boat stolen anywhere on Gotland during the past month,' she said. 'On the other hand, a lot of people don't really keep an eye on their boats in the winter. It's very possible someone might not have noticed their boat was missing.'

'Kyllaj,' said Knutas, then he paused before going on. 'It's been a while since you and I were last out there. Do you remember?'

'Of course I do,' said Jacobsson, feeling her face flush. She knew all too well what he was referring to.

'They've slipped through the net again. Vera Petrov and Stefan Norrström. I'd give anything to know where they're hiding.'

'Uh-huh.'

For obvious reasons, Karin Jacobsson avoided talking about that particular subject. Because of her, the couple who were on all the international lists of wanted criminals had escaped. This was something that only she and Knutas knew. Vera Petrov was suspected of committing two murders on Gotland several years earlier. Her husband, Stefan Norrström, had also been involved. They had fled abroad and had last been seen in the Dominican Republic. Knutas had thought the police were close to catching them but, for some inexplicable reason, they had again managed to get away. He hadn't heard anything more for the past few months, and he was starting to lose hope that they'd ever be caught. Their house in Kyllaj had stood empty ever since they had disappeared.

By the time Knutas and Jacobsson reached the small-boat marina, the crime-scene techs had already arrived. Police tape had been put up, keeping out a few nearby residents who had noticed all the activity going on down at the harbour.

'It won't be long before we have reporters hounding us,' said Knutas with a grimace as he lifted the blue-and-white plastic tape and slipped underneath.

Inside, Jacobsson studied the contents of the trunk without touching anything. She frowned.

'Why didn't the perpetrator make a better attempt to hide the clothes? Why didn't he dump them in the sea or burn them? He should have realized they'd be found eventually. And, of course, they're full of his DNA. But what's that smell?'

Sohlman appeared behind them. He stepped forward and, using a pair of tongs, lifted up the T-shirt so his colleagues could see it.

'See that? There's vomit on the T-shirt. Also on the sweatshirt and the jacket.'

'Puke?'

'That's another way of putting it,' said Sohlman dryly. 'Maybe the perpetrator got seasick on his way over here from Furillen. The wind was blowing at fifty-four kilometres per hour in the daytime on Monday, so the backwash would have been considerable. Probably really rough seas.'

'Or maybe the vomit is a result of what he'd done,' said Knutas thoughtfully. 'I can only imagine what it was like in that cramped little cabin, with blood spraying all around. It would make anybody sick to their stomach.'

'Stop, for God's sake,' Jacobsson said, her face turning white.

'Sorry.' Knutas sat down cautiously on an overturned beer crate. 'But what does this mean? The assailant must have planned his escape in advance, presumably by stealing a boat. He parked his car somewhere in Kyllaj, most likely fairly close to the harbour, since he'd want to get out of here as fast as possible. How long would it take to cross the water from Furillen?'

'According to that writer, Olof Hellström, the boat was very small,' said Sohlman, scratching his head. 'Maybe half an hour?'

'To be honest, I haven't a clue,' said Jacobsson. 'I know nothing about boats.'

'We'll need to find out, at any rate,' said Knutas,

getting up. 'Right now, I want to talk to that Spanish couple. We'll leave you here to work in peace.'

He nodded to Sohlman and went out.

The man from Lergrav had taken Mr and Mrs Morales to a cabin that he owned near the harbour. They both had blankets draped over their shoulders and were warming themselves in front of the fireplace, drinking hot chocolate. They looked pale and blue with cold. Poor souls, thought Knutas. They're not used to our Swedish winter. And it hasn't even started yet.

Jacobsson did most of the talking, since Knutas's command of English was far from sufficient to carry on a conversation, much less an official interview. With much emotion and vigorous hand gestures, Mr and Mrs Morales described what had happened to them, the two of them frequently talking at the same time. The husband didn't speak English, but he kept on wanting to interject remarks in Spanish and add details, which his wife translated.

The interview took twice as long as it should have.

When Knutas and Jacobsson returned to headquarters, they were greeted by the police spokesperson, who was in an agitated state.

'We've been inundated with reporters,' Norrby complained, throwing up his hands. 'Apparently, *Rapport* used its noon broadcast to reveal that Markus Sandberg was having an affair with Jenny Levin. And the news got out that the police have made a macabre discovery in Kyllaj. Now everybody is asking whether the news about the romantic relationship is true, and they want to know what we found in Kyllaj.'

'Okay,' said Knutas grimly. His stomach was growling with hunger. He looked at his watch. 'Call a press conference for an hour from now. In the big meeting room.'

One of the routines that Agnes hates most in the clinic is the mandatory sessions in the warm room. She has tried to talk to Per about it, asked to be excused from the requirement, but he says there's nothing he can do. It's the same for everyone.

There are five warm rooms lined up in a row along one corridor. On the wall outside are shelves holding baskets, each assigned to a specific person. Every basket has a pink label with a patient's name on it. Linda, Erika, Josefine, Sofia, Agnes . . . This is just like in a childcare centre, too, thinks Agnes as she reaches into her basket to take out her own sheet and pillowcase. She has to put them on the bed in the room before lying down. The room is small and has no windows. It reminds her of a prison cell with a round peephole in the door. The nurses can peer inside whenever they like. The room is furnished only with a low bed with a heated mattress, an electric heater and a stool, which is used by a nurse if the patient happens to be feeling particularly anxious. The thermostat next to the door shows that the temperature is 40 degrees Celsius. A lamp with a frosted shade casts a soft glow over the room. And there's not a sound, as if the walls were padded.

She is expected to lie here for half an hour without moving as the warmth spreads through her body. Twice a day, after lunch and after dinner. Thirty minutes of total silence after she has been forced to eat a huge amount of food. The nurses claim that the heat is good for her, that it will decrease the level of her anxiety. To hell with them. Agnes knows all too well what the sessions in the warm room will mean if she follows their orders. With her heart pounding, she opens the door. She hates how diminished she feels in this place, hates how they force her to do things. Do they really believe she's so stupid that she'd agree to lie in this room for a whole thirty minutes and allow the food to invade her body? If she stretches out her legs as she lies on the bed she can even see how they start to swell up from the treatment. They get fatter and fatter with each passing minute.

The first thing she does when she enters the room is to turn off the light so the nurse can't see what she's doing. Since there are no windows, the room is pitch black. She tells them that she finds it much easier to relax when it's dark. Then she turns off the heat and spends the half-hour doing physical exercises. She tries to do sit-ups, but her vertebrae jut out and scrape against the floor. The pain is unbearable. She lies down on the bed and does her sit-ups there instead. Then she raises and lowers her arms and does leg lifts until she runs out of steam. She is soon sweating and out of breath. Her joints ache, making her weep, but she keeps on going. She is locked into these compulsory exercises and can't stop, even though what she wants most is to relax. As she lies there in the dark, frantically exercising, she thinks about how all of this began. How she ended up in this nightmare.

About a year after her mother and older brother died, plunging her into a grief that was as black as night, she started going out and seeing her friends again. One evening in May they happened to go to a club for teens in Visby, and on that particular night there was a modelling contest. On impulse, Agnes decided to enter, and she ended up winning. The grand prize was a trip to Stockholm and a photo shoot with a professional fashion photographer working for the Fashion for Life agency, which had sponsored the contest. Agnes went to Stockholm, where a room had been booked for her at a fancy hotel in the city centre. After checking in, a cab took her to the agency. She was both scared and impressed to see it was so flashy and exclusive, the walls covered with photos of models, all of them unbelievably beautiful.

Everyone she met greeted her cheerfully, with polite smiles. At the same time, she couldn't help noticing the appraising looks they gave her, casting swift, critical glances at her body. This blatant assessment of her appearance made her feel clumsy, and she didn't know what to do with her hands. She tried to suck in her stomach, stand up straight, and look natural, even though she was shaking inside. She was ushered into a studio where she met the photographer Markus Sandberg. The same photographer who was now in hospital, seriously injured after a murder attempt on Furillen. She could hardly believe it when she saw the news on TV. But it was definitely him. In her mind, she pictures him from that first meeting. He was wearing trendy jeans with dozens of pockets and rivets. A simple white T-shirt over his buff torso. He seemed friendly but a bit stressed as he greeted her, running his hand through his unruly hair and smiling. He had very white teeth and at least a day's stubble on his cheeks. He was cute, but old. She had only seen him before in magazine photos of celebrities. It felt unreal to be in the same room as him.

Then it was time for the photo shoot. She felt sick to her stomach at the thought of trying to pose naturally for him in that cold studio. The floor and walls were white as chalk. In the middle of the room a black cloth had been stretched out to serve as a backdrop for the photos. She wasn't given any make-up or asked to change her clothes. They wanted her just as she was. Natural. She tried to move as easily as she could, but the whole time she was terribly conscious that she wasn't any good. Not thin enough, not cute enough, not professional enough. Markus did his best to get her to relax. 'You're beautiful,' he told her. 'You're super-cute. Loosen up. Pretend the camera is a guy you're in love with.' Agnes had just turned fifteen and had never been in love with any guy. But she did her best. Tried to imitate the models she'd seen on TV and in magazines. Twisting one way and then the other. 'Shake your shoulders loose. Put your hand on your hip. Turn your body to the side, but look at me. Flirt with the camera.' The dead lens blinked like an evil eye at her. How was she supposed to flirt with that? She felt stiff and awkward. All she wanted was for the session to be over. When the assistant left the room and she was alone in the studio with the photographer, she felt even more embarrassed. He must think I'm hopeless, she thought, strongly regretting her choice of clothing. Why had she worn such baggy jeans and this loose-fitting top? She probably looked grotesquely fat. As if the photographer could read her mind, he asked her, 'Do you have anything on underneath?' Yes, she was wearing a camisole. 'Take off that big shirt. We can't see how you look.' Hesitantly, she unbuttoned the shirt and took it off, casting a quick glance down at her camisole. White, with a black bra underneath. How embarrassing. What was she doing here, anyway? Unhappy, she looked at the photographer.

Then he put down the camera and came over to her with a smile. Before she had time to react, he took her face in both hands and kissed her on the mouth. She stood motionless, with her arms hanging limply at her sides. She had no idea what to do. Abruptly, he let her go, but his face was still very close, with laughter in his eyes. Her cheeks burned. Playfully, he ruffled her hair; he wore rings on every finger. 'You're beautiful, sweetheart. You taste good. Don't be offended. I just wanted to get you to relax a bit. Okay, let's start again. Think of it as a game, because that's exactly what it is. Not real. Just a game.'

Press conferences were a curse, equally trying every time. Afterwards, Knutas fled to his office and resolutely shut the door. The reporters had behaved like starving wolves, ravenously casting themselves upon each titbit of information the police handed out. Their hunger was insatiable. That was what bothered Knutas the most. The way they never backed down, were never satisfied. Their craving for scandal knew no bounds. Their appetite merely grew as each new fact was presented. New circumstances led to new questions, which led to even more. And always the balancing act that he had to manage, giving the reporters what they wanted so they'd think they'd got it all, but keeping the most important evidence to himself. He didn't want to disclose anything that might jeopardize the investigation, so he had to look out for every trap, every attempt at manipulation, as the reporters tried to coax more out of him than he intended to say.

He was exhausted. He sank down on to his old desk chair and closed his eyes. He was longing for Lina. Wanting to be at home with her in peace and quiet, eating a good dinner and afterwards snuggling together on the sofa in front of the fireplace. Just sitting there, gazing at the fire and holding her close.

But it would be hours before he was able to go home.

He rocked slowly back and forth in his chair. Tried to clear his mind. Out with all the non-essentials that were whirling around in there, so he could think better. The clothes that had been found in the fisherman's shed in Kyllaj ought to give the police some leads. He'd asked SCL, the Swedish Crime Laboratory, to rush their test through. The sight of the shed and the trunk with the bloodstained contents had given him flashbacks to a case involving a serial killer a number of years earlier. In that instance, a young couple had found some bloodstained garments in the storage space under a sofa inside a boathouse in Nisseviken. The clothing had belonged to the female victims. The murderer had stowed them away, wanting to keep them because of some sort of perverse and sadistic sense of possession. This time, the police were apparently dealing with clothing that the perpetrator had discarded as soon as he came ashore.

One thing that Knutas had not revealed to the journalists was that Sandberg's mobile phone had been traced to the Stockholm area. And, more specifically, to the suburbs south of the city.

The police had asked for help from the National Communications Centre, which had picked up the signal from a mast in Flemingsberg. It had not been possible to find out any further details. If the perpetrator lived in Stockholm, why would he have chosen to commit the assault on Furillen? It was such an inaccessible site, nor was it the easiest place to approach or leave without being noticed. If someone wanted to kill Markus Sandberg, why not do it in Stockholm, where the photographer lived and worked? Maybe the assailant had some sort of connection to Gotland, maybe he was from here. Apparently, he knew enough about the area to have managed to find his way out to Furillen without making himself conspicuous.

Knutas opened the top desk drawer and took out his pipe and a tobacco pouch. He knocked out the pipe and then meticulously proceeded to refill it as his thoughts wandered. Sandberg's mobile was not the only thing that had been traced. The phone call from the inquisitive stranger to the Hotel Fabriken, which had been reported by the cleaning woman, had been pinpointed to the Grand Hotel in Stockholm. If the man on the phone was the assailant, this opened up completely new avenues to investigate. The man had made the call from the hotel lobby, so it wasn't certain that he had been staying there. But it did present a strong possibility that the perpetrator had come from Stockholm. Could Sandberg's relationship with Jenny be the motive? The police were in the process of gathering information about the photographer's background and closest relatives, so Knutas hoped they would soon have a clearer picture of the victim's life. He was starting to feel very impatient but, fortunately, the phone rang.

'Yes?' he said.

'Hi. This is Pelle Broström, the helicopter pilot. We've spotted a boat out here, close to Sankt Olofsholm. It might be the one you're looking for.'

Knutas felt his pulse quicken.

'What does it look like?'

'A small dinghy with an outboard motor, brand name Uttern. It's tucked in among the reeds, so we almost missed it. We didn't see it during our search this morning, but we went out again after lunch, and we happened to spot it a few minutes ago.'

'Can you see anything else?'

'No, not from up here in the air. It looks empty, but it's drifting freely. Doesn't seem to be moored to anything.'

'Okay,' said Knutas with enthusiasm. 'Good job. Alert the coastguard and make sure they go out there at once to tow it back to the harbour in Kyllaj. I'll send over the crime-scene techs.'

'Good. Roger that. We'll notify the coastguard.'

A couple of hours later, the police had confirmed that the boat was most likely the one used by the perpetrator out at Furillen. The floorboards were covered with bloodstains and traces of vomit. That was going to make it easy to link the boat to the clothes discovered in Kyllaj earlier in the day.

That evening, the police also received word from an individual in Lergrav who wanted to report that his boat, an Uttern, was missing from its berth in the boathouse.

The shrill sound of a whistle raced across the soggy, muddy football pitch. The members of the Visby women's team were practising their free kicks. Karin Jacobsson stood off to the side, watching her players. It was eight thirty in the evening, and she could sense the listlessness of the team. On a night like this, it wasn't easy to be a coach. The women's league was always assigned worse time slots than the men, who practised from seven to eight thirty. The women had to make do with eight thirty to ten. Equality within the sports world left much to be desired.

She tucked a pinch of snuff under her lip, shivering and stamping her feet to stay warm. The floodlights cast a cold glare over the pitch, it was drizzling, and puddles of water had formed everywhere. The surface had turned into muck that was almost like liquid cement, making it hard for the players to run with any speed. Their clothes were mud-spattered, and almost everyone had been sprayed in the face with gravel. Jacobsson was finding it challenging to keep the team motivated. The previous season had ended, and it felt like the next one would never start. Some of the players weren't even trying; they were merely dashing about and chatting, instead of giving the practice session their full attention. Jacobsson tried to cheer them on as best she could. She had always thought that training on dirt was important. They could at least make an effort. She had divided up the players so that half were wearing blue vests, the other half red. Now they had started practising various passing manoeuvres.

While Jacobsson kept her eyes fixed on the women on the pitch, her mind wandered. Earlier in the day she had phoned Karolinska University Hospital to enquire about Markus Sandberg's condition. He was still sedated, and as before the prognosis was uncertain. All they could do was hope. If Sandberg did pull through, Jacobsson wanted to be the one to interview him, and she had asked Knutas to allow her to do that. She might even have to travel to Stockholm. Their police colleagues in the capital would help out, of course, but it wasn't the same as going there in person, meeting the staff at the modelling agency as well as Sandberg's colleagues, people who knew him and might be able to provide the police with leads.

She also had another purpose in mind. She was hoping to see her daughter in the city. She felt her expression soften as she thought about Hanna.

Six months ago, Karin had met her for the first time in Stockholm. She had been forced to give Hanna up for adoption at birth, but she had always felt a great longing to find her daughter. It was like a dark void inside her heart. And that had probably contributed to her inability to love anyone. Jacobsson had never had a long-term relationship. As soon as things started to get serious and she became so attached to someone that she felt vulnerable, she would flee. Even her friendships were more or less superficial, also with colleagues at police headquarters, people she saw every day. Anders Knutas was the person she felt closest to, no doubt because he never gave up on her. And it was after a conversation with Knutas that she had dared to consider, after so many years, getting in touch with her daughter.

The previous summer, she had finally done something about it. She had already found out her daughter's name, and her address in Stockholm. Hanna von Schwerin. The rather posh name had made her nervous.

Without giving any advance warning, Karin had gone to the address in Södermalm and sat down in a café outside the front entrance of the building to wait. At long last, a young woman and her dog had emerged. Karin knew at once that this had to be her daughter. They were so similar in appearance. Karin had started to cry.

Hanna had studied her in silence for a moment, and then she said only one word: 'Mamma?' She sank down on a chair on the other side of the café table and regarded her with a wary expression. All the colour had drained from her face.

'Is that you? Are you my biological mother?'

Karin noticed how she emphasized the word 'biological', as if she didn't really want to acknowledge the fact that this was her mother. But not her real mother; only her biological mother. Karin couldn't utter a sound. She nodded and looked down at the table. Hanna had glanced over her shoulder, as if afraid that someone might hear. Neither of them spoke. Karin took several deep breaths before she dared look her daughter in the eye.

'I want you to know what happened,' she whispered.

'In that case, you'll have to come with me and my dog, Nelson, to the park. He can't hold it much longer.'

Karin immediately stood up. They were the exact same height and had the same slender build. They both wore jeans, but Karin had put on a more expensive shirt than usual, one that she'd bought in an exclusive boutique in Visby. Hoping to fit in better, considering her daughter's upper-class surname. Giving in to her own prejudices, she had expected to meet an elegant young woman wearing a tight skirt with slits, a blouse with a bow at the neck and a string of pearls. Hanna's casual attire, which happened to correspond to Karin's own tastes in clothing, made things somewhat easier. At least in those first few minutes. Clothes no longer played a role.

They had walked across Mariatorget, crossed Horns-gatan, and strolled along the promenade to the top of the hill. There was a magnificent view of the waters of Riddarfjärden, of Gamla Stan and of the city hall. But Karin didn't even notice. With frequent pauses, she stammered through the story of how she had become pregnant at the age of fourteen and how she'd never had any contact with Hanna's father, not even back then.

'Why not?' Hanna wanted to know, and Karin felt her blood run cold.

Of course, the question was unavoidable. Hundreds of times she had considered this dilemma. Should she tell her daughter that she was the result of a rape? That her father was the riding teacher in town who had attacked Karin?

For a while they walked side by side in silence. A great abyss between them. The dog named Nelson ran on ahead, eagerly sniffing at the ground. Karin slowed down.

'You won't like what I'm going to tell you.'

'No?'

'First of all, your father is dead. He died more than twenty years ago.'

A shadow passed across Hanna's face.

'Oh.'

Then Karin mustered her courage and recounted the whole story, from beginning to end. How her parents had convinced her that the best thing to do would be to give up the baby for adoption. How she had regretted this decision the minute she held her newborn child in her arms, but her parents had claimed that it was too late.

Hanna's expression changed several times as she listened. When Karin finished, a long silence ensued. They kept on walking, but neither of them spoke. Karin was waiting. She didn't know what else to say. She felt completely empty inside. Finally, her daughter spoke.

'I need to be alone to think about everything. It's a lot to take in at once. I need time to process all of it. I don't want you to contact me for a while. I'll phone you when I feel ready. I hope you understand.'

She called Nelson, then turned on her heel and left.

Karin had taken the next flight back to Gotland, her stomach churning with a dull sense of disappointment mixed with worry. Safely back home, she had replayed the whole encounter over and over. Maybe she should have written a letter instead. Given some warning. Allowed Hanna to think about the whole matter and prepare herself. But, after all these years, she had simply popped up like some sort of jack-in-the-box. She'd had so many questions she wanted to ask her daughter. But she hadn't had a chance to do that.

Several times after that first meeting she'd been on the verge of ringing Hanna, but she'd stopped herself at the last minute. Hanna had asked her to wait. That was a request she needed to honour. But, now, her job was taking her back to Stockholm.

Six months had passed. Karin wondered if she would be able to keep her promise and refrain from contacting her daughter. She would probably have to.

The stairs creaked as Jenny quietly made her way down to the kitchen. She knew every creak of every step, and which ones made the most noise. So many times she had crept up these stairs, worried that she might wake her parents when she came home later than she'd promised.

But, to all intents and purposes, she was now an adult. It was both liberating and frightening.

After being discovered by the modelling agency and going to Stockholm, she had left her childhood behind for good. These days, she flew all over the world between assignments and handled everything herself, while money flowed into her bank account. She had whole-heartedly enjoyed her new life, up until the fateful incident on Furillen, which had turned her world upside down. At the moment, she felt completely at a loss.

In the kitchen, she found the dogs curled up in their basket. They yawned as they peered at her sleepily and reluctantly wagged their tails. As if they weren't quite ready to wake up.

She poured herself a glass of water and took a banana from a bowl on the worktop, then sat down at the table. It was pitch black outside, but when dawn came the landscape would be hidden under a haze. At this time of year, everything was grey. The limestone façade of the farmhouse, the bare fields with no trace of vegetation and no sign of snow yet, the cold trees stretching their naked branches upwards, as if entreating, their bark silhouetted against a dreary sky.

A week had passed since that terrifying night on Furillen. The initial shock had faded, only to be replaced by a gnawing anxiety. Not just about Markus, but also about herself. She felt a vague uneasiness, as if she had a premonition that something even worse was about to happen. That was probably stupid, and she'd tried again and again to talk some sense into herself. It was only her imagination; it was just the shock. Nothing like this had ever happened to her before. The psychologist at the hospital had said that she needed to be prepared for some sort of delayed reaction. She had the psychologist's card and phone number, and she had been urged to call whenever she liked.

In her mind, she saw Markus's face. She remembered his laugh earlier in the day, before he was attacked, and the stolen kisses in her room between sessions. Feeling sick to her stomach, she recalled his injured body, the blood all over the inside of that small cabin, his face beaten so badly that it was unrecognizable. The terror and panic she'd felt. Would he survive? Would everything go back to normal? She thought about him all the time. Apprehension flooded over her. She needed to have a cigarette before her mother and father awoke. Even though she now considered herself an adult, she didn't want them to see her smoking. She glanced at the clock on the wall. 5.15. They'd be asleep for a while longer.

She put on her wellingtons and her long black down coat, which she always wore whenever she came home to the farm. She dug through her pockets and found a packet of cigarettes and her lighter. The dogs realized at once that she was going out, and they stood ready at the door, eagerly wagging their tails.

She breathed in the raw cold air as soon as she stepped out on to the porch. She didn't dare turn on the outdoor light for fear of waking her parents. The gravel crunched under her feet. The dogs paused to pee on the lawn, then followed at her heels as she crossed the front garden. The gate squeaked when she opened it. She was used to the darkness here at home; it didn't frighten her. She knew every rock and shrub. Not a sound came from the sheep barn, or the other, older barn. Even the animals were asleep. She walked over to the corner of the sheep barn and stopped there to look out at the fields and the extensive pastures. Off in the distance was the house belonging to her friend David or, rather, to his parents. She hadn't found time to phone him, and she wondered whether he was home. There were no lights on at their farm, and it was only because she was so familiar with the area that she even knew it was there. It was eerie, like peering into a dark void. She heard only a rustling from the bushes as the dogs nosed about. Then a flare of light as she lit her cigarette. And inhaled deeply.

She sat down on a wooden bench next to the wall of the house. This was where her father liked to drink his morning coffee in the summertime as the sun came up. She thought about Markus and felt such a longing to see him. Her parents had thought she should stay at home and recuperate for at least a week. All her assignments had been cancelled, and her boss, Robert, had been so understanding, telling her that of course she should take as much time as she needed.

And Markus was still unconscious, so there was nothing she could do. He had to get well. She had never been so in love before and, right now, her feelings for him seemed even stronger, because of what had happened. Markus was the first real man she'd ever met. What they had together couldn't be compared to any of her experiences with the awkward guys she'd previously dated. What if the worst of all possible things should happen? What if he didn't make it? And he died before she had a chance to see him again? Before she even went to the hospital? Would the sight of his mauled body in the cabin on Furillen be her last memory of Markus? The image of him lying there, stretched out on the floor, his body bloody and beaten? No, no. That was impossible. What was she doing here? She took one last drag on her cigarette and stubbed it out on the gravel. Then she tossed it into the bushes. She had to go back to Stockholm. She refused to wait any longer.

Taking long strides, she hurried back to the house.

The plane landed at Bromma Airport, just outside central Stockholm, at ten thirty in the morning. Markus Sandberg had been under heavy sedation for a week and had undergone several operations, but this morning Knutas had been notified that the photographer was now awake. He had immediately decided to send Jacobsson and Wittberg to Stockholm to interview him. In spite of the doctor's misgivings that Sandberg might not remember anything, Knutas was hoping for a miracle.

Jacobsson swallowed hard as the plane touched down. A car would be waiting to take them to Karolinska University Hospital, yet she wanted nothing more than to drive straight out to Södermalm to try to talk to Hanna. She hoped it would be worth trying again.

When they entered the arrivals hall they were met by a couple of police colleagues who were going to accompany them to the hospital. The doctor had promised to let them speak to his patient for a short time, provided that Markus was sufficiently alert. The Stockholm police could have certainly conducted the interview on their own, but Jacobsson had insisted on being present when they spoke to Markus Sandberg for the first time.

A nurse showed them to the room. Their Stockholm colleagues waited outside the intensive care ward.

'I need to ask you to treat him very gently,' the nurse said as she opened the door. 'Don't try to force anything. Let him take as much time as he needs, and see that he doesn't get upset. He's still in a lot of pain, even though we've given him medication for it. So go easy with the questions. It's not certain that he'll be able to give you any answers. We don't know what he remembers, or if he remembers anything at all. At the moment he's not able to speak or write, so you'll have to find some other way to communicate.'

Markus Sandberg's eyes were closed as he lay in bed under a yellow hospital blanket. His head was heavily bandaged, with two tubes snaking out from under the dressing. His face was swollen, with huge bruises that were various shades of yellow, green and brown. A plastic tube had been inserted in the front of his throat to allow him to breathe. The nurse placed her hand on his arm.

'You have visitors.'

Jacobsson had to take a deep breath and collect herself as she stepped into the room. It was impossible to imagine that the man in the bed was the roguish and charismatic TV host who had often been seen rubbing shoulders with celebrities on the red carpet.

'Just press that button if you need anything,' said the nurse, pointing at a button attached to a cord that hung from the wall. Then she left the room.

'Hello,' said Jacobsson quietly. Then she introduced herself and Wittberg.

She couldn't tell whether Markus was awake. His eyes were still shut, and he gave no indication that he was aware of anyone having come into the room.

She pulled a chair over to the bed, sat down, and cautiously tapped his arm. Then he opened his eyes and turned his head slightly towards her. The expression in his eyes was inscrutable.

'We're from Visby police. We're investigating the assault that left you injured. It's very important that we get your help in finding the assailant, and that's why we wanted to talk to you as soon as possible. We're so happy to see you awake.'

She gave him a little smile of encouragement. No reaction.

'I understand that you're not able to speak, so we have to find some other way for you to communicate with us. Could you blink twice for yes and once for no?'

A long pause. Then Markus blinked twice.

'Do you remember what happened out on Furillen?'

Several minutes passed without a response. Markus's right eyebrow twitched uncontrollably. Jacobsson and Wittberg waited patiently. Finally, Markus replied by moving the palm of his hand back and forth. He seemed to be saying that he recalled at least a little of the event.

'Did you recognize the person who attacked you?'

Markus Sandberg narrowed his eyes.

Two blinks.

'Was it a woman?'

No reaction.

'Was it a man?'

152

He gave her a blank look. As if he wasn't listening or hadn't understood what she said. Jacobsson repeated her question. A trickle of saliva seeped out of his mouth and ran down his chin. He whimpered as if in pain. The next second he uttered a long-drawn-out sound, a howl that rose up from his throat. Jacobsson jumped in fright and was just about to press the call button when the door opened and the nurse came in. Markus raised one arm. Greatly agitated, he grunted and pointed at her. Jacobsson cast a helpless glance at Wittberg, who merely shook his head.

'You need to leave now,' said the nurse firmly. 'As I said, we don't want him to get upset.'

'But we really need to talk to him,' Jacobsson objected. 'It's terribly important that we continue the interview.'

'Not at the moment. He has been seriously injured, and it will endanger his life if he doesn't have peace and quiet.'

The nurse refused to give in.

'You can come back tomorrow if he doesn't get any worse. Now, out!'

She shooed the two police officers out of the door as if they were children.

Jacobsson and Wittberg reluctantly left the hospital ward.

'He's much worse than I thought,' said Wittberg in the car as they drove to police headquarters. 'And he seemed really distraught.'

'He got upset when the nurse came in, and then he pointed at her.'

'But she can't be the one who did it.'

'No,' said Jacobsson. 'But he pointed at her when I asked him whether it was a man or a woman.'

'How could it be a woman?' Wittberg objected. 'The clothes that were found in Kyllaj belonged to a man.'

'I know. That's something we'll have to work out.'

The premises of the Fashion for Life agency were in a beautiful, early-twentieth-century building in a street with trendy restaurants and shops in central Stockholm. Jacobsson and Wittberg had made an appointment to meet with Robert Ek, the agency director. The young receptionist who greeted them had raven-black hair cut in a pageboy style with a fringe that completely hid one of her eyes. Heavy black eyeliner and mascara had been applied to the eye that was visible, which regarded them with some curiosity as she rang her boss. Her fingernails were long and perfectly painted in a leopardskin pattern. Fascinated, Jacobsson couldn't help staring. She was amazed that such women existed. She felt like a twit and a country bumpkin in her jeans, Converse shoes and ugly old army-surplus jacket. If only she had at least remembered to comb her hair and put on some lipstick. Made some sort of effort. But the next second she was cursing herself. What a fool she was. First of all, she was a police officer, not a wannabe model. And secondly, what difference would it have made? In their eyes, her appearance was beyond hope, no matter what she did.

At that moment a man opened a glass door and came in. Jacobsson guessed that he was probably about forty-five. Tall and clean-shaven, with close-cropped hair that gleamed with recently applied gel, as if he'd stepped right out of a toiletries commercial. His face was as shiny as a newly polished copper pan. He wore a light-coloured shirt, leather trousers, red braces and a chic little ascot around his neck. He gave them a big smile, revealing unnaturally white teeth. He wore rectangular eyeglasses with heavy red frames and quite a few rings on his fingers. Jacobsson shook his hand more firmly than usual, as if to make up for her drab appearance and to counteract the antipathy she felt towards this man.

They went to his office. Robert Ek closed the glass door and invited them to sit down on a lime-green sofa. On the wall above it hung an enormous portrait of a woman holding a tartan umbrella as she crossed Fifth Avenue on a windy, rainy day in Manhattan. The woman wore only knickers and a bra, and her long red hair was being blown in all directions, just like the umbrella that she was trying to manoeuvre. Jacobsson immediately recognized Jenny Levin.

'Our new star,' said Ek when he noticed her looking at the photo. 'She's come a long way. Isn't she fabulous?'

'Yes, she certainly is,' said Thomas Wittberg reverently.

Jacobsson merely nodded.

'Can I offer you anything? An espresso? Macchiato? San Pellegrino?'

'What is . . .' Wittberg began, but stopped when Jacobsson poked him in the side.

'No, thanks,' she said. 'We won't stay long.'

'Okay. I understand. So how can I help you?'

If only he'd wipe that damned grin off his face, thought Jacobsson. His top photographer is in intensive care, for God's sake.

'How would you describe your relationship with Markus Sandberg?'

'Excellent. We're on very friendly terms. We've known each other a long time.'

'How long?'

'Oh, it must be about fifteen years now, if I'm not mistaken.'

'Long before Markus started working in the fashion business?'

'That's right. We used to run into each other at various functions. Stockholm isn't as big as you'd think if you were from the provinces.'

He gave Jacobsson another amiable smile, but she did not smile back. This man was already proving to be unbearably irritating. And she was surprised at how unfazed he seemed to be by Markus's present unfortunate condition.

'How do you feel about what happened to Markus?'

As if he'd read her mind, Robert Ek immediately changed his expression.

'It's awful,' he said emphatically. 'Terrible. That's the only word for it. I was so shocked when I heard what had happened.'

As if to illustrate his words, he clasped his hands and opened his eyes wide. Then he shook his head, took off his glasses, and wiped the corners of his eyes with a tissue which he took from a holder on the table. 'We're all hoping that he'll recover, and as quickly as possible.'

'Where were you on the night that Markus was attacked?'

Ek raised his neatly shaped eyebrows. Jacobsson wondered whether he might have dyed and enhanced his eyelashes. They were unusually long and dark.

'On Monday night, a week ago? I was at home with my family. Probably asleep in bed.'

'You're married and have four children. Is that right?'

'Precisely. I'm married to Erna Linton. You may remember her. She was once a very celebrated model. Although that's a long time ago now. The years pass so quickly.'

'Where do you live?'

'In Saltsjö-Duvnäs, right outside Stockholm, in Nacka. We live in my parents' house.'

'What sort of professional relationship do you have with Markus?'

'We don't really see a lot of each other. He's always dashing off on various photo shoots, while I mostly stay here and take care of the administrative work, when I'm not away travelling myself.'

'Do you know whether Markus has any connection to Flemingsberg?'

'Out in Huddinge? No, I wouldn't think so. He has always spent most of his time in the city. Unless a woman is involved, of course.'

'Does Markus have any enemies? Is there anyone who might want to harm him?' asked Wittberg, jumping into the conversation for the first time.

Robert Ek's gaze took in Wittberg's toned and well-dressed figure. He hesitated a moment before answering.

'Not that I know of. He's always been popular here at the agency – sometimes a bit too popular, if you know what I mean. And that has led to a number of problems over the years. I don't know how many models have left in the middle of a job because Markus had just dumped them and started an affair with someone else. It was a big problem, until I finally decided to have a talk with him, six months ago. It's really none of my business, but when I see my models looking unhappy, I have to step in. I tried to explain things and asked him to try to restrain himself. We can't afford to have jobs delayed or adversely affected or, in the worst case, cancelled because he can't control his cock – excuse my French, but that's really what this is about.'

Jacobsson cast a glance at Wittberg. His face was impassive.

'So how did Markus react?'

'He tried to laugh it off.'

'He didn't take it seriously?'

'No, and that's putting it mildly. But I do think that, lately, he's been on his best behaviour. Or maybe he's just been more discreet about managing his love life.'

'But his frequent affairs must have caused other problems,' said Jacobsson. 'Were there any that were particularly significant, or had serious consequences?'

Robert Ek's face darkened. For the first time during the conversation his expression seemed genuine. He looked honestly worried, almost distressed.

'That makes me think of the incident with Marita. A Finno-Swedish model he was dating. Marita Ahonen.'

'And?'

'She was a very promising model who came to us a

couple of years ago. Just under six feet tall, legs like a gazelle, platinum-blonde hair like a wood nymph, her complexion like the smoothest Meissen porcelain, and you wouldn't believe her eyes. They were like Finland's 100,000 lakes all in one glance, so pure that one look could make you blush. She was dream-like, a fairy-tale figure. Unlike anybody else. We predicted a brilliant career for her. The whole world lay at her milky-white feet. Until she met Markus. She fell for him hard. She was so young, only sixteen. I don't think she'd ever had a boyfriend before. It was the classic scenario. He played with her until, as usual, he grew tired of the relationship, and after six months he dumped her for the next cute girl who started working as a model for the agency. I mean, that happens all the time. There are always new girls. Well, Marita was shattered, and she'd also just found out that she was pregnant, but Markus was through with her. He was no longer interested in her or the baby. He persuaded her to have an abortion, and she never recovered after that. She started using cocaine and got very depressed. She let herself go and had to stop modelling a few months later because she wasn't taking care of herself. Towards the end she was more or less high all the time. It just couldn't go on.' Ek's eyes filled with tears. 'I feel so guilty about the whole thing. Haven't been able to put that girl out of my mind. It was awful.'

'What happened to her?' asked Jacobsson indignantly.

'Someone said that she eventually went back to Finland. I haven't heard anything about her since.'

'And when did this happen?'

'It was about two years ago that she came here, and then she disappeared six months later. It all happened so fast.'

'You said her name was Marita? Marita Ahonen?'

'That's right. Just a minute.'

Ek summoned his assistant and asked him to get the file for Marita Ahonen. He looked from Jacobsson to Wittberg as they waited.

'Do you think the assault on Markus Sandberg could have something to do with what happened to Marita?'

'We have no idea,' said Jacobsson. 'But we need to look into every possibility. And speaking of girlfriends, what other women have been part of his life, besides Jenny?'

'The first that comes to mind is Diana Sierra.'

'Diana Sierra?'

'Yes, she's his girlfriend.'

'You mean his ex-girlfriend?'

'I don't know about that. She's working in New York right now.'

'And they're still together?' Jacobsson persisted.

'Yes. That's what I understand.'

'But what about Jenny?'

Robert Ek shrugged.

'This is what Markus always does. He's hopeless. Thinks only about himself. Doesn't give a damn how many hearts he breaks along the way.'

By the time Jenny caught a cab from Bromma Airport, it was already evening and dark outside. She phoned the hospital. Visiting hours were over, so she'd have to wait until the next day. Just as well, she thought. She needed time to prepare herself mentally for seeing Markus again.

The flat where she stayed whenever she was in Stockholm belonged to the agency and was out on Kungsholmen, very close to the water at Kungsholm beach. It was a four-room flat used by foreign models when they were working in the city. Jenny had stayed there many times before. Occasionally, she had the place to herself, but sometimes she shared the flat with other models. It was pleasant and modern, with all mod cons. Right now, she was hoping that no one else would be there. She needed to be alone.

Due to roadworks, the taxi couldn't drive her to the door, so she had to get out quite a distance away, in the dreariest part of Pipergatan, near an office complex down by the Karlberg canal. Since it was past eight, the offices were empty, and the big windows facing the water were all dark. The cab driver apologized, but Jenny assured him that it didn't matter. She had hardly any luggage, so she could easily walk the rest of the way. Taking a firm grip of her carry-on suitcase, she went down the stairs to the street that ran parallel to the canal. Her high heels clacked on the damp stone stairs. The water was black and still. The street was deserted. The street lamps stood at attention like silent sentries along the canal. She heard the sound of her own footsteps, mixed with the roar of traffic from the Sankt Erik Bridge a short distance away.

Suddenly, she noticed a shadow moving among the trees down by the water. Probably someone walking their dog, she told herself, trying to stay calm but casting an uneasy glance at the trees. But the man seemed to be standing still, and she couldn't see or hear a dog. In her mind she saw Markus's lifeless body in the cabin on Furillen. And the blood sprayed all over the walls. What if it was her turn now? The man in the dark might be a lunatic with an axe. Good Lord, pull yourself together, she thought.

After walking on for a bit, she couldn't help turning around. The man was heading in her direction. And she was all alone on the street, which stretched out dark and empty in front of her. Rigid with fear, she walked as quickly as she could without actually running. All she wanted was to get safely inside the flat. And now she was hoping that some other models would be there. Anyone at all. She walked even faster. She could see the building now. She was almost there. Unfortunately, the entrance was not on the street. She had to go around the building and into a small courtyard. She didn't dare turn around, trying to convince herself that the man in the trees had gone off in another direction. Then she went around to the other side of the building and sighed with relief. She rummaged in her purse for the keys and took out a cigarette at the same time. She needed a smoke after such a nerve-racking walk. But now she was safe. Lights were on in all the surrounding buildings.

As she raised the match to light her cigarette, she saw him. He was standing only a short distance away, but the cap he wore shadowed his face.

With a gasp Jenny dropped the match. It went out the instant it hit the ground.

The common room, which is in the centre of the ward, is furnished with sofas and armchairs strewn with soft pillows and stuffed animals. Even though the staff have tried their best to smarten up the place, they can't erase the institutional feel. It seems to be ingrained in the walls. Woollen blankets are everywhere, and placed several metres apart are extra heating units which can be plugged in if anyone is in need of more warmth. Anorexic patients are always cold. Everyone is dressed the same: loose trousers, big warm jumpers and thick socks or fleecy slippers. The TV is always on. Linda is huddled on the sofa under a woollen blanket, watching Oprah Winfrey. Ironically enough, the popular talk-show host has the fashion designer Valentino as her guest. The interview is interspersed with photos of thin-as-a-rake models on the catwalk and comments about how beautifully the clothes drape their bony figures. Agnes doesn't want to watch, but she doesn't dare ask Linda to change the channel. Her request could easily turn into a quarrel. Josefine is sitting in one of the armchairs, frantically knitting, not paying attention to anyone else. And Sofia is sitting in front of the coffee table, studying her maths. No one is talking. It's quiet in the room except for Oprah's ingratiating remarks about how wonderful Valentino is.

They are immersed in their own thoughts, ignoring everyone else.

Agnes is restless and bored. Per hasn't been at work for several days, and she misses him. He's the only one she can confide in here. Not that he ever says much, but he's a good listener. And that's exactly what she needs. The other girls are so paranoid. She has nothing in common with them. She wonders what he's doing right now.

She listlessly leafs through a copy of the women's magazine *Svensk Damtidning*. She's not interested in any of the boring magazines here: *Illustrerad Vetenskap*, *Sköna Hem*, *Kamratposten*, *Min Häst*. All fashion magazines and most weekly tabloids are forbidden, because photos of models and any articles about dieting might have a negative effect on the patients. And yet this is exactly what they're showing on TV. How absurd.

She sighs. On the news this morning there was another report about that horrible assault out on Furillen. Markus had almost been beaten to death. It seemed so unreal. She couldn't believe it was true. The reporter had stood outside the hospital and said that Markus was still hovering between life and death. The girl who found him, Jenny Levin, is from Gotland, but Agnes doesn't know her personally. They're from different parts of Gotland, and Jenny is several years older than she is. Things have gone well for her in the modelling world, unlike for Agnes. And now it was being reported on the news that Jenny and Markus were in a relationship, and that might have something to do with the assault.

Agnes wonders how he's been treating Jenny Levin. She still feels ashamed when she thinks about the things they did together. She even slept with him, although she was only fifteen. After that first kiss, it had been difficult for her to act natural with him. She had felt awkward and embarrassed. Couldn't think of anything else as he photographed her.

That summer she had taken classes on how to pose for the camera. She had learned to walk in high heels, and they had tried to get her to relax. They had also told her that she needed to lose weight, as fast as possible. She was sent to a nutritionist, and they showered her with tips on special exercises and diet foods. She had every chance of becoming a successful model, if only she were thinner. In the autumn, she did get a number of modelling assignments because she was exceptionally beautiful. That's what they told her, but it was obvious that she needed to lose weight. Their clients would not be happy if the agency sent out a model who wore almost a size ten and let her appear in flashy fashion spreads. She understood that, didn't she?

Everyone at the agency was constantly talking to her about her weight. The boss, the staff that booked the modelling jobs, and Markus, too. Whenever he was tired and in a bad mood, he would complain that she was hard to photograph because she looked so heavy. He did the best he could, but even he couldn't work miracles.

Naturally, Agnes wanted him to be happy with her,

admire her, think she was cute. She was in love and lived for those occasions when she was allowed to go home with him. She didn't care that this occurred only on his terms. She would go to his flat late in the evening, and sometimes they'd eat together. Then they'd have sex. At the same time he would taunt her about her figure. He would study her body intently and say, 'Hmm, lose eleven pounds and you'd be almost perfect.'

She was determined to show him.

Agnes's reverie is interrupted by the clanging of something hitting the floor. Josefine has dropped a knitting needle but doesn't seem to notice. She is no longer knitting but instead has turned her attention to Oprah. As she watches, she is jabbing the other knitting needle at the soft flesh between her thumb and index finger. Agnes stares in horror. Josefine is jabbing harder and harder, her eyes fixed on the catwalk on TV. Finally, she punctures the skin and blood runs out.

'What the hell are you doing?' snaps Linda when blood drips on to the sofa. 'Are you out of your mind?'

Josefine doesn't answer, just lets the blood flow, keeping her eyes on the TV. As if she's not really aware of what's just happened.

'I can't even watch TV in peace and quiet in this damned place!' shouts Linda, jumping up with tears spilling down her cheeks. She sweeps a vase of hyacinths off the table and on to the floor, where it breaks into a thousand pieces. A nurse comes running, and another opens the door from a conference room and peers at them, wanting to see what all the noise is about.

'What's going on here?' cries one of the nurses. 'What happened?'

Agnes shrugs. She doesn't want to get involved. The nurse makes a great fuss when she discovers that Josefine's hand is bleeding. She hurries the girl out of the room to be bandaged. Agnes doesn't move a muscle. She has the ability to close down when any quarrels or conflicts arise in the ward. Such things don't concern her. When calm has been restored in the room, she sinks back into her own thoughts. Returning to the memories of her brief modelling career, which ended before it really began.

She had never felt fat before; she'd always been quite pleased with how she looked. But then things had changed, and she started to hate herself. All the sighs and criticisms about her size, all the disapproving looks, made her feel sick to her stomach. She started dieting in earnest and quickly lost weight. At first, the reactions were invariably positive. Everyone praised her new, thin figure. The agency was finally pleased, as was Markus. Agnes took on more modelling jobs, while trying to keep up at school. Her father, Rikard, was both proud and happy. This was an excellent way for his daughter to escape from her grief and give her life new meaning. He was also, gradually, starting to live again. He met a woman named Katarina in Stockholm, and they began seeing each other more and more often. Agnes was happy for her father, even though she had not the slightest desire to meet this Katarina. At the same time, Agnes felt he was beginning to distance himself from her. He no longer gave her the same amount of attention he used to. But if she became a successful model, that would probably change. He would be even prouder of his daughter. She would become as important to him as she'd been before.

'If only Mamma could see you now,' he'd said with tears in his eyes as he admired a fashion spread that she'd done for one of the biggest-selling women's magazines. Agnes was so glad she could make her poor father happy.

She would never forget those words.

Her legs trembling, Jenny Levin entered the lobby of Karolinska University Hospital in Solna on Tuesday morning. She was filled with contradictory emotions. On the one hand, she longed to see Markus; on the other, she was afraid of what she might find. She went to the nurses' station on the ward and gave her name. A young nurse whose brown hair was pulled back in a ponytail and who wore white wooden clogs led the way to Markus's room. Jenny could tell that the nurse knew who she was. It was apparent from the way she spoke to her and because she kept looking at the clothes Jenny had on.

She felt a bit queasy as she noticed the dirty yellow walls, the green linoleum and the hospital smells. The only hospital she'd ever been inside was the one in Visby. That hospital seemed so neat and clean and pleasant compared to this sterile monstrosity. And in Visby there was a splendid view of the sea from most of the windows. Here the windows on one side faced a cemetery, and on the other a busy thoroughfare.

Markus had a private room on the ward. Just that morning he'd been moved there from intensive care. His life was no longer in danger.

'He's still exhausted,' the nurse warned Jenny. 'And he looks bad right now, but things will get better.'

'Does he remember what happened?' Jenny asked.

'It's too early to tell. It was only twenty-four hours ago that he regained consciousness after being sedated. He can't speak. He needs lots of peace and quiet. We don't want him to get upset.'

'I'll just sit with him for a while.'

'That's fine.'

The nurse smiled as she opened the door.

Even though she had mentally tried to prepare herself, the sight of Markus was shocking. She gasped, and her hand flew up to her mouth. The big bandage wrapped around his head, the tubes, his swollen and disfigured face. She didn't even recognize him. At the same time, his body looked so small and thin. As if he'd shrunk several sizes.

'Hi,' she said, giving him a smile. She tried hard not to show how horrified she was. 'It's me. Jenny,' she said as she felt her smile freezing. When she'd thought about everything and tried to picture this first meeting, she hadn't imagined that he would look so bad or be so unreachable. He didn't even glance at her. She was on the verge of tears but managed to hold them back.

She cautiously sat down on the edge of his bed and reached out her hand, placing it gently over his.

'How are you?'

Not even a hint of a response. His head turned away. She waited patiently. The minutes ticked past. Here they sat, like two strangers who had never met before. Only just over a week ago they had been cooking dinner in his kitchen and laughing at the latest Woody

Allen film. Markus had taken her in his arms and made love to her, wildly and passionately, until they were both exhausted. Right now, the very thought seemed utterly surreal.

'Do you recognize me?' she asked.

He still refused to look at her.

Jenny was feeling more and more bewildered. As if she were sitting here with a complete stranger. His face looked awful. This was not her handsome Markus. Nausea overtook her and the room began to spin. She couldn't stay here even a minute longer.

'I'm afraid I have to go now,' she said and set the carrier bag with the grapes, magazines and chocolate on the bed. 'But I'll be back, of course.'

Without looking at Markus, she left the room and hurried down the corridor.

On Tuesday morning Karin Jacobsson and Thomas Wittberg met with their Stockholm colleagues, who gave them an update on the interviews they'd conducted so far. No one knew of any connection that Markus Sandberg might have to Flemingsberg, which was where his mobile had been traced to. The police had done a thorough examination of his life, talking to many of his closest family members, co-workers and acquaintances. They'd come away with a clear and unequivocal picture of the man. An irresponsible womanizer with an appetite for good food, alcohol and a number of different drugs, primarily cocaine, at least when he was young. These days, he might still smoke a joint or snort a line at some party, but his level of drug use was nowhere near what it had been in his youth.

Markus Sandberg was the son of one of Sweden's foremost defence lawyers. He had grown up in a huge flat in Stockholm's Östermalm district, where his parents still lived. He was used to moving in upper-class social circles, and he'd always had plenty of money. Yet he was the black sheep of the family. His three brothers had all followed in their father's footsteps and each in his own way had dedicated his life to the law. They were all married and lived in large homes in the posh suburbs. They had steady jobs within the banking sector and with various law firms. The fact that Markus had chosen photography as his profession had been hard for his family to swallow, and it was even worse when he gravitated towards porn. The family's patience finally ran out when that scandalous TV programme debuted with Markus as the controversial host. When the police interviewed his family members, it became clear that he was regarded as their *enfant terrible* – charming and charismatic, but a temperamental rogue who was impossible to rein in or control. When Markus left the TV show and stopped taking pornographic pictures to become a respectable photographer, as his father expressed it, the entire clan had heaved a collective sigh of relief.

When Markus Sandberg's name began to attract notice in the most exclusive fashion circles, his family finally stopped disapproving of him. Instead, he became the son of whom his parents were most proud. He was not only successful in his profession and made lots of money, he was also a celebrity. A star who hobnobbed with Sweden's elite. And that was what impressed Markus's family most. He was the one son who could measure up to his father's fame, and for that he was greatly admired.

So the brutal assault and its consequences were the worst thing that could have happened to his family. Both parents were utterly distraught, and his father had quarrelled with the hospital every single day, demanding that all sorts of experts be called in. His brothers were better at keeping their composure, although they, too, were worried and upset.

As far as his colleagues and friends were concerned,

they had all told the police much the same story. Markus Sandberg was a well-liked and charming rogue who managed nevertheless to carry out his work brilliantly. Even though he was pushing forty, he still lived very much for the present and didn't seem at all interested in settling down. Nor did he worry about the future. He earned a huge salary, but he spent it fast. There were always new trips, new parties, new girlfriends.

'I wonder where his restlessness comes from,' Jacobsson said as she and Wittberg left police headquarters. 'Markus seems to be constantly on the move, as if he's either searching for something or running away.'

'His behaviour sounds perfectly normal to me,' said Wittberg. 'If you've got the money and the opportunities and don't feel like settling down for the moment, then why not? To me it sounds like a great life – one day jet-setting to Cannes, the next day going to a nightclub in Milan and mingling with Hollywood stars. I could see myself doing that.'

'I'm sure you could,' said Jacobsson, laughing. 'Your life isn't that much different, just on a more modest scale. Surfing at Tofta in the summer, partying at the Gutekällaren, and showing off your muscles at the Kallis beach club. And in the wintertime you keep your summer romances going by taking exotic trips to see Eva in Haparanda, Sanna in Skövde, and Linda in Lund.'

'What about you?' said Wittberg, irritated. 'You should talk. You haven't exactly settled down either.

And don't forget that you're ten years older than me.'

Jacobsson ignored his remarks and merely walked faster. But Wittberg wasn't about to give up.

'You're always so bloody secretive. So tell me. How's it going with that photographer you met – Janne Widén?'

'None of your business,' said Jacobsson, annoyed to feel herself blushing.

They weren't exactly a couple, but they did spend a lot of time together.

At the same time she'd made contact with her daughter, she had met Janne. All of a sudden, two new people had come into her life, which was otherwise quite solitary. And ever since, she'd been preoccupied with both of them, although for very different reasons. Right now, she was looking forward to Janne coming home. But that was nothing compared to how much she longed to see Hanna.

Her thoughts were interrupted by the ringing of her mobile.

'Hi. My name is Anna Markström, and I work on the reception desk at the Grand Hotel.'

'Yes?'

Jacobsson and Wittberg hadn't yet managed to pay a visit there.

'My boss told me that the police are interested in a phone call that was made from here on 15 November by a man who rang the Hotel Fabriken on Furillen.'

'That's right.'

'Well, when I heard about that, I remembered that we had a big fashion show here that day – in the

Winter Garden – and all the models were from the same agency, Fashion for Life. Jenny Levin was one of the models.'

'Are you sure? This was on 15 November?'

'Yes, that's right. I checked to be sure, and that's when it was.'

Jenny came out of the hospital and sank down on to a bench next to the front entrance. She lit a cigarette and took a deep drag, trying to calm down. She quickly realized that she was sitting at a taxi rank, since cabs kept driving up to ask if she needed a ride. After this happened five times, she got up and left. She needed to take a walk, to regain her composure and gather her thoughts. She headed along the path which passed under the thoroughfare, went through a dark tunnel, and then over to Brunnsviken and Haga Park. She wandered along the shore, thinking about Markus. What would happen if he didn't regain his memory? She was filled with despair when she recalled the way he had looked. She tried to tell herself that he'd be better soon. The swelling would go down, his wounds would heal, and whatever disfiguring marks didn't disappear on their own could be dealt with by plastic surgery. She shivered when she thought how vain Markus was and how important his appearance was to him. She sincerely hoped that the hospital staff wouldn't allow him to look in a mirror.

She stopped at the water's edge. Several ducks glided towards her on the smooth surface. Winter was approaching, but they hadn't yet had a proper snowfall, and a few leaves were still stubbornly clinging to the tree branches. The air felt damp and raw. She pulled up the zip on her jacket, then continued walking to stay warm as she tried to clear her head. Again, she pictured Markus's lacerated and bruised face. He simply had to get well. She left the waters of Brunnsviken behind and moved further into the woods. The trees, tall and cold, crowded in around her. The smell of damp earth made her long for home. For her mother and father and all the farm animals: the lambs and horses and dogs. She wanted to bury her face in Miranda's thick coat and forget everything else. Miranda was her favourite ewe. All the sheep had names, and her parents knew every one of them. Jenny had more trouble telling one from the other because she was so seldom home, but she could always recognize Miranda among the hundreds of sheep. She had a shimmering, dark-grey coat and such a gentle expression on her face. Her eyes, set so wide apart, radiated warmth and intelligence. She would always come running on her skinny legs, bleating loudly, whenever Jenny called her name. Jenny had been present in the sheep barn when Miranda had been born five years earlier. The lamb had been in the breach position, so the birth had been difficult and taken a long time. At one point, it wasn't certain that Miranda would survive.

Jenny's reverie was interrupted by the sound of a branch snapping right behind her. She turned around and peered into the trees, but didn't see anything. She realized then that she hadn't seen anyone in quite some time. Near the water, plenty of people had been out walking, some of them with their dogs. But here in the woods no one was about. Just her and the big, mute oak trees. She decided to go back the same way she had come. A few minutes later the path divided and she was suddenly in doubt; she couldn't remember which way to go. She paused and looked around.

Jenny was not familiar with the area. She'd heard about Haga Park, but she'd had no idea it was so big. Again, a snapping sound in the trees. She knew there were deer that lived very close to central Stockholm. She took a chance and chose one of the pathways, picking up her pace. She wanted out of here. The overcast skies made the light dim, even though dusk was several hours off.

After a while she realized that she'd made the wrong decision, because she found herself going deeper into the woods and further away from the most frequented paths. Good Lord, she thought, am I really lost in a stupid city park? In broad daylight? What a joke. She felt both nervous and irritated. What was she doing out here? Right now, all she wanted was to go back to the warmth of the flat, which even had a fireplace. She would make a fire and ring up a friend. Then they could make dinner together. She needed company, didn't want to be alone after everything that had happened. She thought about the man who had seemed to be following her when she'd arrived in a taxi from the airport and had to walk the short distance to the block of flats. He had appeared out of the dark, and stared at her. She had asked him what he wanted, but he merely turned on his heel and left. She wasn't certain that he'd been following her. Maybe she had just imagined it. But there had definitely been something odd about that man.

Now, as she continued on, all alone, her uneasiness grew. She had to find her way back to the main path. How could she feel so isolated when she was so close to the middle of the city? She hurried along. The ground was soggy, and she stumbled over some wet leaves, coming dangerously close to falling, but then she regained her balance. She was aware of how quiet it was all around her. She could no longer hear the traffic.

This doesn't seem much like a park, she thought. It's more like the green belt. Her heart almost stopped when, without warning, a screeching pheasant flew out of the bushes right next to her. She started walking even faster. She needed to calm down. She was in no danger.

None at all.

Karin Jacobsson had just stepped inside her hotel room when Knutas rang.

'Bad news. I spoke to the hospital and Markus Sandberg has suffered another cerebral haemorrhage. He's in a coma.'

'Oh, no. Don't tell me that. And here we were just starting to interview him. Damn.'

'I know. It's bloody awful,' Knutas agreed. 'The doctor said that at the moment they don't know how things might go. Apparently, it could go either way. If Sandberg does pull through, he'll need more surgery. No matter what, it will be a while before we can speak to him again.'

'What terrible luck. We were so close.' Jacobsson sank down on to the bed.

'All we can do is try something else,' said Knutas.

'Of course.'

'How are things otherwise?'

'I already told you everything we've done today.'

'Right. I meant, how are things with you?'

'Okay. But now we're back to square one.'

'I know,' said Knutas. 'Take it easy. We'll talk more tomorrow.'

*

Jacobsson decided not to join Wittberg and a few other colleagues for dinner. She wanted time to herself. She was extremely disappointed about the news of Markus's deteriorating condition, but she was also thinking about her daughter, Hanna. She was trying to decide whether to call or not. She hesitated, because she didn't know if she could stand to hear the response she feared most: *No, I don't want to see you.*

Listlessly, she stared out of the hotel-room window at the black roofs with their chimneys and garrets. Sleet was falling from the leaden-coloured sky. In a few places the snow was sticking, creating patches of white. Her room was on the top floor of the hotel in Gamla Stan, and she was only a kilometre from her daughter's flat. She was feeling too restless to stay here. She glanced at her watch. Ten past seven in the evening. She hadn't had any dinner, but she wasn't the least bit hungry. Without deciding what exactly she was going to do, she went into the bathroom to pee, then combed her hair and put on some make-up. Next, she put on her boots, her leather jacket, her scarf and gloves, and then left the room.

It was bitterly cold outdoors. As she peered inside the restaurants she passed, everything looked so pleasant and inviting, with glowing candles, warm food on the plates and wine in the glasses. She left Gamla Stan and headed towards Slussen, then continued over Hornsgatan hill, admiring the small galleries lining Mariaberget. When she happened to look into a restaurant with big glass windows facing the street, she stopped short.

At a table towards the back of the room Hanna was

sitting with another young woman. They were drinking wine and seemed totally immersed in their conversation. Karin's eyes filled with tears and her heart lurched. She couldn't help staring at them. Then the other girl got up and left, probably to go to the loo. Hanna stayed at the table. She took a sip of wine and looked around. Suddenly, their eyes met. Karin froze. She didn't know what to do. Incapable of moving, she simply stood there, staring at her daughter, this person she had carried inside her body, this person to whom she had given birth. The other girl came back from the loo. Through a fog, Karin saw Hanna put her hand on her friend's arm and lean forward to say something. The next instant she stood up and came towards the door. Karin felt the ground give way under her feet, and she had to hold on to a lamp post in order not to fall.

She saw Hanna appear in the entrance to the restaurant and then take a step outside, a quizzical look on her face.

The afternoon plods along. The afternoon snack is over, and there are still several hours until dinner. The days in the clinic are so monotonous, each day exactly like all the others.

Agnes's father, Rikard, and his girlfriend, Katarina, came to visit in the morning. Or, rather, her father did. Agnes never speaks to Katarina, who had to stay in the day room and wait, as always. Agnes refuses to let her take part in the visits, won't allow any outsiders into her private hell. Yet Katarina stubbornly insists on accompanying Rikard every time. As if she doesn't dare let him out of her sight. Rikard seemed a bit stressed and didn't stay long.

Now Agnes and her room mate Linda are stretched out on separate sofas in the common room. Linda is reading, as usual. Agnes can't understand how she does it. Personally, she's too restless to read even one chapter of a book. She just can't concentrate. The letters seem to leap and dance before her eyes, and the words keep changing places. She can read the same sentence twenty times without comprehending what it says. And that's scary. She used to be such a good student. Now she understands what it must feel like to be dyslexic. She thinks that she's probably just tired and lazy; that's why she can't read anything. Per doesn't read either.

They talked about that this morning. He says he simply doesn't feel like it, can't concentrate properly. Just like her. She finds that consoling. As if the two of them have something in common.

Instead, she absent-mindedly leafs through an old issue of *Sköna Hem*. How absurd to see all these huge mansions and Scanian houses sandwiched in between quaint little cottages and idyllic summer homes. Perfectly set tables in neat and tidy country kitchens. Exquisite flower arrangements, fragrant herb gardens, lilac arbours with hammocks, and drinks made with raspberry juice. As if there were not a problem in the world.

Yet for her, every day is a battle between life and death. A war in which she is always fighting new armies. With a sigh, she lowers her hands and the magazine sinks on to her lap as her thoughts wander.

At the moment the most important thing is to keep the disease inside herself. And not gain any weight. That was exactly the argument she used at the beginning of her brief modelling career. And it had brought her recognition and success, all because she had won the battle against those extra pounds. This spurred her to continue. She would get even thinner, then things would go even better. The skinnier she was, the more successful she would be. Everyone stopped complaining about her weight, and even Markus showed his appreciation and admiration for her increasingly slender figure.

But after a few months all the positive comments began to wane. No one mentioned any more how beautifully thin she was. Agnes came to the only possible conclusion: she needed to lose even more weight. And the transformation had to be so dramatic that no one could avoid seeing the change. Then they would begin to praise her again. That was how she would control her fate and gain control of her life.

Eventually, various people at the agency began to say that she was too thin, that she needed to eat more. Agnes couldn't for the life of her understand their reasoning. In the end, the agency dropped her because she was anorexic.

The disappointment she felt was overwhelming. No matter what she did, they were never satisfied. Yet she personally believed that she needed to be even thinner.

Then things went downhill fast. She continued to lose weight. In hindsight, her father blamed himself for not noticing how ill she was during that time, how she exercised so much and ate so little. Agnes doesn't think it's strange that he didn't notice.

As a carpenter, he had to start work early in the morning, so he usually left the house at 6 a.m. What he didn't know was that his daughter would get up the minute the front door closed and go for a two-hour walk before school. She never ate breakfast. At lunchtime in the school cafeteria she would always pile food on to her plate, though she ate only a little salad and threw the rest out. Dinner proved more difficult. It started with her demanding more wholesome food at home: salmon and bulgur wheat instead of savoury crêpes. She became a vegetarian and refused to eat any sort of fast-release carbs. No bread or pasta or potatoes.

Increasingly, she would go for a long walk at dinner-time.

Agnes began having trouble concentrating in class because she was always tired. She withdrew from her friends and spent more and more time alone. Sometimes she would get up in the middle of the night and exercise, or leave the house and go running in the pitch dark. She always wore baggy clothes, so her father never saw how thin she had become.

That summer, when term was over, things got much worse. Her father worked extra-long hours, since the Swedes who came to Gotland during the summer months were constantly having their cottages re-modelled and there was a lack of skilled workmen. He was always working, except when he went to Stockholm to see Katarina, so Agnes was often left on her own. She lied to him, saying that she was busy doing things with her friends. In reality, she felt isolated and abandoned.

In the autumn she started at secondary school, but after only a few weeks she suddenly collapsed at home. She was taken by ambulance to hospital and then transferred to the mainland and admitted to the anorexia clinic in Stockholm.

She has been here now for three months, and the staff keep complaining that she isn't gaining weight fast enough. The doctor has threatened to increase the amount of food she needs to eat, which is the worst thing that could happen.

Her stomach is still too big and her hips too wide.

Dusk is falling outside. Agnes stretches out her hand to turn on the lamp on the table next to the sofa. She notices how the fat jiggles under her arm. She hasn't done a very good job of cheating today. She ate everything that was served. The nurses have been watching her like hawks.

Tomorrow she needs to do better.

One model after another appeared on the runway that had been constructed in one of Stockholm's most exclusive department stores. Each was more striking than the last. The lights flashed, the music was throbbing and sensual. At a fast tempo and evenly spaced, the models glided across the stage. They moved like suggestive dream women, thrusting their pelvises forward so that their legs and the incredibly high heels they were wearing seemed to precede the rest of their bodies. Hips swaying, their long, slender arms hanging at their sides, earrings dangling, with piercing eyes, fluttering fringe. Their lips were gleaming, their knees slim, their collarbones clearly visible. Straight backs and shoulders, swinging necklaces, glittering nails and sparkling sandals. Breasts that were exposed, without embarrassment, beneath transparent garments. Serious expressions and dark eyebrows.

Crowding together at the first turn stood the photographers. There the models paused and set their hands on their hips. A few twirled around; others posed provocatively; some offered a hint of a smile, an amused glint in their eyes. They were enjoying this. They knew how much they were worth.

The audience was thrilled; spontaneous bursts of applause and shouts rose above the music. The journalists clutched notebooks and pens, watching with accustomed intensity and then frantically jotting down notes.

For the past two weeks, Jenny Levin had once again been working full time. In that short period, she'd travelled to five different countries, criss-crossing the world. Stockholm to New York to the Bahamas to Paris to Munich to Milan and back to Stockholm. Occasionally, she would forget where she was in the constant succession of new airports, new hotel rooms, new people. Frequently, she got only three or four hours of sleep at night, so she had to sleep on the planes. She'd returned to Stockholm and the agency-owned flat feeling completely exhausted. Fortunately she was now going to be working closer to home.

Even though she'd been working hard, it had been wonderful to get away for a while. Away from Markus and everything that had happened. And, somehow, it felt as if her absence had done her good. She now saw him in a new light. He was not the same person as before and probably never would be. He was twenty years older than her. His appearance had totally changed, even though she didn't want to admit to herself that something like that mattered.

And all those rumours about other women. Especially that girlfriend of his named Diana.

Jenny cringed at the thought of meeting her at the agency's traditional Christmas party, which was being held this evening. She'd heard that Diana was back in Stockholm. On the other hand, Jenny was looking forward to the party itself. Drinking champagne, dancing and having fun. Her career was going brilliantly, and she knew that the agency was glad to have her in its stable.

Seconds before she was to appear on the runway for the last time, the lights were turned off and the music silenced. The anticipation could be felt in the whole room.

She was fully aware that she was radiantly beautiful in the gleaming white dress with the neckline that plunged down to her navel. The next moment, she appeared on stage in a cascade of glitter as the music began pounding. The effect was instantaneous. Loud applause, and one by one the audience members rose from their seats and cheered. Jenny felt everyone's eyes on her; even the most experienced and blasé of the old fashionistas gazed at her with admiration.

This was her life now, and she planned to devote herself to it with all her heart.

On Friday afternoon it was snowing hard, as it had done all morning. The streets and buildings were blanketed in white, which contributed to the holiday mood. Knutas left work early so he could go out and buy Christmas gifts. For once, he hadn't left it to the very last minute, and this time he wanted to buy something special for Lina. As a token of his love. She had shown him a beautiful pair of earrings at the silversmith's down on Sankt Hansgatan. That was what he planned to purchase first. But he might get her something else, too, maybe a gift card for a massage. She often complained that her back hurt, and she seldom took the time to pamper herself.

He quickly made his way through Östercentrum and continued on towards Österport. Inside the city walls an entirely different atmosphere reigned. Strung between the buildings were Christmas decorations in the form of glittering garlands with big stars in the middle. Some of the shop owners had frosted their windowpanes with artificial snow and laid pine boughs outside the doors. Several businesses had strings of lights adorning the windows and lanterns with candles inside. At the toy shop 'White Christmas' was thundering from the loudspeakers, and in the big front window a whole winter landscape had been created, with a toy train chugging along between snow-capped mountains. Over by Waller Square some schoolkids were selling ginger biscuits and *glögg*, the traditional mulled wine. Knutas stopped for a moment to chat with a few friends. An enormous Christmas tree towered over Stora Torget, and all the marketplace stalls were busy with customers buying sheepskins, peppermint rock, sausages, honey, mistletoe and wreaths. Warm *glögg* was served from a big kettle. He bought two sausages with bread, which he ate as he looked for the best mistletoe, which they always had in their house. It was an essential part of the family's Christmas celebration.

As Knutas tended to his errands, thoughts of the investigation whirled through his mind. Almost a month had passed since the attempt on Markus Sandberg's life. The photographer was still in a coma, in critical condition. He would probably not be able to tell the police anything for the foreseeable future. According to the doctors, he was going to need several more operations. As for Sandberg's parents and siblings, it turned out that they had very little knowledge about his activities. His contact with his family had been sporadic at best. They celebrated Christmas and various birthdays together, but that seemed to have been the extent of his involvement with them. They had never heard him mention Diana Sierra or Jenny Levin. The police had also interviewed Diana. She was not suspected of committing the attack, since she'd been on a photo shoot in the Bahamas at the time of the assault on Furillen. But she still could have been responsible for initiating it.

Test results had come in from the crime lab. They

showed that the blood found on the boat and on the clothing had come from Markus Sandberg and from another, not-yet-identified individual who was not in any police records. But the blood analysis proved without a doubt that the person in question was a man, not a woman. When it came to the earring that had been found, its story remained a mystery.

The police had followed up on the phone conversation that had been traced to the Grand Hotel. It turned out that the information they'd received from the receptionist was correct. The hotel had hosted a fashion show on that day, and Jenny Levin was one of the models. Markus Sandberg had also been present, taking photographs. The police had talked to everyone who had participated in the show, but no one had noticed anything out of the ordinary. And that was as far as they'd got with the investigation.

It might be worthwhile to interview Marita Ahonen, thought Knutas. No one in Sandberg's family had ever heard of her either. But the agency staff knew all about her love affair with Markus and how deeply it had affected the young Marita. Everybody thought it was tragic, and they sympathized with the Finnish girl, but they hadn't kept in touch with her after she'd returned to Finland last year. The police were having a hard time tracking her down. She didn't seem to have a permanent address, and she'd cut off ties with her mother. Her father was dead, and she was an only child. The search for her was ongoing.

When Knutas had finally made all his purchases and was headed back to Östercentrum, he saw a couple coming towards him. They hadn't yet noticed him, possibly because they only had eyes for each other. The man was tall and slim with gel on his hair. He looked to be in his forties and wore rather trendy clothes, including yellow corduroy trousers and a green jacket. He'd wrapped a scarf around his neck several times. He was walking arm in arm with the petite woman at his side. She was staring up at him with adoring eyes, and they were both laughing. Suddenly they stopped, and the man leaned down to take the face of the slender woman in both hands. Then he kissed her. She pressed her face against his chest, and he put his arms around her, pulling her so close that she almost disappeared.

Neither of them saw Knutas as he passed on the other side of the street. He didn't know what he would have done if Karin had noticed him. His eyes stung, and his knees felt wobbly.

He was at a complete loss.

The ferry was just about to depart from Visby harbour. The three black towers of the cathedral were barely visible through the heavy snowfall. The forecast was for colder weather. It had also been snowing in Stockholm for the past several days, and there was every indication that they would have a white Christmas. As usual, the boat was packed with passengers. The spacious parking area on the dock had been crowded with cars, several horse trailers and quite a few long-distance lorries. Johan Berg couldn't comprehend where all the traffic had come from. It was almost as bad as in the summer.

Johan and his family hurried upstairs to the restaurant to get a good seat next to the window. They had reserved deckchairs, as they always did, but it was actually easier with the children to stay in the restaurant, which had a play area they liked.

'Do you want to eat right now?' asked Johan, putting Anton in a highchair he'd managed to grab. They were much in demand on these ferries.

'Sure. That's probably a good idea. It's going to get crowded later on.'

They were lucky enough to have been among the first to drive on board.

'Could you go and stand in the queue?'

Emma was unpacking felt-tip pens, drawing paper, activity books and various plastic toys so that Elin and Anton could keep themselves amused for the few minutes it would take her to go over and have a look at the menu. There usually wasn't much of a selection: spaghetti with meat sauce, pan-fried fish with boiled potatoes and remoulade, or the day's vegetarian dish. The quality of the food was about the same as in a school cafeteria. And she was sick and tired of that. She might as well just have an open shrimp sandwich. Although these days the restaurant did offer a gourmet option. That might be good.

Johan went first, taking a place in the queue that had already formed. It's almost like being in Ikea, he thought. Practical, child-friendly and no surprises. There were kids everywhere. Many families had already found seats and were unpacking lunches they'd brought along: sandwiches, thermoses and jars of baby food. Not everyone wanted to buy food in the restaurant. Many Gotland residents went to Stockholm to do their Christmas shopping, so they chose to save their money for buying gifts.

Johan was looking forward to going home. That was how he still thought of the city, even though he'd been living on Gotland for several years now, and his family was there. But, in his heart, Stockholm was still home. They were on their way to visit Johan's mother, who lived in the suburb of Rönninge, to celebrate Christmas with her. They planned to stay about a week, and he was looking forward to it. Not just because he'd get to see his mother, with whom he stayed in close contact, but because his four brothers would be there as well.

Somewhat reluctantly, he'd assumed the role of family patriarch after his father had passed away a few years ago. Everyone seemed to turn to him, maybe because he was the eldest of the brothers. This morning, Johan had talked to his best friend, Andreas, who was among those he missed most. They were going to spend a whole evening in town together, have dinner and visit a few of his favourite hang-outs in the Södermalm district. Johan couldn't think of anything he would enjoy more. Part of him would always long to be back in Stockholm.

He said hello to a few acquaintances and watched Visby disappear through the window. There was something about this stretch of water between Gotland and the mainland. In reality, the distance wasn't very great. The trip took less than three hours by ferry. Yet it felt like a long voyage. The crossing almost had an inexplicably exotic feel to it, this passage over the sea. Maybe that was why so many mainlanders loved going to Gotland in the summer. It felt like they were truly getting away, almost like going to another country.

They finished eating their food, which was not much of a culinary experience, but everyone ended up feeling full and content. Then Elin took Anton over to the play area, where a Christmas elf was reading stories to the children. Johan checked the paperback display and bought a detective novel entitled *Unseen*. The plot sounded exciting, so it would do just fine. Emma bought coffee and several magazines. Jenny Levin was on the cover of one of them.

'She looks amazing, but nothing like she does in real life,' murmured Emma.

'What do Tina and Fredrik think about her modelling career?' asked Johan as he skimmed the blurb on the back of his book.

'They're thrilled for her, of course.'

'But aren't they the least bit nervous that she might get involved in bad situations? I mean, with dirty old men, drugs, that sort of thing?'

'I suppose so. But Jenny is a strong girl who has her feet on the ground. She can take care of herself. She's always been very independent. I think she can handle just about anything.'

'What about Markus Sandberg? It sounds like he was just using her.'

'Okay, that was a mistake. But even Jenny is entitled to make a few wrong choices once in a while. Good God, the girl is only nineteen.'

'Exactly.'

'What do you mean?'

Johan stirred his coffee.

'I don't know. I was just thinking that there may be other things about Jenny that we don't know.'

'Like what? And why are we talking about this now? This is the first time we've been on holiday together in I don't know how long. Let's drop it, okay? You're not a policeman.'

'Aren't you interested in finding out what happened? It's your friend's daughter who's ended up in the middle of the whole thing.'

'Of course I want to know.'

Emma reached across the table to take his hand.

'But you're not planning to do any work over Christmas, are you?'

Johan paused before answering. They'd had a rough autumn. The kids had been sick, and the daily routines had seemed particularly dreary. So they really needed a holiday and a chance to relax. He'd already told the children everything they were going to do: go sledding, build a snow cave, make a snowman and snow lanterns. Go skating and cross-country skiing along the wonderful trails near their grandmother's house.

'I'm not planning to do any work, sweetheart,' he said then. 'Of course not. We're going to take it easy, enjoy Christmas, and not think about anything but ourselves.'

'Good,' said Emma, squeezing his hand.

The agency's traditional Christmas party was held in a private flat on Stureplan, which was the centre of Stockholm's nightlife. The flat was directly across from one of the city's hippest clubs, and after dinner the plan was for everyone to go there. Jenny arrived with the agency boss, which caused quite a few people to raise their eyebrows in surprise. Robert Ek was a married man, but known for having affairs. His wife happened to be away, so she couldn't attend the party. Would Jenny be the next in a long line of young models whom Ek had exploited over the years?

The nightclub had promptly announced on its website that the famous modelling agency Fashion for Life was holding its annual party on the premises that evening. Models always enticed people to come to a venue, and it lent the club a higher profile. The agency had several hundred models in its stable, but only the top fifty had been invited to the party, along with the most prominent photographers, stylists, clients and other influential people in the Stockholm fashion world, including designers, journalists and several of the most important fashion bloggers.

Glasses of chilled champagne were served before dinner, and Ek took the opportunity to bid everyone welcome. He stepped up on to a podium to speak to the elegantly clad guests.

'We can look back on a tremendously successful year, both here in Sweden and in the international arena,' he began with great satisfaction. 'Our models have appeared on the covers of some of the world's most prestigious magazines. They opened the most important shows during haute couture week in Paris, and they were first on the catwalk at the big Victoria's Secret show in New York, just to name a few examples. First and foremost, I'd like to thank all the models who are here tonight. In different ways, they have each contributed to the agency's amazing success during the past year. I also want to thank all the stylists, photographers, clients, and everyone else who is part of the fashion world in our beautiful city. You are all incredibly important to the agency, and I hope you know that. I would also like to take a moment to direct our thoughts to our most prominent photographer, Markus Sandberg, who is still recovering in hospital after the attack he suffered on Gotland last month. For all of you who are wondering how he's doing, I can tell you that, for the most part, Markus's condition remains unchanged. But he will undergo more surgery, and we are naturally hoping that he will make a full recovery so that eventually he'll be able to return to working with us. Let's all drink a toast to Markus Sandberg.'

Everyone raised their glasses and fixed their eyes on Robert Ek. The only sound in the room was the light clinking of glasses at the bar. After the toast, Ek continued in a noticeably more cheerful tone of voice.

'This year, I would like to focus on one person, in

particular, who has achieved acclaim that is largely without parallel in the history of our agency. She is a farmer's daughter, from a village on Gotland. During a visit to Stockholm, she was discovered by our scout Isabelle. She had never thought about entering the modelling profession but, by now, during her second season, she has been in more than sixty fashion shows, she has opened Valentino's show in Paris, and she has been on the cover of the Italian edition of *Vogue*. I can also reveal that she recently signed a contract with H&M to take part in their Christmas advertising campaign next year, which means she will be on billboards all over the world.'

A ripple of excitement passed through the audience. Ek paused for effect.

'So let's all drink a toast to Jenny Levin.'

He motioned for Jenny to come up to the podium as everyone applauded. She was completely unprepared for such attention and hardly had a chance to gather her thoughts before she found herself standing in the spotlight next to her boss, who coaxed her towards the microphone.

She managed to ramble off a brief thank-you speech, thinking that she clearly hadn't expressed herself very well, but everyone smiled and again raised their glasses, to drink a toast to her. At that moment she noticed someone she had never met, although she recognized her at once. Markus's former girlfriend Diana was standing nearby, wearing a fabulous creation. The glint in her eye competed with the sequins on her dress, and suddenly Jenny felt an icy gust sweep through the warm and festive room. She stepped off the podium and quickly downed the rest of her champagne. Desperate for more, she snatched another glass from a tray carried by a passing waiter. Several of Jenny's modelling friends came over to congratulate her. Luckily, not everyone was the jealous type.

She noticed Robert giving her an appreciative look. She was glad that he was so generous. His words had warmed her heart and offered some solace after all the misery she'd been through in the past few weeks. He was talking to a couple of designers but kept glancing in her direction. I just hope he doesn't get too interested, Jenny thought. She knew of his reputation, but so far he hadn't displayed those sorts of tendencies towards her. Not at all. He had seemed genuinely happy about her success, although the looks he gave her hinted at his undisguised admiration. She sighed and turned back to her friends, deciding to ignore him for the rest of the evening. She didn't need any more problems. She just wanted to have fun.

The flat that had been chosen for the party was amazing. It was in a beautiful early-twentieth-century building, with high ceilings and stucco decoration, and tiled stoves with blazing fires in every room. Dinner was served in the dining room on numerous round tables elegantly set with linen tablecloths, crystal glasses and elaborate candelabra. The only light came from the glow of hundreds of candles, and there was a magnificent view of Stureplan outside with all the neon lights glittering in the night.

One of the city's celebrated chefs had prepared dinner, which consisted of coquilles Saint-Jacques, veal escalope and lime sorbet.

Jenny was in luck. The other guests at her table were all models or photographers. Seated next to her was Tobias, a cute and very pleasant photographer who was liked by everyone. They had worked together only once so far, but it had been a great experience. Jenny relaxed. Now she was going to have fun, and she happily drank a toast with all the others seated at her table.

An hour later, Jenny needed to find the loo. On her way out of the dining room she came face to face with Diana. She had to admit that the woman was extraordinarily beautiful. She was of Chinese heritage, with a pale complexion and almond-shaped brown eyes. Her hair was black and thick, billowing over her shoulders. She was blocking Jenny's way, staring at her coldly.

'So you're the one,' she said. 'You're the one he was sleeping with.'

'Sorry?' said Jenny uncertainly.

She was in no mood for confrontation. She pushed past and fled to the bathroom. When she came out and looked around, Diana seemed to have vanished.

Jenny needed a smoke, so she went out on the balcony.

She had no sooner lit a cigarette than Diana appeared in the doorway, along with several models that Jenny didn't know. Jenny pretended to talk on her mobile so she wouldn't have to speak to them. Down below was Stureplan, with its neon signs, taxis rushing past in the street, and beautifully dressed city people on their way to various clubs and restaurants.

The next instant, Diana was standing right next to Jenny, her eyes seething with anger.

'Who the hell do you think you are?' she snarled.

Jenny turned her back on Diana and continued her feigned phone conversation, although her heart was pounding.

Suddenly, Diana grabbed the mobile out of her hand. Jenny watched as it was hurled over the railing and shattered on the street several storeys below.

'You need to listen to me when I'm talking to you!' shouted Diana.

'What are you doing? Are you out of your mind?'

At that moment, Robert Ek turned up.

'What's going on here?'

'Nothing. Absolutely nothing,' said Jenny, and she hurried back to her table.

There, she tried to shake off her feeling of unease. Tobias filled her glass with more wine, and she gratefully took a big swallow.

Now the evening could continue.

Ten o'clock is bedtime on the ward, and an hour later it's lights out. Even though she's exhausted after all the travails of the day, she can't fall asleep. Instead, she lies in bed in the dark, thinking about her day. In her mind she weighs up how much she was able to exercise versus how much she has eaten. She goes over everything, hour by hour, from the moment she woke up until now.

First, she had done as much jumping as she could in the bathroom, until the nurse knocked on the door, asking her if she had finished. She had managed to do twenty jumps before the nurse had turned up, and she had to pretend that she was constipated. Not a success, in other words, since she needed to do at least thirty jumps in order to feel satisfied.

Then it was time for breakfast. Lately, Agnes has been allowed to eat in the dining room with the other patients.

No Widget is used at breakfast time. Instead, staff members serve the food portions, and that lends a certain liberating air to the meal. But it also prompts uneasiness and frustration among the patients. It's important to make the right choices and not take too much of any one thing. Nor to get more food than anyone else.

This morning they had been served oatmeal with a choice of half a banana, a pear or a plastic container of plums. The pears were huge and there were no bananas left, so Agnes chose the plums. On a tray stood ten cups lined up, with six plums in each. She examined all of them with great care and only made up her mind when the nurse in charge told her to hurry up. Agnes is almost certain that she managed to choose the cup with the smallest plums.

When the oatmeal was served, she trembled at the size of the portion and she couldn't help protesting. 'That's way too much. She got a lot less than me,' Agnes said, pointing at Erika, who was ahead of her in the queue. The nurse ignored her. The next challenge occurred when she had to pour the milk for the oatmeal. The goal was to make as little milk as possible look like a large amount. Agnes splashed the milk around on top of the oatmeal; that produced the best effect. But then something happened that should never happen. As she stirred the cereal to make it look like a bigger portion, air bubbles formed underneath and all the milk disappeared, slipping away to hide under the cereal. Agnes was filled with panic and on the verge of tears as she tried to explain that she'd already poured at least three and a half ounces of milk into her bowl. But the nurse refused to be convinced, pointing out that she couldn't see any. So Agnes had been forced to add more.

When she finally sank down on to her chair at the table, she was feeling so anxious she could hardly breathe. A nurse was always seated at each table to keep an eye on the patients. But Agnes was still able to remove the cold cuts from one sandwich, along with two slices of cheese, which she put in her pocket. She also spilled several spoonfuls of oatmeal on to the table. All in all, what she managed to avoid eating at breakfast compensated for the ten jumps she'd missed and the excessive amount of milk. In other words, breakfast and her morning exercises were a draw. Feeling slightly relieved, Agnes continued reviewing the day.

After breakfast there was always an obligatory thirty-minute rest period, although they weren't required to go to the warm room. It was enough to sit in the common room or on a sofa in the corridor. She had succeeded in trudging around for at least half of the rest period. When it was time for the morning snack, she was in good shape.

A container with ten ounces of a nutrient-rich drink had to be consumed in fifteen minutes. The same for everyone. Now, an interesting interval ensued. As soon as all fifteen patients had taken their seats at the table, the shaking began. Silence reigned, except for the sound of fifteen drink containers being frantically shaken. Tense muscles, resolute expressions. Everyone was focused on the task at hand. It was important to shake the container as long as possible, since the motion caused foam from the drink to settle on the inside of the packaging, which meant that there was less for the patient to drink. Agnes had also managed to pour some of the drink into the screw-on top. Foam was still in the top when she screwed it back on, so she had even less to drink. The nurse made sure that each container was empty, but it was impossible to detect the foam left inside. Yet another small victory.

*

Before lunch they always went out to get some fresh air. That was definitely the high point of the day. All the patients had to go outside, but there was no question of taking a long walk. Accompanied by two nurses, they took the lift down to the ground floor. It was a relief just to see the Pressbyrå news stand, the hospital entrance, and other people. Outside, they turned left and walked along the paved pathway, past the shelter put up for smokers and maybe two hundred metres further along, moving at a slow pace. At the grove of trees they turned around and headed back. They walked in single file along the path, as if treading an invisible line, all of them following the same crack in the asphalt. More than a dozen young girls who looked almost skeletal, dressed in tracksuit bottoms, fleece shirts, big sweaters, jackets, leg warmers, and knitted caps. Yet they were always cold. Looking pale and solemn, they slowly marched forward. Like a funeral procession. No one spoke to anyone else. Some occasionally took little detours, for instance choosing to go around a pillar in front of the entrance instead of proceeding straight ahead, which would have been more natural. One girl walked on the grass instead of on the pavement because that required more energy; another made a point of veering around every puddle of water. Always the same urge. Each extra step, no matter how small, counted. But it was blissful to be outside and get some fresh air. Any time the daily outing was missed it was cause for hysteria. If it was raining hard or there was a strong wind or the snow was really coming down, the outing would be cancelled. That was the worst thing that could happen. And that sort of decision often led to loud outbursts on the ward. *It's not raining that much, there's hardly any wind, please, oh please.*

In the afternoon, her father had come to visit, with Katarina in tow, although she had had to wait in the day room, as usual. When Agnes and her father went down to the cafeteria on the ground floor, they saw Katarina sitting there, having coffee with Per. He must have taken pity on her. Agnes pretended not to see them.

At least she had been able to skip the afternoon snack, since she was with Pappa. And she'd told him that she'd already eaten. Extra points for that.

Dinner had been a torment, but afterwards she'd managed to slip away to the conference room and spent at least twenty minutes jumping up and down. She'd seen her reflection in the window and that had made her cry. The pain in her chest was almost unbearable. No one had noticed what she was doing.

The feeling of anxiety had eased a bit after that. She'd done much more than she'd expected.

Only when she comes to that satisfying conclusion is she able to relax enough to fall asleep.

'Shall we get together later and have a cosy time? Just you and me?'

The brunette placed her hand on Robert Ek's shoulder as she whispered in his ear. He looked down into her plunging neckline. Then she moved on through the crowd, turning around once to give him a flirtatious smile. She was so voluptuous that he felt weak in the knees. It was now past midnight, and by this time Ek had had rather a lot to drink. He'd spent the past hour hanging out in the club with various models and colleagues as he cast covetous glances at the never-ending stream of young women who passed by. Bare shoulders, trim bodies in tight dresses, long, supple legs, swaying breasts beneath gauzy fabric, seductive glances.

In his capacity as head of the country's biggest modelling agency, Ek was well aware of his high status as a desirable companion, even though he was married. He was rich, he held a not insignificant position of power, and he had a guaranteed place among the elite and famous. He also looked good for his age. He had a smooth complexion, high cheekbones, green eyes with thick, dark lashes, and a lovely mouth with Cupid's-bow lips. Robert Ek was careful to stay fit and keep off the weight. And, in the eyes of many, he had exquisitely sophisticated taste in clothes.

There were so many available women. The only problem was the promise he'd recently made to his wife. That promise had put a stop to any dreams. He truly intended to keep himself under control tonight, because Erna had given him an ultimatum. If she ever found out that he'd again been unfaithful to her, she would leave him for good. This time, she was serious. And she would take the children with her. They were old enough now that they could decide for themselves which parent they wanted to live with. But he knew as well as Erna did what they would decide. All four would choose to live with their mother, who had taken care of them all these years, had always been available, cooking their meals and helping with their homework, showing them love, offering support and encouragement. Robert Ek had always made his job a higher priority than his family. And that had cost him. It was the price he would have to pay if there was ever a divorce. If Erna Linton had not loved her husband with all her heart, they would have separated long ago. But true love could withstand only so much. Even she had finally reached her limit, and Ek realized that his wife would no longer forgive his transgressions or ignore what was going on. 'Good Lord, we're both close to fifty,' she'd told him. 'I can't do this any more. I want peace and quiet and harmony. I want to reap my rewards after all the work I've done with the children. I want to travel, go to the theatre and the cinema, and enjoy good meals. To put it simply, I want to enjoy life. And if you can't accept that, then we need to get a divorce and I'll do it on my own. I don't want to be sad any more. Or feel hurt and disappointed.'

If only this party had been a couple of weeks earlier, the doors to an extramarital fling would have stood wide open. The situation couldn't have been better, with the agency's annual Christmas celebration coinciding with his mother-in-law's eightieth birthday up in Leksand. The whole family had gone to Dalarna for the weekend, and he had had the house to himself. Since he lived so close to town, it was a simple matter to invite people over. And the house was set sufficiently apart from the neighbours that no one would notice who was coming and going – something that had made his escapades in the past that much easier. He wasn't tempted to go to a hotel; that seemed too tawdry. It didn't bother him in the least that he played out his sexual desires in his family home. 'What someone doesn't know won't hurt them': that was Robert Ek's philosophy. And, besides, the house belonged to him. He had paid not only for the house itself but for every single thing inside it.

Yet now he was planning to give up all such amusements. He didn't know if he dared take the risk of defying his wife. The thought of becoming a lonely old man frightened him, and in his heart he had to admit, however reluctantly, that Erna was right. How long could he keep carrying on these affairs? And did he really want to be unfaithful? The thought of sitting all by himself in a flat somewhere without any family or sexual desire scared him out of his wits. So there was only one thing to do: stop having these flings. Even though that seemed nearly impossible in this situation.

And it wasn't that he and Erna had no sex life; when it came right down to it, they enjoyed making love to each other. But a sense of excitement was missing, the titillation of going to bed with someone new, someone he didn't know. He wasn't sure he was going to be able to keep his promise. He could feel the effects of the alcohol and, faced with all the available women around him, his resolve began to weaken.

He slipped off to the loo. After relieving himself, he stood at the sink and splashed cold water on his face. Then he stared at himself in the mirror. Should I or shouldn't I? Erna wouldn't know a thing. The thought of finding himself in the arms of that brunette was getting more and more enticing. He was interrupted when his mobile phone began ringing in his jacket pocket. Wouldn't surprise me if that's Erna, he thought. She can probably sense what I've been thinking.

He took out his mobile. When he looked at the display, he froze. The message was not from his wife.

It was from a number he hadn't used in a long time. The number belonged to Markus Sandberg.

It took only a few minutes for Robert Ek to walk from the club to the agency. He tapped in the security code at the front of the building then stepped inside. He wasn't fond of lifts, so he decided to take the stairs. As he passed the entrance to the courtyard, he noticed that the door was ajar. Someone's been very sloppy, he thought, and carefully closed the door. He checked several times to make sure it was locked. They didn't want any homeless people or drunks getting inside the building.

He unlocked the door to the agency and turned on the lights in the hall and kitchen. Several bottles of champagne stood next to numerous empty glasses on the worktop. The staff had gathered here to have a drink before the party, along with some of the models, including Jenny. Now that he thought about it, she'd seemed unusually lively tonight, almost flirtatious. He felt desire burning inside him. He'd experienced a momentary confusion after reading her message, but then he'd sent back a text, saying that he would wait for her here. Any hesitation about being unfaithful had vanished completely. This was an opportunity he couldn't pass up. He would never forgive himself if he did. He looked at his watch. Ten more minutes until she'd arrive. He should have enough time. Eagerly, he unbuttoned his shirt and hurried to the shower room. All sorts of images whirled through his head as he lathered himself with soap. Jenny, of all people. He felt dizzy at the thought of touching her body, caressing and kissing her. Her message had surprised him. It said, 'Meet me at the agency in half an hour. Hugs. Jenny.'

At first, Ek had been puzzled to see that the text had been sent from Markus's mobile. But then he decided that Jenny must have taken possession of the phone when she found Markus in that cabin on Furillen. And after that she'd probably taken it home to recharge it. A bit odd, perhaps, but what the hell. Women were always coming up with the strangest ideas. And Diana had tossed Jenny's mobile over the balcony railing.

It never occurred to him to question why Jenny would have brought Markus's phone to the Christmas party. He was preoccupied with entirely different thoughts.

He quickly dried himself off and put on more aftershave. At the same time, he told himself that this was going to be the absolute last time that he was unfaithful to Erna. When he was dressed, he checked to make sure the agency door was unlocked so that Jenny could easily get in. Then he went to the staff lounge, lit a few candles, took a bottle of champagne from the fridge and washed two glasses. Glanced at his watch. She would be here any minute. He poured the champagne, turned off the ceiling lights and sat down on the sofa. All right, he thought, filled with anticipation. He was ready.

The minutes ticked by, but Jenny didn't appear. He

sipped his champagne. When almost an hour had passed, he sent a text:

'I'm here. I'm waiting for you.'

After a while he went to his office and sat down at the desk, switching on the lamp. He might as well take care of some of the paperwork he'd been planning to take home over the Christmas holiday. He looked at the clock on the wall. Already 2.45 a.m. He'd stayed at the party longer than he'd intended. Old habits were hard to break. He'd always been a night owl.

Ek had nearly finished his work when he heard a sound. The front door opened and closed. Finally. He decided to stay here in his office and let her come to him. His heart was beating hard. Another minute passed, and she still hadn't made her appearance. For a moment he was puzzled. He didn't hear any footsteps. Was she playing with him? Maybe she was hiding somewhere. Maybe she had stretched out on the sofa and was waiting for him there.

He got up and padded across the floor to peek inside the staff lounge. She wasn't there. The agency offices weren't big enough to offer many hiding places. And he should have heard her by now.

'Jenny?' he called, filled with anticipation. 'I'm in the staff lounge.'

No answer. He stood in the doorway for a few minutes. Motionless, his lips parted, his eyes open wide. Expectant and confused. Gradually, doubts began to form in his slightly hazy brain. He listened tensely. He thought he'd heard someone pressing down a door handle. But now there was only silence. Quickly, he returned to his desk and sank down on his chair, reaching out his hand to turn off the desk lamp. The room was cloaked in darkness. He sat still, waiting. When a couple more minutes had passed and Jenny did not turn up, he realized he'd been tricked. Slowly, he got up from his chair, hearing the faint creak of the leather seat and thinking that he was not dealing with some run-of-the-mill burglar. Who had pretended to be Jenny, and why? And how did the person in question happen to have Markus's mobile? There could be only one explanation.

Ek tried to make as little noise as possible as he made his way through the kitchen towards the office of the booking agents, which was right next to the reception area. That was when he heard it. A creak. There was no doubt about it. And the sound came from the office. He could make out the furniture and the counter. He hurried as fast as he dared towards the front hall.

He touched the door. Panic sank its claws into him as he realized that the door was not only locked, but the key was missing. He turned around. And then he froze as someone reached for the switch on the wall and the hall was suddenly bathed in light. Robert Ek saw at once that his suspicions were correct. The person who had broken into the agency was no ordinary burglar.

Not at all.

When Jenny awoke, she had no idea where she was. The first thing she noticed was that the duvet felt different. It was heavier than her own and the covering was made of silk, as was the sheet underneath her. The bed was big and soft. At home, all of her bedlinen was cotton. Cautiously, she opened her eyes, which felt as if they were filled with sand and her lashes stuck together. She squinted at the window, which was covered with a heavy curtain. She could make out the faint sound of traffic in the distance. Slowly, she turned over and discovered next to her a muscular shoulder with a tattoo she didn't recognize. Straggly blonde hair. She let her eyes wander onward. Further away, she saw a leg that couldn't possibly belong to the person with the straggly hair. It was lying at the wrong angle. Her brain was sluggish; her thoughts crawled along. Again she looked at the leg, noticing that it was slender and nicely shaped, without a trace of hair. The toenails were painted black. So the leg must belong to a woman. She stared at the leg, trying to gather her thoughts. When she shifted her body, she realized that she was lying on a waterbed. Good Lord. Who had a waterbed these days? Where was she? How had she ended up here? She tried to get up, but the movement immediately brought on a splitting headache. She sank back against the pillows, trying desperately to remember what had happened last night. Some fragmented images appeared in her mind. The confrontation with Diana, Tobias's warm eyes, wild dancing at the club, drinks at the bar, a white pill in the palm of her hand. Had she taken it? That's what she must have done. Her head felt so muddled. What on earth had happened? At the club she'd met a big bunch of people she didn't know; they were drinking champagne in the VIP room, laughing uncontrollably and having fun. She had danced, while her friends had disappeared. She didn't know where Tobias had gone either. She thought they might have all gone home together, but he had been dancing with some blonde.

Blurry memories of the group leaving the club in the wee hours of the morning. Several girls and guys who had all crammed into one large taxi. Or was it a limousine? She recalled hands reaching under her shirt. She didn't know who they belonged to, but she didn't try to stop them. She was so drunk she no longer cared. She just passively went along with it. Let things run their course. It didn't matter any more. She was beyond thinking about possible consequences or that she might put herself in some sort of danger or relinquish control. She remembered a staircase, music, a bare-chested girl, hands on her body. Then everything went black. No matter how hard she tried, she couldn't recall anything else. All that remained was an aching feeling in her head and between her legs. And that spoke volumes.

Panic came creeping over her. She had to get away. She had to get out of here. Away from these people she didn't know. What had they done to her? She started crying and sat up, making the bed shake. She staggered to her feet and managed to find her clothes in the dim light. Then she noticed a huge sectional sofa at the other end of the room. Two men and a woman, all of them naked, were sprawled on top of each other, sound asleep. When she went downstairs, she saw that it was broad daylight, or at least as light as it ever got in December. She looked out at a neatly maintained garden and caught a glimpse of water in the distance. She was clearly in someone's luxury home. In the high-end kitchen with the panoramic views, she found her jacket and boots. Her handbag was on top of the dishwasher. To her relief, she found a packet of headache tablets in the loo and an unopened bottle of the energy drink ProViva Active in the fridge.

She decided to take it with her. Then she fumbled with the lock and opened the door to feel the fresh suburban air come gusting towards her.

Two days passed before anyone discovered what had happened to Robert Ek. His wife and four children stayed the whole weekend in Dalarna, and his friends who had spent the night after the party in his house went their own way after regaining consciousness on Saturday afternoon. As agreed, they left the house key in a pot under the veranda stairs at the back of the house.

When the family returned home on Sunday, they found clear signs that a raucous party had gone on inside the house. And no one had bothered to clean up afterwards.

Someone had slept in the children's beds. One or more people had also used the master bedroom, since the bedclothes were in disarray and several glasses, half filled with wine, stood on the bedside table. The last straw was when Erna Linton found a thong in the woodpile next to the fireplace. At that point she turned on her heel, gathered up the children and dog, and left the house. She phoned her sister, who had also spent the weekend with their parents in Dalarna and who lived nearby. At her sister's house she left the dog and the children, who were happily surprised to find that they were going to have more time to play with their cousins. It was only a short while ago that they'd said goodbye at the service station where they had all stopped to have refreshments on their way home from Leksand.

Erna Linton then headed over to the agency. She was boiling with rage. Robert had promised never to do this again. He'd kept his promise for only two weeks, maybe even less. Over the weekend she'd tried to reach him several times, both on the home phone and on his mobile, but without success. Now she realized that he'd been busy with other things.

With a grim expression she drove her SUV through the Söderled tunnel and towards central Stockholm. Since it was Sunday evening, and the Christmas holiday had begun, it was easier than usual to find a parking spot. Normally, that was no easy task in Östermalm, where most of the streets were one-way.

She found a spot on Riddargatan, only a block from the agency. She had a strong sense of foreboding as she walked along the street and turned on to the lower section of Grev Turegatan.

She tapped in the security code and the heavy, polished door of the building opened with a faint buzzing sound. The door to the agency was decorated with a big wreath of lingonberry branches and red bows. She rang the bell. Waited a minute. No answer. She held her breath as she pushed down the door handle. The door opened. The floorboards in the hall creaked under her feet. A quick glance in the mirror. She looked pale and tired.

She surveyed the floor in the front hall. No shoes, or any coats lying about. She peeked inside the room where the bookings were done. Everything was neat and tidy. She continued on to the kitchen. On the work-top were a dozen empty champagne bottles, along with a number of glasses, some with lipstick on the rim. And a bowl with a few cashews left in the bottom. A sour smell hovered over the kitchen.

The agency's most beautiful room had a tiled stove at one end and a large sofa. On the coffee table she saw two glasses filled with champagne and a bottle in a wine bucket. Candleholders had been set on the table.

The door to her husband's office was ajar. When she looked into the room she noticed at once the congealed blood on the oak parquet floor.

She would have given anything to avoid seeing the scene that now confronted her.

When the phone rang late on Sunday evening, Knutas was at home, having fallen asleep on the sofa while watching a film on TV. Lina was working the night shift at the hospital, and the children had, for once, gone to bed early.

Still feeling groggy, Knutas recognized the voice of Martin Kihlgård, his colleague from the NCP, the National Criminal Police, in Stockholm. Kihlgård had worked with the Visby police many times.

'Hi, Knutie. Sorry to disturb you so late, but there's been a major development here.'

Knutas chose to ignore the fact that he hated being called Knutie. Fortunately, Kihlgård was the only person who ever used that nickname.

'What's going on?'

'Well, you know that modelling agency – I think it's called Fashion for Life? Tonight, the boss, Robert Ek, was found murdered in his office there. It was his wife who found him.'

Knutas stood up abruptly. He was suddenly wide awake.

'You're kidding me. How was he killed?'

'With an axe. Apparently, he received blows to his head as well as to his body. Kurt's the one who asked me to ring you, because he's got his hands full at the moment. Over here at the NCP we're already working on the case.'

'Okay. What have you found out so far?'

'Not much. According to the preliminary assessment the medical examiner did at the crime scene, the victim has been dead at least twenty-four hours. The agency had a party on Friday night and, as far as we know, nobody has seen him since then. His death is probably connected to the party.'

'Where was the party held?'

'In a rented flat on Stureplan, only a few minutes' walk from the agency. The body is being taken to the pathology lab. The whole area is already crawling with journalists, of course, and they'll probably be ringing you up as well. Do you want to send someone from your team to Stockholm?'

'Definitely. Jacobsson and Wittberg will catch the first plane tomorrow morning.'

Knutas pictured Kihlgård's face lighting up. He was very fond of Karin Jacobsson.

'Great. Tell them to give me a call. I've got to go. But at least now you know what's going on. Talk to you later.'

Knutas informed his colleagues on the investigative team about what had happened. Then he checked the news reports to see what the media were saying about this development. All the reports were largely the same. A man had been found dead in an office in central Stockholm, and the police suspected that it was a homicide. At this stage, that was really all the journalists were saying, and Knutas was grateful for that. Robert Ek's children and parents might not yet have been told what had happened to him.

An hour later, Karin Jacobsson and Thomas Wittberg were sitting in Knutas's office. He made a pot of strong coffee and offered them some ginger biscuits. There wasn't anything else available at this time of night. The vending machine with sandwiches had been emptied before the weekend started.

'This puts a whole new light on the Markus Sandberg case,' said Jacobsson. 'I don't think there's any doubt that it's the same perpetrator. Or at least we have to assume that the two cases are connected.'

'Right,' Wittberg agreed. 'My first thought is that the motive has something to do with their profession and the agency.'

'The only difference is that, this time, the assailant succeeded in killing his victim,' said Knutas grimly.

'I'm sure he intended to do the same in the cabin on Furillen,' said Jacobsson. 'When the perpetrator left, he probably thought that Sandberg was dead.'

'But who would have a motive to kill these two individuals?' Knutas rubbed his chin. 'Someone in the fashion world? Or could the motive have roots further back in the past?'

'That's certainly possible,' said Wittberg. 'For instance, both men seem to have had an extremely active sex life. Robert Ek was apparently notoriously unfaithful to his wife. And Sandberg has had plenty of affairs.'

'Have you heard that either of them was ever mixed

up in anything irregular? I mean, did they have any ties to criminal elements, for example?'

Jacobsson shook her head.

'No. You can say what you like about Sandberg's career with all those porn photos and tits-and-bum shows on TV, but there's nothing illegal about any of it.'

'At least so far,' muttered Wittberg. 'But it wouldn't surprise me if—'

'Did you say something?' Jacobsson said sternly.

'No, no. Nothing.'

Wittberg held up both hands as if to ward off any criticism and then took a few more biscuits from the plate on the table. He was too tired to do any of the usual sparring with Karin. He'd met a girl on Friday night, and they'd spent all yesterday in bed. Which had proved far from restful.

'Who phoned from Stockholm?' asked Jacobsson, to change the subject.

'Kihlgård. And he sends his regards to both of you.'

Jacobsson's face lit up.

'Martin? How nice. But why did he make the call? Is the NCP already involved in the case?'

'Apparently. He'd like you to contact him as soon as you get to the city. The two of you will be leaving first thing tomorrow morning.'

Jacobsson and Wittberg exchanged glances. It was three days before Christmas Eve.

'That's fine with me,' said Jacobsson. 'I was thinking of going to Stockholm anyway. Hanna has invited me over for Christmas Eve.'

A big smile appeared on her face.

'That's wonderful,' said Knutas warmly.

'Yeah, that's great,' Wittberg agreed. 'But I can't say that a visit to Stockholm was part of *my* holiday plans. Of course, this means I won't have to eat any of the brawn that my grandmother always serves, and that's a positive thing. Plus, there's a bird or two in the city I could always ring up.'

'It's not certain that either of you will have to stay there over Christmas,' said Knutas. 'But I think it's important for you to be on the scene as soon as possible so you can get your own impression of the situation. The perpetrator might be from Gotland. At this point, we just don't know.'

Jenny sat on the sofa in the flat on Kungsholmen and stared into the dark. It would soon be daylight, but she hadn't slept at all. A sense of unease had kept her awake. She still didn't have a clear idea of what had happened after the Christmas party. The scattered images that she'd had upon waking up in the waterbed in the stranger's bedroom kept coming back, but that was all she could remember, no matter how hard she tried. The ache in her pelvic region had gone, but an unpleasant feeling remained because she had only a fragmentary idea of how the evening had ended. What had she got herself mixed up in? And where had she been?

The house stood in a secluded spot, with no neighbours close by. Without her mobile, she couldn't even ring for a taxi. After walking several kilometres along the road, she'd finally entered a residential area with more houses.

She stopped at an intersection, pausing to consider which way to go. Apparently, she had looked bewildered enough that a female driver pulled over and rolled down her window. When Jenny asked where she might find the nearest bus stop, the woman had offered her a lift. Jenny found the whole situation so embarrassing that she gratefully accepted the offer without asking where she was. The woman was driving into town and was kind enough to drop Jenny at the front door of her building.

As luck would have it, the other models who had spent the night in the flat had already left. She bought a take-away pizza and rented a film on Saturday evening, trying to shake off all thoughts of the unwelcome experience of the night before.

On Sunday she slept until one in the afternoon and didn't leave the flat for the rest of the day. She hardly had the energy to move at all. She was glad she didn't have her phone, so she wouldn't have to talk to anyone. She was just waiting for Monday to arrive so she could go back home. She was going to spend the Christmas holiday with her parents on Gotland and didn't have to return to Stockholm until the 26th. She was longing to be with her parents and feel safe on the farm.

She had gone to bed early but couldn't fall asleep. Finally, she gave up and went into the living room to sit on the sofa. She could sleep when she got to Gotland. Her plane was due to depart at ten thirty in the morning. She had already packed her bag and cleaned up the flat. She looked out of the window, catching a glimpse of the canal below. The water glittered in the light from a solitary street lamp but, otherwise, everything was wrapped in darkness. No people were visible on the narrow pathway. With a shiver she recalled the last time she'd walked along that path. And the man who had appeared out of the dark. But he hadn't spoken or done anything, so she had decided not to tell anyone about it. She didn't want to alarm

her mother for no reason; she was neurotic enough
as it was. But Jenny had definitely found the incident
unsettling.

Overcome with restlessness, she decided to go out
to Bromma Airport as soon as possible. She couldn't
bear to sit here waiting, drinking coffee and reading
the morning papers. She wanted to get out of this flat.
Away from all this shit. She looked at the clock on the
wall and saw that it was four fifteen. She really couldn't
see herself getting there before six.

So she took a shower and washed her hair. Then she
spent time rubbing lotion on her skin and putting on
some make-up, which made her feel more alert. In the
kitchen she turned on the radio and hummed along
with the tune that was playing. At five o'clock the music
was interrupted by the *Eko* news report. By that time
she had sat down at the table with a bowl of yoghurt.
As she listened to the news, she lost her appetite.

*On Sunday evening a man in his forties was found dead
in an office in central Stockholm. The police suspect foul
play. The office belongs to one of Sweden's biggest modelling
agencies, Fashion for Life. This is the same agency which
employed Markus Sandberg, the well-known fashion
photographer. In late November he was the victim of a
brutal act of violence on Gotland when he was assaulted and
seriously injured. The police refuse to say whether they've
found any direct links between the two cases, but they won't
rule out a possible connection.*

Then a police spokesman was interviewed, giving a
terse and unrevealing account of the investigation.

Jenny jumped to her feet. This couldn't be true. She
refused to believe it. She dashed into the living room to

turn on the TV. The early-morning news bulletin was longer on television than on the radio, so the report about the murder at the agency was still on. A reporter was shown standing in front of the agency building. He said that it was the wife who had discovered her husband's body inside. The victim could be only one person. Robert Ek.

The footage then shifted to another scene, and Jenny could hardly believe her eyes. She was looking at a luxury home with police vehicles parked outside it. In spite of the darkness, sections of the façade were visible, along with the front entrance, which had a lion sculpture on either side of the door. The disembodied voice of the reporter echoed hollowly:

The victim lived in this house in Nacka outside Stockholm. The police have searched the premises and apparently found evidence that an unknown number of people spent the weekend here while the victim's family was out of town. The police would be grateful for any information from the public regarding any individuals who were seen in the vicinity of the home over the past few days.

Jenny recognized at once the house where she'd found herself on Saturday morning. And she felt her throat slowly closing up.

'Hi, sweetie.'
Her father looks happy, as usual, but she notices concern in his eyes as he swiftly appraises her thin figure to see if she has put on even a tiny bit of weight. He gives her a cautious hug. Katarina makes no attempt to hug her. She knows that Agnes would not welcome such a gesture. Instead, she gives her a quick, uncertain smile and whispers hello. Katarina is so pathetic.

Agnes takes her father by the arm and turns to head back to the ward. She has been longing to see him. Last night, she hardly slept. She lay in bed thinking about the murder of Robert Ek, who was head of the modelling agency she once worked for. She'd heard about it on the evening news. She had met Ek several times. Now she wants to talk to her father and find out what he knows. Probably more than she does.

She expects Katarina to trudge off to the day room, as she always does. But she sees that something is up with her father. His feet seem to be glued to the floor.

'Well, er, you see, Agnes,' he says, 'I was thinking that, uh . . .' He casts a quick glance at Katarina. '. . . we were thinking that Katarina would come with us today. With you and me. Is that okay?'

Agnes is completely unprepared for this request. Why would she want to spend time with that woman? She isn't the least bit interested in the idea and can hardly bear to look at her. For a moment, no one speaks. Agnes stares at her father as she struggles with herself. The two adults wait for her to answer, exchanging looks with each other. She can sense their nervousness seeping through their coats.

But she doesn't want to behave like a stubborn child. That would merely confirm Katarina's preconceptions about her. Before she manages to say anything, Per appears, like a guardian angel.

'Hi. Come on in.'

As if he understands the difficulty of the situation, he leads the way down the corridor, and the others follow. Agnes's cheeks are burning with shame. So far, she has simply ignored Katarina, pretending not to see her at all. That's going to be harder to do now. She's also disappointed because today she won't have any private time with her father.

They take seats in the common room. Per goes to the kitchen to get coffee for all of them. Agnes's father sits next to her on the sofa while Katarina sits in an easy chair.

'It's very nice in here,' she says appreciatively, looking around the room.

Agnes gives her an icy glare but doesn't say anything. Her father nervously shifts position.

'So, how are you?' he asks in his gentle voice, placing his big, dry hand on top of hers.

'I hate this place. You know that,' she snaps, pulling away her hand. 'And I feel shitty, in case you want to know.'

He ignores her tone of voice.

'Grandma and Grandpa send their love.'

'Huh.'

She's already regretting her attitude. She doesn't want to appear weak in Katarina's eyes. Or as if she cares about her being there. Agnes casts a surreptitious glance in her direction. Come to think of it, Katarina actually looks rather nice. Dark hair under the beret she's wearing. Brown eyes and a fresh complexion with rosy cheeks. Distinctive features. Pale-pink lipstick. Agnes shifts her gaze to her father and is suddenly seized with tenderness. He looks tired. His calloused hands are fidgeting. She notices the faint scent of his aftershave.

Per brings them their coffee. The china clinks and his hands tremble slightly as he fills their cups, one by one. It takes for ever.

'Why don't you join us?' Agnes suggests. 'You would ease the situation a bit. It's rather tense, as you can tell.'

The next second, Katarina is on her feet, her lips pressed together in a tight line.

'I can see this isn't a good idea. I don't think Agnes is ready.'

'Don't go,' Rikard pleads as she leaves the room.

'It's okay,' Per tells him. 'I'll go after her.'

He hurries after Katarina, who is angrily striding down the hall.

'Was that really necessary?' Agnes's father gives her a reproachful look. 'Couldn't you at least try?'

'She's so highly strung,' Agnes defends herself. 'Can't stand even the slightest criticism.'

'This isn't easy for her either. She's been sitting in

that day room for three months now. Don't you think it's about time you cut her a little slack?'

'Why should I do that?'

'Because Katarina and I are together and have been for quite a while now. How do you think I feel when you ignore her, pretending that she doesn't exist?'

'What about me? Don't I mean anything to you?'

'Agnes, sweetie. You're everything to me. But I need to live my own life, too. I have my work, but everyone else has a family they can go home to. I don't want to sit at home alone every evening and every weekend. And you're here. And you don't seem to be getting any better. Don't you want to get well?'

'Of course I do. But it's not that easy.'

'I spoke to the head of the clinic, and she says that you're resisting the treatment. That you're not helping yourself.'

'Huh.'

Her father looks deep into her eyes, then reaches out to caress her cheek gently. She's on the verge of tears, but she fights against it.

'My beautiful daughter,' he says tenderly. 'My beautiful little girl. You're the only one who can make yourself well. Nobody else can do it for you. What's so awful about gaining weight? What are you afraid of?'

She shrugs. The words lodge in her throat.

Then she says, 'I don't know how to act if I'm not anorexic. I can hardly remember what I used to be like.'

'Before all this happened, you were a happy, sweet girl who had lots of friends and enjoyed going to school. Until those damn fashion people came into the picture. Katarina agrees that it's awful how they destroyed your life. I hate them for what they did. She does, too. She thinks it's terrible how they treated you. I want you to know that Katarina cares about you, even though you don't think she does. But you can have your life back, and everything can be the same as it was before. Don't let those cold, calculating people win. They've already caused enough harm.'

Johan Berg was about to have his morning coffee when he switched on the TV, as he usually did on Mondays. It made no difference that he was on holiday and staying at his mother's home in Rönninge. He still had to watch the news. It was in his bones.

'What the hell?'

He reached for the remote control to turn up the volume. His colleague from the Stockholm office Madeleine Haga was on the screen. She stood in front of a building in the city centre.

There is speculation that the murder may have had something to do with the staff Christmas party, which the agency hosted on Friday evening at a club on Stureplan, only a stone's throw from its office. Robert Ek may have lain dead in his office all weekend. But the police are also asking the question . . .

Emma came into the living room, carrying a mug of coffee. The children were still asleep in one of the guest rooms upstairs. Johan's mother wasn't yet awake either.

'What is it?' she asked, sitting down on the sofa next to Johan.

'The head of Fashion for Life is dead. He was found murdered at the agency.'

'Really? Good Lord, this is too much.'

'I know. His body was discovered last night. And they haven't caught the killer.'

'That's unbelievable. What's going on with that agency? And Jenny works for that place. This is starting to get really scary. I need to call Tina.'

She got up and left the room.

In the meantime, Johan rang his boss, the editor-in-chief, Max Grenfors, in Stockholm. He sounded out of breath. Johan could picture him running along the corridors of the huge television building.

'What a bloody mess! The morning meeting starts in a few minutes, and after that we'll decide how to tackle this story. Right now, Madeleine is on the scene, and I've got two reporters working on it here in the office. I'll phone you back after the meeting and we'll work out how to handle the Gotland angle.'

'What are you hearing?'

'There's speculation that it's some sort of personal vendetta against the two victims – that they were involved in some shit together, and that's what provoked the attacks. They share a long history.'

'Is that right? I didn't know that.'

'I'll brief you later. Haven't got time to talk right now. But since you're here in Stockholm, why don't you drop by the office? This could be a big story.'

Johan could hear excited voices talking in the background. Apparently, there were others who wanted Grenfors's attention. Johan yearned to be there, in the midst of it all. He wondered what Emma would say about Grenfors's idea.

He went back to his mother's kitchen, which was elaborately decorated for the holidays with red curtains,

Advent stars, Christmas elves and a gingerbread heart which hung in the window. The whole room was still fragrant from the ginger biscuits they'd baked the day before.

It was two days before Christmas Eve.

Karin Jacobsson and Thomas Wittberg were sitting in a conference room at police headquarters in Stockholm, along with Detective Inspector Martin Kihlgård of the NCP. They had just arrived from Visby and were about to get their first report on the situation. Outside the window, the light was fading, even though it was only eleven in the morning. Snowflakes were briskly tumbling down from the gloomy sky. In the big windows facing the park, someone had placed electric candles, which produced a warm glow against the hazy backdrop. Stockholmers hunched their shoulders as they hurried along the street in the snowstorm. No one paused or glanced to the side or bothered to meet the eye of other pedestrians. It was too cold for that. In these days before Christmas, everyone deadened their senses by spending too much on gifts and decorating their homes in a desperate attempt to withstand the darkness.

Martin Kihlgård reached out his hand to take a saffron bun from the basket of pastries on the conference table. He was famous for his appetite, and he was almost always eating something. He was solidly built, without being obese. Jacobsson thought his rotund appearance gave him a certain air of authority. And confidence. She had liked him from the very first time they met, several years ago, when he came to Gotland to help hunt for a serial killer.

'How much do we know?' she asked him now.

'Robert Ek was found in his office at the Fashion for Life agency, murdered with an axe. He had been brutally attacked and had multiple wounds on his head and body. His skull had been split clear down to his eyes. It was one of the worst things I've ever seen.'

Kihlgård shook his head, making his cheeks quiver.

'What about the perpetrator?'

'Not yet apprehended. But we did find some interesting items in the rubbish early this morning, including what appears to be the murder weapon. A bloodstained axe.'

Wittberg whistled.

'Damn. Is it the same one that was used on Furillen?'

'We don't know yet. It was sent to the lab for analysis. The forensics guys also found Ek's mobile phone. And it turns out that he received a text message from another mobile on the night of the party. And not just from anybody. The message was sent from Markus Sandberg's phone! At 1.10 on Saturday morning.'

Wittberg and Jacobsson stared in astonishment at their colleague.

Kihlgård paused for dramatic effect before he went on.

'This is what the message said: "Meet me at the agency in half an hour. Hugs. Jenny."'

'Are you serious?' exclaimed Jacobsson.

'Yup. That's what it said. Word for word. I have the transcript here. And the next minute, Robert Ek sent a reply, saying that he would wait for her. Fifty-one minutes later, at 2.01 a.m., he sent a text saying, "I'm here. I'm waiting for you."'

'So that means the cases are definitely connected and, judging by the text, it's the same perpetrator,' said Jacobsson. 'The question is whether Jenny Levin wrote it, or whether the killer pretended to be her in order to lure Ek to the agency. Sandberg's mobile has been traced to Flemingsberg ever since Markus was assaulted, and Jenny hasn't been anywhere near there, at least according to her. What does she say about all this?'

'The problem is that we haven't been able to reach her, but we just heard from her parents that she's on a plane heading for Visby right now,' said Kihlgård, casting a glance at his watch. 'She should be landing any minute. I've asked our colleagues in Visby to contact her as soon as possible. From what I understand, she was one of the last people to see Robert Ek alive. Witnesses told us that the two of them were seen talking together at the bar during the party, around midnight. So that was about an hour before he left.'

'What did the crime scene look like?' asked Wittberg.

'Lots of blood, of course. The SOCOs found footprints, but no fingerprints. There was no sign of a struggle, or any indication that someone had broken in. So either Ek left the door unlocked or the perpetrator had a key.'

Wittberg raised his eyebrows.

'Is there anything that might lead us to think that one of the employees is the murderer?'

'It's far too early to say. We need to question more people and then put together the information from the interviews we've already done. The work has just started.'

'What about the footprints?' asked Jacobsson. 'What can you tell us about them?'

'They're from a heavy shoe with a rubber sole. A rather small size. Five and a half.'

Jacobsson and Wittberg exchanged glances.

'The same as on Furillen. We found footprints that were the same size.'

'Interesting,' murmured Kihlgård, biting into another bun. 'One more thing,' he said as he chewed. 'There were two glasses filled with champagne and a bottle of Taittinger in a wine bucket on the table in the staff lounge. And he seems to have set the mood with candles.'

'Taittinger?' enquired Wittberg.

'A type of champagne,' Kihlgård clarified.

'Do we know what time Ek left the party?' asked Jacobsson. 'And did he leave alone?'

'The bouncer and the cloakroom attendant both say the same thing. He left the club around 1 a.m. and they think he left alone. There was a lot of coming and going, because people kept leaving to have a smoke. So they weren't a hundred per cent positive, but he was alone when he picked up his coat.'

'Was he drunk?'

'He'd definitely had a few, but he wasn't too bad.'

'Since he was such a ladies' man, he had plenty of opportunity to take someone home with him that night. His wife and kids were away, so he had the whole house to himself. Why didn't he ask Jenny to go home with him?'

'That's a good question,' Kihlgård agreed. 'Although he'd already invited some people to stay the night. Maybe he didn't want them to see her. At any rate, Robert Ek wasn't planning to be at home alone. He'd invited a couple of male friends and given them a key. They brought along some girls from the club.'

'How do we know this?'

'His wife, Erna, could tell that there'd been a party in the house. She gave us the phone numbers of several of Ek's closest friends, and they were quick to answer our questions. One of them, who also happened to be at the Christmas party, had borrowed a key to the house. We interviewed him late last night. He said that a bunch of them went to Ek's house for an after-party, thinking that he'd turn up later on. When he didn't, they assumed that he'd decided to stay with some girlfriend instead. This friend left the house on Saturday afternoon and put the key inside a pot at the back, as he and Robert had agreed. He didn't give it any more thought.'

'How many people were in the house?' asked Jacobsson.

'That's a bit vague. This guy doesn't seem completely trustworthy. He claims that he was really drunk and can only name one of the women, who also happens to be his girlfriend. He didn't know the others. They were people he'd met at the club and had never seen before. He can't recall exactly how many spent the night, but he thinks five or six. When he and his girlfriend woke up on Saturday, everybody else was gone.'

'What's the name of his girlfriend?' asked Wittberg.

'Katinka Johansson. She lives in Bagarmossen.

Twenty-seven years old. Works at the 7–11 on Grev Turegatan.'

'Has anyone talked to her yet?'

'Yes, but she really had nothing to say. Could hardly remember where she'd spent the night, and she couldn't name a single person who was there, except for her boyfriend.'

Wittberg looked at Kihlgård.

'What about surveillance cameras? There must be some at the entrance to the club or along the street on the way to the agency. The building is smack in the middle of Stureplan.'

'We've already thought of that. The club has cameras at the front entrance, but we didn't see anything of interest. We're checking the whole area and should have more information later in the day. We can only hope we find something useful.'

'What about the other tenants in the building?' said Jacobsson. 'Did anyone see or hear anything?'

Kihlgård was starting to look annoyed.

'We don't know yet. Robert Ek's body was only found last night, damn it. Of course, we've got officers knocking on doors and questioning the neighbours.'

'Okay, okay.' Jacobsson waved her hand, trying to calm him down.

Kihlgård drank some coffee and leaned back in his chair.

'Naturally, our first thought was that the murder of Robert Ek and the assault on Markus Sandberg must have something to do with the fashion world,' said Wittberg.

'I agree. And Jenny Levin is involved in both cases,'

said Jacobsson. 'I wonder how she figures in the whole thing.'

'Sure. But it could also be a coincidence. All these people work together. And the attacks might have nothing to do with the fashion industry. The motive could have something to do with women. Ek has a reputation for being a ladies' man, just like Sandberg. And what about Ek's wife, Erna Linton? She's also an ex-model. What was her relationship with Sandberg? It's clear that she had a motive for killing her husband. Or at least the desire to do so – if she knew about his escapades.'

'Does anyone know how he's doing now?' asked Jacobsson. 'I'm talking about Markus.'

'I spoke to the hospital this morning,' said Kihlgård. 'His condition is unchanged, so it's impossible to question him. And, apparently, there's no light at the end of the tunnel, so to speak. Unfortunately. As for Erna Linton, so far we've only conducted a brief interview with her. We're going to meet with her here after lunch. You can sit in as witnesses, if you like. But she does have an alibi. She was visiting her parents in Leksand all weekend.'

'But the murder occurred well after midnight,' countered Wittberg. 'How long does it take to drive from Leksand in the middle of the night when there's no traffic? Three hours? Let's suppose that she left around eleven or twelve on Friday night. Arrived in Stockholm around two or three in the morning. Maybe she'd pretended to be someone else in order to set up a rendezvous with Ek at the agency. And then she killed him. Afterwards, she drove back. If she left the city around three thirty, she'd be back in Leksand by six thirty. She could have done it.'

'You could be right,' Kihlgård admitted. 'We'll have to take a closer look at her alibi. And I have no idea where she was when Markus Sandberg was assaulted.'

He gathered up the papers lying on the table.

'So, are you starting to get hungry? There's a new place down on Kungsholmstorg that serves great home cooking.'

'Just a minute,' said Jacobsson. 'There's one more thing. I was thinking about that Finnish model Marita Ahonen. The one that Markus got pregnant. Do you have any material from the agency here? A catalogue showing the models and information about them? I'm thinking in particular about their shoe size.'

'We confiscated all sorts of material – computers, and the like – yesterday. It's over in the technical department,' said Kihlgård, clearly worried that lunch might be delayed another hour. 'Wait here.'

He left the room, grabbing another saffron bun on his way out. A few minutes later he was back, his face flushed.

'I found out about that Marita Ahonen. She wears a size five and a half shoe.'

Karin Jacobsson was sweating in the lift on her way up to the fifth floor. This was the first time she'd been invited to her daughter's flat. Even the front entrance had made her nervous. It had to be one of the poshest buildings in all Stockholm, with its stucco flourishes and embellishments. A thick red carpet adorned the steps of the grand marble staircase in the vestibule, and on display in one corner towered a stately Christmas tree decorated with ornaments and lights. Marble sculptures stood in several niches, and a crystal chandelier hung from the ceiling. She had never seen anything like it. Thankfully, she knew that Hanna was not a pretentious person, or she would have been terrified.

On the top floor of the building there were two flats. One of them belonged to Hanna.

Jacobsson smoothed down her hair, took a deep breath, and rang the bell. She was clutching a bouquet of white tulips, which she held out in front of her.

The heavy door opened almost at once.

'Hi, Karin. How nice. Welcome!'

Hanna's sunny smile calmed her, and the warm hug helped even more. The dog came over, wagging his tail, clearly delighted with the visitor as he leapt about on his long legs.

'Okay, Nelson. That's enough.'

Karin handed over the bouquet.

'Thank you. Come in.'

Hanna led the way to the kitchen, which faced Mariatorget. Karin couldn't help pausing on the threshold. It was as far from a traditional kitchen as it could possibly be. A long counter made of black marble against a bright-yellow mosaic wall, an inverted zinc basin that served as the ceiling lamp. And the walls were decorated with old-fashioned Swedish enamel signs trumpeting various products such as Mazetti cocoa eyes, the orange soda Loranga, oatmeal from AXA and Tre Ess margarine. No refrigerator, freezer, or kitchen cabinets in sight.

Hanna pulled on a handle that was the same colour as the mosaic to reveal a spacious, ultra-modern fridge. Karin realized then that all the appliances and cabinets were built into the walls. Hanna took out a bottle of white wine.

'Would you like a glass?'

Karin nodded.

'What a beautiful kitchen. And there I was thinking you had simple tastes.'

'Appearances are deceptive,' replied Hanna, laughing.

They went from room to room. Karin saw that the flat was even bigger than she'd thought. The grand balcony that she'd seen from the street ran the full length of the flat. They took a tour of the dining room, living room, home office, guest room and bathroom. A lovely oak staircase led up to the floor above. There, Karin saw two large bedrooms, a huge bathroom with a sauna and its own little balcony, and yet another living room, which looked more like a library, with a fireplace and countless bookshelves holding both books and DVDs.

'This is amazing,' said Karin with a sigh. 'How big is this flat?'

'Just over 250 square metres,' said Hanna. 'I inherited it from my uncle. He died of cancer three years ago, and he insisted that I should have it. We were very close. The one condition was that I had to take care of his dog and stay here for as long as Nelson is alive. So I can't sell the flat. He didn't want Nelson to have to move. He thought it was traumatic enough for the dog to lose his master. He was a bit eccentric, my uncle. But he had a heart of gold. He also left money in a bank account that was to be used for only one purpose. To renovate the entire flat according to my own taste, because he knew I'd want to do that. He hadn't done a thing to the place in thirty years, so it was really run-down and outdated. And he also made sure that the managing agents' fees were paid for the next twenty years. He overdid things a bit. I realize that. He knew that Nelson couldn't possibly live that long.'

'What an incredible story. And what about your parents? How are they doing? If it's okay for me to ask,' she hurried to add.

'Of course. They still live in our house in Djursholm, where I grew up with my little brother, Alexander. He's two years younger than me. They'd been trying for years to have a baby when they adopted me. And it wasn't that long after they brought me home that Mamma got pregnant. They're still married.'

'What sort of work do they do?'

Mari Jungstedt

'Pappa has his own company. He's in the construction business. Mamma is the head of an advertising firm. We get along well, and I'm especially close to my father. It's largely because of him that I became a structural engineer. I suppose I've always been Pappa's little girl. But now I think the food is probably ready.'

They went back to the kitchen. Hanna busied herself at the hob while Karin sat down at the counter.

'We're having vegetarian lasagne. I haven't eaten meat in ten years.'

'Okay. Why not?'

'I don't like the way the animals are treated. I won't eat anything that has a mother or father.'

'But where do you draw the line? For example, do you eat eggs?'

'No. And not shrimp, either. They have parents.'

'Right.'

Karin sipped her wine. There was so much they didn't know about each other. They were strangers. Even so, she felt an odd sense of connection. Maybe it was just her imagination, but she wanted to hang on to the feeling. Savour it as she sat here, in Hanna's kitchen. She could sit here for all eternity, just looking at her daughter. Fixing her eyes on her.

For as long as possible.

256

Robert Ek's wife was an attractive woman, tall and elegant, dressed in a bright-pink rib-knitted tunic that reached almost to her knees and heavy turquoise tights that were barely visible above her black, high-heeled boots. Her taste in clothes is just as colourful and striking as her husband's, thought Jacobsson.

Erna Linton sat down on a chair in the interview room, which was similar to the one in Visby, although bigger and with a view of Agnegatan. Wittberg and Jacobsson were seated in a corner of the room and would take part only as witnesses. Detective Inspector Martin Kihlgård was handling the interview. He'd arranged for coffee, water, and a plate of ginger biscuits. Typical Kihlgård, thought Jacobsson. Always so thoughtful.

Even though they'd worked together many times, she'd never sat in on an interview with Kihlgård. This opportunity excited her almost as much as the thought of hearing what Erna Linton was going to say.

'Would you care for milk or sugar?' asked the inspector.

'Milk, please. Thank you.'

Erna crossed her long legs and stirred her coffee. She blew on the hot liquid for a moment before raising the cup to her lips. Only then did she look Kihlgård in the eye. Her expression changed from wary to slightly alarmed when Kihlgård calmly dipped a biscuit in his coffee and then took a bite of the soggy *pepparkaka*. He gave the woman across from him a kindly smile.

'Tell me about Robert. What was he like?'

Erna's slender white hand shook as she considered the question.

'What do you mean?'

'What sort of interests did he have? What did he enjoy doing in his spare time? What did the two of you do together for fun?'

'I don't really know,' she replied hesitantly. 'He worked so much at the agency. And we have four children, so they take a lot of my time. There's not much left over for anything else.'

'I see.'

Kihlgård fell silent for a few moments. Erna picked at a cuticle, then shifted her position.

'Have a biscuit.'

'No, thank you.'

'A little sugar can be very soothing.'

'Okay.'

She bit into the biscuit and then proceeded to eat the whole thing.

'How are you holding up?' he asked with a friendly expression.

'Not so good.'

'I understand.'

Again, silence.

Erna's eyes narrowed. 'What are we waiting for?'

Kihlgård shrugged without speaking. Jacobsson and Wittberg exchanged glances. What was he up to? In

front of him sat a woman who had just lost her husband in the most brutal and awful way imaginable.

Erna moistened her lips with her tongue before she
spoke again.

'So maybe you think that I'm the one who did it?'
she said, clearly ready for a fight. 'Is that why you're
using this silence tactic? You think that if you just
wait me out, I'll confess? Or else what the hell are
you doing? I have four children at home who are very
upset. I don't have time to sit here and stare at the
walls. So tell me, what do you want? What do you
want me to say?'

She threw up her hands and half rose from her chair.
Kihlgård didn't take his eyes off her face. But still he
said nothing. The seconds ticked by.

'Okay, I was fucking furious with him. He was unfaithful to me, but I'm sure you already know that, don't
you?' She turned to look at Jacobsson and Wittberg,
who were huddled in the corner. 'I was totally furious
with him! Our youngest child is only nine years old,
for God's sake! But he didn't care about that. He just
followed his prick wherever it took him, without a
thought for me or the children. His family! Then he
liked to come home and sit down at the dinner table to
play the darling father. And what's the last thing that
he does? The very last thing? He goes and gets himself
murdered. And what does he leave behind? A sex orgy
in our home, and preparations for a romantic interlude
at the office, while the children and I are away at a
family gathering. That's what he leaves behind for me.
That's the last memory I'll have of him.'

Erna Linton sank back in her chair. Tears were

running down her cheeks. Kihlgård reached out and patted her hand.

'There, there.'

'He was unfaithful,' she sobbed. 'All the time. There were always new women.'

'How do you know that?'

'I've known for a long time. I'd have had to be blind and deaf not to know. He would stay over at the office, he smelled of perfume, he had an unreasonable number of late business dinners or parties he had to attend. New models he had to take care of. My God. I was in the fashion business myself for ten years, so I know how things work.'

'What do you mean?'

'Come on, now. You can't be that naive. It's all very competitive. You have to make an impression and meet the right people, cultivate the best contacts, get powerful men on your side, make them like you and value you so that you'll get the choice assignments. They're the ones who can boost your career. And a model is always hungry. It can drive even the smartest and most grounded person insane. If you want to be a model, you have to be prepared to be constantly hungry for at least ten years, or however long your career lasts. To satisfy the ideal of the world's biggest fashion designers, you have to have the hip measurements of a twelve-year-old. How do you think all those models accomplish that? Not by eating full meals every day. Hunger is blind and deaf and drives a person to do the most hair-raising things. Why do you think my husband, who was almost fifty, was able to sleep with models who were only eighteen or nineteen? Do you think it was because of his fabulous personality? Hardly!'

At this point, Erna paused and loudly blew her nose on a tissue she took from her handbag. The salvo she'd fired, which had ricocheted off the cold walls, had now faded, leaving behind a bitter emptiness.

The emotional outburst had surprised the police officers. They were literally speechless. Silence settled over the room, and the air felt heavy. No one could think of anything to say.

The walls waited. Jacobsson and Wittberg waited. The table and chairs waited. Even the Christmas star in the window held its breath. When Erna Linton finally spoke again, her tone of voice had changed completely.

'It's true,' she said calmly and matter-of-factly. 'I could have strangled him with my bare hands when I saw that wine bucket with the bottle of champagne. But I didn't. I didn't kill my husband.'

The fashion editor Fanny Nord studied the proofs for the next issue of the prestigious women's magazine, which had been pinned up on the wall. Mini versions of page after page had been added as the layout was finished. Now she had the entire March issue, which was the big spring fashion issue, in front of her, and she was able to get a complete overview. From page one to page three hundred and sixty. With a critical eye she scrutinized the pages. She was primarily interested in the fashion reporting. They had four major fashion spreads, but was that enough? If only their biggest competitor didn't have more. The nightmare scenario would be if they put six fashion spreads in their spring issue, which would make hers look terribly skimpy in comparison. The mere thought made her shiver. On the other hand, she decided that the mix they'd chosen looked good. It was a real juggling act, trying to appeal to older readers, including the editor-in-chief, while also being sensitive to the latest trends and staying on the cutting edge. It was a task filled with contradictions, and not always easy to handle.

The magazine couldn't feel too young, and the models couldn't be too thin. Yet she always tried to get the coolest and hottest names.

She and her colleagues had found the inspiration for

the fashion spreads in this issue at the Hermès and Yves Saint Laurent shows in Paris during the late summer and early autumn. She was especially pleased with the spread she was personally responsible for, which had been inspired by the new French designer whose name was on everyone's lips: Christophe Decarnin, for the fashion house of Balmain. Twelve pages in the magazine with a chic rock 'n' roll theme: short black leather dresses, rivets, shoulder pads, the models' hair pulled tightly back in sleek styles. Punky and decadent. Cheeky. If only it doesn't seem too harsh, she thought uneasily. It might be too much for our older readers. Forget it, she thought in the next second. If we're going to be Sweden's biggest fashion magazine, we can't satisfy everyone. And the younger readers are important, too.

She went back to studying the proofs, then frowned with displeasure. Why had they put such an ugly, full-page advert right there, in the middle of the spread? It ruined the impact. But the worse the economy, the more important the adverts. She sighed and turned away. In spite of her reservations about certain details, she was generally pleased with the issue. Especially because they'd managed to get Jenny Levin for the more subdued fashion spread for which her colleague was responsible. The perfect counterpoint to the Balmain spread. And since Jenny was considered one of Sweden's top models, it was a real coup to have her in a big spread again, even though she'd been in the Christmas issue. She was truly exceptional.

On her way back to her desk, Fanny Nord went past her in-tray and grabbed a bundle of letters. She sat down at her desk in the big, cluttered room she shared with the other fashion editors and a number of assistants. Clothes hung on hangers everywhere. On the floor stood scores of boxes filled with clothing, while papers, books and magazines were scattered about. Their work was so frenzied and intense they never had time to clear things away. Fanny began opening envelopes, while keeping an eye on her computer and the emails that had come in during the morning. One letter she'd received in the post caught her interest. Initially, she saw only that it contained a card, or rather a folded piece of heavy paper, with a message inside, formed from words cut out of a magazine.

Her first thought was that it was yet another invitation to a fashion show. No doubt from an unusually creative new designer who wanted to attract attention with this sort of invitation. Hoping it would stand out. Then she read the text. There were only four words: 'You are all killers.' Surprised, she read the short sentence again.

She turned over the envelope. Was it really addressed to her? Yes, there was her name. She glanced at her co-workers, sitting around the room, all of them absorbed in their own projects. She called to her colleague Viktor, motioning for him to come over.

'Look what I got in the post.'

Fanny handed him the card. He read the message in silence, then frowned. He pulled up a chair and sat down next to her.

'What the hell is this?' he said, keeping his voice low.

He didn't want to upset the assistants unnecessarily. Then they both leaned close and stared at the cryptic message. Fanny felt a shiver race down her spine. Considering recent horrible events, she couldn't help feeling alarmed as she reread the four accusatory words. She thought about the big issue they were now in the process of putting together, and she felt her blood run cold when she remembered the contents of the Christmas issue. At the last moment they'd included the fashion spread from Furillen as a supplement. Another photographer had edited Markus Sandberg's amazing shots of Jenny Levin. And, as a tribute to Markus, they had included an article about him and his career at the end of the fashion spread. Was that why she had been sent this message? And what did the sender mean by saying they were killers? Fanny Nord didn't understand. It was all very unpleasant.

'We need to talk to Signe,' she said.

'Absolutely,' Viktor agreed. 'This is fucking serious.'

Editor-in-chief Signe Rudin had a private office next door. She paused to clean her glasses before she read the message.

'I don't think we should make a big deal out of this,' she finally murmured.

'What do you mean?' objected Fanny indignantly. 'This is damned scary. He could be coming after *us* now – or me, since it's my name on the envelope.' She sank on to the visitor's chair in front of the editor's desk. 'I don't understand. Why is he sending this message to me?'

'It does seem odd,' Signe Rudin admitted. 'If he was out to get the fashion world in general, or the magazine in particular, he should have sent the letter to me.'

'Good Lord. What have I done? Why is he threatening me? I don't get it!'

The editor-in-chief studied the ordinary white envelope. The address was handwritten, in black ballpoint. A cramped, sprawling script. And, of course, the name of the sender was missing. Then she looked at the card that had been inside. A plain folded card that could be bought in any stationery shop. Four whole words had been cut out and pasted down – not individual letters, as she had seen in films and on TV shows.

Signe Rudin took off her tinted reading glasses, pushed back a lock of hair, and looked at Fanny.

'Let's not blow this out of proportion. As you know, it's not unusual for us to receive threatening letters. This could be referring to just about anything. We have no idea what's behind it. And the message is not specifically directed at you. No one has issued threats against you personally.'

'No, but I still think it's nasty. And very unnerving. I won't dare even go out on the street any more.'

'Let's not be too hasty about all this.'

'But we should call the police. Don't you agree? Considering what's happened.'

'I'll speak to the publishing director first and see what he thinks. Then we'll decide what to do next.'

Signe Rudin closed up the card and put it back in the envelope.

Fanny felt both dismissed and powerless. As if this threat against her was not going to be taken seriously. But when the editor-in-chief spoke in that firm tone of voice, nothing would change her mind.

Her legs trembling, Fanny went back to her desk. She

sat there, staring into space. Maybe it was just as Signe had said – maybe the note was merely another in a series of crazy letters sent to the magazine. She tried to convince herself of that.

But the uneasy feeling refused to go away.

Agnes awakes to the sound of a traditional Swedish Christmas song blaring from the radio downstairs in the kitchen. She has been given permission to spend the holiday at home on Gotland. Her pappa came to fetch her from the ward – luckily, without Katarina – and pushed her in a wheelchair. The staff don't want her to walk anywhere when she is away from the clinic because her heart is so weak.

They flew to Visby, and Agnes started to cry as the plane made its approach for landing because she could see the Gotland coast below. That was when she realized how much she had missed home.

She has been granted five days' leave. And, best of all, she and her father will be on their own. Just the two of them. She had assumed that Katarina would insist on spending the holiday with them, since she'd come along every time Rikard had visited the hospital. But when they last spoke Agnes's father had told her that they'd be alone, just like last year.

She looks up at the sloping ceiling, enjoying being in her own comfortable bed at home in Visby. She burrows her face in the pillow that feels so soft against her cheek. She's had this old pillowcase and duvet cover for so many years. It makes her feel safe and cosy and reminds her of another time. Back when she had a mother and a father and an older brother. When she was healthy and had friends. When she went to school, like everybody else. She can't get all of that back, but she can snuggle under the old duvet cover and pretend for a while. Daydream back to that time and let the memories wash over her.

Usually, when her mother and Martin pop up in her thoughts she tries to push them away as quickly as possible. Make them disappear. She doesn't want to remember, can't bear to see their faces or hear their voices. But here, at home in her bed, she allows herself to think about them. And, in a sense, it feels so liberating. She pulls the covers over her head, breathing in the familiar scent of home. She summons up pictures of her mother. Crawls into a make-believe world, her own safe cocoon, allowing herself to be wrapped in the warmth of the duvet and the cover that her mother bought for her at Ikea when they went to Stockholm long ago. It's still here, but her mother is not. The very idea is absurd. How can a simple duvet cover outlive a person? But she refuses to think about that now. She wants to sink into her daydreams, go back in time a few years. Pretend that everything is the way it used to be when she was twelve. Soon she'll get out of bed and have breakfast with her family; then she'll leave for school. Her best friend, Cecilia, always used to stop by to collect her, waiting in the doorway for her to put on her coat. Then they would walk to school together. Now, it all seems like a dream.

She studies the pattern on the wallpaper and feels more cheerful than she has in a long time. Pappa has said that they'll take their time over breakfast and then go for a walk, like they always used to do when Mamma and Martin were alive. Agnes and her father had both burst out laughing when he said the part about 'taking their time' over breakfast. With Agnes, every meal lasts a long time, since she can't be hurried. And going for a walk means that he will push her in the wheelchair as best he can along the snowy streets. But it doesn't matter. They will be together, Agnes and her father.

She runs her finger along the ceiling beam above her head where the wallpaper is coming loose. When Agnes was younger her mother had scolded her for poking holes in the paper. Now she pictures her mother's face, still so vivid in her memory.

She remembers very little of the period right after the accident. Or how they managed to get through the days. Outwardly, Pappa had seemed able to cope with the daily tasks, but at night she would hear him sobbing in the bedroom he used to share with his wife. Every morning he would get up early and leave for work, as usual. Relatives and friends tried to persuade him to take some time off, but he stubbornly refused. He clung to his regular routines, which gave some semblance of order to the chaos. He didn't want to talk to a psychologist; he thought he could handle things on his own. Agnes worried about her father being so alone. She stayed home from school until after the funeral. She couldn't bear to see the look in everyone's eyes or answer all their questions.

The funeral was a horrible, anxiety-filled experience that she would prefer to forget. In the cemetery, when the two coffins were lowered together into the ground, side by side, she realized for the first time that Mamma and Martin were really gone for ever. They were never coming back. And it was suddenly all too much for her, as everyone stood there, all clad in black and with big white snowflakes falling around as they watched the coffins disappear into the dark earth. It felt as if strong hands had seized hold of her throat and were trying to strangle her. Everything went black and she collapsed on to the damp, cold ground.

Fortunately, during the weeks following the funeral, Agnes received a great deal of help from her friends, especially Cecilia. She would sit with Agnes for hours and let her talk about her mother and Martin. Cecilia never grew tired of listening or offering support. She helped Agnes as best she could. That was before Cecilia gave up on her. Agnes aches when she thinks about that now. She has no friends left any more.

She had found it touching that her father showed such concern for her. She knew that he must have been suffering terribly, yet he was careful not to burden her with his grief. Only on a few occasions had he wept openly after the funeral. For instance, when they finally began cleaning out Martin's room and packing his belongings in cardboard boxes.

Up until then, Pappa hadn't been able to throw anything out. He had washed Martin's clothes, which he'd found in the laundry basket, then neatly folded them and placed them back in the chest of drawers and wardrobe. But he left out one garment, a blue sweatshirt, which he would hold close, breathing in the scent, if he thought no one was watching. Agnes had also saved one of Martin's T-shirts. She kept it in a dresser drawer. Now and then she would bury her face in the fabric.

As long as Martin's scent lingered, part of him was still alive. A small fragment she could cling to for as long as it lasted. She had cried all night when she discovered that the smell had gone.

On that Sunday when they'd decided to pack up Martin's belongings, they were sitting in his room upstairs as the rain pattered on the rooftop. They put one thing after another into boxes. They worked slowly and carefully, both of them wanting to see and touch each item. It was excruciating. Martin was everywhere in that room. The bed he'd slept in, the desk where he'd done his homework, the TV on the wall. He'd been so proud of that TV, which he'd bought with the money he'd earned working at the ICA supermarket in the evenings and at weekends. Agnes remembered seeing all the notes he'd made in his schoolbooks and on his calendar. The writing was still there, but Martin was not. He was never coming back.

Cautiously, Agnes gets out of bed. With the thick down duvet draped over her shoulders, she pulls on another pair of tracksuit bottoms over the ones she slept in. Then she puts on two thin cotton shirts, a fleece jumper, her warm slippers and, finally, her mother's old knitted tunic that she used to wear out in the country. Agnes goes into the bathroom.

The radio is on downstairs in the kitchen, with the volume turned up, as usual. Yet she can hear her father talking on the phone. His insistent tone penetrates through the loud music, and she catches a few phrases here and there. 'But you have to understand, Katarina . . . Agnes needs . . . I know you're lonely . . . No, that won't work . . . We agreed that . . .'

Agnes stands still to listen. Her father's voice grows more urgent, then entreating and gentle, filled with tenderness, and finally annoyed and angry. 'But you can't possibly understand . . . Agnes is seriously ill . . . She needs me . . . I know it's difficult for you because you don't have children, but . . . children always come first in every situation, and that's how it should be, that's our duty as parents, we have a responsibility, even though you're having such a hard time understanding that.'

His voice rises, and now Agnes can hear every word.

'No, you can't come here. No, Agnes and I need to be alone. We've already talked about all of this. Don't call me again, do you hear me?'

Agnes hears him slam down the phone. The next second the radio shuts off. Nothing but silence.

She waits for a long time before she goes downstairs.

There was a sense of anticipation in the conference room as Knutas took his usual place at the head of the table. It wasn't enough that the director of Fashion for Life had just been found murdered. Over the last few hours, all sorts of speculation had been swirling through the air in the criminal division. Everyone was aware that there had been some new and important development in the investigation, but nobody knew what it was. Knutas had kept his office door closed, and talked on the phone all afternoon, and no one had dared disturb him. By the time he abruptly called together the team for an emergency meeting late on Monday afternoon, everyone was eager to hear what was going on.

All eyes were on the investigative team leader as he told them about the threatening message that had been sent to the editor of the fashion magazine.

'Apparently, it's not unusual for the editorial staff to receive hostile letters,' Knutas explained. 'According to the editor-in-chief, this might happen if the magazine shows a model wearing furs, and then the animal-rights activists react. Or people might accuse the magazine of being racist because there are rarely black models on the cover. Or the magazine is blamed for encouraging anorexia. But this particular letter arrived in their offices the day after Robert Ek was found murdered. And it wasn't sent to the editor-in-chief or to the magazine in general. The name on the address was the fashion editor Fanny Nord,' he told his colleagues.

Crime-scene technician Erik Sohlman was the first to comment on the actual message.

'Letters cut from a newspaper or a magazine – that's an age-old tactic. But the fact that the sender took the trouble to cut out the letters and yet wrote the name and address by hand seems awfully amateurish.'

'Although he didn't bother to cut out separate letters. Instead, he cut out whole words,' Knutas pointed out. 'Four words, in different colours and typefaces, but they seem to be from the same publication. Some sort of magazine. The fact that he wrote the address on the envelope by hand does seem to indicate that we're not dealing with a professional. Would it be of any use to contact a graphologist to study the handwriting?'

'Not really,' said Sohlman. 'We have nothing to compare it to. I assume that the letter has already been sent to the lab for DNA analysis. Where was it postmarked?'

'In Stockholm. Yesterday. So it was probably mailed after Robert Ek was murdered.'

'If the words were all cut out of the same publication, it shouldn't be impossible to work out which one it was,' said Jacobsson. 'Do you have a photo of the message?'

'They're sending us one,' said Knutas. 'And I'm sure the Stockholm police are working on that angle. But we shouldn't get our hopes up. Even if we identify the magazine, it doesn't mean it will give us a lead in the investigation. Just think how many magazines there are in this country.'

'The words didn't come from that fashion magazine?' asked Jacobsson.

'Apparently not.'

'What about fingerprints?' asked Sohlman.

'There are a lot of prints on the envelope, of course. But none on the card itself. The sender wore gloves.'

'So the question is whether the killer we're looking for sent the letter. And also, what does it mean that it was addressed to Fanny Nord?' the spokesperson, Lars Norrby, summarized with a solemn expression.

'What do we know about her?' asked Smittenberg, turning to Knutas.

'Not much,' he replied, leafing through his papers. 'She's twenty-nine years old, and in spite of her young age she has worked at the magazine for ten years. It seems she started as an assistant right after secondary school. Then she worked her way up and is now both a stylist and a fashion editor. Which means that the magazine pays her to work with models at fashion shows and on photo shoots. She also does the planning and layout for fashion spreads. And she writes articles as well.'

'Sounds like you managed to find out quite a lot,' said Smittenberg, smiling.

'Well, she was very talkative and pleasant, that Fanny Nord. Although nervous. She's worried that the person who sent the letter is a madman and that, for some reason, he's after her. And of course she's asking herself why it was addressed to her when the message says: "You are all killers."'

The main offices for Regional News were located in the big Swedish TV building near Gärdet in Stockholm. When Johan Berg stepped through the glass doors on the day before Christmas Eve, he felt his stomach flutter. The TV building never lost its thrill.

As he walked down the long corridor on his way to the editorial office, he ran into several former colleagues, who greeted him warmly, stopping him to chat. It took him fifteen minutes just to get to the Regional News office, so he was almost late for the morning meeting. Everyone else had already taken seats at one end of the big room. He was greeted with happy shouts and thumps on the back when he joined his co-workers. Johan was quite touched by such a welcome. Suddenly, it didn't matter that he had to work on the day before Christmas Eve. Unfortunately, Emma took a different view of the matter. She wasn't happy about being left with her mother-in-law in the house in Rönninge, even though they got on well together. He would have to make it up to her later. But he couldn't say no to his boss now that there were such major developments in the case. Max Grenfors had decided that Johan should come into the office and stay for as long as necessary, depending on how the murder investigation evolved.

As usual, Grenfors first reviewed the previous night's

news broadcast. Everyone discussed what was shown and offered critiques of what hadn't been entirely successful. The big topic of conversation, of course, was the murder of Robert Ek.

'It's going to be the top story today, too, if nothing else important happens,' Grenfors explained. 'Johan is going to be working with us here in Stockholm, and we're very happy about that. He'll be primarily responsible for research. Andreas and Madeleine will, of course, continue to cover the case, in cooperation with Johan. The morning papers gave the story front-page attention, and this is what the evening papers look like today.'

He reached for a copy of the major Stockholm paper. The front page was dominated by a big photo of Robert Ek's blanket-covered body being carried out of the agency's building. The headline, in big black type, said: 'FASHION FOR DEATH'.

'Very clever,' said Grenfors dryly. 'Yesterday, we covered the press conference and interviewed the police spokesman. Today, I want to focus on the agency staff. I'll leave that to you, Andreas. Madeleine can chase down the head of the investigative team and any criminologist or criminal profiling expert who can say something about what the next steps will be. I mean, both victims were viciously attacked with an axe. What does that say about the perpetrator? Johan will dig up any connections between Robert Ek and Markus Sandberg. That's a good start, until we see how things develop as the day goes on.'

'What are we doing about the Christmas party the agency had on Friday evening?' asked Johan. 'Doesn't it seem likely that Ek's murder was somehow connected with it?'

'So far, the police haven't confirmed anything like that, but you're right. Andreas, see what you can find out, since you're going to be talking to the staff.'

'Was Jenny Levin at the party?' asked Madeleine.

'I think so.'

'Shouldn't we try to get in touch with her? She was the one who found Sandberg, after all. And now she's involved in this case, too.'

Madeleine turned to Johan.

'Don't you have a contact for her?'

'Yes, I do. Emma is good friends with Jenny's mother, Tina Levin. I'll try to reach her today. Although she may have gone home to Gotland for Christmas. If so, Pia can always interview her. We've already inter-viewed her once before.'

'Good,' said Grenfors, clapping his hands. 'Let's get going.'

The meeting broke up. Together, Johan, Andreas and Madeleine went to get coffee out of the machine as they discussed how best to divide up the work. Johan realized how much he missed working with a large group of colleagues. The hubbub and fast pace. Chatting with co-workers from all the other editorial offices in the building. He'd been assigned a desk next to Madeleine's. He cast a surreptitious glance at her as they sat down. She was as attractive as ever. Hadn't changed a bit in the ten years he'd known her. She looked exactly the same, pretty and petite, with full breasts, big blue eyes and almost black hair. They'd had a brief fling years ago, before his relationship with

Emma got serious and he had ended up being posted to Gotland. He had to admit that Madeleine's feminine charms still had an effect on him.

He reached for the phone. Right now, he had other things to think about.

Knutas studied the words in front of him. He'd kept a photocopy of the threatening message that had been sent to the lab for analysis. Those four words stared up at him: 'You are all killers.'

He got out a magnifying glass from his desk drawer and examined the typeface. The words had been sloppily cut out, as if done in a hurry or under stress. Again, he read the brief sentence. What on earth did it mean?

He'd ordered back issues of the fashion magazine for the past year, thinking he might find a lead. The magazine was published fourteen times a year. He started in on the pile, spending the next few hours carefully leafing through each issue. He gave special attention to the pieces written by the editor-in-chief and to the fashion articles and columns that Fanny Nord had been responsible for.

When he was finished, he had a slight headache and he'd had his fill of fashion and beauty tips. He honestly wondered how women could stand all that rubbish. The readers of this magazine must be a small clique of wealthy city-dwellers who had nothing better to do than think about their appearance. It was like a competition to see who was the prettiest and most fashionable; a beauty pageant that never ended. He simply couldn't understand it. The women in the photos were as different from his down-to-earth Lina as they could possibly be. But he was well aware that the magazine's target audience was women just like her. A woman in her forties with an income high enough that she could afford to buy the clothes shown in the flashy pictures. If she was at all interested, of course.

He sighed heavily and put aside all the magazines except for the latest one. The Christmas issue had a supplement with the photos taken of Jenny Levin on Furillen. These were the last pictures that Markus Sandberg took before he became the victim of a murder attempt.

Against the bare backdrop and in the remarkable bluish-grey daylight, Jenny and the clothes she wore took on a special look. There was a bewitching atmosphere in those pictures, a captivating quality that drew the eye like a magnet. Fascinating, thought Knutas. Though he wasn't sure whether it was because of everything that had happened to the individuals involved since those photos were taken, or whether the images themselves possessed an inherent sense of mystery all on their own. In certain pictures, Jenny stared into the camera with a hint of a smile in her eyes and on her lips. In others, her expression was serious, her eyes seductive and intense. He forgot to look at the clothes she was wearing. He saw only her. Who was Jenny Levin, deep inside? It was easy to be enticed by her exotic appearance, and that was probably why she was a model.

Earlier in the day, Knutas had spoken to her on the phone at her parents' house. Her mother had begged the police to allow her daughter to celebrate Christmas in peace, so they had agreed to do the interview by phone. Jenny had no idea what had happened to Markus's mobile, so she could not have sent the text message. For some reason, Knutas believed her.

Again, he studied the pictures. Markus Sandberg had done the photo shoot, completely unsuspecting, putting his whole soul into his work to make the images as good as possible. A few hours later, he was almost killed. What was the connection?

At the end of the fashion spread there was an article about Sandberg. Quite a handsome fellow, thought Knutas. No wonder women were attracted to him. His face nicely suntanned and slightly weather-beaten. Clear blue eyes, his teeth as white as in a Colgate advert. The article was about Sandberg's career and how he'd gone from being a porn photographer with a tarnished reputation to a popular national celebrity and one of Sweden's hottest and most respected fashion photographers. Now it seemed unlikely that Markus Sandberg would ever be able to work again.

Knutas had spoken to Dr Vincent Palmstierna earlier in the day. If anything, Sandberg's condition was worse than before. He'd undergone yet more surgery, but that had resulted in further complications, and the doctors were still uncertain about the prognosis. The patient was still in a coma. It was tragic. Knutas put down the magazine and leaned back in his chair. He filled his pipe as he ruminated. Had the fashion spread from Furillen and the tribute to Markus Sandberg prompted the threatening letter sent to the magazine? He tapped in the phone number for the editor-in-chief and asked her when the Christmas issue had been published.

'We put that one together very quickly,' explained Signe Rudin. 'Usually, we require three months to do the layout, but after the horrible attack on Markus, we wanted to include the fashion spread as soon as possible. We didn't know how things would go for him. At first, it seemed very unlikely that he would survive. And since he'd done so much work for us over so many years, well—'

'You wanted to be the first to print his story?' Knutas finished her sentence.

'That's not at all how I'd express it,' said the editor-in-chief indignantly. 'We thought it was important to pay tribute to a photographer who'd been such a big part of the magazine. And it felt right to publish the photos from Furillen.'

'I was struck by the way a certain line was phrased in the article.' Knutas read it aloud: '"The last photographs taken by Markus Sandberg – this is how a master photographer worked." It sounds like he's already dead.'

'Considering the injuries that Markus has sustained, I think we can all agree that he's not going to do any more photography work. And you could also interpret that sentence to mean the last photographs he took before he was attacked. You'd understand that if you read the whole article.'

Signe Rudin was starting to sound cross.

'Right,' said Knutas curtly. 'But what I really want to know is how soon the public had access to this fashion spread. When did this issue go on sale?'

'The twelfth of December. The day before the Lucia Day celebration.'

'A week before Robert Ek was murdered,' said Knutas.

'That's right,' said the editor-in-chief.

He could now hear a slight nervousness in her voice.

'Do you think we received that threatening letter because of the article?'

'At this stage, it's mere speculation,' replied Knutas. 'But the fashion spread and the lengthy tribute to Sandberg might have provoked our perpetrator.'

'But how does Fanny fit into the picture? Why was the letter addressed to her? She had nothing to do with that fashion spread or the article. A different stylist was assigned to the Furillen photo shoot. And I wrote the article about Markus myself.'

'That's exactly what we need to work out.'

The glittering lights from Gannarve farm could be seen from far away. Torches burned on both sides of the lane of old, gnarled oaks that led up to the buildings. Lanterns had been hung on the outside of the old barn and the sheep barn, casting a soft glow in the winter darkness. The snowfall over the past week had added to the drifts already covering the fields, giving the residents of Gotland a white Christmas, which was highly unusual. On Christmas Eve, the farmhouse was full. Close family members and other relatives had come from far and wide to celebrate the holiday together. Candles were everywhere, fires blazed in all the fireplaces, and the whole house was fragrant with the smell of Christmas cooking, *glögg* and the special *pepparkakor* biscuits.

A cheerful hum of conversation filled the room as everyone sat down at the long dining table to enjoy the meal. Both Jenny's siblings were there, along with several cousins and other relatives, including her maternal grandparents. The dinner was so pleasant that, for long periods, Jenny managed to forget about all the awful things that had happened recently. It was great to be home.

She had been shocked to discover that she had spent Friday night in Robert Ek's bed. The very night that he

287

was murdered. She started to wonder if she was the target of some sort of conspiracy. Why was it on that particular night that she'd ended up being drugged, when that had never happened to her before? And why was Markus assaulted when he was on a photo shoot working with her? Why had the killer pretended to be her in the text that he sent to Robert, in an attempt to lure him to the agency? Was it just a coincidence that she had found herself nearby when both victims were attacked? Or was there some premeditated plot behind it all? Time after time, she thought about the man she'd seen outside the building on Kungsholmen.

She still hadn't told anyone about that incident. She didn't want to worry her parents. Yet the murder of Robert Ek had shaken her badly. Maybe she should talk to someone. Maybe even the police. Superintendent Knutas seemed very nice. Although that seemed a fairly drastic measure. He might even laugh at her. After all, the man hadn't done anything. He hadn't threatened her or even come close enough to speak to her. She was probably just imagining things.

She felt the warmth of everyone around her as she listened to them talking and laughing. All those horrible events couldn't possibly have anything to do with her. She was just a model who worked for the agency. One of many. She could even switch agencies if she liked. Although she wasn't yet prepared to go that far.

She needed a cigarette, but she didn't want to go out into the cold to have a smoke right now. Instead she accepted another glass of wine and decided not to think any more about all the craziness at the agency.

She had a couple of minor jobs in Stockholm during the coming week, and then she'd be going to New York for a prestigious show for Diane von Furstenberg. And after that, Paris. The whole world lay at her feet, and she had no intention of letting what had happened at the agency stop her. On Christmas Day she would go into Visby with all her old friends. She was longing to see them again and to be plain old Jenny. At least for a while.

'Are you all right, sweetie?' Agnes's pappa bends down and cautiously kisses her on the cheek as she lies on the sofa. He straightens the blanket that is wrapped around her.

'You're not cold, are you? I'll be back in plenty of time to watch *Donald Duck and His Friends Celebrate Christmas*, and then we'll have coffee. Are you sure you don't want anything?'

'No, thanks. I'm fine.'

It's Christmas Eve, and he's going to drive over to his parents' house to deliver their gifts. They wanted Agnes to come, too, but she doesn't have the energy. They live over in Klintehamn, and Pappa has explained to them that Agnes is too weak. She talked to her grandmother on the phone, and they agreed to see each other on Christmas Day instead. She hasn't seen them in several months.

The front door closes as her father leaves the house, and the only sound is from the TV. He has rented several films for her, since she doesn't feel up to doing much else. She is watching an American comedy that seems very stupid. She can't really concentrate. Pappa has piled pillows and blankets on the sofa. But she's feeling restless. Her gaze shifts, and she looks at the walls in the room. Her father has brought out the old

Christmas star they always put up in the living room. It's a bit fancier than the others. He has even bought a Christmas tree, a sweet but rather lopsided tree, which they decorated last night as they both shed a few tears. The holiday always brings back memories of Mamma and Martin. This is the third Christmas without them. It feels strange to be lying here on the sofa, home alone. It's like going back in time. The sofa, the wallpaper and the coffee table are all the same. Mamma embroidered the cloth on the table. Agnes leans forward and sniffs at it. As if it might still hold her mother's scent. On the bookcase there is a photograph of Mamma and Martin. Next to it, Pappa has set a family photo from Greece, taken the summer before the accident. The whole family, sunburned and laughing, with Naxos harbour in the background. They had rented a house on the Greek island with another family for two weeks. That holiday was the best they'd ever had. Agnes remembers how they would sit in the shade on the terrace in the late afternoon, playing cards after a long day at the beach. They had talked about going back there. But life had made other plans.

She feels tears welling up, but she doesn't want to cry any more. She sits up straighter, takes a sip of water from her glass, and tries to focus on the film. But she can't. She breaks out into a cold sweat and the prickling sensation in her hands and feet is getting worse. She's hungry. They've just had lunch, but when Pappa's mobile started ringing in his jacket pocket in the front hall and he left the room to take the call, she dumped half of her food in the rubbish bin. Afterwards, she felt guilty. She did want to get well. Deep in her heart, she really did. Maybe it was dumb to throw out her food. Maybe that's why she is feeling so weak right now. She ought to eat something. Just a little. Then she'll feel better.

She goes into the kitchen and opens the fridge. Hunger is screaming inside her. She's just going to look at the food. Just look. And maybe choose a small piece of something so she won't keep feeling so ill. The refrigerator light casts a gentle glow in the dim kitchen, and she hears its faint, familiar droning sound. She holds on to the door for support as she inspects what's inside. Everything looks so good. She sees cheese, ham, beetroot salad, Christmas sausages. Her eyes stop on a bowl of homemade meatballs, big and dark and slightly irregular in shape. Just like they're supposed to be. Just like the ones Mamma made, which Agnes always loved. Pappa said that he had made them according to Mamma's recipe. And they look just as good. But she can't eat them. If she does, she will be utterly lost. If she eats one, she won't be able to stop herself from eating the whole bowl. She wishes someone would come in and force her to eat them all. Then she wouldn't have to decide for herself. On the shelf underneath is a carton of cherry tomatoes. They seem less dangerous than anything else. She takes a few.

Then she discovers a dish of red Christmas apples on the worktop next to the fridge. Those crisp, shiny apples that are a dazzling white inside and taste so sweet. She chooses the smallest apple, takes out a plastic cutting board and a knife, and then sits down at the kitchen table. She cuts the apple into two pieces. It should be okay for her to eat half an apple; it doesn't have many calories, and she's really feeling awful. She eats half. It tastes better than she imagined. The moment she swallows the last bite, she realizes she has upset the entire day's routine. So she might as well continue. She eats the other half of the apple, too. It tastes amazing. She has to have another one. She gets up and brings over the entire dish, setting it on the table. She takes another apple, not bothering to slice it in half this time. Sweet apple juice runs out of her mouth. Greedily, she eats the whole apple. It tastes so good, yet she is filled with feelings of shame and disgust. She starts to cry. Now she has lost all control. She eats fast, finishing off two more apples as tears run down her face.

A suffocating sensation abruptly sets in. She feels stuffed. Her stomach is heavy. What on earth has she done? Quickly, she clears away all traces. She puts the dish back on the worktop with the few apples that are left. She wipes down the chopping board and washes the knife. She has to try to throw up. She doesn't usually do that, but it now seems the fastest solution. She goes to the bathroom, raises the toilet lid and kneels on the floor, sticking two fingers down her throat. She tries several times without success. Then she stuffs all the fingers of one hand as far down as they'll go, but she still can't vomit. Why is it so damn hard? She is sobbing in despair. She has to get rid of those apples. It's absolutely essential. Good Lord, she has eaten four of them.

She dashes out to the kitchen and pulls open the drawers, looking for some sort of tool. She takes a spoon back to the bathroom and sticks it down her throat. That should activate the gag reflex. But, after several attempts, the only thing that happens is that she feels nauseated and a tiny little piece of apple comes up. Nothing more.

Desperate and distraught, she finally stands up and catches sight of her face in the mirror. What she sees is frightening. Her face is bright red from the strain, her eyes are swollen and bloodshot. She realizes there is only one thing to do. Her mind is working frantically. How many calories are in an apple? She did throw out half of her lunch, so that means the situation isn't really so dire. She checks her watch. Quarter to one. At best, she has at least two hours before her father comes home. She does a quick calculation in her head, figuring out how many jumps and sit-ups she needs to do to burn off all the fruit. Then she'll be back where she started.

She knows she can do it.

She takes up position on the soft rug in front of the TV and starts jumping.

The temperature had plummeted in Stockholm, and it had snowed all night. Karin Jacobsson had booked a room at the same hotel in Gamla Stan where she usually stayed. She'd been given an address in Södermalm and the name of a café; that was all. She was supposed to turn up there at eleven o'clock on the morning of Christmas Eve.

For the first time, she was going to celebrate Christmas with Hanna, but not at home in her flat on Mariatorget. That much, Karin understood. The door slammed behind her as she stepped out of the hotel and into the quiet lane glittering with snow. Christmas decorations hung between the beautiful old buildings in Gamla Stan, and the windows of the small shops gleamed. The narrow streets were covered with snow, which creaked under her boots in the cold. A few other people were walking along the main street of Västerlånggatan. Almost everyone she met gave her a friendly look and nodded a Christmas greeting. That hadn't happened to her before in Stockholm – strangers saying hello. In a plastic carrier bag was her present for Hanna, the first she'd ever bought for her daughter. It hadn't been easy to choose what to give her, since she hardly knew Hanna. But the old enamel signs in her kitchen had given Karin an idea.

In a little antique shop, she'd found an old advertising sign for Göta chocolate. She had decided that was the perfect present. She didn't want to go overboard this first Christmas. She needed to proceed cautiously. The situation was still so fragile.

She walked south across the bridge at Slussen and continued up Katarinavägen. Across the water to the east was Djurgården and the frozen ground of Gröna Lund with its roller-coaster, now motionless. It would be months before the ride was once again filled with people. From there, it was easy to see how narrow the lanes were in Gamla Stan, spreading out like octopus arms from Stortorget in the centre and down towards the wide avenue of Skeppsbron. The rooftops and ground were blanketed with snow, and all the church towers reached for the sky.

She took a detour through Vitaberg Park, which was bustling with life. Children were sledging down the steep slopes, laughing and shouting, and their parents seemed to be having as much fun as the kids. Some youngsters had launched themselves headlong down an ice slide, and she was alarmed to see them bouncing over a rock at the bottom.

Karin continued through the pleasant neighbourhood locally known as Sofo, meaning south of Folkungagatan. Quiet streets with hardly any traffic but plenty of small shops, cafés, bakeries and restaurants.

She finally found the café she was looking for. It was on a corner, only a stone's throw from Katarina Church. In spite of the sign, which read 'Closed on Christmas Eve', the door was unlocked and a bell chimed as she stepped inside. Hanna popped up from behind the counter.

'Hi, Karin!'

'Hi! Merry Christmas!'

Hanna put down what she was holding.

'I see you found the place all right.'

'Sure. No problem. It's amazing how beautiful Stockholm is. I'm more impressed every time I come here. I walked through Vitaberg Park.'

'I know what you mean,' said Hanna with a laugh. 'A big crowd over there, right? We went sledging in the park yesterday. It was great!'

They gave each other a hug. A quick and slightly awkward embrace.

'So, have a seat. Would you like coffee?'

'Please.'

Karin took off her cap, gloves and scarf, then removed her big anorak, looking around. The room had an intimate feel to it. The walls were painted warm colours, and the café was furnished with old, worn sofas and easy chairs. The lamps all had interesting shades from the fifties and sixties. And there were candles everywhere. Against one wall stood a long table where stacks of plates, glasses and cutlery had been placed. A copiously decorated Christmas tree stood in the corner with a big pile of presents underneath.

'Looks like everything is ready for Christmas in here,' she called to Hanna, who had disappeared into the kitchen.

'You better believe it.'

'Why aren't you celebrating Christmas with your family?'

'Mamma and Pappa are spending the holiday in Brazil. They invited me and Alex to come with them, but neither of us wanted to go. He has a new girlfriend, and so do I.'

Hanna came back from the kitchen carrying a coffee mug, but she wasn't alone. She was holding hands with a young woman who Karin immediately recognized as Hanna's friend from the restaurant on Mariaberget.

'This is Kim,' said Hanna, and Karin instantly understood. She stood up to shake hands.

'Hi. I'm Karin. Hanna's biological mother.'

This was the first time she'd introduced herself as Hanna's mother. It felt good. Hanna handed her the coffee mug.

'So tell me,' said Karin, 'what's going to happen here in the café?'

'Well, the thing is,' Hanna began, 'Kim and I had this idea to arrange a Christmas for the homeless instead of just sitting in the flat and enjoying ourselves in our nice, cosy, safe bubble. So we rang up Situation Stockholm and various shelters. But they told us that if there's one day when the homeless don't need more meatballs and ham sandwiches, it's on Christmas Eve. Because so many of the churches in town organize a Christmas meal for them. So we asked ourselves: Who are the most needy in this society? Who are the ones that nobody ever thinks about? And we decided that it has to be women with children staying in residential shelters and LGBT refugees. There are a lot of gay young people from other countries in Stockholm, and they can't go back home because of their sexual orientation. They've been disowned by their families. And then there are also all the illegal workers who are invisible in society and hounded by the police. So we've invited them here for a Christmas celebration. Could you possibly forget that you're a cop for one night?'

'That's fine. Don't worry,' said Karin, smiling.

This wouldn't be the first time she had broken the rules.

They went into the cramped kitchen, which was overflowing with food. Ovenproof dishes held potatoes *au gratin*, as well as the traditional casserole Jansson's Temptation – sliced herring, potatoes and onions baked in cream. Next to them were multiple platters of pickled herring, salmon and boiled eggs. On the two hobs Karin saw meatballs frying in big pans and potatoes simmering in enormous pots. The kitchen benches were piled high with boxes of chocolates, cartons of table napkins and candles, tins of ginger biscuits, and loaves of sourdough and rye bread, along with packages of saffron buns.

'How did you manage to collect all this food?' asked Karin, impressed.

'We asked for donations. You wouldn't believe how generous people can be. We went around to the local supermarkets, bakeries, restaurants and shops. They showered us with food, and they also gave us a lot of really nice toys for the kids.'

'And how did you find the people that you've invited?'

'We have our contacts,' said Hanna slyly.

*

They started setting out the food. It was just about time for the party to begin. A short time later, a red-bearded man with a shaved head and tattoos covering both arms appeared in the kitchen doorway.

'Merry Christmas, girls. Anything to eat for a guy before we get started?'

Hanna gave him a hug and introduced him to Karin.

'This is Mats. He's going to be our doorman for tonight. You never know who might try to barge their way in. A lot of the women are scared to go out because their husbands may come after them. And there's always a risk that some drunk might turn up. Since there are going to be children here, we can't have any heavy drinking going on.'

She filled a plate with meatballs, beetroot salad and potatoes and handed Mats a Christmas beer.

'Here you are, Mats. But you'll need to sit out there in the café. As much as we love your company, you'll just be in the way here in the kitchen.'

An hour later, the first guests arrived. A short, dark-haired woman with four children of varying ages stopped outside the big café window that faced the street. She paused to glance in both directions before stepping inside. She had a frightened look in her eyes, and she seemed nervous. The children were well-dressed but silent, their expressions solemn. Much to Karin's surprise, Hanna began speaking fluent Spanish with the family. The woman's face lit up, and for a moment she seemed to forget her fear. It turned out that they were from Chile, and the woman had been abused and harassed by her ex-husband. After he threatened to kill both her and the children, they'd gone to stay at the shelter for battered women a few blocks away. Now, she'd mustered enough courage to venture out to attend this Christmas party, for the sake of her kids, who ranged in age from five to fifteen. Their eyes opened wide when they saw all the food and the big pile of presents under the tree.

Hanna pointed at the various dishes arranged on the buffet, and Karin assumed that she was explaining what they were. The woman held the hand of her youngest child. She murmured and nodded, constantly casting wary glances out of the window. After a while she seemed to relax, and they helped themselves to the food. Karin sat down at a table with them. The woman spoke only broken Swedish, but the kids were fluent in the language and had almost no accent, even though they gave only brief answers to Karin's questions.

People dropped in all evening. A few men, but mostly women and children living under assumed names. Three gay guys who looked to be no more than eighteen or nineteen sat down next to Karin. They wore elegant trousers and neatly pressed shirts. They told her that they were from Iraq and had been forced to flee; their lives had been threatened because of their sexual orientation. It wasn't immediately obvious that they'd been disowned by their families and were all alone in the world. But it was impossible to miss the sorrow in their eyes.

There were refugees from Eritrea, Pakistan, Iran and Afghanistan – all of them now stateless and unable to return home. And several Swedish women who were victims of domestic violence and who now lived in shelters in the city. Several Finnish women turned up with a big group of kids who were excited about the Christmas tree and all the treats, happy to be with adults who were kind to them.

Hanna was a big hit as Santa, handing out presents, to the delight of the children. Karin watched her as she sat with two kids on her lap, chatting with them in incomprehensible Spanish.

And she's my daughter, thought Karin.

The dance floor was crowded in the venerable restaurant Munkkällaren, which was located on Stora Torget in Visby. There were no traces of a peaceful Christmas celebration. The bar was filled with youths who'd been drinking heavily and had a great need to party with their friends after spending so much time with all their relatives during the holiday. The loudspeakers were reverberating with throbbing rock music that was as far from tranquil Christmas carols as you could get. Christmas Day was a big party day for all the Gotland young people – both those who had left the island to work or study on the mainland and had now returned to celebrate Christmas, and those who still lived here. It was an opportunity to get together and catch up on what everyone had been doing since summer. To hang out with friends they seldom saw any more.

Of course, most of them were familiar with what had been happening in Jenny Levin's life. She had enjoyed remarkable success, and the island was a small place; everyone talked about it whenever someone from Gotland became nationally known. And the shocking incident on Furillen, in which Jenny had played a key role, had naturally led to an explosion of magazine and newspaper articles over the past month. Her name and photo had figured in countless tabloids, and rumours were rampant on the internet. The attention only escalated after Robert Ek was murdered. The press devoted endless column space to speculation in which her name constantly appeared. Even though Jenny was afraid of running into reporters, she wasn't about to break with tradition and decline to go out with her friends on Christmas Day. She refused to allow her evening to be ruined. It was one of the high points of the year. Besides, the journalists probably didn't frequent Munkkällaren, which was the sacrosanct rendezvous for young people on Christmas Day.

Although, this year, things seemed different. It was noticeable the moment Jenny walked in the door. She had been careful to dress simply and with very little make-up so as not to give the impression of a diva. Yet everyone knew who she was, and she was aware that they were all staring at her. Her old friends tried to treat her the same way they always had, but she could still see what they were thinking. Had all the success and celebrity gone to her head? Was she really the same old Jenny? She realized that this was only natural, and she would have reacted the same way in their place, so she tried to relax and have fun. She recognized a lot of people, but most were merely acquaintances or friends of friends. The guys seemed even shyer than the girls and hardly dared come near her, though she could see the admiring look in their eyes. As if she were some sort of unapproachable icon. No doubt that would change with the increased alcohol intake.

Several times during the evening a girl that Jenny remembered from school looked in her direction, as if she wanted to talk to her but didn't dare. She was attractive and petite, with long blonde hair. She was standing at the bar with a glass of white wine, talking to some friends, but she kept glancing at Jenny. Finally, it became so obvious that Jenny went over to her.

'Hi. Do we know each other?'

The girl looked both surprised and embarrassed.

'No, we don't. We both went to the same secondary school, but I was a year behind you, so . . .'

'Oh, okay.' Then Jenny introduced herself and they shook hands.

'My name's Malin,' said the girl, smiling uncertainly.

'I had a feeling that you wanted to talk to me, but maybe I was mistaken.'

'No, you're right. I do want to. Talk to you, that is. Is that all right?'

'Of course.' Jenny felt both curious and uneasy.

'Could we sit down over there?'

Malin pointed to another room that wasn't as noisy.

'Sure.'

They sat down on a sofa. Malin's expression was completely different now as she turned towards Jenny.

'Do you know Agnes? Agnes Karlström?'

Agnes is examining her hands and arms as she waits for the first therapy session after Christmas. Her veins are big and very noticeable. They swell up if a person doesn't eat. And her whole body is covered with downy hair. Like a little monkey. When a person is starving, hair grows out of their pores. It's probably some sort of protective mechanism. She has started fretting about her appearance. At home, she had a shock when she saw herself in the mirror, since there are no mirrors on the ward. Her face wasn't so bad, but her body looked awful. The sunken chest, jutting bones and vertebrae; her gaunt shoulders, which made her think of starving children in Africa; her hips and the swollen little belly that she knows in her heart is not a result of fat but because the musculature of her body can no longer hold up her intestines, so they've sunk down into a heap at the bottom of her abdomen. She doesn't want to look like this.

Her reverie is interrupted as Per opens the door to invite her into his new office, which is at the very end of the corridor and much bigger than the one he had before. She feels warmth sweep through her at the sight of him.

'Hi. I see you found it.'

'Uh-huh. Hi.'

She's dismayed to feel herself blushing.

It's a bright room with a window facing the city centre and all the high-rise buildings nearby.

'You can even see my flat from here,' says Per, pointing to one of the small windows lined up in a symmetrical pattern on the smooth grey façade of a building. 'That's my kitchen window. Do you see the Christmas star? And the red curtains?'

He points, and Agnes turns to look.

'Uh-huh. I see them.'

She sits down on the visitor's sofa in the newly renovated office. It still smells of fresh paint.

'It's nice in here,' she said.

'So how was your Christmas?' he asks, looking at her with his tired blue eyes.

'Fine. It was great to go back home and spend time with Pappa. We had a good time together. I almost felt normal. It was a relief to get away from the clinic.'

'What did you and your father do?'

'He cooked, and we went for walks.' Then she corrected herself. 'Or rather, Pappa pushed me in the wheelchair. And we watched TV.'

'Did you see any of your old friends?'

'No,' she says dejectedly. 'Not that I expected anyone to get in touch with me, but I was sort of hoping to see Cecilia.'

'Did you happen to run into anybody else? Visby isn't a big place, after all.'

'A few people came over to say hello, but others didn't dare. They don't really know what to say. They just look away. But I did see Cecilia's big sister, Malin. I talked to her a little.'

'Okay. So how's your father doing?'

'Good, I think. He seems to be getting along okay. He has started running again, and he's thinking about taking up orienteering. He stopped all that after the accident, even though he has done orienteering his whole life. He talked more than usual, and even told a few jokes. But maybe he was just making an extra effort for my sake.'

'What did the two of you talk about?'

'About Mamma and Martin, and about life in general. About his girlfriend, Katarina. I don't really like her much.'

'I know that.'

'At first I was angry because he'd found a girlfriend so fast. As if Mamma didn't mean that much to him. Then I got scared that he'd care more about her than me. But I don't think that way any more.'

'What's changed?'

'I happened to overhear my father quarrelling with her on the phone. She was upset because he wouldn't let her come over to spend Christmas with us, and it was fantastic to hear Pappa cut her off like that. She didn't have a chance.'

'She came to the clinic on Christmas Eve.'

'She did?'

'Yes. She brought over a flower arrangement for the staff and then ended up staying all evening. She said she had nowhere to go except back home.'

'She doesn't have any children, but I know that she has a sister who lives in Norrland.'

'I see. Well, at any rate, she was here. And I was on

duty, so it was nice to see her. Not many people are here during Christmas.'

'What did you do?'

'Not much. Watched a little TV. Had some food. I don't think you should judge her so harshly. She hasn't done anything to you, has she?'

'No, I guess not. But the very fact that she exists is too much for me.'

Agnes feels her annoyance growing. She really has no desire to sit here talking about Katarina.

'There's one more thing,' she says.

'What's that?'

Agnes tells Per about her eating frenzy on Christmas Eve, even though she doesn't want to. The most shameful thing about it was losing control like that. A real nightmare.

'I understand how tough that must have been. But it's not so strange.'

'But I don't want to be like this. I don't want to go through that again. Never again.'

Agnes can feel the tears coming. She's so tired. So deathly tired of all this shit.

Per gets up from his desk and comes over to sit next to her on the sofa. He puts his arm around her shoulder and lets her lean against him.

'Go ahead and cry. But don't be sad. I'm going to help you. I promise you that. I'll do everything I can.'

Even while he was still on Lidingö Bridge Knutas could glimpse across the water the extraordinary sculptures placed on tall pillars and looming against the sky at Millesgården, the former estate turned art museum. He hadn't set foot there since he and Lina had spent their honeymoon in Stockholm almost twenty years ago. Back then, they couldn't afford to travel to some exotic destination but, for them, a trip to the capital and staying in a hotel had seemed exciting enough. Lina was from Denmark and had never been to Stockholm, while Knutas had been there mostly as a student, although occasionally his work had taken him to the city. So he'd never had the time or the desire to do any sightseeing. They had spent a marvellous summer week taking a boat ride around the archipelago, visiting the most important sights, and going for endless walks along the numerous wharfs. Millesgården had been a high point, with its fairy-tale garden built on various levels and the flagstone terraces set into the steep cliffs facing the water.

Jenny Levin had a photo shoot out there that was going to last all day, and Knutas wanted to take the opportunity to speak to her in person about the circumstances surrounding Robert Ek's death. Their brief phone conversation on the 23rd had proved less than satisfactory.

Knutas parked and then got out, to stand in bewilderment in front of the shuttered entrance. A sign stated that the museum was closed on Mondays. There wasn't a soul in sight. Across the way was a hotel, but that, too, seemed silent and deserted. Knutas stamped his feet on the ground. It had been a cold night, with the temperature dropping to minus twenty Celsius. Suddenly, a wrought-iron gate opened and a long-haired man wearing green overalls came out. Knutas introduced himself and showed the man his police ID.

'Follow me,' said the man. 'They're taking the photos indoors. It's too cold out here.'

They went inside the building that had once been Carl Milles' home and proceeded through a gallery with a beautiful marble floor and sculptures placed in niches along the walls.

The photo-shoot crew was working in a big studio, an immense white space with a ceiling that looked to be close to ten metres high. The room was filled with plaster models of Milles' sculptures. In the centre towered an impressive work that Knutas recognized: *Europa and the Bull.* Leaning against the bull's stout neck was Jenny Levin, though he could hardly recognize her. She was wearing a horizontally striped dress that was practically a body stocking and bright-blue shoes with sky-high heels. Her hair was pulled up into a tall, cone-like shape on top of her head. She was heavily made up, and she kept changing her pose in front of the camera with slight, deliberate movements. An entire array of spotlights had been positioned around the room, and the photographer had three assistants who ran about fine-tuning the lights and holding up reflectors. The make-up artist and stylist watched everything like hawks, and in between takes they would rush over to Jenny to touch up her make-up, apply more powder and adjust her dress. Knutas was fascinated by the whole drama. He'd never seen a photo shoot before, and he was impressed by Jenny's professionalism in front of the camera. It was obvious she was in her element.

It took a few minutes for her to notice him. She froze for a moment but then calmly continued to pose.

'Okay. I'm happy with that,' said the photographer after a while. 'Good job.'

'Maybe we should break for lunch,' suggested the stylist. 'What time is it?'

'Five past twelve.'

'Okay. Lunch until one o'clock. There's food at the hotel next door.'

Knutas went over to Jenny.

'Hi. I'm glad you have a break right now. I need to talk to you.'

'You'll have to do that while Jenny eats lunch,' the stylist interrupted them. 'We're on a really tight schedule.'

'That's fine with me.'

'I just need to change first,' said Jenny.

'I'll wait.'

A few minutes later, they walked across the court-yard to the hotel, where a buffet lunch was laid out.

Knutas and Jenny each filled a plate with food and then sat down at a vacant corner table some distance away from the others.

'There are a few things I need to clear up. That's why I wanted to meet up with you today,' Knutas began. 'You told me on the phone that you didn't know what happened to Markus's mobile. Is that right?'

'Yes. I wasn't the one who sent that text message. It wasn't me. I haven't seen Markus's mobile since the photo shoot on Furillen. I've tried to remember if I saw it in the cabin, but I don't think I did.'

'And you have no idea who could have sent that text to Robert Ek?'

'Absolutely not. I think this whole thing is horrible.'

In spite of her make-up, Jenny looked pale, and she was nervously fidgeting with her knife and fork.

'According to the medical examiner, Ek died sometime between one and five o'clock on Saturday morning. What I want to know is this: what were you doing during that time?'

Jenny's eyes filled with tears, but Knutas refused to be swayed.

'Where were you between 1 and 5 a.m. on Saturday, 20 December?'

'Do you think I did it?' she stammered in fright. 'Do you think I murdered Robert?'

'It's too soon for us to be drawing any conclusions. But we need to know where you were during that time period.'

Jenny pushed aside her plate of food and took several sips of water. She refused to look him in the eye.

'Let me think. I was very drunk. And there were so many people. A bunch of us spent a long time in the club, talking. I think Robert was there, too.'

Knutas nodded encouragingly.

'Go on.'

'Some guy invited me to dance, so I did. I don't know for how long. Then we sat down on a sofa somewhere. I think it was in the VIP lounge. And a lot of other people came in.'

'Who were they?'

'I have no idea. I didn't know them. After that, my memory is pretty hazy. The fact is that I think someone put something in my drink, because I really don't remember anything after that.'

'Where did you spend the night?'

Jenny turned to look out of the window. She hesitated for a long time before answering.

'To be honest, I have no idea. I woke up in bed with some guy, and I didn't even know his name. It was embarrassing. He was still asleep when I slipped out of the flat. I wanted to get out of there as fast as possible.'

'Where was this flat?'

'Somewhere in Östermalm, on a little side street. I'm not all that familiar with Stockholm. I wandered about for a while, and suddenly I found myself in Karlavägen and then I knew where I was. I took the subway to the agency's flat on Kungsholmen.'

'Was anyone else there?'

'No. It was empty, and I was grateful for that. I felt terrible all day.'

'What did you do?'

'I just stayed indoors, except for going out to rent a

film and buy a pizza. The same thing on Sunday. On Monday I went home.'

'And you really have no idea who you spent the early-morning hours of 20 December with?'

Jenny gave Knutas a worried look.

'No, I don't.'

'Is there anyone who might know? Someone who was at the club?'

'I don't think so. The place was packed.'

'So that means you have no alibi for the time of the murder. Is that right?'

Knutas was interrupted by the stylist calling from the photo crew's table.

'Five more minutes, then it's back to work!'

Jenny looked like she was going to throw up.

Signe Rudin had just got to the office when the post was delivered. Ever since the arrival of that threatening letter, her heart had skipped a beat every time she emptied Fanny's in-tray. She was glad that Fanny had gone abroad. It bothered her that the letter had been addressed to her colleague personally; she was one of the best editors Signe had ever worked with in her long career. It would have been better if she'd received that letter herself. She was more thick-skinned. Signe had hoped that the letter would be a one-off, but the moment she looked inside Fanny's in-tray, she realized that was not going to be the case. She recognized at once the sprawling and somewhat feeble handwriting. She took a deep breath, then opened the envelope. Words cut out of a magazine, just like before. This sentence was equally short. 'I am a killer.' She automatically turned the paper over, but there was nothing on the back.

Thoughts began whirling through her head. There were a few people working in the editorial offices, but no one in a position of authority. No one she could turn to for advice.

Should she ring the police herself? She read the brief sentence again. It could only be regarded as a threat. But what did this person mean? 'You are all killers.' 'I am a killer.' Should she call Fanny and tell her about this letter? She had the right to know. Yet Signe didn't want to bother her while she was on holiday in Thailand. She really needed time to unwind. Fanny had sent a few text messages to ask if anything new had happened, or if the murderer had been caught. Unfortunately, Signe hadn't been able to give her any positive news. She couldn't understand why the police hadn't made any progress in the case.

Filled with annoyance, she studied the envelope again. What kind of idiot would do this? And why on earth would he be targeting the magazine, or rather, Fanny Nord? If it was the same person, that is. The sender could be anybody; maybe someone who was goaded by all the attention the crime had attracted.

Suddenly, Signe Rudin had an idea. She put down the letter, closed the door to her office, and pulled down the blinds on the window facing the corridor. That was the signal that she didn't want to be disturbed. Next she switched off her phone for incoming calls and set her mobile on vibrate. Then she began looking through the file folders on the bookcase. She had decided to wait to ring the police.

First, there was something she wanted to check out on her own.

After his visit to Millesgården, Knutas drove to police headquarters on Kungsholmen. From there, he rang Dr Palmstierna to find out how Markus Sandberg was doing. There was no change in his condition. With each day that passed, hope diminished that Sandberg would be able to help by shedding any new light on the investigation.

Knutas had arranged to have lunch with Kihlgård and Jacobsson. Karin had now been in Stockholm for a week, and he was looking forward to seeing her. He had missed her more than he liked to admit. He didn't feel the same satisfaction with his work when she wasn't in the office – although he was annoyed that she had such an effect on him. He was ashamed of the emotions that had been provoked in him when he saw her in town with that man before Christmas. He realized that he must be Karin's new boyfriend. Knutas felt like a jealous teenager, even though there was nothing going on between him and Karin. And never had been. He really couldn't understand his reaction.

When they met in Kihlgård's huge office, she gave him a warm hug. She felt so small in his arms.

'Hi. Long time no see.'

'Uh-huh. I think it's time for you to come back home, before you get too comfortable here.'

'Not a chance,' said Jacobsson with a laugh. 'I'm planning to fly home tomorrow.'

'You are?' he said, sounding absurdly overjoyed. 'Then maybe we can travel together.'

'Okay, enough of the small talk,' Kihlgård interrupted them. 'We need to compare notes over lunch. And I'm starving. Let's go.'

They went across the street to a local pub. Knutas told them about his meeting with Jenny Levin at Millesgården.

'So that means she doesn't have an alibi for the night of the murder,' said Kihlgård, chewing on a piece of freshly baked bread as they waited for their food. The place was noisy but pleasant. Kihlgård had taken the trouble to book a table at the back.

'She doesn't have an alibi for the assault on Furillen either,' he went on.

'I have a really hard time picturing Jenny Levin being involved in any way,' said Jacobsson with conviction. 'Besides, we know that it was a man who attacked Sandberg. That's what the lab determined from the blood on the clothes that were found in the fisherman's shed.'

'Keep in mind that the clothes could have been planted there to throw us off the scent,' Kihlgård pointed out. 'By a strategically minded and far-sighted perpetrator – male or female. I know that sounds like a long shot, but we can't rule out the possibility.'

'At any rate, the same murder weapon was not used in both cases,' Jacobsson said. 'We've had that confirmed by the lab. The axe that was found in the rubbish bin is not the one used on Furillen.'

'Any evidence?' asked Knutas eagerly.

'No fingerprints, unfortunately. And blood only from the victim.'

Jacobsson took a swig of her light beer, thinking, and looked at her colleagues.

'Something doesn't add up when it comes to Jenny. I have a feeling she has nothing to do with any of it. Something else is behind all this. She's probably embarrassed about spending the night with some strange guy when she doesn't even know his name. It sounds like a stupid thing to do.'

'Don't forget that she's only nineteen,' said Knutas.

'Right. I know. But she's also a girl who has recently been discovered and is on her way to becoming a top model. So I have a hard time believing that she would get mixed up in such vicious attacks. Besides, she was in love with one of the victims and very fond of the other. Apparently, she and Robert Ek had an unusually close relationship. As friends, I mean.'

'Maybe from her point of view,' said Kihlgård, 'but what about him? All it took was a brief text message for him to leave the party, rush over to the agency, and open a bottle of champagne. He didn't exactly get what he was hoping for, the poor devil. Speaking of which, I can tell you that we've reviewed all the footage from the surveillance cameras in the area, and we didn't find a thing. Ek isn't in any of the pictures.'

Kihlgård cast an envious glance at the plates piled high with great-smelling food that were being served at the next table. His own lunch hadn't yet arrived.

'Okay. So what about the Finnish woman Marita Ahonen?' asked Jacobsson.

'Our Finnish colleagues finally got hold of her. She was summoned to an interview at police headquarters in Helsinki, but she never showed up. They're still trying to track her down. But I don't really put much faith in that lead. It seems too far-fetched. She may well have been angry with Markus Sandberg because he'd dumped her, but why would she want to kill Robert Ek?'

'Because he was head of the agency she worked for?' suggested Jacobsson. 'Maybe she was disappointed that she didn't get more support from her employer. And there could always be something else we don't know about.'

'We've already asked Ek's wife and the agency staff, and none of them knows of any long-standing quarrel between Marita and Ek. I know we need to keep an open mind, but I don't think we should waste energy on a bunch of irrelevant rubbish. This investigation is already taking us in a million different directions.'

Kihlgård's face lit up when he saw the waitress approaching.

'Our food is here!'

They had ordered fish casserole with scampi, and all three hungrily dug into the beautifully served food.

'Maybe we're looking in totally the wrong direction,' said Jacobsson after a while. 'When it comes right down to it, maybe these attacks have nothing to do with Sandberg and Ek personally. It could be that we should disregard their private lives, their family relationships, and any dubious events in their past. The key to the whole thing could be in that threatening letter that was sent to the magazine.'

'Fanny Nord, who received the letter, has gone to Thailand. At least we managed to interview her before she left. But, unfortunately, she didn't have much to add. She couldn't recall ever feeling threatened or harassed, nor could she think of anything out of the ordinary happening recently,' said Kihlgård.

'But let's take a moment to consider the message,' said Jacobsson. '"You are all killers." Why would anyone send something like that to an editor of one of Sweden's biggest-selling fashion magazines?'

Knutas wiped his mouth on his napkin.

'When is Fanny Nord expected back in Sweden?'

Agnes and Per are sitting on one of the sofas, playing cards. She is studying him, although he doesn't seem to notice. She likes his face. He has a distinctive appearance. His eyes always look tired, as if he stays up too late or is thinking about something else when she talks to him, though she knows that's not true. He has small, pale hands with a tattoo on the back of one of them, some sort of beetle between his thumb and index finger. His hair is ash blond and cut so short that it's almost bristly. He has blue eyes with long lashes, a fair complexion and thin, pale lips. He has a long face and a small, nicely shaped nose. Not a trace of pimples or any other blemishes on his skin. Almost no sign of stubble. One earring. Today, he's wearing a checked shirt and a pair of dark DKNY jeans that look brand new. His white trainers also look new. He's thin but quite muscular, and not very tall. Maybe only two inches taller than her.

Her thoughts are interrupted when a nurse comes into the room.

'Agnes, you have visitors.'

'What? Now?'

She looks up in surprise, first at the nurse, then at Per. It can't be her father. He's on Gotland with Katarina.

'Who is it?'

323

'Two girls. They said they're friends of yours from Gotland. I thought I recognized one of them.'

Agnes gives a start. How is this possible? None of her old friends have visited her even once since she's been at the clinic. The only person who came to see her was Markus, who visited right after she was admitted. As if he suddenly had a guilty conscience. He brought her flowers but clearly felt awkward and uncomfortable, and he hadn't known what to say. It was embarrassing and just made her feel bad. Finally, Per had asked him to leave.

Most of her friends had disappeared long before she ended up here. After the accident, many of them hadn't known how to act around her or how to offer sympathy, and they gradually retreated. The others left when she got ill, and the anorexia took over. She knew that it was largely her own fault. She was the one who had withdrawn. She could no longer think of anything else to do; she didn't even try to keep up with the activities of her friends. Eventually she became so obsessed with exercising and controlling what she ate that she had no time or energy for anything else. But still.

The person who had disappointed her most was Cecilia, her best friend. They had stuck together through thick and thin in school but, in the end, Cecilia had also turned her back on her old friend. Agnes had made a few clumsy attempts to restore contact, but with no response. When she was at home for Christmas, she hadn't even felt like trying. The closest she'd come to Cecilia was when she and her father had run into her big sister, Malin, and they'd exchanged a few words. And she'd once seen Cecilia off in the distance with some old classmates in the Östercentrum shopping mall. But she couldn't bear to go up to her. Sitting there in her wheelchair, Agnes had pulled up the blanket that was draped over her legs and then sunk further down into her thick scarf, pretending not to see them.

Now, she drops the cards she's holding so they fall on to the table.

'Who do you think it is?' she asks Per.

'I have no idea.'

He gives her a smile as he gathers up the cards. He seems happy for her. Agnes glances at the clock on the wall. It's 4.05 in the afternoon, and darkness has already fallen outside.

'Do you think it's Cecilia?'

She looks at him, filled with hope, her cheeks burning.

'Maybe. That would be nice.'

'If it's Cecilia, then I think it's a sign.'

She gets up from the sofa. She feels like she could almost race out of the room, down the long corridor, and over to the entrance and the room where all visitors have to wait for the patient they've come to see. She proceeds under her own steam, doesn't want to use a wheelchair. I wonder how I look, she thinks, glancing down at her worn slippers and her shabby cardigan. Her tracksuit bottoms have a small hole in one knee. She discreetly sniffs at her armpits. She hasn't showered today; she usually waits until evening. Her hair is lank and wispy; she has lost most of it due to malnutrition. She senses Per trailing behind her. He's probably curious to see what Cecilia looks like, since Agnes has talked so much about her. In her mind, she pictures Cecilia in a succession of idyllic images, remembering all the fun things they did together – summers spent out in the country, shopping in town, giggling and whispering in bed when they slept over at each other's house, and the way Cecilia had offered her support after the accident. And her undisguised joy when Agnes won the modelling contest.

By the time she reaches the door to the waiting room Agnes is brimming with excitement, and her heart is leaping in her chest. So she pauses for a moment to lean against the door jamb, and then stares mutely at the two people sitting inside. All sense of anticipation seeps away, to be replaced by a dull and leaden disappointment.

One of the young women hesitantly stands up.

'Hi, Agnes,' she begins. 'I've thought so much about you since the last time we met, and I just wanted to stop by and say hello. I'm still in Stockholm for the New Year holiday, so I thought that . . .'

Agnes stares vacantly at Cecilia's older sister, Malin. She can't understand why Malin is here and not Cecilia. Without saying a word, she shifts her gaze to the other visitor, who has also stood up. She is tall and radiantly beautiful, her red hair hanging loose over her shoulders, shining in the light from all the Advent candles and Christmas stars. Agnes recognizes Jenny Levin from the fashion photos she saw in the magazines when she was at home for Christmas. There are no such magazines here on the ward, but the supermodel from Gotland had been on the TV news. And she had also been with Markus. The man who had robbed Agnes of her virginity as light-heartedly as he brushed his teeth. The man who had given her an inferiority complex about her body. The man who was partially responsible for her being in this clinic right now, looking like a living skeleton. And here she stood. Jenny Levin herself. Dazzling everybody with her beauty.

'Oh, this is Jenny,' Malin hurriedly added. 'She's from Gammelgarn and went to the same secondary school we did. And she works for the same agency you used to work for. Fashion for Life.'

Jenny smiles nervously as she shakes Agnes's hand.

'Hi. Nice to meet you.'

Agnes manages to murmur something that's meant to be a greeting. Her head is spinning. She's trying to understand why Jenny Levin is here. The nurse who announced the arrival of the two young women comes to her rescue.

'How nice for you to have visitors from home, Agnes. Come in. Can we offer you anything? Would you like coffee?'

'Yes, please,' the young women say in unison and then gratefully follow the nurse, their high heels clacking. Out of the corner of her eye, Agnes notices that Per has come to a halt in the middle of the corridor. He looks completely bewildered by these imposing feminine creatures. No wonder, thinks Agnes. Such a cruel contrast between these wholesome-looking beauties and the ghosts who roam the halls. She can hardly fathom that they've even been allowed to come inside. They seem to fill the whole ward with their presence.

Without knowing how it happens, all three of them are sitting at a table in the deserted day room with cups of coffee and a plate of ginger biscuits. Agnes stirs her coffee. She is looking down at the table and can't think of a single thing to say. Malin is chattering nervously.

'Cecilia sends her best wishes. She couldn't come with me to Stockholm this time because she has a floorball tournament – it's the Midwinter Cup, you know. It's always between Christmas and New Year's.'

Agnes used to play floorball, too, on the same team as Cecilia. They've done that ever since their first year at school. And she has competed countless times in the Midwinter Cup. She makes an effort to sound polite.

'Thanks. How is she?'

'Good. Really good,' Malin hastens to say. She seems grateful that the conversation finally seems to be rolling along after the fumbled beginning. 'She complains about all the studying she has to do, says it's much harder than before. But she's done brilliantly. And she has a boyfriend now. She's dating Oliver, you know. He was in the same class with you.'

'Oh.'

'Not bad, huh?' Malin laughs shrilly. 'He was the cutest boy in school, and he still is. They've been together for two months.'

'Oh.'

Agnes fidgets. She doesn't want to be reminded of everything she could have been doing. Or who she used to be. Jenny clears her throat and leans forward. She holds out a package wrapped in shiny paper.

'This is from the agency. Everyone wanted to say hello.'

Agnes slowly unwraps the gift. It takes some effort to remove the ribbon. Her fingers won't really obey her properly, and the wrapping paper has been well taped. Per, who is standing a short distance away, pretending to be busy with something, hurries to bring her a pair of scissors. Inside is a box. She opens the lid and finds a card with a cheerful message to get well soon. All the staff members have signed the card, except for Robert Ek, of course. Agnes feels her blood run cold.

She takes out the paper under the card and gasps at what she sees in the box. A stack of pictures of herself. Professional photographs from various photo shoots she did before she fell ill. A close-up of Agnes with her hair slicked back and wearing trendy sunglasses. Agnes in a bikini. Agnes wearing an evening gown and high heels. A picture taken in a studio, showing her laughing merrily at the camera, wearing only black tights and a bright-pink camisole. Her hair is thick and glossy.

Agnes is breathing hard. She feels the room start to sway, the photos grow blurry; Malin's voice fades into the distance as she eagerly comments on the pictures: 'Look how beautiful you are in this one, and here . . .'

Something rises up inside Agnes, surges into her throat. The scream echoes off the walls in the ward as the two well-dressed young women exchange frightened looks and then scramble to gather up their things, while Per and the other nurse rush forward and seize hold of Agnes. Someone stuffs the pictures back in the box and puts it away. The two visitors jump up from the sofa and flee to the hallway, murmuring words of alarm. There, they fumble with the door and finally leave the ward. Only then does Agnes stop screaming.

After the visit, Per sits on the edge of her bed and holds her hand. He brings dinner to the room and stays with her until she falls asleep.

Signe Rudin had begun going through all the assignments Fanny Nord had handled during the past year to see if she could find some reason for the threat, but she hadn't had time to complete the task.

On the morning of New Year's Eve she got up early and left home after drinking a quick cup of coffee and eating a piece of toast. She left a note for her husband, who was still asleep, asking him to buy some champagne and a bouquet of flowers for their hosts later that evening, since they'd been invited out for dinner that day. Signe was a very determined woman, and she liked to finish whatever she started.

She still hadn't found anything significant. Yet her review of all the files had proved eye-opening in another respect. Fanny had worked incredibly hard during the past year. Signe needed to find some way to reward her and show her appreciation. Maybe a weekend trip for her and her boyfriend to a romantic country hotel, or maybe a day at a spa. She was worth it.

Signe decided to go even further back in time. She glanced at her watch. She and her husband wouldn't have to leave Stockholm until after lunch in order to head for the archipelago to visit their friends.

When she came to October of the previous year,

she found a modelling job which the magazine had uncharacteristically scrapped, even though all the work had been done. This rarely happened, since the profit margin was so small and a photo shoot was expensive. Not because of the models' fees, since they were often poorly paid. The editors frequently exploited the fact that a fashion spread in this particular magazine could raise the models' profile, and it could prove valuable on their professional résumés. So the models willingly worked twelve hours for a measly few thousand kronor. The real expense was in all the preparatory work, all the time spent in setting up the site, getting the clothes, and looking for the right model. The photographer demanded a sizeable hourly fee and often had to be hired locally. A typical one-day photo shoot cost the magazine at least forty thousand kronor, so it was highly unusual simply to chuck the work aside. But, in this instance, that was what had happened, and that made it memorable. Now Signe recalled why.

The girl that the agency sent was too fat. They had expected a model to wear the usual size eight, but she'd been closer to a ten. Signe clearly recalled how Fanny had complained when she came back from the assignment. None of the clothes had looked good, so the photographer had been forced to take partial shots when they actually needed a lot of full-length shots. Fanny had worked like a dog to get the clothes to fit, unbuttoning the trousers, leaving the shirts untucked even though they weren't meant to be worn that way. She had been forced to toss out half of the collection and use some replacement garments, simply because the clothes were too small. The shoot had also taken far too long. The model was aware of the problem, of course. She'd felt awkward and uncomfortable, which further hindered their work. Finally, she started to cry, and Signe could hear Fanny's voice when she reported on the whole fiasco:

'I tried to comfort her. I told her that it was the agency's fault, not hers. They have to realize that they can't send over a model who is too big. Nothing fits well, and it's impossible for the photographer to get any good shots. Nobody can do their job. And it's no fun for the model either. I gave the agency a piece of my mind afterwards, and it turned out, as I thought, that they'd underestimated her waist and hip measurements when speaking to us earlier. And the girl had also gained weight since she'd been photographed for the agency file. Good God. We really tried our best to make it work, but I'm afraid we're not going to be able to use any of those photos.'

It turned out that the pictures just weren't up to standard; no matter how much the photographer retouched and edited them, they weren't very good. So, finally, the magazine was forced not to publish them.

Signe Rudin couldn't remember who the photographer was. She checked the notes to see who had been working that day. When she saw the name, her mouth went dry. Markus Sandberg. Signe paused a moment before reading further. The model worked for the agency Fashion for Life, which was run by Robert Ek. Her name was Agnes Karlström. What had happened to her? She tapped in the phone number for the agency and, as luck would have it, one of the staff members who did the bookings was in the office. Signe asked her for information about Agnes. The woman, who was a new employee, didn't know the name, but she offered to look the model up on the computer.

Signe waited tensely.

'Agnes Karlström worked here for only about six months, and never full time,' said the woman on the phone several minutes later. 'She was so young that she was still in school. But during a period of a few months I see that she had a lot of photo shoots, and things seemed to be going well for her. Then the jobs dropped off drastically. Someone's added a note here. Wait just a moment.'

For several seconds there was only silence. Then the woman was back.

'In fact, she was let go. It seems she was suffering from anorexia.'

On the last day of the year Jenny woke up early in the flat on Kungsholmen. She went into the kitchen to make coffee. One of the bedrooms was occupied by a Finnish model she knew but, thank goodness, she was still asleep. Jenny had no desire to chat.

Malin had invited her to come with her and a friend to a big party in Södermalm. Jenny had already received invitations to various trendy gatherings, but she knew that a lot of models and other people in the fashion world would be attending. She just couldn't handle that sort of thing at the moment. Especially after visiting Agnes Karlström at the anorexia clinic the day before.

She thought about the repulsive sight of that bony, hollow-eyed girl who looked like a twelve-year-old. Jenny had only seen her in fashion photos, so she hadn't expected such a drastic difference in her appearance, even though she knew that Agnes was anorexic. Jenny had never met a skinnier person in her life. It was terrifying when she thought how Agnes had looked only a year earlier. How in the world could something like that happen?

Then she'd been dumb enough to think that she could do something positive for Agnes by visiting her and showing that she cared, that the agency cared.

Maybe she'd imagined that the pictures might have a positive effect, that Agnes would be encouraged to start eating again if she was reminded of how she could look, and of all the possibilities that would be open to her in life.

Malin had persuaded Jenny to come along, even though she didn't actually know Agnes. She was convinced that Agnes would appreciate knowing that people still remembered her, that her old friends on Gotland were thinking about her. And she also thought that Agnes would be happy to see that the agency cared, and that Jenny had taken the trouble to visit. How wrong they both were.

Agnes hadn't seemed to understand the purpose of their visit at all. She had screamed like a madwoman. Her eyes were completely wild; maybe she really was mad – mentally ill in some way. A person didn't end up in that sort of place without there being a reason for it.

Jenny shook off her uneasiness and paused in front of the mirror. That made her feel better. She really *was* attractive; now, she understood what it was that everyone admired about her. She looked lively and alert, even though she had just got out of bed. The sun was cresting the horizon, and she could make out a few pale rays of light. She couldn't remember the last time she'd seen the sun, so she decided to go jogging. She had a good pair of shoes for running in winter.

I should make use of the light, she thought. And there's no way I'm going to let all this shit bring me down. I'm only going to allow good things to happen today, and I plan to be happy. At least until I fall into bed tonight, after a party that's hopefully lots of fun.

Feeling invigorated by these thoughts, she gulped down a cup of coffee then put on long underwear and her lined jogging coveralls. A cap, gloves, spiked trainers, and she was ready to go. It was only eight thirty in the morning, and the cold, fresh air gusted towards her as she stepped out of the door. She started running towards the city hall and then continued along Norr Mälarstrand. She smiled at the sun, and her steps felt as light as air. At Rålambshov Park she turned off and ran under Väster Bridge and out on to the promontory near Smedsuddsbadet. The sandy beach was covered with snow.

Unbelievable that people actually went swimming here in the summer, she thought. In the middle of the city. She followed the rocky path along Fredhäll and then ran back through the park and along Norr Mälarstrand. When she reached the front door of her building, she paused to catch her breath. Standing near the bank of the canal, she spent some time stretching her muscles.

On the wharf, which stuck out some way into the water, there was a bench. A couple sat there, arms around each other and their backs to her. They seemed to be in love, sitting there so close to each other. Jenny felt a pang of jealousy. She longed to experience that again, to be part of a couple. To be hugged and loved. She was looking forward to the party this evening, hoping that it would stop her thinking about such things at least for a little while. She raised one leg, grabbed the heel with both hands and stretched the muscles in her thigh, staring at the couple on the bench. It was an effort to keep her balance. She noticed they were sitting very still.

When she switched legs, something happened. The man suddenly turned to face her and waved. He picked up the woman's arm and waved that, too.

That was when she realized the woman was not a real person. It was a doll. A photo had been taped over the face. Jenny looked at the picture. When she understood what it was, she lost her balance.

She was staring at herself.

It was snowing heavily in Visby on the last day of the year, covering the streets and the buildings in a thick white blanket. Knutas and Lina were going to welcome in the New Year with good friends in Ljugarn. Their children were old enough now to have made their own plans. But the whole family started the day by having a late breakfast together in their house on Bokströmsgatan.

Knutas had baked scones in honour of the day, and he and Lina had made a big bowl of caffè latte for each of them. For Christmas, the children had given them the espresso machine they'd both been wanting.

'What's this? A bowl of pudding?' asked Petra when she shuffled into the kitchen in her dressing gown, her hair dishevelled.

Lina laughed.

'No, dear. It's caffè latte. I just overdid it a little when I tried to froth the milk.'

'Mmm.' Petra sat down and took a sip of the hot drink. 'That's good. And you've outdone yourself, Pappa.' She cast a grateful glance at Knutas as she reached for one of the fragrant, piping-hot scones.

Nils joined them, and soon they were all sitting at the kitchen table in the glow of the candles. Knutas looked around the table at his family, feeling warm inside. How carefree everything seemed here at home right now.

'So what are your plans for the day?' he asked his children. 'You're going to hang out with some friends, is that right, Nisse?'

'Yeah. Oliver is having a party. His parents went to the Canary Islands.'

'How many are coming?'

'No idea.'

'Good luck,' muttered Petra, rolling her eyes.

'What?' countered Nils, ready for a fight.

'A party in their gigantic house, which is only a stone's throw from the city wall? And his parents are out of town? What do you think is going to happen? Word's going to spread like wildfire. Is his sister home? What's her name again? Sandra? She's such a geek. Not that I'm trying to be negative, but that party is not going to end well.'

'Come home and sleep in your own bed, at any rate,' said Knutas. 'It's so close.'

'Okay,' muttered Nils.

'What are you doing for dinner?' asked Lina.

'Nils and I were thinking of eating here at home,' said Petra. 'Then I'm going over to visit Elin and Nora.'

'Pappa and I are leaving around five. What are you going to eat?'

'Could we do our own shopping? I feel like making my recipe for pasta with beef and truffles in cream sauce.'

'That sounds delicious,' said Knutas. 'And what are you going to drink?'

'You don't want to know, Pappa dear,' Petra teased him, pinching his cheek.

'Well, you can't—'

'We know that. Don't worry. We'll drink nothing but soda – the whole evening.'

She hurried to change the subject.

'But first I'm going over to the club. They're having a New Year's gathering at four o'clock for everyone who does orienteering. We're going to ring in the New Year a little early. It's also a welcome-back party for a former leader, a man I really like. Rikard Karlström. Do you remember him? He's not really new, since he's been involved with the club for years, but he stopped participating when his wife and son died in a car accident a couple of years ago. It happened outside Stenkumla. Remember?'

'Oh, right. That was awful,' said Knutas, who recalled the accident all too well. 'They both died instantly.'

'And that's not the only thing,' Petra went on. 'He has a daughter named Agnes. She's a year younger than us,' she said, looking at her twin brother. 'You know that girl Cecilia Johansson, who's on the floorball team? Well, she used to be really good friends with Agnes, but then they lost touch because Agnes had anorexia. She was supposed to be in secondary school, but she had to drop out. Cecilia told me that she collapsed at home and was taken by ambulance to hospital. She only weighed ninety-five pounds.'

Knutas was just about to reach for the butter.

'Did you say anorexia?'

'Uh-huh. And it's so terrible, because she got it after she was discovered by a modelling agency. Agnes won a contest at the Burmeister. It was arranged by that agency, Fashion for Life. The one you're investigating right now. And she was forced to lose weight to be thin enough to be a model, but things got out of hand.'

'What a sad story,' said Lina. 'How's she doing now? Do you know?'

'I heard that she's still in the anorexia clinic in Stockholm. But she must be doing better, as Rikard is coming back to the club.'

Knutas froze. He sat there motionless, the butter knife in his hand.

Knutas had phoned Jacobsson and Wittberg, and they were now all seated in his office at police headquarters, which was otherwise deserted. Not many people worked on New Year's Eve. He quickly told them what Petra had said about the unfortunate Rikard Karlström and his anorexic daughter who had worked as a model for the agency Fashion for Life.

'You've got to be kidding,' exclaimed Wittberg. 'Where is the daughter now?'

'I haven't looked into that yet,' said Knutas. 'I wanted to talk to both of you first.'

Jacobsson glanced at her watch. It was one thirty in the afternoon.

'I'll ring the agency. We can only hope that someone is still working after lunch today.'

'I'll try to get hold of Rikard Karlström,' said Wittberg. 'I think I might've met him once. He's a carpenter, if I'm not mistaken.'

'In the meantime, I'll talk to Kihlgård. Come back here when you've finished.'

An hour later, they again met in Knutas's office.

'Karlström isn't answering his phone, but I did get hold of someone else at the orienteering club,' Wittberg began. 'She confirmed that he'll be coming to Svaidestugan around four o'clock today. If we don't get in touch with him before then, I'll just drive over there. The woman also said that Agnes was admitted to an anorexia clinic in Stockholm, but she didn't know which one.'

'Good,' said Knutas. 'Drive over to his house first. Maybe he just doesn't want to answer the phone. But don't go alone. You never know.'

Wittberg nodded.

'I talked to the agency,' said Jacobsson. 'Agnes worked there for only a few months before she was dropped because she was anorexic.'

'Do they know where she is now?'

'Afraid not. But I did find out something interesting.'

'What?' said Wittberg and Knutas in unison.

'Earlier today, the woman I spoke to had received another phone call regarding Agnes Karlström.'

Knutas stared at his colleague in surprise.

'And it was from none other than the editor-in-chief of that big fashion magazine. Signe Rudin.'

'What did she want?'

'The same thing we do. She wanted to know where Agnes Karlström is now.'

Johan and Emma were back on Gotland to celebrate New Year's with their friends Tina and Fredrik Levin in Gammelgarn. They were also going to spend the night there. And without any children, for a change. The younger kids were staying with their maternal grandparents on the island of Fårö. They were too little to care about New Year's. Sara and Filip were spending the holiday with their father.

'How beautiful it is out here,' sighed Emma as they approached Gannarve Farm. 'The Östergarn countryside is so marvellous.'

'It really is,' Johan agreed. 'Maybe we should move here.'

For a long time they'd been talking about buying a new house that would be completely their own. Johan liked the house in Roma well enough, but he still felt as though he could sense the presence of Emma's ex-husband, Olle, in the walls. There was no getting around the fact that the house had been theirs for a long time. They had bought it when they still shared dreams about their married life; their two children had spent their early years there. It had been Emma and Olle's house for many years before Johan appeared on the scene.

He longed for a different place, and he read with

great interest all the listings of houses for sale. He'd always had a weakness for the eastern part of Gotland.

The dinner they'd been invited to was going to be a big affair, with forty guests. The farmhouse wasn't especially large, but the renovated old barn, which had been converted into a gallery and shop for selling sheepskins and art, had been turned into a banqueting hall for the evening. It was already crowded with guests, all of them dressed in their finest and filled with anticipation. Candles were everywhere, and the welcome drinks were served by young people from the area who wanted to earn a little extra money on New Year's Eve.

As their hosts greeted them in the doorway, Emma could tell that something was wrong. Fredrik and Tina gave everyone warm smiles, the tables were beautifully set for the party, and a crackling fire blazed in the hearth. But Emma saw that Tina looked strained, and her face was pale in spite of the make-up she had so carefully applied. Had they quarrelled? Fredrik also seemed stressed as he mingled with the guests. As soon as she had a chance, Emma took Tina with her to the kitchen.

'What's happened?' she asked.

Tina bit her lower lip.

'Something terrible is going on. I don't know what to do about it. Can we go outside and have a cigarette?'

Emma looked at her friend in surprise. She never smoked.

'Of course. Whatever you like.'

They slipped out the back so they could be alone.

'It's just crazy,' Tina began. 'We almost cancelled

the party, but then we remembered that some people were coming all the way from the mainland. So we both agreed we had to carry on. Although, now, I can tell that this is going to take more of an effort than I thought.'

Tina told Emma about the man with the doll who had been sitting outside Jenny's building that morning.

'She ran inside and, luckily, he didn't follow her. But she was terrified and rang me right away. She was crying on the phone. Thank God another girl is staying in the flat, so she wasn't alone. But that man scared her out of her wits, and I suppose that was what he meant to do.'

'Did she phone the police?'

'No. I think all she wanted to do was come home as fast as possible. Fortunately, there was a three o'clock flight that still had seats. I called the police in Visby, and they wanted us to come over to headquarters as soon as I picked Jenny up at the airport. They questioned her and said that they would provide her with police protection but, since it's New Year's Eve, they can't do anything about it today.'

'Did Jenny recognize him? Had she ever seen him before?'

'That's the worst part. Because she had seen him before. But this was the first time she mentioned to anyone that, several weeks ago, she'd had a feeling that a man had followed her to the front door. But she wasn't certain. Now, she realizes it was the same man she saw this morning.'

Tina shook her head.

'How's Jenny doing?' asked Emma.

'She was worried and upset, but eventually she calmed down and had something to eat. She's really worn out and doesn't want to see anyone tonight. She's upstairs in her room with the dogs, watching TV.'

Tina took a deep drag on her cigarette and gave Emma an anxious look.

'Do you think the murderer is after her?' Tina asked.

'I think that would be very unlikely. As far as I know, neither Robert Ek nor Markus Sandberg received any threats before they were attacked. In Jenny's case, this man seems to have settled for scaring her. To me, he sounds more like a stalker, someone who's been set off by all the reports in the media. Jenny isn't exactly unknown. Almost half the Swedish population knows who she is, and anyone who reads the papers or watches the news on TV would realize she knew both victims.'

Tina looked a bit calmer now.

'I hope you're right.'

Lina ended up having to drive out to Ljugarn alone, even though she did so reluctantly. Knutas said he might be able to join her later in the evening. Given the new situation, celebrating the New Year was the furthest thing from his mind.

As soon as the meeting was over, he rang editor-in-chief Signe Rudin. She didn't answer her phone. Damn the woman, he thought. It was so frustrating to know that she had apparently ferreted out some important piece of information and he didn't have a clue what it might be. Something that had led her to Agnes Karlström.

He rang the airline, only to hear that there were no more afternoon flights from Visby to Stockholm. The ferry wasn't operating at all on New Year's Eve. He booked himself a seat on the first flight out the next morning and decided to go with Wittberg to Svaidestugan. He was much too restless to sit in his office. His colleagues had dropped by Karlström's house on Endre väg, but no one was home.

Svaidestugan was a few kilometres outside Visby in a popular open-air recreation area. It had been the location of the orienteering club for years.

As soon as they turned on to the bumpy road that

led to the building, they could see plenty of activity. The car park in the woods was filled with vehicles, and the small red-painted wooden buildings that housed a sauna and changing rooms were decorated with wreaths made from spruce boughs and coloured lights that glowed in the winter darkness.

Knutas and Wittberg went into the clubhouse. It was crowded with people holding cups of coffee and mugs filled with *glögg*, chatting in small groups. Everyone looked so healthy, with their rosy cheeks and sporty clothing, as if at any moment they might set down their drinks and go out for a hike. Knutas didn't much care for the whole club and orienteering scene, even though he was fully aware that it meant a great deal to a lot of people. The spirit of camaraderie was all well and good, but he couldn't ignore the slightly sectarian feeling he'd noticed. There was something exclusive about their meetings, no matter how pleasant and lively everyone might seem outwardly. It was as if only those who fitted the mould could belong – those who were fit, healthy and upstanding citizens. With set routines, everything in its proper place, everything neat and tidy. Preferably no weaknesses. If you're not as healthy and fit as we are, you're not good enough. Eat oatmeal, muesli and whole-grain bread. Keep your back straight, wear barefoot trainers on your feet. Hallelujah.

Knutas and Wittberg had barely stepped inside when a woman in her sixties came over to greet them. She introduced herself as the club secretary, Eva Ljungdahl. She was the one Wittberg had spoken to on the phone. She was a wiry woman with a firm handshake. Her suntan told them that she had celebrated Christmas somewhere at a much warmer latitude.

'Rikard is here. He's in the kitchen. Come with me.'

They made their way through the crowd to the kitchen. Knutas immediately recognized Rikard Karlström.

About forty-five, Knutas surmised. The timid type. Short, slender and sinewy. Typical runner's physique. On his shaved head he wore a cap that said 'O-Ring' on the peak.

They formally introduced themselves. Karlström seemed self-conscious, and his anxiety was obvious. As soon as the woman left the kitchen, he spoke.

'What's this about?'

'I assume you know about the assault on Markus Sandberg on Furillen in November, right? And the murder of Robert Ek, which occurred just before Christmas?'

Karlström nodded.

'Both of them worked for the agency where your daughter, Agnes, worked before she fell ill.'

'She was only there a short time,' stammered Karlström. 'She hardly knew those awful people. They kept talking about her weight. I think that's what caused the anorexia.'

'Where is Agnes now?'

'She was admitted to a clinic in Stockholm. It's called the Anorexia Centre.'

'How long has she been there?'

'Since the end of September. So about three months.'

'And how is she doing?'

Rikard Karlström's expression softened a bit.

'Better. She was home for a few days at Christmas, and I think that did her good. For the first time, it seems like she might get well. She's started to respond to the treatment, and I'm really happy about that.'

'Have you or Agnes had any contact with the modelling agency since she stopped working there?'

Karlström paused to think.

'I know that I talked to someone there a couple of times. It had to do with money that Agnes was owed, and photographs of her they wanted to send.'

'Do you know who you talked to?'

'Her name was Sara. I don't remember her last name, but it's in a folder I have at home. She was extremely pleasant. Nothing wrong with her.'

'What about Agnes? Has she been in contact with the agency?'

'Not that I know of.' Karlström rubbed his chin. 'Wait a minute. I was there when someone came to visit her, right after she was admitted to the clinic. She'd only been there a few days.'

'Who was it?'

'A photographer, I think. Dark hair. About thirty-five.'

Knutas and Wittberg exchanged glances.

Markus Sandberg.

Agnes's father had asked her whether she wanted him to come over on New Year's Eve, but she told him that he could celebrate with Katarina if he liked. She assured him that she really didn't mind. She was always so tired and probably wouldn't even stay up until midnight. And they'd already had such a nice time together at Christmas.

She'd felt a little guilty when Per told her that Katarina had come to the clinic on Christmas Eve. She hadn't realized that her father's girlfriend was so alone. And if there was one thing that Agnes understood, it was loneliness. That was the worst thing about anorexia. You lost all contact with other people.

Even though Agnes doesn't really care for Katarina, she has decided to try to make an effort to be nice. Maybe that's part of the process of getting well. Lately, she has noticed that things have begun to turn around, that she has been feeling a greater urge to get well. She still suffers from a hellish anxiety whenever she has to eat anything, and she can't stop herself from exercising, but she doesn't do it as much. She doesn't cheat, or exercise as often, although the process hasn't been totally smooth sailing. Sometimes she feels so panicked that she thinks she might fall to pieces.

She detests this sense of duplicity. On the one hand,

she wants nothing more than to put on weight so that she can leave the clinic and start living again. On the other hand, that is exactly what scares her most.

The eating frenzy she experienced at home on Christmas Eve has increased her motivation to get well. She doesn't want to live like that. She never wants to go through that sort of torment again. Yet the episode also reminded her that the anorexia is harming not only her but her father, too. She is all that he has. And Katarina, of course. She thinks it's fine for them to celebrate the New Year together. If only for Pappa's sake.

Besides, Per has said that even though he actually has the day off, he's going to spend the evening with her. They'll think of some way to celebrate.

He turns up right after lunch, looking cheerful and like he'd just stepped out of the shower. She is sitting on her bed listening to music when he sticks his head in the door. As luck would have it, Linda has moved out, so Agnes now has the room all to herself.

'Hi. Can I come in?'

'Sure.'

She's suddenly nervous. What's going on? Her despair after yesterday's visit from Cecilia's big sister, Malin, and Jenny Levin has faded. Now, she just feels ashamed at her outburst.

'I'm sorry I was such a nuisance yesterday.'

'That's okay.'

'Maybe I should ring Malin to apologize. I know she meant well.'

'Of course.'

A shadow passes over his face.

'But maybe not today,' she adds. 'I can call her to-morrow.'

Agnes would rather forget about the whole thing.

He looks relieved. It was hard on him, too, even though he's used to outbursts from the patients. But something special seems to have developed between them lately. Agnes wonders if he has noticed it, too.

'I thought we could go out for a walk, or rather I could push you in the wheelchair,' he suggests.

'Great.'

Agnes hasn't been outdoors since she came back from Gotland. The daily walks have been cancelled between Christmas and New Year's.

'Just let me go to the loo.'

With an effort she gets up from the bed and stumbles into the bathroom. Now she's annoyed that there is no mirror. She splashes water on her face, brushes her teeth, and pinches her cheeks, hoping to give them some colour.

The air is clear and cold. Per pushes the wheelchair through the slushy snow. Agnes is bundled up in two pairs of long underwear, several woollen jumpers, heavily lined thermal trousers, and a big white down jacket that makes her look like the Michelin man. On her head she has a Russian hat with ear flaps. It's wonderful not to be freezing as she feels the fresh air biting at her cheeks. They head up the hill towards the centre of town. There are people everywhere, doing their last-minute shopping for New Year's.

'Would you like to see my place?' he asks.

'Okay.'

He pushes her in the chair over to a block of flats with a blue-painted façade. The stairwell smells a bit musty. The lift is modern and has plenty of space for the wheelchair. They go up to the sixth floor.

A long corridor with a series of doors. The third one has a sign on it with white plastic letters. 'P. and M. Hermansson. No junk mail.'

Agnes is momentarily startled. Does Per live with someone?

'Who is M?' she ventures as he pushes the chair over the threshold.

'M as in Mamma,' said Per with a laugh. A dry, mirthless laugh. 'Margareta, actually. My mother. But, sadly, she has passed away. So now I live here alone.'

Agnes is relieved, even though she feels sad on his behalf.

'Oh. I'm sorry. I didn't know your mother was dead.'

'Cancer. She was a nurse in the infectious diseases clinic at the hospital. She was the one who got me the job on the ward.'

'Was it just the two of you living here?'

'No. I have a sister, but she moved away from home when she turned eighteen. She and my mother didn't really get along.'

'What about your father?'

'My parents divorced when I was a kid. Would you like some coffee?'

'Yes, please.'

'It's two o'clock. Time for your afternoon snack. The question is, what have I got in the kitchen?'

He parks the wheelchair in the hall and she gets up.

'Shall I show you around first?' he asks. 'It's not a big place, but . . .'

Now he seems almost shy. Agnes finds that endearing. The flat is nice and bright, with windows facing in two directions. Everything is neat and clean. Attractive, but a bit boring. Nothing very personal about it. They go through to the kitchen, which is completely ordinary, with grey cabinets. A pine table and four chairs stand next to the window, which has red curtains and a Christmas star made of straw with a red ribbon.

'Do you recognize that?'

Agnes nods. He had pointed out the window from the ward, and she now sees the same star and red curtains.

Next to the kitchen is a small bedroom.

'This is where I sleep,' says Per. 'This room is much smaller than the other one, but I can't bring myself to sleep in Mamma's room. Do you think that's weird?'

'No, not at all.'

The furniture in the living room looks like it's from the seventies. Bookcases made of dark-stained pine with built-in lighting and a drinks cabinet. A sofa with brown-and-orange upholstery that has a rough texture to it. A coffee table with brass legs and a tinted-glass top.

They move on to look at a bigger bedroom that has been turned into a gym, with mirrors and several exercise machines.

'This is my workout room,' Per explains proudly. 'I don't really need much living space, and I like to work out. So, this way, I save having to pay for an expensive gym membership.'

'Cool,' says Agnes, not sure what else to say. 'When did your mother die?'

'Eight and a half months ago.'

'Have you thought about getting a smaller flat?'

'Yes, I have. But I feel comfortable here. I've lived here all my life. It's my childhood home. And the rent is low. I pay the same for this two-bedroom as I would for a one-bedroom in the city. So I'd rather stay here. And, besides, it's close to work.'

Per makes coffee and they eat a few crackers. It's pleasant sitting there with him in the kitchen, looking out at the hospital. Being on the other side. On the healthy side.

That's where she longs to be.

It was 6 p.m. by the time Knutas got back home after talking to Rikard Karlström. Wittberg was in a hurry to get to a New Year's Eve party. As for Karin Jacobsson, it seemed she was spending the evening with Janne Widén. Knutas didn't know why he felt so uncomfortable when he thought about that.

He'd tried several times to reach Signe Rudin, but she didn't answer her mobile or her landline at home. When he rang the magazine, he got a recorded message wishing everyone a Happy New Year and telling him to ring again after the holiday. He realized there was nothing more he could accomplish, so he phoned Lina, who told him that they hadn't yet sat down to dinner. The hosts were just about to offer their guests some champagne. Maybe he felt like toddling over there and spending a little time with his wife on New Year's Eve?

Knutas realized that, if he hurried, he could get there before dinner was served. He took a quick shower and put on clean clothes. Then he got in the car and drove east. Just as he reached Ljugarn, his mobile rang. It was Signe Rudin.

'Hi. I'm terribly sorry for not calling you back, but I'm visiting good friends in the Stockholm archipelago, and I left my mobile in the bedroom, and . . . Well, you know. I thought I should be able to leave the job behind, since it's New Year's Eve, and all. But I was planning to ring the police tomorrow morning.'

'Oh, really? What's on your mind?' asked Knutas, forgetting for a moment why he'd been trying to call her.

'The thing is, we received another letter.'

Knutas almost drove off the road.

'When did it arrive?'

'Yesterday.'

'Just a minute.'

Knutas had to pull over and stop. Quickly, he got out his notebook and a pen. Annoyed that Signe hadn't notified the police about the letter earlier, he said curtly, 'What did it say?'

'Just four words, like last time. But instead of saying "You are all killers," it said, "I am a killer."'

'And was it the same as last time? I mean, words cut out of a magazine?'

'Yes. And the type looked the same as before, so he must have used the same magazine.'

'Who was it sent to?'

'Fanny Nord. Just like last time. And the address was handwritten. No sender's name.'

'Anything else that was different from the first letter?'

'No. The handwriting on the envelope looked the same. The same pen, too. The same kind of envelope.'

'Where is the letter now?'

'I have it here with me.'

'Could you possibly scan the message and email me a jpeg image?'

'Sure. No problem. My friends have their own business, so they have a lot of computer equipment.'

'Scan the envelope, too.'

Knutas gave her his email address.

'Before you go, I'd like to know one thing. Why did you phone Fashion for Life this morning and ask about Agnes Karlström?'

For a moment, Signe Rudin didn't speak. She was clearly surprised by his question.

'Well, I found out that, last year, Fanny was responsible for a photo shoot that ended up being a disaster because the model was too big. As a result, we couldn't use any of the pictures. And it turned out that the model's name was Agnes Karlström. The photographer was Markus Sandberg.'

Knutas leaned back and closed his eyes.

'Okay,' he said at last. 'Email me those pictures as soon as you can.'

Then he turned the key in the ignition. Just beyond the next bend in the road was the house where the New Year's party was in full swing, but Knutas turned the car around and drove back the way he had come.

New Year's Eve is turning out much better than Agnes could have imagined. There are only four other patients on the ward, and two of them are so ill they don't feel like getting out of bed. Per has gone home to change his clothes while she takes a quick nap so she'll be able to stay awake until the stroke of midnight. They have agreed to meet again at seven o'clock.

It almost feels like a date. Agnes has found a skirt and top that she hasn't worn since coming to the clinic. Per has never seen her wear anything but tracksuit bottoms and a sweatshirt. He has decided that they should sit at a separate table from the other patients. Dinner is pasta with pork in a cream sauce, but Agnes hardly touches the food. It's nice to be sitting here, and on this one evening she is allowed to do what she likes with the food. Her Widget is not in use on New Year's Eve. Per has arranged for linen table napkins and candles.

'You look so nice,' he says, lowering his eyes.

'Thanks,' she says, embarrassed. 'It feels great to wear something other than tracksuit bottoms and sweat-shirts.'

She thinks Per looks very handsome. He is wearing a checked shirt. On his wrist she notices a silver chain she has never seen before.

'Nice bracelet. Is it new?'

'Yes, actually. It's a New Year's present.'

'Oh. Who's it from?'

'Guess.'

Agnes gives him a hesitant look.

'It's not from a girl, if that's what you're thinking.'

Agnes changes the subject. She doesn't know much about Per's personal life but, clearly, he must have relatives, friends and others who care about him. She doesn't want to seem nosy.

They talk about all sorts of things, avoiding any mention of her illness. Films they've seen, what they like to do in their free time. Per tells her that he used to work only part time while he was going to college, but last autumn he was offered a full-time position replacing someone who'd taken a leave of absence. So he decided to give up his studies. He found college boring, anyway, and he hadn't been doing very well.

'It was my mother who was always talking about me continuing my education,' he says. 'She thought I should make something of myself. And I can understand that. She was a nurse, after all. My sister started her studies before I did, even though she's two years younger than me. So that really put the pressure on me.'

'Just think, neither one of us has a mother,' says Agnes.

'I know.'

For a moment, they both fall silent.

'I think a lot about her during the holidays, like today,' Agnes goes on. 'Mamma loved New Year's Eve. We always went out to visit friends, or else we had a party at home. My mother was such a happy and social person. She loved being with people. She always talked louder and laughed longer than anyone else.'

Agnes smiles at the thought. Per looks at her with that preoccupied expression of his.

'My mother wasn't like that at all. She was quiet and reserved. She did her job but, otherwise, she just stayed at home. I can see Mamma sitting on the sofa, wearing an old dressing gown, with some knitting on her lap as she watches TV. That was her daily routine. But I think she was happy.'

Per raises his glass and looks at Agnes, a little smile tugging at his lips.

'You're beautiful, you know. You really are. Here's to you, my girl. Cheers.'

'Cheers.' Agnes smiles at him.

The apple juice tastes good.

An hour later, Knutas was sitting in front of his computer with two meatball sandwiches and a beer. The only one who seemed happy that he'd returned home was the cat, who jumped up on his lap and curled up contentedly. Lina, who had been expecting her husband to come through the door and join the party at any moment, was furious and abruptly cut him off when he rang her again. She didn't even want to hear his explanation. It was enough for her to know that he'd driven all the way out to Ljugarn only to turn around again. Nothing could be so important on New Year's Eve that it couldn't wait another day, or at least until after midnight. That was what she had shouted in his ear before ending the conversation and dismissing him for the rest of the night. Lina was usually very patient about the irregular hours required by his job, but even she had her limits.

Knutas shook off his feeling of discomfort and took a bite of his sandwich. He'd had better meals on New Year's Eve. And better company, too, he thought as he petted the cat.

Then the email appeared in his inbox. His heart pounding, he clicked it open and looked at the image of the message. Exactly the same typeface as before. The words glared at him. 'I am a killer.' Who are you?

he thought. Who the hell are you? And who are you thinking of killing next?

Knutas ate his sandwiches and drank his beer, letting the thoughts whirl through his head. It would be another week before Fanny Nord returned home. He had a good mind to go out to the airport and meet her in person. Maybe he'd be lucky enough to find this bastard out there. He was still staring at the message on the screen. What did it tell him? He clicked on the print icon and then took the printed text into the living room. He lit a fire in the fireplace, put on a favourite CD by Simon and Garfunkel, and got another beer out of the fridge. In his mind, he pictured Lina's face. She wouldn't be any happier tomorrow when she came home to an empty house. His plane to Stockholm left at eight thirty. Before settling down on the sofa, Knutas went back into his home office to fetch his copy of the first letter. Then he sat down on the sofa and compared the two print-outs. Who had written them? Rikard Karlström was a possible candidate. Erna Linton was, too. And Marita Ahonen. Or was the perpetrator some unknown individual they hadn't even come across?

With these thoughts in his mind, Knutas fell asleep on New Year's Eve, with still a whole hour left until midnight.

When Agnes goes to bed on New Year's Eve, she is feeling more light-hearted than she has in a long time. The fireworks were fantastic. She had joined the few patients on the ward who were still awake, along with the staff, and they had all gathered in front of the conference-room windows to watch the colourful pyrotechnic display. It felt magical to be standing there next to Per and seeing the whole sky exploding with shooting stars and glitter. The two of them together, standing very close.

He arouses strange feelings in her, but they're not unpleasant. She gets a tingling in her body whenever she looks at him, but it's not the same prickling sensation she used to have. And with a combination of joy and alarm, she realizes that she is falling in love with her personal nurse. Which is insane, of course. I wonder if he feels the same way, she thinks, smiling to herself. He gave her such an odd look when they drank a toast at midnight. She couldn't tell what he was thinking.

Her father had phoned shortly after midnight to wish her a happy New Year. When Agnes asked him about Katarina, he said that they'd quarrelled, so he'd driven her back to the airport earlier in the day. He said that their relationship might be over, slurring his words a bit. But in the next breath he told her it didn't really matter. Katarina wasn't an easy person to be with. She was very controlling and had a bad temper. So the truth finally came out, now that he was slightly drunk. He'd never said a negative word about Katarina before.

But he wasn't complaining, he assured Agnes. He was celebrating New Year's with some of his co-workers from his construction job. And that was just fine with him.

Agnes has to admit to feeling a certain relief.

She leaves the light on for a while. She's not sleepy at all, even though her body is aching with fatigue. She's glad that Linda has moved out. She doesn't have to take anyone else into consideration. She's thinking about Per, and that makes her happy. She pictures his face and his weary eyes, which fascinate her. He told her that he has the next few days off, so he's going to Gotland to visit a friend. An old classmate from school. But he has promised to phone.

Agnes can't understand why he seems to care so much about her. She has started thinking about the future. First, she has to get well as fast as possible. If she does everything right, it shouldn't really take so long, even though she realizes that she is so underweight that it's going to take more than just a few months. But maybe she'll be okay by summer. She thinks about venturing out and socializing again, going to the beach and swimming. Will she be able to handle that? Her worst nightmare is having to get undressed in front of other people. But if she gets well, then . . . No, not *if*, she corrects herself. *When* she gets well. She is looking forward to jumping into the water with Per at Tofta

Strand. She giggles at such an unrealistic thought.

Suddenly, she's roused from her reveries. The heavy curtain in front of the window sways. It's just a vague movement which she sees out of the corner of her eye, so she's not sure it even happened. Did the curtain really move? She fixes her eyes on the velvety fabric. She must be imagining things. The alarm clock on the nightstand is discreetly ticking. 1.20 a.m. She hasn't been awake at this hour in a very long time. She hears footsteps out in the corridor which pass her room and then disappear. The night staff are probably still celebrating. Before she came back to her room, she noticed that they had set out a cheese platter and lit some candles in the common room. Maybe they were even drinking wine. They probably weren't so strict about the rules on New Year's Eve. Poor things. Even they needed to relax once in a while. She wonders if Per is with them, and feels a pang of jealousy. No, she doesn't think he is. He's leaving for Gotland early in the morning.

Slowly, she runs her finger over the downy skin on her arm. Back and forth. She wonders what it would feel like to kiss Per. He has nice lips. His teeth are a bit uneven, but that doesn't matter. She thinks it's charming.

Then the curtain moves again. Just slightly, but enough for her to realize it's not her imagination. She sits bolt upright in bed, without taking her eyes off the curtain. It's heavy and reaches all the way to the floor so that it will keep out the light, as well as blocking the cold and any sound. Her heart is beating faster. Is there that much of a draught from the window? She listens for the wind, but hears nothing. The room seems suddenly filled with danger. A tangible, menacing feeling, but she doesn't know why. She tries to reach for the alarm button.

But that's as far as she gets.

Early in the morning on New Year's Day, Knutas was awakened by the doorbell. Groggy with sleep, he stumbled out to the front hall and opened the door to find his son, Nils, standing there. His face was white as a sheet, and his hair was sticking out all over.

'Sorry. I forgot my key. Happy New Year.'

'What?'

It took a moment for Knutas to remember what day it was, and then he realized that he must have fallen asleep on the sofa.

'Are you home early? Or is it late?'

'It's six o'clock, and I just left the party. I'm going to bed. Where's Mamma? I thought you were both going to stay in Ljugarn.'

'We were. But something came up and I had to work.'

'That figures. Good night.'

Nils quickly disappeared upstairs. Knutas blinked his eyes in confusion. Where was Petra? Wasn't she home yet? He looked around and caught sight of her boots in the hall, and next to them was her jacket, where she had dropped it on the floor. He breathed a sigh of relief. Then he went back to the living room. It was lucky he hadn't lit any candles last night. The fire in the fireplace had burned out on its own.

He sank down on to the sofa. Checked his mobile.

Lots of calls and texts with New Year greetings at midnight. One from Lina, too, which made him happy. He looked at his watch. Only 6.10. Too early to phone her. His eyes fell on the print-outs. All of a sudden he thought he recognized the typeface of the letters. He was certain he'd seen those very words before. Somewhere in the back of his mind, he'd known it all along. Lina had a tendency to save everything, including old magazines – for recipes that might come in handy, tips about how to re-upholster a chair, redo a fence, or plant a shrub.

Again he looked at the words that had been cut out and pasted on the card. He got up and shuffled through Lina's stack of magazines. It didn't take long before he stopped. There they were. Right in front of his eyes. To think it could be that simple. It was now crystal clear. No doubt at all. Slowly, he picked up the magazine. The words had been taken from the cover, where a number of headlines screamed their messages.

A publication that was read only by members of a specific group. The magazine was called *The Nursing Profession*.

The plane from Visby landed late at Bromma Airport because the wings had to be de-iced before take-off. Knutas immediately caught a taxi to the anorexia clinic. It was an overcast morning and bitterly cold, with a frigid wind blowing from the north. He hurried into the hospital. After losing his way a few times he finally located the clinic, which was in a separate building of the huge hospital complex. In the lift, it occurred to him that he should have phoned ahead. But it was too late for that. He was here now.

When he finally reached the ward, he found the glass door locked. He rang the bell. A woman looked up and then pushed a button to let him in. With a faint whirring sound, the door opened.

The woman came to greet him, introducing herself as the clinic supervisor, Vanja Forsman. She looked nervous, and Knutas hurried to show her his police ID.

'My name is Anders Knutas, and I'm from the Visby police. I'm here to see one of your patients. Agnes Karlström.'

Vanja Forsman looked as if she might faint.

'Agnes?' she repeated weakly. 'How could the police already . . . Did someone phone you? Did you say the Visby police?'

She leaned forward to look at his ID again.

Knutas gave her an enquiring look.

'Excuse me, but I don't understand,' he said. 'I know I should have called ahead, but there wasn't time. I really need to speak to Agnes as soon as possible. It has to do with a murder investigation.'

Vanja Forsman's face went white.

'A murder investigation? You want to talk to Agnes about a murder investigation?'

'Yes, that's right,' said Knutas, relieved that she seemed to understand him at last.

'I'm afraid you can't. I'm afraid that's not possible.'

'Not possible?'

The woman's lower lip began to quiver.

'The patients are only now getting up. We agreed that anyone who stayed up to watch the fireworks could sleep in today. And Agnes . . . Agnes isn't with us any more. Just ten minutes ago we found her in bed. And she's dead.'

He was sitting at the gate for the Visby flight, casually leafing through the previous evening's papers. He'd arrived at the airport with plenty of time to spare and had already checked in and gone through security. One of the papers had an article listing all the major crimes that had been committed during the past year. The assault on Markus Sandberg was on the list, along with the murder of Robert Ek. Too bad they won't get to include what's going to happen next, he thought. It would be a real gem for their morbid little compilation.

He knew that Jenny Levin had flown home to Gotland. On the afternoon of New Year's Eve, after he had taken Agnes back to the clinic, he'd returned to the modelling agency's flat on Kungsholmen. He had a few hours before he and Agnes would eat dinner together.

He rang the bell and a Finnish girl opened the door. That was a serious disappointment. He felt both foolish and angry. But, luckily, he quickly regained his composure and pretended to be a friend of Jenny's. The Finnish girl told him that she'd left for Gotland a few hours earlier. That definitely complicated matters. He'd be forced to go there and rent a car again, but what the hell. As long as he was able to complete his plan.

He had put the last letter addressed to the magazine

in the post box outside the airport. Today, there was no postal delivery, so it wouldn't arrive until tomorrow. He had no intention of carrying out his threat, but he wanted to make those monsters suffer a little longer. That bitch Fanny Nord was going to shit her pants again. And she deserved it, even though he'd changed his mind when it came to her. He had other things to think about now.

Fury surged inside him when he recalled what Agnes had told him about the photo shoot with Fanny Nord. That woman had kept complaining about how fat she was until Agnes finally broke down. And that disgusting Markus Sandberg had kept snapping pictures as he added his own criticisms. He complained and grumbled about Agnes's figure, but that hadn't stopped him from fucking her. What a scumbag. That man got what he deserved.

At first, he'd been furious and disappointed that the bastard hadn't had the sense to die. And he was angry at himself for not making sure that he'd finished Sandberg off. But, later, he'd read in the magazine about the injuries the photographer had sustained – the article said that he would probably suffer terrible pain for the rest of his life, that he was badly disfigured, and that he would never be able to work again. That made him feel like things had turned out even better than planned. That conceited, pompous idiot who had criticized Agnes's appearance was going to experience at first hand how it felt to look like a monster. Now that he thought about it, he couldn't have asked for a better outcome.

He looked up from the newspaper and checked his

watch. The minutes were crawling by. He had arrived much too early. The airport was practically deserted. Not many travellers on New Year's Day. He went back to reading the article and saw Robert Ek's sunny smile in a photo taken at some flashy fashion show. You haven't got much to smile about any more, he thought harshly. He grinned to himself as he thought about how easy it had been to lure Ek to the agency. Offer him a little young flesh and the man came running with drool running down his chin. He felt sick when he thought about what that pig had done to Agnes, threatening not to represent her any more if she didn't lose weight. He remembered the fear in Ek's eyes when he turned up at the agency on that night. He'd felt a thrill of excitement as he hacked away with the axe. It was liberating to do the job properly. And, this time, he'd made sure that his victim was dead. Now there was only one thing left to do in order to complete his mission. Then Agnes would be avenged.

She and her father's girlfriend, Katarina, were the first people who had meant anything to him since his mother had died. He twisted the new bracelet on his wrist. Katarina had even dropped by the clinic on New Year's Eve and left him the bracelet as a gift. She really cared about him. She was almost like a mother to him. He hoped that Agnes would eventually accept Katarina. He loved both of them. During the past three months, since Agnes had been admitted to the clinic, he'd spent many hours with Katarina. And it felt like a genuine friendship had developed between them. They had hit it off from the very beginning, and it didn't take long before they could talk about every imaginable topic. Sometimes, it almost felt as if they were mother and son. Katarina didn't have any children of her own.

She had sympathized with his outbursts about the modelling agency and the cold-hearted people who worked there, and how they had slowly but surely broken Agnes down. She never tired of listening to him, and she added her own comments and offered insightful advice, which he would never have been able to think up on his own. Katarina was a smart woman. She had made him believe in himself and realize that he shouldn't simply accept the shit that was happening all around him. She had convinced him that he had the power to change things. That he was capable of putting things right.

The rest of the world could go to hell. Including that Jenny Levin. She had some nerve turning up at the clinic. She'd come waltzing in, wearing her trendy jeans and those bright-red boots. Tossing her hair about and tilting her head and pretending that she cared. That was her way of mocking them. 'Look at me. See what a success I am.' It was no wonder Agnes got upset. As if she hadn't suffered enough already. It had taken several hours to calm her down.

He had decided to make Jenny his last victim. Fanny Nord had no idea how lucky she was. Taking that trip to Thailand had saved her life.

He sighed with relief when the departure time finally appeared on the board. The flight to Visby would leave on schedule, and he could now begin his journey towards the end. After that, everything would be fine.

The body had been left in the bed while they waited for the medical examiner. Since the death had occurred unexpectedly on a hospital ward, and the patient had suffered from psychiatric problems, it was routine to summon the ME. The doctor on call lived close by and would arrive shortly.

Rikard Karlström had been notified and would be taking the next flight to Stockholm from Visby. Knutas dreaded seeing Agnes's father under such terrible circumstances. Yet he wanted to stay in the clinic to speak to the ME. The staff told him that Agnes had gone to bed after watching the fireworks at midnight, and that she'd actually had a few sips of champagne. She had seemed fine when she went to her room. In fact, she had been unusually cheerful, almost lively. The nurses who had worked the evening and night shifts had all gone home before her death was discovered.

'It's so sad,' said Supervisor Vanja Forsman. 'I don't believe she would kill herself. Agnes had finally started to get better, and she was responding to the treatment. We had hopes that she would recover, even though she was still very ill. No, I don't believe it. She wouldn't have committed suicide.'

She shook her head and blew her nose loudly.

'What else could it be?' asked Knutas cautiously.

'Her heart must have stopped. Patients with anorexia have such weak hearts. All their organs shrink from malnutrition – the brain, lungs, heart, everything. Most likely, her heart simply gave out. But it's awful, considering that she was doing so much better. She's seemed calmer ever since she came back from Gotland. She'd gone there for Christmas, to be with her father. And she was so happy when she came back, and—'

They were interrupted by the arrival of the ME.

It was a woman about the same age as Knutas. He hadn't worked with her before. They briefly introduced themselves.

'I'd like to see the patient's case file,' she said to a nurse as they headed for Agnes's room. 'You can come with me, if you like,' she said, giving Knutas a nod.

When the sheet covering the body was pulled back, Knutas couldn't help gasping. Agnes was so small. And so young. She was the thinnest girl he'd ever seen, lying there in her childish pink nightgown with a heart on the front. Her ribs were clearly visible under the fabric. Her emaciated arms lay at her sides. Her face was beautiful but rigid, and her skin had a greyish pallor, lacking all lustre. Her eyes were closed, her cheekbones unnaturally pronounced. It was a child's face. Knutas could have cried, but he pulled himself together. He sat down on a chair in the corner and let the ME do her job.

She worked in silence, lifting the eyelids, checking inside the mouth. Knutas didn't say a word. After a few minutes, a nurse brought the case file.

'Was the patient's pulse, temperature and blood pressure checked during the past few days?' asked the ME, keeping her eyes fixed on the body.

'Yes,' replied the nurse.

'And there was nothing out of the ordinary?'

'No, not that I can see.'

'What about her blood? When was the last blood test done?'

'Yesterday.'

'And how were her electrolyte levels? Sodium, potassium, calcium and phosphate?'

'Totally normal.'

The ME slowly straightened up and took off her glasses. She turned to look at Knutas.

'Agnes has pinpoint bleeding in the whites of her eyes, which indicates a strong death struggle and deep breathing. There are also subtle injuries in the oral cavity. She has discrete haemorrhaging from her teeth on the inside of her lips and millimetre-sized ruptures on the folds of the mucus membranes inside her mouth as a result of pressure.'

'Pressure?' Knutas repeated, puzzled.

'Naturally, I don't want to draw any hasty conclusions, but there is every indication that Agnes was murdered.'

Knutas immediately sounded the alarm and contacted his colleagues in both Visby and Stockholm. According to the ME, the nature of Agnes's injuries indicated that she had been smothered, most probably with a pillow that was pressed over her face. The ward had been cordoned off, and all staff members had been summoned for questioning. The interviews would be handled on site, and no one was allowed to leave the building.

The crime scene technicians inspected Agnes's room thoroughly, paying particular attention to her pillow. Suffocation with a pillow was especially hard to prove, but if they found the slightest evidence, that would be enough. There might be fibres, skin scrapings, or something else left by the perpetrator on the pillow, as well as saliva or blood from the victim.

Knutas accompanied the supervisor back to her office and shut the door. Vanja Forsman was visibly shocked and upset that a murder had occurred on her watch.

'According to the ME, Agnes died sometime between one and five in the morning,' Knutas began. 'How could an unauthorized individual get into the ward?'

'All the doors are locked. No one is admitted without permission, and there were no outsiders here yesterday.

Not during the day and not at night.'

'Who was in the clinic last night?'

'Five patients and the night shift. They start at nine o'clock. There's an overlap of an hour before the evening shift ends. Well, they're supposed to stay until ten, but they can leave as soon as they're finished. Yesterday, most of them were in a hurry to go since it was New Year's Eve.'

'So who was on duty during the night?'

The supervisor looked through her lists.

'Let me see now. Elisabeth, Ulrika and Kerstin. Per was here, too, but he left early, around one in the morning. He actually had yesterday off, but he came over to take care of Agnes all day. And he stayed on in the evening, too.'

'Why is that?'

'He's Agnes's personal nurse. Every patient is assigned a special contact, a personal nurse, as we call them. Someone they have regular meetings with to discuss the treatment; someone they can turn to with any problems or if there's something they want to change. Per asked to take care of Agnes on New Year's Eve, as his only patient. He did it voluntarily, and without pay. She wasn't doing very well, you see.'

'I thought you said that she was getting better.'

'She was, but the day before yesterday she had some unexpected visitors, and that threw her off balance.'

'Who came to see her?'

'An old friend from Gotland, and she brought along that famous model, Jenny Levin.'

Knutas looked stunned.

'Jenny Levin?'

'Agnes worked for the same agency, you know. That place that's been so much in the news lately . . . What's it called? Fashion, something, or—'

Knutas interrupted her.

'What happened during their visit?'

'They were all having coffee in the day room and everything seemed fine. But the nurse told me that, all of a sudden, Agnes had some sort of fit. I wasn't there myself. She started crying and screaming, and there was a big scene. Agnes was completely beside herself, and Per was the only one who could calm her down.'

The supervisor suddenly looked uncomfortable.

'He sat with her until she fell asleep,' she said hesitantly. 'As I mentioned, they had a special relationship.'

'What does this Per look like?' asked Knutas.

'Just a minute. I'll go and fetch the staff manual.'

A few moments later, she was back.

'Here he is. Per Hermansson.'

The man was staring solemnly at the camera. He looked about twenty-five, thirty at most. Shaved head, yet that was a popular style these days. A slightly babyish face, very fair skin, clean-shaven, nice, big blue eyes, although there was something a bit preoccupied about his expression. As if he were thinking about something else and didn't really give a damn about the photographer. Red T-shirt, denim jacket. An earring in one ear.

Shaped like a little beetle.

Tina Levin was sitting in the kitchen drinking coffee when Jenny came downstairs. Everyone seemed to be sleeping in, and she had spent the whole morning in her room, watching old episodes of *Desperate House-wives* on DVD. That was about the level of what she could handle right now.

'Happy New Year, sweetheart. How are you?'

Tina got up to give her daughter a hug.

'Okay. Happy New Year.'

Jenny looked around the kitchen, which was cluttered with dirty plates and glasses.

'Wow, what a mess.'

'I know. At five in the morning a few people got hungry. We'll clean up later. Have you eaten lunch?'

'Uh-huh. I had a few sandwiches while I was watching TV. I was thinking of taking the dogs for a walk. I need some fresh air. I'll go out of my mind if I stay indoors any longer.'

In reality, she was longing for a smoke, but she kept that to herself.

'I'll come with you.'

Tina was already getting up from the table.

'No,' said Jenny, and it sounded harsher than she'd intended. 'I mean, I'd really rather be alone. I need some time to think, Mamma.'

'Are you sure?' Tina said uneasily.

'Yes. And don't worry. I'm just going for a short walk, and I'll have the dogs with me.'

'Okay. There's still a lot to clean up in here, and in the barn, too. And we have to feed the sheep.'

'Did you have fun at the party?' asked Jenny, trying to make up for her curt response.

'Yes, it was a big success. I hope we didn't disturb you too much.'

'Not at all. I fell asleep in front of the TV.'

'Did you see the fireworks?'

'Yes, I did. From my window. What's the temperature outside?'

'Minus ten. Can you believe how cold it's getting?'

'It's incredible.'

Jenny went to the front hall and put on her long down jacket. Then she wound a heavy scarf around her neck several times. She rummaged in a drawer to find a pair of Lovikka mittens, and checked her pockets to make sure the pack of cigarettes and lighter were still there.

'I'll help you later, after I get back.'

'You don't need to do that, honey. Johan and Emma are here. They'll help out when they get up.'

Jenny whistled and the dogs instantly came running.

'Oh, by the way,' said Tina, 'leave Semlan here. We're going to need her. A sheep has wandered off somewhere.'

'Okay.'

Jenny took Sally with her and shut the front door in the face of the older sheepdog, who whined with disappointment.

*

The cold struck her like an icy wall as she stepped outside. It was cloudy, with a light wind, but she had on warm clothes and the air felt crisp and fresh. She glanced over towards David's farm. She would have liked to go and visit, but he'd been out partying like everyone else and had sent her a text at midnight. She didn't want to disturb him. He might not even have slept at home.

Instead, she headed in the opposite direction, waving to her father, who was sitting on the rumbling tractor. Then she continued down the lane to the road. The young dog, Sally, happily dashed about in the snow, rolling around and burrowing tunnels into the drifts. Jenny couldn't help smiling at the dog's obvious delight. It was unusual to have such a heavy snowfall on Gotland. Luckily, her father had cleared the road. Otherwise, no one would have been able to get through. High banks of snow towered up on both sides.

Her mood was already improving. No doubt everything would work out in the long run. Given Markus's situation, she knew he would never fully recover. Their relationship was over, but they could still be friends. Hopefully, he would regain his ability to speak.

Most importantly, the police needed to catch the murderer, who was still on the loose. A shiver raced down her spine when she pictured the man with the doll again. She hardly dared think that he might be the killer. No matter what, she just needed to get away until the police caught the man. Fortunately, she was due to leave on her next trip abroad very soon. She would talk to the agency and ask them to change her tickets so she could leave from Visby, then change planes in Stockholm to fly on to New York. There was no way she wanted to set foot in that flat on Kungsholmen again.

It started snowing. She had turned on to a smaller road, heading towards the woods. She'd been so lost in her own thoughts she almost forgot why she'd come out here. By now, she was far enough away from the farm not to be seen and she dared smoke. She took out the pack of cigarettes, looking for somewhere to sit down. For some reason, she didn't like to smoke while she walked. She wanted to sit down and smoke in peace and quiet.

Up ahead, next to the road, she saw a dilapidated farm. From what she remembered, no one lived there any more. She decided to sit on the rickety front porch. It should hold her, even though the boards looked like they might be starting to rot through. On the porch, she would also have a roof over her head, and that suited her perfectly, since it was now snowing harder. She trudged over to the farmhouse and cautiously went up the crooked stairs. The porch swayed alarmingly under her feet. She sank down on to a wooden bench and lit a cigarette, sighing with pleasure as the smoke filled her lungs. Exactly what she needed. The dog disappeared around the side of the house.

Jenny took another drag on her cigarette, letting everything that had happened in the past few weeks pass through her mind: Markus beaten to a pulp and lying on the floor of the cabin on Furillen; Robert murdered; and waking up in his house after the hazy and unwanted sexual escapade, whatever it was. She still couldn't remember a thing about it. And the distressing visit to Agnes at the clinic. No matter how hard she tried, she couldn't erase from her memory the image of that emaciated girl with the big eyes. Her screams still echoed in her head.

It was snowing even harder, and Jenny realized that she ought to head home. She whistled, but Sally didn't appear. She called her several times. No response. She started to feel annoyed. She really wanted to go back now. So she got up and stubbed her cigarette out on the railing.

It was quite a large farm, with several buildings scattered about. Maybe the dog had found a dead animal or something else of interest. She was only a puppy, and still unreliable.

Jenny went down the steps. She plodded through the deep snow around the side of the house, again calling Sally. Now, she saw a trail leading under a stairway to a cellar door on the other side. With a sudden feeling of foreboding, she went over to have a look. The door was ajar. Slowly, she approached, trying to shake off her fear.

The moment she reached for the door handle, someone grabbed her arm and pulled her into the dark.

With a thud, the door closed behind her.

On New Year's Day Johan didn't wake up until the afternoon, and with a noticeable hangover. Emma was lying in bed next to him and still seemed sound asleep. The guest room, which was small but cosy, was upstairs, with a view of the wintry-white fields and meadows. Several sheep with thick woollen coats were crowded around the gate. It had started to snow. He sat up and saw that it was feeding time. Tina and Fredrik drove up on the tractor to put out hay for the sheep, who stayed outdoors year round. Johan thought to himself about the life his friends led. Hard physical labour every day, even after a big New Year's bash. The party was still going on when he and Emma had withdrawn to their room at around five in the morning, although the guests had dwindled to a small group in the kitchen, looking for a snack. He had fallen asleep listening to them talking and laughing downstairs. He wondered when their hosts had finally gone to bed.

The party had been a huge success. They had enjoyed a sumptuous three-course dinner of lobster and steak, and far too many bottles of excellent wine. At midnight, they had all gone outside to the small hill behind the sheep barn to set off fireworks, and had watched the firework displays in the surrounding area at the same time. Then there was dancing into the early hours. He hadn't caught even a glimpse of Jenny all night. She must have decided to stay in her room, exhausted after that frightening experience in Stockholm. And that had put Johan in a real dilemma. Even though the threatening incident had high news value, he had promised not to pursue the story until after New Year's Eve. Today, they would have another talk about it.

He let Emma sleep and climbed out of bed.

Downstairs in the kitchen he found the worktop cluttered with dirty plates from the party, along with glasses holding the dregs of wine and champagne. He wrinkled his nose at the smell, but decided to ignore the clutter for the time being. A lamp had fallen over, and the telephone lay on the floor. It looked like things had got quite lively down here.

There was fresh coffee, so he poured himself a cup. Then he opened the fridge and took out some cheese and butter. He cut a few slices of bread, turned on the radio, and drank several glasses of water. After eating some bread and cheese he'd probably feel a lot better. He hated having a hangover. Fortunately, it didn't happen very often these days.

He sat down at the table and began eating his breakfast, enjoying the peace and quiet. The radio was replaying requests from the past year.

Then the theme music started up for the news programme, and the announcer spoke: 'It's two o'clock, and here is the news for Gotland. A sixteen-year-old girl from Visby was found dead this morning in the Stockholm clinic where she was a patient. The cause of death has not yet been determined, but the police suspect that the girl was murdered. Foresnsics officers are now conducting a search of the crime scene. No suspect has been apprehended.'

Johan immediately rang the editorial offices of Regional News. No answer. There was no regional broadcast on TV on New Year's Day. Damn. He tried Grenfors's mobile but got a busy signal. A Gotland girl had been found murdered in Stockholm the day after the threatening incident Jenny had experienced. Was there a connection? Had the two girls known each other? Johan dashed upstairs to Jenny's room. A 'Do Not Disturb' sign hung on the door handle. He ignored it and knocked. No response. Was she still asleep? Cautiously, he pushed down the handle and opened the door.

The room was empty. He looked at the bed, which had been neatly made. No trace of Jenny.

The hunt for Per Hermansson, who was wanted for murder and attempted murder, was immediately launched on all fronts. A quick check revealed that he'd had several days off from work, both when Markus Sandberg was assaulted and when Robert Ek was killed.

And, during this first week of the New Year, Hermansson was supposed to be on holiday, although no one knew what his plans were. He was not in his flat, and he didn't answer when any of his phone numbers were called. The police swiftly obtained permission to search his home, and broke the lock on the door. Knutas had just left the anorexia clinic and was sitting in a taxi when Jacobsson rang.

'We've checked with the airlines. At ten o'clock this morning Per Hermansson took a plane from Bromma Airport to Visby.'

'Bloody hell. How could he know that Jenny had gone to Gotland?'

'Yesterday afternoon, a guy rang the bell at the flat on Kungsholmen that's owned by the agency. Another model was there, and she spoke to him. He asked for Jenny, so she told him she'd gone home for the holi-day.'

'Damn it! And I just found out that Agnes had a visit

from Jenny and a girl named Malin Johansson the day before New Year's Eve. For some reason, the visit made her very upset, and it was Per Hermansson who calmed her down. Have you talked to Jenny's parents?'

'No. They're not answering their mobile phones, and there seems to be a problem with the landline. We still haven't been able to get in touch with Jenny.'

'Do you know when the next plane leaves for Gotland?'

'If you go out to the airport right now, you can catch the one-thirty. I'm sure it's not fully booked.'

'Okay. Can you pick me up in Visby?'

'Of course. There's just one thing I don't understand. Why would Hermansson murder Agnes?'

'A mercy killing?' suggested Knutas.

The grip on her arm was so strong that she whimpered in pain. The man's face was only millimetres away from hers in the dark. She could feel his breath, hot and damp against her cheek. His lips grazed her ear as he whispered.

'How nice that you decided to come over, Jenny Levin. And here I thought that I'd have to break into your house, but you've saved me the trouble. This makes everything much easier for me. Thanks for that, my lovely fashion model. But now it may not be much fun being Jenny Levin any longer. Now, you're just an ordinary girl, you see. Nothing special. No cameras flashing. No catwalk lights. Just little Jenny.'

His voice changed from feigned regret to scornful hatred.

He shoved her away with such force that she tumbled across the cellar and landed on the cold cement floor.

He stared at her. She could just about make out his face in the dim light. He was younger than she'd thought, but she recognized him. And his cap.

His eyes were filled with insanity, or maybe cold, suppressed rage. She wasn't sure which. Maybe both. Maybe the man was a psychopath.

'What do you want?' she stammered.

'What do you think I want, sweetie?' he snarled. 'You sweet little model.'

He softly hummed a tune about a little model and a carousel.

'What do you want with me?' she said. 'What have I done?'

He went over to her and squatted down so his face was only a few centimetres away from hers. He took off his cap. Jenny flinched.

'Do you recognize me?'

His voice was unnecessarily loud in the cramped cellar room, and he exaggerated the enunciation of each word.

'Yes,' she whispered. 'You were in the anorexia clinic with Agnes.'

'Exactly,' he replied. 'A-n-o-r-e-x-i-a c-l-i-n-i-c,' he spelled out. 'Where Agnes is still a patient, thanks to people like you.'

'What do you mean? What have I—'

She didn't get any further before he punched her in the mouth.

'Shut up,' he spat. 'Who the hell do you think you are? You come waltzing into the clinic wearing your high heels and tossing your hair, pretending that you really care about Agnes. But you were just mocking her, and all the other patients, too. You know that as well as I do!'

Jenny lay on the floor, pressing her hands to her bleeding lips.

'But I just wanted to—'

His fist slammed into her face. For several seconds, everything went black. She was paralysed with terror.

She was alone here with this madman, completely helpless. And the farm was deserted. No one lived here, no one ever came here. Now he was standing over her. She could see his black, shiny boots right next to her face.

'Just wanted to—?' he hissed. 'Just wanted to—? Let me tell you why you and I are here right now. The whole insane fashion industry nearly killed my girl. Do you understand? The only person I've ever cared about. Agnes was thin and beautiful, but she wasn't good enough. They told her she wasn't good enough. Do you hear me? They shattered her self-confidence. She was a sweet young girl with her whole life ahead of her! But they told her that she wasn't beautiful enough. She needed to lose weight. And did she ever lose weight! She almost starved herself to death. She weighed ninety-five pounds when she arrived at the clinic. And Agnes is tall. She's five foot nine. Do you know what that means? Ninety-five pounds. Do you have any idea what happens to someone who's anorexic? Do you? Their heart shrinks and they go into cardiac arrest. Do you realize that we have patients who are so weak that they can't even raise their head? Can you even comprehend that?'

'But I have never—' Jenny ventured, her voice a whisper.

'You have never—?' he snapped. 'Oh, right. You've never hurt a fly, have you? You're lily white and fucking innocent. Don't you get that you're part of the whole thing when you go swishing around and posing for all those fashion photos? Do you realize what a complex you give young girls who try to live up to the image you're projecting? And that's exactly what you are – an image, an illusion, a dream. You're not *real*. You're a symbol for that whole stinking industry. Even worse, you're a symbol for that bloody agency which destroyed Agnes's life and almost succeeded in killing her. That's why you're going to die, you fucking, deceitful nobody. And that's precisely what you are: a nobody, with no substance whatsoever.'

Jenny lay still, incapable of moving a muscle, panic-stricken, listening to his strident outpouring of words.

Then, abruptly, he stopped talking. He walked resolutely over to the door, and for a moment she hoped that he would open it and disappear. Instead, he leaned down and picked something up.

And the next second she saw what he was holding.

He turned to face her but stopped at the sound of loud barking from outside.

'What the hell?'

Jenny didn't move. She was frozen in place on the floor, hardly daring to breathe. Now she remembered his name. Per. He was Agnes's personal nurse. She had spoken a few words to him at the clinic.

He crouched down and leaned his back against the wall. For several minutes, he merely sat there, seeming to weigh up what he should do next. He glanced at Jenny, and then apparently decided to deal with her later. He stood up and peered out of the window.

'I fucking hate dogs,' he muttered.

He opened the door just enough to slip out as the dog growled and barked wildly.

'Fucking shit!' he shrieked, presumably because Sally had dug her teeth into him.

Good Sally, Jenny thought. Good dog.

She listened tensely. It lasted only a few seconds. A loud commotion, a thud against the wall, then the barking suddenly changed to a quiet whimper.

Per came back in and gave Jenny a cold look. He was holding an axe in his hand. She saw that there was blood on it.

'Don't,' she pleaded. 'Please. Don't.'

Half an hour after Jenny had left for her walk, Sally came limping into the farmyard. Without Jenny. The dog was bleeding from a wound on her head, and her left rear paw was injured. She was in very bad shape.

'What in the world . . . ?' cried Tina, who had just returned from the field. She climbed down from the tractor and squatted down to examine the nasty-looking wound on the dog's head. A bloody gash, as if she'd been stabbed. The dog whimpered. Tina's throat went dry. Where was Jenny?

She stood up and looked in the direction her daughter had taken. The snow was really coming down, making the visibility worse every minute that passed. She could see only a few metres, and then the landscape vanished, as if in a heavy fog. Johan came out of the house.

'Jenny's not in her room. Do you know where she is?'

'She was just going out for a walk,' Tina said in bewilderment. 'With the dog.'

Tears began running down her face as she again fixed her eyes on the road.

'Oh, good,' said Johan, sounding relieved. 'I was worried that she didn't sleep here last night.'

'She did. But she wanted to go out for a walk. With

Sally. But now the dog is back and covered in blood. Oh, Johan, what could have happened to her?'

Tina started to sob, tugging at the sleeve of Johan's jacket.

'Where is Jenny?'

Before he could answer, several police cars drove into the farmyard. Jacobsson and Knutas were the first to get out. They briefly introduced themselves.

'What's going on?' asked Jacobsson.

'Jenny went out for a walk with the dog, but now the dog is back, injured and bloody,' said Johan. 'And Jenny is missing.'

'When did she leave?'

'About half an hour ago.'

'Which way did she go?'

The snow continued to fall, effectively erasing any footprints. The police spread out and set off in different directions. Knutas and Jacobsson hurried down the lane and then took the tractor path that led towards the woods, since Tina had said Jenny might have gone that way. The path had been cleared. They walked at a set distance from each other, each surveying one side of the road, but the visibility was very poor. And dusk was already settling in.

Further along, the path divided, and they split up. Knutas took the fork into the woods. Before long, he came to an old abandoned farm. The cladding on the dilapidated buildings was grey with age, and a thick layer of snow covered the roofs. He gave a start when he saw footprints leading towards the farm. His heart started beating faster. He took out his service weapon and trudged over to the porch. But the footprints continued around the side of the farmhouse. He followed them, noticing the tracks of an animal as well. Maybe a dog. When he came to the back of the building he realized at once that someone was there. A cellar door was ajar, and light glimmered from a little window. Slowly, he crept over to the door and peeked inside. Inside the dim cellar room he saw that a candle was burning in a lantern. Jenny Levin was huddled on the floor in a corner, and Per Hermansson was pacing back and forth, hefting an axe in one hand. He was saying something that sounded almost like a chant, although Knutas couldn't make out the words.

He tore the door open, his gun drawn.

'Police!'

Then everything happened very fast. Per threw the axe at Knutas, who ducked to avoid being struck. That gave Per enough time to shove him to the floor and then rush through the door. Knutas quickly got to his feet and raced after him.

'Stop! Police!'

Hermansson disappeared around the side of the house and ran into the fields. Out of the corner of his eye, Knutas saw a car parked a short distance down the road. He ran as fast as he could.

'Stop!' he repeated. 'Or I'll shoot!'

The fleeing man paid no attention, just kept on running. All of sudden he was swallowed up by the twilight and the swirling snow. Knutas fired a warning shot in the air and shouted into the void, 'Stop!'

Clearly, he had no hope of catching up with Hermansson. He caught sight of a shadow off in the distance, then it vanished at the edge of the woods.

Knutas ran in that direction and soon found himself among the trees. He followed a path, holding his gun in one hand, and in the other a pocket torch, which he had luckily brought along. It was easier going in the woods, since he was no longer blinded by the falling snow, and he was able to track the fresh footprints on the ground. His heart was pounding in his chest. The only sounds he heard were his own laboured breathing and branches tearing at his clothes as he moved forward. After a few minutes, he discovered drops of blood next to the footprints. Silently, he cheered. The man must be injured. Maybe the dog had bitten him.

Suddenly, Knutas's odds of catching the perpetrator had improved substantially. And he saw more and more blood. If he was lucky, eventually, Hermansson might be forced to stop.

Abruptly, the trail he was following ended. The young man must have veered to the right, going deeper into the woods. Knutas paused for a moment to catch his breath. The silence was broken by the sound of wailing police sirens off in the distance. Thank God, reinforcements were on the way. The police dogs would find Hermansson in no time. Knutas shone the beam of his torch on the spot where the footprints had vanished among the trees. He flinched as he heard a rustling sound only a few metres away. He stopped, listened intently, unaware of the cold. He noticed a dark silhouette in among the trees. That was where he was hiding.

Knutas took a few cautious steps in that direction. Hermansson no longer had the axe, but he might have other weapons. Maybe even a gun. Knutas knew that the killer must have seen him by now and was probably watching him approach. The beam of his torch could be seen from far away. So there was no longer any need for silence.

'Per!' he shouted into the darkness. 'How are you doing? Are you injured?'

No reply. No sound except his own breathing. And, in the distance, the slamming of car doors. A crow cawing. A faint rustling in the trees. The snow was still coming down, but it was caught by the branches of the spruce and pine trees.

'You need help, Per,' Knutas said. 'You're injured. I can see that you're bleeding.'

He waited a moment. Suddenly, he saw that Per was very close.

'Put down your gun,' he heard a tense voice say from behind the trees.

'The police are here,' Knutas told him. 'The roads are blocked. We know who you are. You took care of Agnes, and she was very fond of you. We know that. Everyone at the clinic said that the two of you had a special relationship. But now Agnes is gone. It's time to give up, Per.'

A brief silence.

'Gone?' said the voice hollowly. 'What do you mean, Agnes is gone?'

Knutas felt his blood run cold. Per had no idea that Agnes was dead. A shiver ran down his spine. He didn't know anything about it!

'Agnes was found dead this morning in her bed at the hospital. She was murdered. Smothered to death.'

Silence.

After a moment, a man stepped forward, his face pale among the trees. A man holding his hands in the air, staggering towards Knutas, dragging one leg behind him. A man with a look of hopeless despair in his eyes, his lips quivering as he tried to speak. Finally, he managed a whisper, barely audible.

'Dead? Agnes is dead?'

'I'm afraid so.'

At that moment, Knutas forgot that he was standing face to face with a murderer. He saw before him a young man whose expression openly revealed his grief. His eyes displayed a sorrow so deep and so heavy it almost felled him to the ground. Per Hermansson shook his head, slowly at first, then with increasing vigour.

His scream started far away, then surged up through his throat and out. A wail that resounded through the dark, silent woods.

The flat in the seaside town of Hammarby was right on the water, at the foot of Hammarby Terrace, with a view of Södermalm on the other side. She went into the kitchen to make coffee. She took the latest photo album from the bookshelf in the living room before she sat down at the kitchen table. She listened to the laboured hissing and gurgling of the coffeemaker as the water dripped through the filter.

She opened the album, which was bound in black leather. It had been expensive, but the contents were worth it. This was her favourite album. Hers and Rikard's. Tears filled her eyes as she looked at the pictures. She'd always cried easily. There was a photo of Rikard smiling at her. It was taken last summer. He was suntanned, wearing shorts and a checked shirt with short sleeves, standing on the dock on the island of Ljuströ. They'd been island-hopping for a week, seeing Stockholm's archipelago together. There he was, sitting on a rock in the evening. How handsome he was. A real man. And there they were together. They had asked the waitress to take their picture in the restaurant where they were having dinner.

To think that, just yesterday, she had almost torn up all these photos. Luckily, Rikard had phoned and stopped her. There was still hope for them. Especially now. Since it was just the two of them. She had done what she had to do. Agnes was keeping her from the love of her life, the man she had finally found. And, besides, the girl didn't really want to live. Everything was going to be fine. She felt very calm inside. What a difference compared to how she'd felt on New Year's Eve. For the thousandth time they had quarrelled about Agnes. As usual, Rikard's spoilt and obstinate daughter was standing in their way.

But then she had pulled herself together. Seen an opportunity, now that the police were still hunting for a murderer. And she'd known for a long time who he was.

Late in the afternoon on New Year's Eve she had gone to the clinic with a gift for Per. But she didn't go home. She found a patient's room that wasn't being used over the holiday, and that was where she hid. The rest had been easy. She was quite pleased with herself. She had removed what was hindering their happiness. She knew that she could handle this. She'd always been able to get herself out of tight spots. She had the power to govern her own life. And Rikard would be more dependent on her than ever. Now that he had no one else.

She got up and poured herself some coffee. Then she took out the box of Aladdin chocolates that had been in the fridge since Christmas.

She felt like treating herself to something sweet after all she'd been through.

She had just eaten the first chocolate praline when the doorbell rang. Her heart leapt with joy. Was he already here? She patted her hair and cast a quick glance in the mirror before she went into the front hall to open the door. She was so impatient she forgot to look through the peephole, as she usually did. She opened the door to find two people standing there. She didn't know either of them. One held out a police ID.

'Police. Are you Katarina Hansell?'

Acknowledgements

This story is entirely fictional. Any similarities between the characters in the novel and actual individuals are coincidental. Occasionally, I have taken artistic liberties to change things for the benefit of the story. This includes the pre-press process of a fashion magazine, Swedish TV's regional coverage, and a few other things. The settings used in the book are usually described as they exist in reality, although there are some exceptions.

Any errors that may have slipped into the story are mine alone.

First and foremost, I would like to thank my husband, journalist Cenneth Niklasson, who is my most important sounding board, for all his support and love. And my wonderful children Rebecka (Bella) and Sebastian, who are warm rays of sunshine in my life.

Also thanks to:
Sofia Åkerman, author and lecturer
Isabelle Kågelius

Lovisa Carlsson

Åsa Sieurin

Ankie Sahlin, Mando Anorexia Clinic, Huddinge
  Hospital

Maria Bejhem, supervisor, Capio Anorexia Centre,
  Löwenströmska Hospital

Magnus Frank, detective superintendent with Visby
  police

Martin Csatlos, the Forensic Medicine Laboratory in
  Solna

Johan Gardelius, detective inspector with Visby
  police

Ulf Åsgård, psychiatrist

Lena Allerstam, journalist

Johan Hellström, owner of Furillen

Jenny Mardell, agent and model scout, the Stockholm Group

Emma Sahlin, stylist, fashion editor, *Damernas Värld*

Haddy Foon, model

Lina Montanari, Grand Hotel

Lars and Marianne Nobell, Gannarve farm, Gotland

A big thanks to all the professional staff at Albert
Bonniers Förlag – especially my publishers Jonas
Axelsson and Lotta Aquilonius, and my editor, Ulrika
Åkerlund.

Thanks to:
  my media agent, Lina Wijk, and publicist, Gilda
    Romero
  my cover designer, for the Swedish edition, Sofia
    Scheutz

my agents Emma Tibblin, Jenny Stjärnströmer and
   Poa Broström

And thanks to all my wonderful author colleagues for
support and encouragement and for all the fun that we
have!

Mari Jungstedt
Stockholm, March 2010

Discover more from Mari Jungstedt

THE DOUBLE SILENCE

A group of close friends holiday on a remote
Swedish island every summer. But this year,
their trip won't go as expected.

A terrible series of tragedies unfolds, seemingly
random, somehow all connected. To find the truth,
Detective Superintendent Anders Knutas will have to
look into the friends' tangled pasts.

What malevolent force has followed
them to the island?

Or was it amongst them all along?

DARK ANGEL

Family ties can be dangerously tight.

Viktor Algard was in love. Reckless in the grip of passion, he left his wife and grown-up children to be with his new lover. His last act was a celebratory drink at a glamorous party . . .

Inspector Anders Knutas must find out who on the island of Gotland hated Algard enough to poison him. At first Algard's spurned wife seems like the obvious suspect. But a second attack confirms his suspicion that there's a more complex motive behind the murder.

If Knutas is to catch the killer, he must discover the truth that lies hidden at the heart of a broken family – and face some secrets within his own.